Ennarisi Unite

*Children of Ennaris*
The Children Return
The Blood Rises
Ennarisi Unite
Children of Destiny

# Ennarisi Unite

## Children of Ennaris III

James K. McVey

James K. McVey

# CONTENTS

CONTENTS

CONTENTS

For Stephanie, whose support and encouragement made this and many other things possible.

Prologue

The being that was known to its children as The One examined its universe and would have grimaced had it features to form the expression. A myriad events were under way, spanning unimaginable distances and innumerable places and uncountable numbers of peoples, its children and its children's children.

The One allowed its children significant leeway and made sure that they did the same for their own children. On a small number of occasions its children were unable to stop their own children from destroying themselves. The One grieved with its children on those occasions and reminded itself that it was not omnipotent, nor all-knowing. It was, however, as much higher in development compared to its children as they were above their own children's development.

The One knew that some of its first children were treading a difficult path between allowing their own children to take responsibility for their world while trying to make sure that they did not destroy it.

The One was pleased with this group of its children, as it had just told them. But, to be sure, it had staged its own intervention, as recommended by one of its siblings. So it had caused a Prophecy to be formed such that its children took note and altered their behaviour accordingly, and so allowed the time for the children's children to be ready, as it seemed they now were.

Satisfied, The One turned its attention to other problems momentarily. For in this universe that The One inhabited, that The One had created, in fact, each galaxy had its own issues. With its new understanding about when to intervene and when to stand aloof, The One paused to consider some of those other problems with new thoughts, new considerations. This was something to discuss when next it met with its siblings from their own universes.

Odruf felt the feather touch of The One fade and smiled. He knew that the actions of the Guardians of Ennaris met with approval and had even been instrumental in actions his own parent - parent in spiritual terms, at least - had taken elsewhere in its universe. He knew very well that the Guardians had to tread carefully. The Ennarisi had reached a peak long ago and the fall had been horrendous and harrowing. But Odruf also knew that the Ennarisi and their children were likely to grow further than they had previously should the current events be handled correctly.

Odruf knew when Goroth was freed from stasis, for it was Odruf who caused those chains to loosen, as the Prophecy told him to do. *For when the Children take their place then will the bound one be released, and the dark shall take its place once more.* Odruf was sure that *the bound one* was Goroth and that the time was right. The Children were taking their places. Accordingly, he caused the stasis chamber to eject Goroth. Goroth, of course, would believe that it was his own power that caused the stasis chamber to fail.

Odruf also knew that Likud had departed the Andorethi home world, which provided an opportunity to begin repairing the damage Likud had done. Therefore, Odruf sought out Orish, one of the Guardians who had spent his time away from Ennaris in repairing the ill work of Likud on world after world that had fallen prey to the fallen Mage. Subtle was Orish. Although his Ennarisi persona usually involved strong drink and licentiousness, that was an invention by Balgor at his most mischievous, for Orish was sober and quiet, respectful of all creatures, of all worlds. Odruf discussed his idea with Orish, who considered briefly and agreed, as did the Guardians when it was presented to them as a group.

Thus, as Likud sped towards Ennaris with the entirety of his armed might, Orish left Ennaris and sped on his way to Andoreth, to establish a new presence for the Guardians and commence his work to guide the Andorethi back to the right path.

On *Starfire,* Jord was called to the bridge by Kiri. The fleet remained at general quarters, although little had happened so far.

"Sir, one of those bolts of energy just emerged from the planet and headed off into space," Rork said as Jord stepped up behind him.

"It had no problems getting through the planetary defence?" Jord asked thoughtfully.

"No sir, it just zipped through and took off."

"Any reaction from our friends over there?" Jord asked, inclining his head in the general direction of the Empire fleet's remnants.

"None, sir."

"Any idea where it's going?"

"Well, assuming whatever it is has no concerns about hiding its route, an extrapolated path takes it to the Shadow's home system."

Jord nodded. "Interesting. And just when the Grand Admiral seems to be expecting Likud and the whole Empire fleet to arrive any time." He pondered, pursing his lips as an idea emerged and was swiftly examined. "Kiri, send a coded signal to Fleet headquarters suggesting that monitoring of the Shadow home world should be stepped up. And that we may want to be prepared for diplomatic efforts in the near future."

"Sir?" Kiri asked, perplexed.

"I know, sounds strange, but I have the oddest feeling that this represents an opportunity rather than a threat. And Kiri," Jord said as his first officer turned to carry out her orders, "sign the dispatch Grand Admiral Mavin Serra. That should get the attention of someone."

Jord had a wicked grin as he turned back to the display showing the forces deployed around the planet below. Somewhere back at Fleet, someone who had been trying to make things very hard for the Union forces was about to get the fright of their life.

## 1. Portals

Blaine frowned as his hrss trudged along the dusty road heading back to the Citadel. They were two days out still. The two Warriors of the Light were returning from the Free Cities of Algol after thwarting efforts at infiltration, but with little addition to Corm's forces as a result. They had been back on the large plateau on which the Citadel was located for a tenday now. It had been an uneventful journey from Telsith via several villages and small towns. The Premptor of Telsith had provided them with hrss and provisions, and they had been able to make good time.

He was hot, dusty and uncomfortable but Blaine knew that the journey had been of immense value. Potential sources of danger had been negated in Frelor and Telsith. In doing so, and in the short time that they had been travelling, they had learnt much about this part of Ennaris, had met quite a few people and extended the Faero's influence. He was not sure what that would add up to militarily, however. The Sergeant may be able to spare some of the criminal element of Frelor but Telsith would be unable to assist.

Of course, other key accomplishments were discovering the portal and making contact with *Starfire*. That was not something they had envisaged doing and both had been surprised to find that they could do so. Jalor's suspicions about the ban on technology seemed to be valid - that interdict seemed to be selective, or at least incomplete. They had returned to the location of the portal the morning after hearing that strange sound, a sound without noise and only heard by them, it seemed, only to find the portal's tunnel had been cleared of the rock fall somehow, revealing a smooth, unblemished wall.

Senasarra - Sensor Array 413 - had informed Jalor that full communication had been re-established and security protocols were reinstated but had little further information to add, referring them to the Archmage. A few more questions elicited the information that Senasarra - oddly, the portal continued to respond to the name given by the villagers - was not equipped with a gate, where larger, more centrally located ones, were. Using his new authority as a member of the Council of the Guides, Jalor had directed Senasarra to continue to assist Hunder and the villagers, to which the portal had acceded.

The Warriors discussed the changes on their way back to Manis Reach. Putting two and two together and hoping they made four, they decided to make their way back to the Citadel with greater haste. Blaine made a mental note to return to Manis Reach when it was possible to do so and see how Hunder was doing with his efforts. Possibly he could lend a hand and help the Ennarisi advance once more. Blaine was finding that he quite enjoyed his time with these people, most of whom were genuine and lived far from ostentatious lives. Once you got past the murderous magical beasts, of course, Blaine thought to himself with a snort. But that, he hoped, was something he could do something about.

Jalor was similarly preoccupied in thinking about recent events. He was now certain that he and his team had been manipulated, but whether that was by Serra or the Guardians or some form of fate he could not tell. From the moment they had landed on Ennaris, the plan had gone out the window, which, he reflected ruefully, was pretty much the norm anyway. Usually, though, he had a chance to stay somewhat to the script they had formed, but here the script had been torn from his hands, ripped into shreds and scattered on the winds. They were being led towards a future battle with a foe who was, supposedly, the most powerful disruptive force in the galaxy, excluding the Guardians from the equation who had already said via Balgor that they would be non-combatant.

The episode with Senasarra - whose designation, Sensor Array 413, Jalor thought may have indicated that there probably were at least 412 others, and likely more - both rankled Jalor and provided food for thought. It rankled because the technology should not have worked if the interdict had been in place as they thought. The fact that it *was* functional indicated that some agent was interfering, and Jalor had not been able to determine exactly who or what that may be. It was food for thought, though, because it had been allowed to provide a valuable service to the Warriors, obviously after checking back to a central command location. And now it seemed to have returned to something like normal operations.

The fact that he and Blaine had been admitted to the Council of the Guides, which meant they were part of Flin's structure, also required some thought. It may mean nothing, but there had been statements and further hints that he and Blaine, like Varna, were singled out, because of their genetic heritage, for some form of 'gift'. Varna had almost succumbed to the effects of her gift or gifts, and Jalor was a little uncomfortable that he had lost touch with his more vulnerable team member, but he also knew that there were times when you went with the flow and times when you bucked it. This time he had decided to go with it, and he hoped it was the right decision. He wondered, both privately and openly in discussion with Blaine, whether the fact that they could hear that odd tone and no-one else did was also because of their genetic heritage. In part it was because he suspected that it might be so, and also that some sort of event had occurred that was important, that he had decided on a faster return to the Citadel.

As they rode, both men maintained the watch for danger that was so ingrained in them as to be automatic and continued to reflect on their situation. Both felt that the time for action was approaching but neither was sure about what form it would take.

Had Jalor seen Varna at that time he would have been doubly concerned. Naked as the day she was born, arms and legs outstretched and hair floating free in a sort of nimbus surrounding her head, her eyes were closed, and she floated impossibly in a chamber of the Tree. Her senses registered nothing physical, for the field in which she floated allowed for nothing to reach her - there was no sound, no smell, nothing could touch her, she could see nothing, nor could she taste anything. Instead, she was learning to use her new senses via telepathic instruction.

Floating with her was Eresh, still trying to find a way past whatever was blocking Varna from achieving full control. Part of the issue, she still suspected, may have been because Varna had been raised in an environment where gifted people, those with 'magic', were thought to be charlatans, fakers or tricksters, and the existence of the gifts was denied. Eresh knew that gifted individuals, or those suspected of performing magic, had been targeted for persecution and death in the history of Varna's civilisation. So, perhaps there was a cultural blockage to break through. That was do-able because it was nothing more than a conditioned belief system, and sufficient evidence would deal with that.

But there was something else, and Eresh had been surprised, then shocked, to find that she was unable to break through it. In fact, she was unable to get a clear understanding of what it was. For two tendays of Ennaris time now they had tried. Varna was much more proficient at reading the world around her but still was unable to tap into the depths of her gifts, and from what Eresh saw those gifts were going to be prodigious. Those two Ennaris tendays had been stretched to six tendays for Varna in virtual time while the Guardians worked to release her powers. Eresh was convinced this woman had depths never seen before. The force lying latent behind some form of wall was immense, she could tell, but the shape of that power and its extent could not be properly judged.

Eresh had discussed it with her fellow Guardians. They had debated whether to task Balgor with the effort, given the obvious intimacy the two had achieved and the affection now openly displayed, but it was felt that the fact of the intimacy may be an obstacle. Not that any of the Guardians were opposed to their relationship - most if not all of them had had Ennarisi lovers in the past, which had resulted in the greater strength of the gene pool - but they were both wary of the effect of it on Varna's efforts to break through her blockage and, likewise, were aware that it offered a refuge for her when her efforts were unavailing. Therefore, Eresh continued, sometimes supported by Lak and Menra, two of her fellow Guardians with some experience in helping those with blocked gifts to break through their blocks, and at other times by Fernis, Ogun and Odruf himself.

What was clear to all of the Guardians was that Varna would have to make the breakthrough herself. Eresh kept trying to unearth any influences that may have caused the blockage, to get through the stubbornly hard-held inner thoughts, into deep memories. Already they had investigated the difficulties Varna had experienced during her time at the Union academy, and the experiences of being accused of using her supposed psi powers to cheat, only to be exonerated. They had worked through the discovery that the man she thought had been supporting her had, in fact, been active in seeking to have her expelled from jealousy of her achievements. Varna had learned more about herself already, about how she had sought companionship and physical comfort from various men without really forming commitments - Eresh thought that was because the same blockage caused latent anxiety to bubble through.

Now they were digging through her earliest history. Varna objected that she had been able to do the same herself, but Eresh was insistent. And now, deep in her past, they found an episode whose details Varna had hidden from herself, from a time when she was very young. Her father had been away on duty and her mother took a break from her work at a local hospital when two men broke into the house and attacked Varna's mother. Varna, too young to truly understand what was happening, did understand that these men were trying to hurt her mother and she tried to stop them. One slapped her away, causing Varna to hit her head and almost lose consciousness but she fought back, and a surge of power rose through the core of her being. Without realising what she did she slapped the man in retaliation and pushed him, hard, across the room. The man collapsed, unmoving, against the wall. The second man, shocked, turned to confront the young girl only to be hurled across the room to smash into the main control panel of the house. With a great clap and flash the panel burst into flames and the house caught fire quickly. Varna, trying to get to her hurt mother, could not get through the flames and the neighbours who rescued her had to fight her from entering the house, which by then was an inferno. Her mother died in the flames.

Investigators had tried to piece the events together but could only come up with the fact that Varna's mother had fought against her attackers - for Varna had been able to describe them breaking in - and in so doing had somehow started the fire. Varna was unable to explain further and, while the few visible scars were treated and disappeared, the mental scarring was extreme and deep. She turned inward, even when her father rushed back from his tour of duty, blaming herself for her mother's death and having no-one to turn to but her distraught father, whose own emotions were fractured.

Eresh was sure that she had found the trigger for the block but was unable still to break it down. Varna, now forced to relive the episode, rediscovered her grief and was inconsolable for a time. She still blamed herself for the outcome. Despite the Guardians' sympathy and their reiteration that the young Varna was merely reacting to events forced upon her by the unscrupulous men, it seemed that the blockage was strengthened. For some time she avoided her sessions to learn further control, although Eresh was sure that she had been taught all that could be taught by the Guardians. The rest would be up to her own efforts, and they were dependent on Varna forgiving herself.

If not, if the power locked away in Varna could not be released to aid Drewflin and the others, then Eresh was afraid that Ennaris may be doomed!

Dalresar was in another part of the seemingly unending Tree, with Ogun. Dalresar's own memory block remained. Ogun had taken it upon himself to train Dalresar in weapons and warfare before tackling the blockage. Both Flin and Varna had thought that to be unnecessary, having seen how well he had handled weapons during the several fights they had been through. Still, Ogun was insistent, and so there they were.

Dalresar was presented with scene after scene of enemies to be fought, which he did with clinical precision. Flowing, spinning, jumping and pirouetting through bands of creatures from nightmares, or against individuals with skills almost matching his own, Flin's apprentice dispatched them all. And throughout every battle scene he fought without expression, fiercely but dispassionately, as though this was what he knew from a past life. But for Dalresar to play his part in what was to come that would not be enough. He would need to rediscover himself. After a time, Ogun decided he needed help and he, too, called on Menra.

Menra revelled in warfare. She had been the one to teach several very early Ennarisi tribes how to defend themselves from other aggressive tribes, reasoning that the strength that would result was what would be needed for the future. She had worked hard with a small group of very early Guides who had extreme agility, ensuring that they were better prepared to deal with any enemy. It was this group of Guides, or their descendants in arms, who had formed the guard for the Faero in the early days of Ennaris' unity, and who continued to do so up to the rebellion, many long ages after Menra had ceased to train them. When forced to leave Ennaris, Menra had sought out a particular world, far away from the centre of the Ennarisi civilisation on the furthest rim of the galaxy. There was a nascent civilisation where the women were stronger and better fitted than the men, and Menra made them the best hand to hand warriors in the galaxy. These warrior women did not seek power for themselves but were only interested in being the best. Menra had worked with generation after generation of these women. She would return once the well-being of Ennaris was settled. She was looking forward to the time when the warrior women of Atal met the advanced human civilisation that was spreading slowly through the galaxy.

Menra had little patience for most people, but in Dalresar she recognised a warrior spirit that was being held down. Intrigued, she agreed to work with Ogun, but in her own blunt style.

"He is damaged," Menra said to Ogun after their first session. "He knows how to fight and has the best skills of any I have seen, but he is damaged."

"Yes," Ogun agreed. "He has no memories of a time before the Archmage found him and recognised something within him. Drewflin was unable to establish just what the damage was."

"Perhaps the blast from the mine used to destroy the attackers when he landed on Ennaris has addled him," Menra suggested. "From what Odruf told us that was quite a destructive device."

"Perhaps, but I think not. I've spoken with Varna," Ogun responded, "and she told of finding sensor images of him carrying another of the first team away from the blast zone. Varna remains unaware of his identity, however."

Menra narrowed her eyes in thought. "A woman?"

"Possibly. There was one in that team."

"I'll examine that as a thread. I feel that there are memories here also that are causing him to hold back. He's the best I've ever come across," she reiterated.

"You realise his mission to Ennaris was over fifty cycles past, don't you?" Ogun said evenly.

Menra pursed her lips. "Yes, and that indicates that he's of the Children also. There is a different power hidden deep, as Drewflin surmised, and I think when we get it out it will be ... impressive."

"He is the Champion," Ogun said. "For both of his peoples. The Stone selected him from among all available in his home civilisation."

Menra nodded, thoughtful once more. "Then we need him to come back to us," she replied.

Ogun gave a return nod and faded away, leaving Menra to ponder.

Archmage Drewflin could move quickly when it was needed. He made his way to the Council Chamber and was surprised to find that the facility was fully lit, with all consoles active. Moving from one to the other, he noted that the planetary sensor array was online completely, as was the moon facility. He glanced at the arrangement of the two fleets in space above Ennaris and quirked an eyebrow at the ship docked on the side of the moon away from the fleets. He could see activity under way to re-establish defensive arsenals and with some surprise noted that the sensor array on Ennaris was also on-line.

That had interesting implications, for it may mean the interdiction against technology had been lifted. And that would mean Goroth was free. After so long, time was passing quickly, and Flin sensed that he did not have enough time for all preparations to be made.

However, it also meant that he could move around more easily, assuming the portals and gates had also come on-line, which another glance told him was the case. That caused him to sit and ponder for a while. The portals had been in place well before the rebellion, and that would mean some of them would be destroyed or damaged beyond use. Some may be in places one did not want to go, like the bottom of the new inland sea. Thoughtfully, he called up a map of current Ennaris and overlaid the portal locations, nodding to himself as he saw locations against more modern cities and towns, or in some cases wilderness.

Abruptly, he changed his mind. He had been thinking of heading back to the Citadel, but now he had another goal in mind. He pointed to one of the portals and a status panel popped up against the portal's icon. Flin smiled sadly. This one reminder of what had been lifted his spirits a little, although his smile faltered when he considered how small a sliver of that life it was. Once again Flin nodded, considering his next step. He needed further information so, without further consideration he made his way to the library.

It was not long afterwards that Flin exited the library and made his way down two levels to the portal. In the Council Chamber the portal was intended to serve multiple roles, so it was larger than many of the ones dotted around Ennaris. He moved to the control pad and tapped in a set of coordinates as he liked to do in the past, waiting for the few moments while the portals synced and the gate entrance turned a pale grey. With a quick glance at the control panel to ensure that a stable connection had been made, Flin walked through the portal gate.

He emerged from a smaller portal gate in a stone-sculpted building, obviously long disused. Soft lighting awoke as he appeared. Several lights showed a pale and wan glow, while others delivered strong light. A panel against one wall lit, showing Flin the layout of the building. He took a moment to examine it, recalling with a little effort the layout of the land around it from times long past. He moved to the exit door in the wall facing the portal, which slid open. It was a little jerky in its movement but Flin was impressed that it moved at all. He walked through and stood, staring at his surroundings.

Gone was the fertile valley that he recalled, with the many rows of vines and plots of orchards growing all kinds of fruit. He knew that such would be the case but, still, the reality shocked him for a moment. What he now stood on was a rocky pile thrusting up from the ocean. Craggy rocks stood out of the rolling waters. Huge waves threw themselves on the rocky island to be shattered into spray and spume that was thrown high into the air only to fall back into the ocean and be replaced by the next wave. The surface of the water heaved for as far as Flin could see, a huge swell lifting and falling.

Flin turned away from the sight and walked to one corner of the building where a staircase, treacherously slippery after thousands of cycles of sea spray and neglect, led up to a flat deck atop the building. From there, he watched the long waves rolling across the surface, with this islet being the only obstacle in their journey. Each wave split as it reached the island. The wave threw itself against the rocks, only to regain its energy as the rest of the wave rolled past and thus continued across the ocean. Below, behind the building, a curved rocky spit had been left behind, thrusting into the ocean.

After a time spent watching the hypnotic rhythm of the rolling waves, Flin descended the staircase once more and walked carefully around the building. The old path was shattered and dropped into a cavern of sorts. Once again he stopped and considered, then carefully stepped down the rocky incline and into the cavern. His path was made clear by light coming from a large opening at sea level. Through the opening he could see a tall spire of the fractured rock, standing on the end of the spit. Flin walked to the opening and stood still, his gaze carefully moving across the small beach that was in front of him to where the spit began. The water was calm and smooth inside the small cove that was formed by the spit and a rocky out-thrust near the cavern's mouth. He mapped out in his mind a path to use and started out. Drawing his staff to its full length and using it as a walking stick, he made his way slowly through the rocks and boulders to the small beach. Then, with a slight smile, he walked to the water's edge. The calm beach was illusory, he knew, for from the deck atop the portal building he had seen that the water depth increased rapidly even inside the sheltering cove.

He held his staff in his right hand, raising it slightly before lowering it so the foot of the staff was in the water. The stone flared and Flin sent out the call, one that he had never used before, a call that had not been made for thousands of cycles. He had no way of knowing if the call had been received, or if any remained to receive it and understand it, but after a long moment he lifted the staff once again. The stone extinguished its light as he did so. He walked to one of the larger stones along the tiny shoreline and sat, composing himself to wait.

Flin held off the cold wind with a small buffer of thickened air, looking over the heaving water and thinking back over the recent few tendays. He had been so sure that he was in control. His preparations had been proceeding at what he called a measured pace, and he was con-fident that he would be ready for what would come. He had expected to encounter difficulties, of course, but his confidence was dealt a blow on waking from stasis to find that he would not have Marjory to stand with him. Now, he had also lost that sense of control and was having to re-establish some sort of plan. The Guardians were taking a part, which was not expected in any way, and the Children had not panned out exactly as he expected. To be fair, he was not sure what to expect, but he certainly did not expect to have three such varied individuals. The fact that Varna was favoured by the Guardians and appeared destined to be a force was a shock, given her rocky start on Ennaris. Blaine and Jalor each had their own capabilities, and Flin suspected that he was not aware of just what they may be. The Prophecy mentioned several individuals by role, and the Warriors could fit into any of several. So, how could he make the best use of those around him? He also had in Dalresar an enigma that he hoped the Guardians could help with, a new Faero who was untested and raw, three Mages along with himself and what seemed to be a clutch of young Ennarisi with gifts breaking through. There were two fleets in orbit and the technology that had seemed unavailable suddenly seemed to be working again.

Round and round his thoughts went. Uncertainty built on concern and was swallowed by fears for his planet and its people. It took him a moment to realise that a long, wide, huge body had appeared and was floating towards the spit, slowly propelled by enormous flukes. Flin had known of the leviathans, of course, and Marjory had spoken of her dealings with them, but he had never realised that there were Guides left amongst them. And the size of this one was breath-taking. After a moment when he just stared, Flin stood and walked to the water's edge once more. The huge creature made his way as far as possible before turning slightly and extending one great fluke over the shallow stretch of water to hover uncertainly in front of Flin. In awe, Flin slowly reached out and placed one palm on the fluke, which was held in place for a time and then slowly drawn back. The leviathan slid back into deeper water, submerging temporarily before re-emerging to float atop the water. One great eye watched Flin.

*Well met, Archmage.* The thought was transmitted to Flin. *My name is Ooshmin. I am the last Guide of the Seas of Ennaris. I am also the last Mage of the Sea.*

"Well met, indeed, Ooshmin," Flin replied gravely. "I deeply apologise for not having taken the trouble to meet with you before now. I was not aware any Guides of the Sea survived the rebellion, let alone that there were Mages."

*Ana has informed me of your plight, Archmage,* Ooshmin replied. *I received the chime of the revelation of the Archmage. My heart is full, now we have an Archmage once more.*

"I thank you Ooshmin," Flin said. "There are very few of us to do what must be done."

*Indeed,* the leviathan replied with a wry tone. *But I have started to train a new generation and some will be ready to take the oath shortly.*

"So soon!" Flin said, surprised. "We have uncovered gifts of varying kind but amongst the young only. How are you able to do this so quickly?"

*Our method is more direct, Archmage. We have the ability to link mind to mind and so pass on the learning far more rapidly.* Ooshmin paused a moment, considering. *We have much to discuss, Archmage. Would you consider linking your mind to mine, as was done in the days past?*

"I'm not aware of how to do that," Flin confessed.

*I am well aware, as I did so often with the Guides of the Land. Would you trust me with this? We do need to touch.*

Flin did not hesitate. He stepped into the cold water, to the edge of the shallow, to make it easier for Ooshmin to approach.

"It would be my honour."

Ooshmin once again rolled slightly and extended his fluke, more easily this time because Flin was closer. Flin reached forward and once again placed his palm on the fluke. A moment passed and then Flin felt a gentle touch on his consciousness, a feather only, as though Ooshmin was asking permission. Which, Flin thought, he probably was. Opening his mind in assent, Flin found himself sinking into Ooshmin's mind, the two Mages merging their consciousnesses in an experience unlike anything that he had had before. In wonder, Flin saw Ooshmin's world, and was shown memories of the time before the rebellion. He was shown events in the oceans since then that included the passing of all other Guides and the continuing efforts of Ooshmin and his newer brethren to repair the damage caused by Goroth and his allies. Flin shared grief with Ooshmin, and experienced the joy of Ana returning, ending with the exhilaration of receiving the chime as Fernis placed the Enchara on Flin's head.

Humbled at the thought of this great being being made so happy by virtue of his own recognition, Flin in return let Ooshmin into his own memories of the changes to the land since the rebellion, the despair of the Guides and their decline to a handful, of Flin's own despair when he found Marjory gone, and of the events of recent times.

The two beings shared wonder after wonder in communion with each other, on a rocky island far from the north continent of Ennaris, losing track of time as they did so. And in doing so, an unshakeable bond was formed.

Corm was concerned, although he tried not to show it. It had been many tendays since he was acclaimed Faero, and he had neither seen nor heard from Jalor or Blaine for much of that time. True, he had been drilled, hard, by Almin Bor and several others, including the warrior woman Helt. He knew that he was much improved in his sword-play and other aspects of warfare, but he felt that he needed the appointed general of the forces to actually be around for part of the time. The twins had drummed into his head fact after fact about Ennaris, the Faeros of the past and the little that was understood of the Prophecy, and they had explained about how Ennaris had been a galactic power far, far in the past.

The twins seemed to be much more engaged since that strange episode when they heard what they claimed was the sound of the Arch-mage being appointed formally by the Guardians. What was surprising to many, the twins not the least, was the number of other people who had heard the tone, including Corm. Ragnor had started an investigation to find out how many people had heard or felt that odd sound to some extent and his excitement had grown as an increasing number of Faeronar had come forward. Raglin told Corm that it meant the gifts had not died out as much as was feared, although few people acknowledged them.

Corm's guard had grown and was now more properly called an army, small though it still was. Almin Bor had started to select more officers and the recruits were being sorted depending on skill levels. The Citadel was bustling and apartments that had been long closed were being re-opened. New businesses had sprung up to cater for the increase in population, not the least of which being several new inns and taverns, while existing businesses had put on extra staff.

Refugees had also continued to arrive, if not as many as before. Rumours told of a haven for displaced people, especially women, that had been established at a place called Anhard Springs, where some sort of talisman had been left to protect the village by one of the Children of Ennaris, who had returned as foretold in the Prophecy. Corm was not sure what to make of it, but the rumours said the talisman had saved the villagers from being wiped out by ghazrak, with the Child wielding the sword of the last Faero before the rebellion. He asked Raglin about the sword, and was told that the smaller ceremonial sword had disappeared along with several other artefacts and had been presumed lost when the land changed. Perhaps that was not the case. But, if it was one of the Children, then it had to be Varna.

Events were moving around him. The Faero was restless as he watched yet another small group enter through the Gate of Balgor, a name given to the entry to the Citadel after the events of the battle with the ghazrak had been made known. Balgor said he hated it, of course, which in the perversely humorous way of the Faeronar meant that it stayed that way. This group, a heavily muscular man with a tall, spare woman and three children of varying ages, were gathered up by one of the reception teams that Corm had established and taken to be questioned to understand their skills, whether they had any gifts and what they could offer to the Citadel.

The family were followed by two dust-covered men riding equally dusty hrss, and it took Corm a moment to realise that they were Jalor and Blaine. Corm was amused by the efforts of one of the reception team to herd the two away from the main square, resulting in Jalor giving her a penetrating glare before Almin Bor appeared to intervene. Corm was amused also to see Helt appear, seemingly from nowhere, and take a place to the left of Blaine as they left their hrss with a guard recruit and walked across the square.

"Jalor, Blaine," Corm acknowledged as they drew near to where he stood leaning against the stone front of the administration building. "I was beginning to think you had disappeared," he said with some of his frustration leaking through.

"Hello Corm," Jalor replied. "I apologise for the time spent away. It was longer than we expected but a few things came up that we had to help with. I'll fill you in over a meal if you like?" At Corm's nod he continued. "And there are a couple of things we need to discuss with the twins that you probably need to hear. I think we may have a way to gather your army faster than we thought."

Almin Bor sighed. "The army is growing already," he said, "and that will cause problems soon. I've been getting the basic organisation going but we will need to make that happen faster. And if it gets much bigger then the problem gets worse."

Jalor nodded. "We can deal with that also. I need to clean up, and I'm guessing Blaine does also. Can we get together after that? Maybe away from what seems to be a lot more ears than there were?"

"I'll arrange that," Almin Bor said. "I'll inform the twins also."

With a nod Jalor headed off to his quarters, trailed by Blaine and Helt, neither of whom had said a word to each other yet. Corm stared after them, a smile tugging at his lips, while Almin Bor walked away with a grin of his own.

Sitting across a satisfying meal, Jalor had told of the various events on their recent journey, and had reached the discovery of the oracle in Manis Reach.

"An oracle?" Raglin asked, looking askance. "Someone telling tall tales and such?"

"Not quite," Jalor replied. "The oracle is called Senasarra by the people of the town. It was found in what they thought was a mostly blocked-in cave and was being used to tell them the weather forecast as well as giving hints about how to better make metal alloys. The blacksmith is an avid user of its advice."

"Alloys?" Corm asked.

"A blend of different metals to make a stronger metal, in this case for ploughshares," Jalor explained.

Raglin watched Jalor through slitted eyes. "And what are you waiting to tell us? You have the look of a borus that got the cream."

Jalor smiled. "Senasarra's proper name is Sensor Array 413."

The twins exchanged a single surprised look before Ragnor stood and hurried away from the group. Corm was perplexed, as was Almin Bor and Helt. Blaine sat back to wait, both expectant and hopeful, while Jalor took a segment of fruit like a mango and bit into it, wiping away the inevitable trickle of juice that made its way down his chin. Neither offered an explanation.

Ragnor returned a short while later and nodded to Raglin. "The array is active," he said.

"How long have you known it is there?" Jalor asked.

"Since it was built, but it went dark when the technology interdiction was imposed. The Citadel was built before the rebellion ended, remember, so the array was installed as normal and the portal with it."

Blaine relaxed, only then realising that he had been keyed up. The existence of working portals and gates was crucial to Jalor's plan. He smiled at Corm's continued confusion, reflecting how odd it was to have advanced technology in an almost medieval setting. There would be a lot of confused people for a while.

"Would someone please tell me what this is all about?" Corm asked plaintively.

"Better that we show you," Jalor said, rising. "Ragnor, would you guide please?"

The twins nodded, as though he had addressed them both, and the whole party left the table. Ragnor made his way confidently through the corridors to a staircase at the back, in a dark corner. A single heavy wooden door was pushed open, allowing access to the stairs and the group trooped down three flights, passing a door on each flight. Another door at the end was pushed open and Blaine noted a corridor with glowing lights. Guttering brands hanging from wall sconces interspersed the steadily glowing lights. Of course, he thought, the technology is coming back. These lights had been dormant for millennia and just switched back on. The Warrior shook his head as he considered the advances this civilisation that had almost died could provide to the galaxy, even in its current state.

The corridor ended at another door. Blaine calculated that they must be close to the edge of the Citadel, a surmise proved correct when the door was pulled open to reveal what obviously was the roots of the Citadel wall, dug deep into the earth and sitting on bedrock. A large room was revealed. Patterned tiles covered the floor in a huge mural, showing what Blaine thought were fanciful scenes of a futuristic city with tall pointed spires, where light and airy bridges spanned gaps between structures. Large open spaces were surrounded by gardens, fountains and a few people enjoying what looked like a fine day.

Corm gasped and stopped, examining the floor before asking, "What is this?"

Raglin sighed. "Arbogast, before the rebellion," he said sadly. "Just a small portion of it, of course. This was the Square of Light."

Blaine stared, then looked up to see Jalor with a bemused expression. This had been real? This is part of what was lost?

"Indeed yes, Blaine," Raglin replied to the questions that Blaine now realised he had asked aloud. "But the tiniest part of what we lost as a result of arrogance and greed. And Arbogast was not the most advanced of our cities, for it was the administrative hub of Ennaris. Arbotan was truly beautiful, and the island city of Arbolith was a hive of artistic expression. All gone now for these thousands of cycles."

Jalor and Blaine, no strangers to advanced architecture and technology, stood amid the image of the lost city. Corm and Helt, with Almin Bor, walked slowly around the large chamber, each alone, stopping to examine parts of the mural. Helt turned to Blaine, who was surprised to see tears running down her face.

"We must get this back," she said quietly. "We cannot allow this to die completely."

"This is part of what we will be fighting for," Almin Bor said in response. "All of us who join with Corm to oppose Goroth and his kind. I never realised what was lost, and I vow to do my all to bring it back. I speak for the Blood."

Corm nodded, acknowledging the sentiment, then started at the sound of a heavy blade being drawn from its scabbard. He turned to find Helt advancing on him, naked sword drawn. Blaine made to step forward but Almin Bor stopped him with a light hand on his arm.

"Corm, I have been grateful for the acceptance by the Faeronar where others refused me. I have fought with your guard for your father and now you, because that was what I wished to do. I now see that you have a higher purpose and I would be part of that." Helt reversed the sword, holding the hilt towards Corm as she dropped to one knee in the centre of the Square of Light, and continued in a formal tone at odds with her usual banter. "I, Princess Anhelter of Escar, do pledge my service to the Faero of Ennaris for so long as is required to overcome the evil besetting this land. Do you accept my pledge, Faero?"

Corm stared, as did all but the twins, who merely looked satisfied. Corm reached out and took hold of the sword hilt, lifting it from Helt's grasp, before turning it again so the hilt faced Helt.

"Princess Anhelter of Escar, I accept your pledge," he responded in a similarly formal tone. "Now please, arise and take back your sword. It's heavy!" he ended in a lighter tone of voice.

Helt grinned as she stood and, with a flourish, took her sword back and sheathed it in a single movement.

"Show off," Corm muttered with an answering grin. "Now, this is all very good, but what were you going to show me here?"

Ragnor gestured to one side wall, which had no stone-work and was dark. A single tiny light showed in a panel at the edge nearest the Citadel wall. The party moved to stand near the panel. Ragnor waved his hand over the panel and the single light was joined by a small set of varying coloured lights.

"Mage Ragnor recognised." A male voice said from somewhere.

Ragnor turned to Corm. "This is part of the heritage of Ennaris. This is a portal, and it allows access to the artificial intelligence that controls parts of the Ennaris defence systems, as well as information resources. It can answer many questions, and has access to much of the knowledge of Ennaris of the past. It also controls sensors, which are like watchers scattered around the area so you can be made aware of certain things when you have need. There is a panel like this in your chambers, which I will show you shortly. This portal also has a gate." He waited until Corm nodded, although obviously he was still mystified, before continuing. "Sensor Array 935, recognise Corm Ramesa, Faero of Ennaris. Corm, say something so the array knows your voice."

"Uh, um, hello, er, sensor ray," Corm stammered.

"Recognise Corm Ramesa, Faero of Ennaris," the array responded, and then the voice changed to the same female voice Jalor remembered from his previous interaction. "Council Assistant recognises Corm Ramesa, Faero of Ennaris. Access to all systems available. Update. Planetary defence grid online. Sensor arrays online, multiple failures being investigated. Offensive array online. Planetary weapons platforms generating and at eighty percent effectiveness. Two fleets in orbit of Ennaris. Targeting system locked. Awaiting orders."

Corm looked helplessly to the twins and then Jalor, who grinned. "It will take a little getting used to, I'm afraid," Jalor said.

"Recognise Flight-Colonel Vinca Jalor," the Council Assistant broke in. "Access to all defence and offence systems available, by order of Archmage Drewflin."

"Thank you Council Assistant," Jalor said. "Is the portal network functional?"

"Yes, Flight-Colonel," was the reply. "The portal network is functional, although because of geographic changes several portals are either off the grid or located in sites that represent danger to users and thus have been disabled."

"Can you plot the portals with gates on a map of Ennaris, please? A modern topographical map with the major cities."

The wall to the left of the control panel came on, showing a map of Ennaris. Corm exclaimed and stepped forward, while Helt's eyes opened wide and she also moved closer. The map showed the two continents of Ennaris, with the narrow neck of land at the eastern side joining the two continents and the large sea that occupied the space between them. A narrow opening led from the inland sea into the western ocean. Major rivers were shown, along with the desert and steppes, mountain ranges and forest and jungle areas. A single point showed in yellow at one end of the large plateau in the northern continent, and then a jumble of blue points appeared, scattered over much of Ennaris. A second wave of points, red this time and far fewer in number, were added, most of them showing in the ocean or around the mountain ranges. Finally, diamond icons were displayed, with names against them.

"The blue points indicate working portals and the red inactive ones," the Council Assistant said. "The diamonds are working portal gates."

"Escar!" Helt exclaimed, pointing to one of the diamonds.

Jalor examined the map intently. Most of the main cities of the present day were coincident with, or very close to, a portal gate. But there was no real way to know just where the portals may be in those cities. Several of the blue points with diamonds were in what seemed to be the wilder regions, including two in the northern steppe and one near the centre of the desert in the south. He noted one point in the ocean west of the landmass, and considered it for a moment - probably an island that survived. There were four blue points and two red ones in the furthest north, where the map showed ice extending beyond the land mass. Only one of the blue points showed a diamond.

"Raglin, Ragnor," Jalor called, bringing the twins from where they were having a private discussion. "Which are the major cities or regions we need to convince to join Corm for defence? Other then those we have already visited."

Raglin stepped forward and considered for a moment. He looked to Ragnor and lifted a hand with five fingers splayed, his eyebrows asking the question. Ragnor shook his head and held up six fingers, at which Raglin nodded.

"There are six major cities. Most of the smaller ones will follow, although there may be the need to convince a few that it's not a ploy to absorb them into the larger domains. Escar is important, especially militarily. Frankly, Ensert could take over most of the north with relatively little effort, other than the steppes, of course, but he doesn't want to. We expect he will support Corm, although maybe not as an overlord of sorts." He smiled as Helt nodded decisively, and then pointed to a second diamond, at the eastern end of the steppes. "Escar is facing an immediate challenge that we will discuss. Harhaven is less a city and more of a meeting place for the Clan people of the steppes. The various Clans don't really consider Hartik to be a queen, more a leader of equals, but they may join as a whole. I think Corm will have to convince them that he is strong enough for them to follow. They've never lost a war, at least in their collective memory, so they feel confident they can defeat anyone ultimately."

"Okay," Jalor nodded. "But we would have to visit with Ensert also. What is his position? King, I assume, if Helt is a princess?"

"He is king," Helt replied, agreeing with what was almost a snarl. "From a long line of kings who believe women can only cook, wash and give birth!"

Jalor smiled, answering Blaine's broad grin. "I'll remember that. Will having you as one of the officers of the army cause problems?"

Helt's snarl became a gasp. She was nonplussed. "Me, an officer of the army? But, but I get into trouble all the time."

"Well, that's probably because you were allowed to get away with it. Not in my army you won't. Besides, from what I'm told you have a good head for strategy, once you stop charging into the middle of every fight with sword swinging." Jalor turned from Helt, who still looked like someone had struck her from behind, and back to the twins. "Who's next?"

Raglin pointed to a point in the south. "This is the desert. Like the steppes there's no real city, and the sand just keeps rolling over most places anyway. So, the desert tribes tend to gather once a cycle at the Vale of Morrig..."

"Oasis of Morrig," Ragnor broke in.

"What?" Raglin said, to the amusement of the others who had never seen the brothers lacking in synchronised speech. It seemed the shock went both ways.

"When she came back Morrig renamed it the Oasis of Morrig. Apparently that's what the desert-dwellers were calling it and she saw no reason to change it."

"Oh." Raglin shrugged, back on an even keel once more. "Well, then they meet once a cycle at the Oasis of Morrig. It's almost in the exact centre of the desert. They meet at almost the same time as the herders of the steppes, oddly. They may or may not need convincing. They were devoted to the memory of Morrig, so her word may be telling."

"And both places have portal gates nearby?" Jalor asked, considering the array of blue points on the map. "Convenient. Is it coincidental?"

"Not really," Ragnor said. "The Oasis of Morrig is where she was reputed to have her dwelling, even before the desert was there. Even when she was forgotten as an actual being. It was the rebellion that caused a rapid change there, but Balgor told us that she had been helping the gardens to stay alive for some time, anyway, so when her power was lost the sand took over. As for the herders, the grass steppes had been there for a long time as farmland and pasture, and the portals were how the Guides were able to meet with them. It was the bread basket of Ennaris. Lots of grain crops and such. We kept a permanent presence there, and the portals are all that will be left. We've not been to them for a very long time, so we have no idea what they're like now."

"Right. That makes sense." Jalor was looking at the map. "Next?"

"I hope you like the cold." Raglin again pointed to the sole blue point with a diamond at the top of the north continent, well within what was displayed as an arctic ice zone. "Xylar. It's a permanent camp more than a city, largely a base where supplies are stockpiled and on-sold to those who live in the remote parts of the northern reaches. The Junda are a particularly hardy group, but how they would go as an army I have no idea. If they joined up. They also are very individualistic in many parts of their lives."

"Which Guardian do they look to?" Blaine asked.

Raglin nodded appreciatively. "Lak. She will support our cause without question. Well, I think all of the Guardians will, but some may see the need to be more even-handed. Lak will favour Corm."

"Oh? Why so certain?" Jalor asked.

"Um, well, the story goes that quite a long time ago Lak took a liking to one of the then Faero's sons. He was not likely to be in the line of succession so no-one bothered with it, if they even knew who she was. There was a son, who did not have significant gifts. But, after a couple of generations the Faero's line died out, so that branch took the burden." Ragnor paused, glancing to Corm. "The line has been essentially that branch since, even when Faeros died without children and the family sought a surviving sub-branch."

Corm stared from one to the other. "Wait! Are you saying one of my forebears was a Guardian?"

"Yes, so the story says," Raglin said with a grin.

Jalor laughed. "Well, that's one way to get influence. And number six?"

"In the mountains, very high up. The old walled city of Umber." Ragnor pointed to a blue point and diamond in the midst of the mountain peaks. "The mountain people pretty much never leave the mountains but no-one has ever defeated them. Or rather, no-one has ever defeated the mountains. The mountain people may even be more hardy than those of the ice. This portal is a distance from the old city, in what was once a garrison town, although there was no real planetary military."

"Garrison against what?" Blaine asked. "I thought Ennaris was all one happy family before the rebellion."

"Yes and no," Raglin replied. "There were differences still, as the events leading to the rebellion showed. Many in the mountain area were not supportive of the Guides and accepted the Faero on sufferance only. Luckily the Rocs did support us, and they held a lot of sway with the mountain folks."

"Rocs?" Jalor's head was starting to spin. "I don't believe I have heard of the Rocs. What people are they?"

"Not people. Birds!" Ragnor said. "Big birds! They have their eyries amongst the peaks of the mountains. Very intelligent, resourceful and devoted to Kunas. I assume he has returned also. He may have received a frosty reception though. From what Balgor told us they were un-impressed with him leaving them after the rebellion. They suffered huge losses."

"So," Jalor said. "We have scattered locations on both continents where we need to get support, or at least exert influence to get what we can. Nothing in the jungles?"

"No, nothing of size," Raglin said, shaking his head. "Likki is back there and expelled the priests who tried to bring back the old practices of sacrifice and cannibalism, but that's all I heard. There are actually very few people who live in the jungles, we believe. Most live in small settlements along the coasts. Port Killnar and Killfor are called twin cities but they're only half the size of Escar together."

"What about the other towns and small cities?"

"As I said, many of them will follow the lead of the larger city that they look to for leadership. Some few may be less inclined to help, but most will listen. The Tellers have been primed to remind the people of their lessons from history. Hopefully, the last few cycles of the old stories being told will have an effect." Raglin shrugged. "There are a lot of people in those towns. Even the small cities are more like large towns, although some of them have played larger roles in their regions than they may do today. And pride still exists in many of them. Frelor and Telsith in the free zone of Algol are the ones you already know about."

"And this area of the map where there is a blank? I see there are several portals listed as damaged or off-line."

"That's where we believe Goroth's people are," Ragnor said bleakly. "We think they have completely corrupted the people of Kresh and Ingten. They grew out of the remnants of the lands of the old forests after the rebellion. The forests did not survive, and the people were struggling to survive when we tried to help them. They blamed us for the destruction and drove us away. They probably were incited by Goroth's supporters. It was one of the areas that strongly supported Goroth - it was his home, by the way. It's now known as the twin kingdoms of Kresh and Ingten. The land up there is hard and unrelenting, rocky and barren. The people who were with the ghazrak were from there by the looks of them. That's also where the red gold comes from. It's actually gold that is blended with traces of iron ore, by the way. In the far past that region was where iron was made, before we took the mines and factories off-planet."

Jalor nodded, considering. The group remained quiet while he did so. Helt wandered away again, looking at the mural. Corm stood and looked at the map, marvelling at what he saw and, at the same time, feeling completely out of his depth. Conversely, it was obvious that Jalor, Blaine and the twins were at home with these instruments. He sighed to himself. He was going to be a figurehead, and would have to rely on these people for everything. He wondered if his father had ever felt like that, and felt a pang at the loss. How he would love to be able to turn to his father for advice now. Too late, all too late!

"Okay, so this is how we'll play it," Jalor said. "There are details to be worked out but I think Corm or I or both of us will go through the portals to each of the main cities. Raglin or Ragnor, can you ascertain when the gatherings for the herders and the desert people will take place? We need to use that as the timing foundation. And we will have to have one of you with us. Corm, I'm sorry but you are going to have to put on a show to try to get as many of these people with us as we can."

Corm nodded.

"Don't feel that this is making you a figure-head though," Jalor said, noting Corm's surprise at the statement, and feeling he had been correct in thinking that was exactly what Corm would have felt. "You are the Faero and you need to be the Faero. Blaine and I are here to do a job, and this now appears to be part of it. But when we leave you need to be in charge."

Corm nodded again, standing straighter.

"Almin Bor has been working with you about strategy," Jalor continued. "Part of a strategic approach to warfare is for the leader not to be in the front line, at least not all the time. In a world such as you have here you need to balance that with being seen as someone to follow. That is what we need to work on. But don't ever feel that you are anything less for not being at the front all the time."

"The King of Escar always leads his men into battle," Helt said, with a display of haughtiness that Blaine had not seen before.

"How many kings have fallen in battle," Blaine asked quietly.

"Many," Helt replied, proudly.

"And what happened to Escar each time?"

Helt faltered. "Well, sometimes there was internal strife, and other times a new family branch took the throne via acclamation."

Blaine nodded. "And sometimes Escar lost battles or even the war because of the loss of the king. Am I right there?" He waited while Helt nodded reluctantly. "Leading in battle is fine if there is a suitable structure to pick up the leadership when the leader falls, even if only injured rather than killed. Corm does not have that structure, nor does Ennaris."

Corm picked up the thread of the previous discussion. "So, what's the plan?"

"That's something we need to work through in some detail," Jalor replied. "But we need to visit those cities or meeting places and speak with the people involved. You need to show them a Faero, while I show them your general. Meanwhile, Raglin, you said there's a terminal in the Faero's rooms?"

Raglin nodded. "Yes, I can show you. It's been covered over but may be working."

Jalor smiled. "Assistant, is the portal in the Faero's quarters active?"

"Yes, Flight-Colonel," came the instant reply.

Jalor smiled to the twins, who grinned ruefully. "In fairness, we've not had the portals operational for thousands of cycles," Raglin said in defence.

"Or we would have thought to do that," Ragnor finished the thought.

"Then let's gather in Corm's quarters tomorrow morning and go through the detail of the program. Blaine, I'm thinking you stay here and work with Almin Bor. But I may take Helt with us." Jalor cocked an eyebrow in Helt's direction, who nodded in response.

"Nothing makes people take notice more than someone in a metal suit," Blaine said blandly.

"Well, I need something to eat and a good night's sleep, but first I think Almin Bor and I need to go over what's happening with the guard, or army as we need to start to call it."

The group left the portal chamber, Corm and Helt both giving backward glances at the former glory of their world. Almin Bor was already starting his update to Jalor as they walked.

# 3. Sirius

Admiral Mika Sancer grunted as he watched the time count down. There were still a few seconds to go but he held out no hopes of his ship meeting it. Just as they had not met it the last twenty-seven times.

"Admiral, all positions report ready," Captain Heris Morgal reported, struggling to keep his face smooth.

And failing. A broad smile broke out on the *Sirius'* captain's face. He had worked endlessly on getting *Sirius* back into trim as a fighting ship. Finally, the ship had met what was, admittedly, one of the oldest tests in the book - a battle stations test.

*Sirius* had been close to falling apart. The Admiral and captain were both summarily discharged and replaced, a large proportion of the Warrior team had been found to be compromised to the point where the whole team had been stood down from duty. The command staff were thought to be compromised also, as were the medical and logistics staffs, especially after the attempts to kill Varna Barr, the Warrior who had brought the situation to light by exposing her team leader as an Empire collaborator. And she was the new admiral's daughter. The infection was felt to be wide enough that there was thought of scrapping the Fourth Fleet entirely, taking the loss and rebuilding the fleet complement entirely or breaking it up and retiring the fleet's colours.

It had been the new admiral who came up with the best answer to the difficult problem. After several weeks of trying to uncover all those involved, and dealing harshly with many of them, he had taken himself off to Earth without warning, returning a few days later with a stone.

But not just any stone. This was the Shakar, the stone used to choose the Champion.

Over the next month every member of the fleet from the highest to the lowest were rotated through the *Sirius'* security section for interview. Each was instructed to hold the stone. The interview consisted of a single question: *are you an Empire collaborator?*

The result was as breath-taking as it was shattering, even for the more seasoned of the security teams. Over one hundred collaborators who had not already been identified were now unmasked. The effects of the Shakar drove some of them over the edge, mentally. Most of the rest of those exposed were badly shaken by the experience. Not a few attempted suicide over the next two weeks while they were prepared for incarceration. As a purge it was extremely effective.

The effect on the fleet's morale, however, was staggering. Many of those who were exposed had held command or bridge positions, and more Warriors were uncovered. The fact was that everyone in the fleet found that they had been working alongside women and men who had been active enemies of the Union. People who had been trusted, who were close friends, lovers, partners, those to whom lives had been entrusted, all had been shown to be the enemy rather than a friend.

Captain Morgal had joined *Sirius* from the Fifth Fleet, with a reputation for running efficient and effective fighting ships. Immediately, he had been tasked by Admiral Sancer with getting *Sirius* into shape. The task was huge. Morale was the worst anyone in a fleet position had ever seen or hoped to ever see again. Requests for transfer from the fleet tripled once the interviews ended and Sancer was confident that the traitors had all been discovered. Most were granted. Retirements more than doubled. Counsellors were working overtime and their numbers had to be bolstered to help to rebuild the self-regard of those who remained as well as those who wished to leave, for there was no desire to create problems for other fleet commanders.

The fighters were another story. The Warriors went through the classic sequence of grief and those who came out the other side were noticeably harder. These were people who dealt with adversity repeatedly, and managed uncertainty and challenges every day of a deployment. Now, they were forced to dig deep to counter the effects of what had been uncovered. Anger at Varna, which had been contrived and fostered by some who were then found to be traitors, was replaced by a deeper admiration as her story became known more broadly. The Warriors who remained now *knew* that they could trust those who remained with them and became a closer knit group with a deep, visceral need to prove themselves once again.

The pilots had a different reaction. Oddly, none of the pilots had been proven to be compromised, but all were deeply angered and frustrated. They worked their anger and frustration out via massively increasing their training load, by hitting the gyms, by hitting the bars, by hitting each other - charges for fighting among the air crews rose noticeably - until Admiral Sancer had called them all together and informed them in no uncertain terms that if they did not put a lid on it they would be confined or fired. The counsellors had been horrified. The support staff who had borne the brunt of many hot-tempered pilots were amused. The pilots themselves were either incensed or humiliated, or both, at the effects of their own actions. But the admiral had made the address while wearing a pilot's flight suit, and he ended his very blunt description of the pilots' attitudes with an invitation to join him in target practice in a nearby asteroid field. Many asteroids died that day.

Then came the receipt of the signal.

"Admiral, copying a signal sent to Fleet headquarters from *Starfire*," the communications specialist reported.

"And is that of interest to us?" Sancer asked. "How did we get it anyway?"

"It was broadcast rather than tight beam, Admiral. Almost as though it was meant to be heard."

"Okay, so meant to be picked up. What is the message?" Sancer turned to look at the comms station.

"*Starfire* suggests that the Shadow home world should be monitored for possible diplomatic overtures, sir."

"Odd, but not anything to be too concerned about," Sancer replied.

But the communications specialist seemed to be agitated. She was new to the ship, one of the many recent replacements. She was one who had proven herself to be adept and confident in her skills. In his limited experience with her she had exhibited nothing but professional calm.

"Lieutenant, what's so special about this message?" Sancer asked.

"Admiral, it's the signature. The message is signed by Grand Admiral Mavin Serra."

Silence descended on the bridge. Sancer merely sat in his command chair and considered, allowing the silence to lengthen while he played through the scenarios in his head. He had met the Grand Admiral as a very young officer but he knew and had known and worked with many who worked with her. She was back, somehow, and apparently had taken over Denton's fleet.

"Lieutenant, do you have an approximate location for that signal's origin?"

"Aye, Admiral."

"Put it on the main board, please."

The large screen at the front of the bridge changed from showing a view of surrounding space to a star chart, with a point lit in a section of the galaxy quite a distance from *Sirius*. Sancer thought some more, working his own keypad. A new point lit up, close to the first. Sancer noticed the quizzical look from the Lieutenant.

"It's the site of an old space battle. Where *Sunburst* was lost." He mused a little more. "Tactical, where are the Empire fleets to the best of our guesses?"

"There's reported to be an Empire fleet in the near vicinity of *Starfire's* location, Admiral, exact location unknown. Preliminary reports are of the Empire's Main Fleet moving also. Direction is uncertain but it could be in the same direction. And the Outer Fleet seems to be moving also, possibly to the same location. Hard to tell, but it's slow if it is. Adding the best guess to the plot, Admiral."

"Thank you," Sancer replied.

From that point the training and preparations for the Fourth Fleet had stepped up dramatically. Sancer drove his captains mercilessly, demanding performance improvements across the board. His tactical staff were charged with maintaining an up to date plot of both Empire and Union fleets. Something was happening and if *Starfire* was involved, then so was Varna. But more than that, Sancer had a feeling …

Now, finally, the Fleet appeared to be coming together. The battle stations readiness test was simple, but it involved everyone doing what they needed to do as a team, to work as a unit. Each ship had to be in its correct position for either defence or attack, and the ship complements had to be in their designated places to fight or defend their ship. It was only a short time before that the Fourth Fleet was unable to get close to that coordination. Now, it had been achieved. It was a massive improvement and Sancer knew the effort that it had cost his own staff and those of the other ships. Fleet logistics were difficult things to manage well. When it was done well it was like a ballet in space. When it was not done well, it resembled nothing more than an upturned ant colony.

"Comms, send to all ships. Well done and congratulations. Simulation successful." Sancer sat back, satisfied at what had been achieved.

"Admiral," Tactical reported.

"Yes?"

"You asked to monitor movements. Second Fleet has left Earth Base Three. It's heading takes it in the direction of *Starfire*."

Sancer nodded.

"Admiral, in addition, the Empire Outer Fleet has moved, potentially to intercept but maybe just heading in the same direction."

"Both plotted?" Sancer asked.

"Aye, Admiral, the plot has been updated."

"Tactical, am I reading that right? Are they cutting through the Lancing Cluster?" Sancer examined the star chart closely. The Lancing Cluster was not far from *Sirius*.

"Aye, Admiral," Tactical said, glancing back to Sancer with a grin approaching feral. "They're heading through the Cluster."

"Sound General Quarters. This is not a drill. Tactical, estimate course and time for interception of the Empire fleet please. Captain Morgal!"

"Aye, Admiral," *Sirius'* captain growled as he moved towards the admiral. "We're ready, Mika."

"Let's see if we are," Admiral Sancer replied. "Fleet to configuration Delta-5. Tactical, send the plot and the course to all ships."

"All ships report ready, Admiral."

"Very well. Proceed."

As a space battle it resembled a school punch-up. If ships could be said to have pent-up frustrations then the Fourth Fleet's ships let that frustration out in spectacular fashion.

The Empire's Outer Fleet was significantly smaller than the Main Fleet, but still it comprised four capital ships and more than twenty smaller vessels that ranged from corvettes to supply vessels. It was moving quite a bit below normal sub-light speed because of the known obstacles in the Cluster, and because those known obstacles had a disconcerting tendency to move position. Going through that huge region rather than going around it would save time even at much slower speeds. But slower speeds also meant that the ships were exposed.

*Sirius* and the Fourth Fleet made it to the Cluster with time to spare. Two of the mine layers looped around the likely entry and egress points of the Empire fleet, dropping a broad net of passive sensors that would inform the Fleet of the presence of the Outer Fleet. The sensors were interspersed with additional sensors that had been devised some time ago but never used. The Empire commanders did not handle "new" well, so Admiral Sancer thought these may have a decided impact.

Mika Sancer made an odd tactical decision in his preparations for the space battle. Massed ships tended to slug it out as fleets because of the orthodox view that capital ships needed to maintain overlapping shields to protect the smaller ships. Sancer, as befitting one whose early training had been given by those who were themselves trained by Grand Admiral Serra, usually treated that orthodoxy with scepticism, even while conforming to it, mostly. Now, he departed from it. His three capital ships were dispersed at strategic locations through the cluster on the expected line of travel. It was a gamble, especially with the Fleet being untested since the purge, but inside the Cluster the massed ships would be unwieldy anyway.

"Admiral, sensors show the leading ships entering the range," Tactical reported. "They're moving slowly, standard configuration."

Sancer acknowledged. Standard configuration for such a transit meant two or three cutters acting as a point patrol with a full sensor sweep leading the way, followed by the capital ships in a staggered line astern and the screening vessels arrayed around the four sides. Essentially, it formed a type of cylinder of ships. Sancer breathed easier. He glanced to Morgal, who gave a brief smile and nod. So far the gamble was paying off.

"All ships of the fleet are within the sensor field," Tactical reported in a hushed tone, as though by speaking too loud the enemy may hear. "Screamers have commenced the count-down."

Seconds ticked away. The large plot ahead of the bridge crew showed the Empire fleet picking its way through the region of the Cluster that Sancer had selected as the site of battle. Eyes were glued alternately to the plot and the countdown timer at the bottom right corner of the screen.

"Three ... two ... one, screamers active," Tactical reported.

The plot changed to show a riot of activity. The screamers were sensors that had been given a larger than normal power source and emitters that caused them to appear to be Union ships. Now, all thirty-seven of the screamers lit up along the path of the Empire fleet. The effect was astonishing.

The Empire commanders must have reacted with astounding speed, Sancer thought, or they were all on edge with fingers on triggers. The corridor along which the Empire ships were travelling became a mass of energy weapon signatures. Every Empire ship was firing at what their screens probably told them was a superior force, expending huge amounts of power in doing so. Ships moved out of line. One ship actually moved into the line of fire of one of the capital ships and was torn apart. Its destruction sent pieces of its hull onto collision courses with other ships, causing them to move out of formation further. It could not have worked better.

"Hold," Sancer said as Tactical held her finger over the communication nub. "Hold, wait … wait … now! Engage!"

The nub was pressed firmly. No more than two seconds elapsed before the Union ships moved out of their hiding places behind an array of planets, moons, asteroids and scattered debris fields that made the Cluster such a difficult place to navigate and that degraded most ship-based sensors' performance. The corvettes and cutters carved through the outer Empire ships as the latter's energy weapons were drained. They wreaked havoc on the smaller Empire vessels, while *Sirius* and the two destroyers, *Helica* and *Borealis*, moved on the capital ships. Union fighters exploded into the midst of the Empire fleet, seeming to appear out of nowhere. The screamers continued to emit signals of Union ships. The Empire commander was besieged by what appeared to be overwhelming numbers.

One of the Empire screen ships, a smaller ship similar to a torpedo boat, was destroyed as the fighters swept into action, followed in short order by two of the corvette class ships. Empire weapons had a short re-charge cycle, but all had expended their energy stores quickly and were forced to rely on point defence systems. Two Union fighters were lost to those point defences as they streamed past the ships. *Sirius* concentrated on the second capital ship in the fleet. The fleet commander usually occupied the second position, it had been found. The Union energy weapons ran into the Empire ships' deflectors and were neutralised, as expected, but they were followed by shots from *Sirius'* single main rail-gun. *Helica* and *Borealis* each occupied one of the remaining capital ships and the fourth, the lead capital ship, was harassed by three of the Union corvettes, dodging and darting through the growing debris field as the battle toll grew rapidly.

On the bridge of *Sirius* the messages were coming fast. The plot was updating in near real time but the bridge crew maintained a steady litany of updates.

"*Ursul* reporting major damage," Tactical reported, "Withdrawing to try to repair the worst."

"We've lost *Ygras*, Admiral. No survivors."

"Empire cutters *Hurg* and *Nilk* destroyed."

"*Helica* has lost one of her secondary defence arrays. Re-orienting to compensate. Still on *Hreb*, though."

"Enemy cruiser *Saq* venting to space. Its reactor is going critical. *Borealis* is moving clear and engaging the *Hreb*."

"Admiral, engineering reports *Sirius* port defence array is down to sixty percent available."

"*Hreb* is breaking up. *Borealis* and *Helica* are converging on *Tak*. *Saq* will blow any moment now."

"*Jupiter* and *Dresdil* are both disabled and being targeted by Empire torpedo boats. *Borealis* moving to shield and assist."

"*Sirius* is clear of *Peduk*, Admiral. Engaging *Tak*."

The reports kept coming but the tale of the battle was becoming clear. The Fourth Fleet had destroyed all four of the Empire capital ships and many of the support vessels.

"*Saq* has imploded, Admiral," Tactical reported. "*Peduk* is drifting into the path of the asteroid debris field."

"Escape pods?" Sancer asked, knowing the answer.

"No pods, Admiral, and not many from our ships, either."

"The remaining Empire ships are orienting, Admiral. Moving to jump speed."

"Inside the Cluster?" Tactical asked incredulously. "That's suicide."

"*Ursul* re-engaging."

"Five Empire vessels have reached jump velocity. Jumping."

"Maintain a watch on their projected course, please," Sancer said evenly. "What's the count?"

"Four Empire cruisers destroyed. Twelve support ships destroyed and another three are disabled. Make that fifteen destroyed. The self-destruct fail-safes seem to have kicked in for those three. The five that bugged out were all that remained capable of flight." Tactical paused. "Three likely impacts reported along the trajectory plotted. It would appear at least some of the escapees ran into something."

"Our ships?"

"*Ygras, Jupiter, Nerku's Pride* and *Kirkas* are gone, Admiral. Escape pods are being recovered from *Kirkas* and *Jupiter*. *Sirius* has damage to our secondary defence array but it's repairable quickly. Damage reports are still coming in though. *Helica* is down to fifty percent offensive and defensive capability. *Borealis* reports little damage. *Ursul's* damage is significant but she managed to get mobile again. We've lost thirty-three fighters. The rest are recovering to their ships. *Jupiters's* fighters are coming to *Sirius*."

"Casualties?"

"One thousand, three hundred and twenty seven confirmed dead so far, Admiral," Tactical reported. "Medical reports serious injuries across many of the ships. *Antilles* is entering the field and has started to receive the worst of the injured."

"Make sure *Antilles* gets whatever she needs," Sancer ordered.

"Admiral, we have twelve ships that are too banged up to fight for some time. But they should be able to limp back to one of the bases if they take it easy. That would include *Helica* to act as shield as its repairs are made." Captain Morgal stood by Sancer's chair.

Sancer turned from the casualty reports streaming across his personal screen. He had lost people before and space battles were never pretty, but the list of names kept coming. He sighed. Now he looked up at Morgal, considering. *Sirius* and its fleet had come through this battle with serious hurt, but it remained a fighting force and had proven itself once more. Sancer snorted to himself, drawing a raised eyebrow from Morgal.

"Open a channel to *Helica*, please," Sancer ordered.

"Channel open, Admiral. Captain Fellas responding."

"Herm, how are you going with repairs?" Sancer said to the grizzled veteran whose image came up on the screen.

"We've taken worse, Admiral," Captain Fellas replied. "This one will be a bit of a struggle to get cleaned up quickly but we'll be back in form soon."

"It won't be soon enough, Herm. You know that," Sancer looked at the image of *Helica's* captain eye to eye. "The damage is too much to be done with quickly."

"We can still fight, Mika."

"I know that, but you can't get there fast enough and at the moment you can't fight long enough. Which is why I'm sending you back." Sancer maintained eye contact.

Fellas thought for a moment and then grimaced and shook his head in resignation.

"Okay, Mika. You're right, of course. Do you want us to act as shepherd?"

"Yep. You'll have a slow trip back with about a dozen ships. I'm sending *Antilles* with you, too. We'll top off the stores for all ships and you can take all but one of the supply ships."

"Fighters?"

"What do you need?"

"Transfer all of the fly-able damaged units to me and take the ready birds with you. We can make repairs as we go and the repairs can fly patrol as they come online." Fellas nodded. "I think that will see us home."

"Agreed. You did well, Herm. Now take the kids home safe."

"Aye, Admiral. In case I don't get the chance to say this later, you turned this fleet around, Mika, and for that each of us is grateful. Admiral, it has been an honour."

The link to Helica winked out. Sancer gave a thin smile as he turned back to Morgal.

"Divide the fleet please, Captain. Restock the ships and get the worst of the wounded to *Antilles*. Let's get the fighters re-armed fully and then find berths for them all on the fully fit ships."

"That will take the better part of a day, sir. What then?"

"As if you don't know," Sancer scoffed. "I understand there's a Grand Admiral over there somewhere" ... he waved a hand in the general direction that the Empire ships had been taking ... "who may need a hand. I met the Grand Admiral long ago but always wanted to spend more time with her. Now seems like a good time."

# 4. Eastern Army Raised

In the time before the rebellion and its disastrous aftermath, there were three main groups of people east of the great north-south mountain range that cut the northern continent into two unequal parts. The section east of the range was only a fraction of the size of the area west of the range. The range had existed from the time of the early forming of the planet, but the damage from the rebellion had lifted some parts and shifted the land northwards. To both west and east of the range the changes caused passes to be blocked and trails to be destroyed.

The eastern coast of the northern continent had been the centre of maritime services before the rebellion. They largely represented a pleasant pastime given the ability to move around Ennaris readily via portal gates or the application of high technology to vehicular transport. Between the east and west sides of the northern continent was a vast ocean, one that had proved itself to be unnavigable given the lack of technical aids since the world was shattered. Over the cycles since, there had been many attempts to sail from the east coast to the west coast, and all had failed. Navigation from the bottom of the eastern part of the northern continent was also fraught, as the huge destructive forces had caused great maelstroms to form, effectively blocking any way to sail from the east to the south.

Trying to sail around the north of the continent proved to be impossible, with the solid sheets of ice forming a permanent barrier. It may have been possible to walk across the northern ice, and the Junda people may have done so, but if they did, then they told no-one about it.

To the south the currents were such that sailing or oar-driven ships found themselves turned away from rounding the southern tip of the eastern section of the northern continent.

Consequently, the people east of the high peaks had nothing to do with those to the west from the time of the rebellion's end. Common to both the eastern and western areas was the collective rage felt at the damage to their world, and the massive loss of life. Cities were destroyed and regions shattered. Food stocks were decimated and water sources were reduced to trickles. The easterners took their anger out on the Guides as much as the westerners did, if not more so. The Mages who normally would have tried to exert an influence over the people were isolated on the western side of the ranges, having all been engaged on one side or the other of the battles that raged, culminating in the fight to subdue Goroth. When the technology interdiction was enacted, the few easterners who remained alive in the west were unable to return home. Those who tried failed.

The Guides perished. In this, the mobs were egged on by Goroth supporters among the general populace. As the remnants of civilisation started to be dragged together once more, it was the descendants of the Goroth faction who took the lead, and who set the tone for the recovery efforts that occurred.

Pestilence, famine and illness all took their tolls, but through it all the new leaders of eastern Ennaris disseminated their view of the struggle, a very different view to that espoused in the larger western Ennaris. Even though the west persecuted the remaining Guides and Mages, the view in the west was that all of the gifted were at fault, not just one side. In the east, the Council of Mages was blamed for the events, and Goroth and his supporters were painted as those fighting the heroic battle and seeking to save the world.

Here, too, a Prophecy took hold, this one being the mutterings of a dying priest of the god Groks, who usually was depicted as a snarling face with dark horns emerging from a head devoid of hair but with bright red and orange streaks. In a somewhat rare, more complete image, the cloven hoofs that served as feet were below legs that became more Ennarisi-looking as they rose to a muscular torso with a barrel chest, thick neck and thickly-muscled arms. The arms ended in odd four-finger hands that were more like claws. The full image showed Groks' masculinity in all its glory, an impossibly thick appendage that hung from a crotch bereft of hair. In fact, there was no hair on any image of Groks. Groks' eyes seemed to leap from any image and stare at its followers as they worshipped it.

Over two thousand cycles Groks became the dominant god in the east. All challengers were destroyed, their religions cast away via a deliberate policy of aggression and destruction of places of worship. Groks' high priest became the *de facto* leader of the eastern regions until, finally, civil and religious power was joined. The Groks religion's greatest hero was Goroth, the greatest Mage ever to set foot on Ennaris, the one who tried and failed to hold back the destructive forces of the Council of Mages, who was imprisoned unjustly and who would return when Ennaris was most in need of its heroes. And he would be aided by the other heroes of Groks, Grensor and Likud. When that time came the followers of Groks would be summoned, and the religion of Groks would spread across Ennaris while all others would be struck down.

For so the Prophecy of Groks said, and thus, so it would be.

The three troops of ghazrak pushed through the last of the thick overgrowth and emerged into the early evening dark. It was past twilight but not yet full dark. The ghazrak carried crudely made swords strapped to their broad backs, and equally crudely made spears were clutched in claws. Behind them came an old and apparently frail man, leaning on the arms of two other men, with a further two in close attendance behind them carrying the pieces of a sedan chair. Seven Andorethi followed, gliding over the ground in their full-length hooded robes. The ghazrak stopped, turning outward and sniffing the air, while one troop leader moved further down the strange path that had met them when they emerged, until he rounded a bend. Several minims later he returned. He grunted a few words to the old man and then gestured to his troop to follow.

This they did, the odd group moving boldly down the centre of the path. The other two troops would remain where they were. If all went well they would stay in the east.

Grensor looked around and nodded to himself, even while being helped along the path, apparently well pleased. All this time, he had sought to get back here and had failed, but now with the passageway beneath the mountains having been revealed it was possible. That the lights were working was something to consider. If the technologies were coming back into use then his own power nodes may have done so also. And that meant he could accelerate his work.

It had been a very long journey from the waste lands and he hoped it would be worthwhile. He had no real idea about how the culture in the east had evolved. He and his followers had tried to set a direction before they joined Goroth for what became the final battles, and he had some inkling that they had been successful when he received reports about an expedition that had made its way into the mountains, only to have all of the members die in the treacherous heights.

The ones who stumbled across the corpses had reported to their community leaders that the people appeared to be strongly built, with no hair, and all carried amulets with what appeared to be effigies of a demon. The tale had made its way across the wilderness areas, transmitted by word of mouth, until it had been picked up by a spy and reported to Grensor. That had been almost three thousand cycles ago. Grensor had hopes that it meant they had succeeded. He intended to find out.

The ghazrak troops moved off the path and found a place where they would spend the remainder of the night. Grensor's helpers put up a small tent after putting the sedan chair together and Grensor crawled in after eating a poor meal. Still, he reflected, it provided energy that he would need.

The morning dawned with a light overcast and a misty feel. Grensor glanced left and right as he emerged from his tent. The ghazrak were up and eating their gruel. Grensor stopped by the small fire and accepted a bowl of the same gruel and a spoon, which he used to eat the unappetising but energy-dense mixture. By the time he had finished his breakfast, the troop that would accompany him was ready to move and the tent was packed away. Grensor passed the bowl to one of the assistants and walked slowly to the troop leader.

"Remember, Gakk, we're not here to kill everyone," Grensor said slowly and clearly. "We need the people here to accept us and agree to listen."

Gakk snarled but nodded shortly. "No kill," he growled. "Yet."

A hooting grunt sent the troop down the path, spreading out to form a skirmish line. Grensor shook his head and followed, supported by his two helpers, one of whom was juggling Grensor's empty bowl into his pack. Grensor stepped onto the sedan chair and the party set off.

Five hurs later, with two stops to allow Grensor to regain some required energy, the troop came upon a town. *A small city, perhaps,* Grensor thought. The first indications were the smells of fires, although the many and varied aromas of a settlement soon followed. The troop bunched slightly. The original skirmish line folded back to be little more than a line abreast across the path. Of itself, the pre-rebellion road they followed was impressive to Grensor. He was surprised that the road could have survived both the rebellion and the long time since in such condition, but evidently it had. Almost certainly there would have been no maintenance capability in the east, so it must just have been a peculiar set of circumstances that allowed it to remain in good condition.

As they rounded a final bend the ghazrak were confronted by a body of ten armed men - all men, Grensor noted - who stood and stared wide-eyed and open-mouthed at the ghazrak, as though in stunned recognition. The ghazrak stopped also at a signal from Gakk, before moving to match the men's spread. Spears were dropped and swords pulled off their back mounts.

*Interesting*, Grensor thought to himself when seeing the reaction of the armed men, thinking back to the amulets that had been discovered with the doomed easterners all those cycles ago. *This may work.*

With an effort Grensor exited the sedan chair and stood as upright as he could. He walked forward slowly until he reached the line of ghazrak facing the easterners. For a moment he was unsure as to who led this band. All wore the same uniform of red quilted blouse with a heavy leather breastplate, loose black trousers, what looked like supple leather boots and open-faced helmet that had some sort of studded metal band. Then he noticed one of them wearing an armband in a different shade of red where the others had none and decided he must be the leader.

"I am Grensor," Grensor stated, directed at the armband wearer, and waited.

Wide open eyes darted between the ghazrak and Grensor now. The band's leader tried and failed to find voice and Grensor, amused more than annoyed and encouraged at the effect, waited for a few microns more.

"I am Grensor," he repeated. "I have great need to speak with your leaders. Are you able to take us to them?"

"Uh, uh, uh," stammered the band's leader. "I, I, I am Qanirar." He pulled himself together to some extent. "How can you prove that you are Grensor? It is a grave offence to take the name of Groks' heroes in vain."

"Groks?" Grensor repeated, thinking back to the time of the rebellion and the use of the demon's name and image to cause dissension and fear. "It was Groks who ordered me to come to the east, to raise the banner for the return of Goroth and to prepare for the final battle against the westerners. It is well that you remember Groks' name."

*But just what does Groks mean here?* Grensor asked himself. The image on the amulets were what had encouraged Grensor to try to raise an army in the east, but he had no real idea about the extent of any sort of Groks worship that may exist. *Ah well, the only thing to do is to push on.*

"As proof of what I say and who I am, what would you have me do?" Grensor asked calmly, gesturing as he asked the question but using one of the signals to Gakk to be ready. "You already see that I am accompanied by ghazrak, modelled on Groks and its fellow Kindred."

"Kindred?" Qanirar asked.

"Groks is from a race of, er, gods called the Kindred," Grensor explained. "Long ago Groks deigned to take the role of the god of Ennaris. Goroth, Likud and I are the chief disciples of Groks and have been since before the Council of Guides caused the destruction of Ennaris."

Grensor waited. Qanirar obviously had no idea how to test whether Grensor was who he said he was or not, and Grensor decided to take the initiative.

"How about if I cause that hill over there to collapse?" he asked offhandedly.

"You can do that?" Qanirar asked, shocked.

"I am Grensor," Grensor said, as he turned to Gakk. "Gakk, I need a sacrifice."

Gakk grunted, turned and walked back to where the ghazrak waited, arrayed against the eastern troop. He walked past one ghazrak, who continued to stand and stare at the opposing group and reached back to pull his crude sword from the mounting point on his back. He grunted and the ghazrak stepped forward between the two lines and knelt. Gakk stood behind him, close to the facing men. With a snarl he lifted his sword high above his head, pivoted and beheaded the nearest of the men facing the ghazrak. The easterners stood, shocked, as Gakk and the ghazrak who had been kneeling each grabbed an arm of the dead man and dragged the body to where Grensor waited.

Grensor nodded and rolled back the sleeves of his robe, revealing very white arms with wiry muscles that were sagging slightly. He reached down and allowed his hands to be covered by the blood of the slain man as it pumped sluggishly from his body. He reached inside himself, feeling the life blood of the sacrifice seeping into his very being. The blood of a freshly killed man allowed him to reach beyond the bounds of the corporeal, beyond anything he had been taught as a Mage and into the dark realms. The fresh blood was absorbed into Grensor, leaving no signs of it on his hands. Grensor's eyes glowed with a red cast. He turned towards the hill he had indicated and saw into its depths where the foundations were locked together. With a thought he shifted a few large rocks, pushed against a channel in the rocks and then, deeper still, found the large subterranean cave that he had hoped to find. This whole area had been tectonically active much later than other parts of Ennaris, and there were caverns and caves deep below the ground level. With a focused thought he caused a cave-in. The cave was filled with the rocks and dirt that Grensor had worked on, and the effect rippled upward. A deep rumble was felt as much as heard. As the astonished men watched, the hill collapsed on itself.

Qanirar stared at the hill and then back at Grensor. He prostrated himself in front of the old man, as did the men of his troop. Grensor waited for a few moments before signalling Gakk. The ghazrak each pulled their swords from their backs and killed the men who were still prostrate, most by driving the sword through their prone torsos, some by smashing the edge of the sword against their heads. Qanirar was spared but he stared aghast at his whole squad lying in their own spreading pools of blood. The ghazrak hacked the men's heads off, picked up their spears and drove one head onto each spear.

"Qanirar," Grensor said, "this is because you questioned me. Never do so again."

The next day, Grensor reached the high temple of Groks in Yster. Qanirar had sent runners from the first village through which Grensor and his troop passed with their grisly trophies on open display. The people of the villages through which the strange procession passed were made aware by Qanirar that it was none other than the hero Grensor who accompanied him. Many of the villagers were sceptical that this old man was the Grensor of legend but, when Qanirar explained that the trophy heads were because he had questioned Grensor's identity, the villagers all tended to accept that this old man truly was the great hero of Groks.

Grensor had another ace as well, for one of the norther men who accompanied Grensor now carried a banner, one of Goroth's old banners, modelled on the ceremonial banner of Ennaris of old. The deep blue background was edged in white. Five white orbs equidistant from each other formed a circle in the middle of the banner. To this Goroth had added a ring of ten stars, which Goroth claimed represented the main worlds that Ennaris owned, for once civil war had become a reality Goroth had abandoned Ennaris' doctrine of allowing client civilisations to make their own way and adopted one of Ennaris being the empire of the galaxy.

This was the flag that had flown when Goroth had fought against the Council. This was the flag under which all of Ennaris' most beautiful cities had been destroyed. And this was the banner that flew when Goroth met Drewflin and Marjory, with the lesser remaining Mages, and was defeated. Grensor had used his dark arts to spirit himself and a few of his own retinue away from the site of battle, taking the standard - this standard - with him.

Many did not recognise the standard. The First Prophet of Groks *did* recognise it, however. Sitting on his dais high above the huge courtyard of the Great Temple, having squeezed his enormous bulk into the ceremonial chair used on rare occasions, the First Prophet was more than sceptical, until the standard was carried into the courtyard. It was followed by the troop of ghazrak carrying their grisly trophies and staring aggressively at anyone nearby. Then came the old man sitting in a sedan chair carried by four husky men. Held in the most closely guarded part of the Great Temple was a small room where the greatest treasures were housed. In that room were images of the great Goroth and his lieutenants from several vantage points. In several of the images Goroth's flag featured. The Great Prophet had one of those paintings by his side now. Even from the distance and with rheumy eyes that were failing, he could see that the flag being carried by one of the strangers was the same flag. Admittedly, anyone could put a flag together, but when combined with the ghazrak the chances diminished rapidly. He could not make out the features of this old man but the Great Prophet decided not to take the chance.

A sharp signal brought his handlers to him and they levered him out of the ceremonial chair and helped him to make his way down the great steps leading from the dais to the floor of the courtyard. Slowly, with ponderous effort, the First Prophet staggered his enormous bulk step by step until he was able to stand on the flagstones of the courtyard. The sedan chair had been placed on the floor not far from the steps, thankfully, and the First Prophet made his way across the short space, peering at the old man as he did so. *Strip away the cycles and yes,* he thought, *this old man may well be Grensor.* The First Prophet knew of at least one defining feature of Grensor and he sharpened his gaze. There it was. On the old man's throat, on his left side, was a distinctive mark, a purple stain about the size of a five cycle old child's palm. Legend told that Grensor had earned that mark while defending Goroth from attack, although the First Prophet was more inclined to believe that it was nothing more than a birth mark.

Everything pointed to this being Grensor. For a moment that thought, that this was the fabled Grensor, caused the First Prophet to freeze. At no stage had he considered that Grensor may be alive, and certainly not that he would appear without warning at the Great Temple. When he was able to think again, he had no idea *what* to think. So, the First Prophet stood alongside the sedan chair staring at Grensor.

Grensor, in turn, looked over the grossly fat figure in front of him. *If this is what the east is turning out then there may be problems,* Grensor reflected sourly. Still, the goal was to obtain an army that would harass the Faero's forces and make him split them when the norther armies met them. The ghazrak would not be enough by themselves and the small number of mid-weight gifted northers that Grensor could put in front of Goroth could not carry the fight alone. There remained the need for additional armies to fight, especially while technology had failed in most places. Grensor had not seen true armed forces on his journey from Yster to the tunnel opening, but that did not mean they did not exist. Grensor needed to get this First Prophet on side to take what advantage he could.

To the surprise of everyone, including Grensor, the First Prophet signalled to his retainers and then slowly, ever so agonisingly, was assisted to kneel before Grensor. The latter stared for a moment and then slowly exited the sedan chair and stood in front of the kneeling First Prophet.

"Hero Grensor," the First Prophet said in a thick dialect that Grensor had never heard before. "The Great Temple of Groks welcomes you. I, the First Prophet of Groks, welcome you. What is ours is yours."

Grensor considered his words. Unlike Goroth, he had never been one to honey-coat words. Diplomacy had never been a strong suit although he knew the value of careful speech. He wished Goroth was with him but, he thought as an aside, it could be worse. He could have Likud with him. That one's idea of diplomacy was shoving a bigger gun in anyone's face.

"First Prophet," Grensor said, enhancing his vocal reach with a technique he had learned as a trainee much more than a hundred thousand cycles past. "On behalf of Goroth and the true Mages of Ennaris, I accept your welcome."

Grensor waited as a ripple of chatter passed through the gathered crowd before continuing.

"I come with great tidings," Grensor said, turning to look around the courtyard, making it clear that he included all in these words. "For the time has come for Goroth to return to us. The time of the Prophecy has come. The Children of Ennaris have been called home and await Goroth to lead us to victory over those who caused the great destruction of Ennaris."

Another ripple. None here, nor their forebears going back more than a hundred generations, had the first idea about what had been lost, but still the language was important and the idea even more so.

"And so, as promised long ago to the First Prophet, I have returned to fulfil my vow and to allow the army of the people of Groks to join with us. The way to the west has been opened again after such a long time closed. Together we will prevail against those who would oppose us in what the Prophecy tells us will be the deciding battle. I thank the First Prophet for his welcome and bid you to stand, for we are as brothers in this venture."

Grensor made a lifting gesture to accompany his words. The First Prophet was helped wheezing to his feet. The two old men stared at each other, although the First Prophet could be more correctly thought to be glaring. This was not what he was expecting at all. Goroth returning? Final battle? Army? There was no army! The First Prophet had his secret police and guard force but that was to deal with the occasional unrest and minor infractions that occurred. However, the First Prophet was aware of the promise made by the original First Prophet, one who had been with Grensor before the time when Goroth was taken by the evil Drewflin and Marjory. That promise had been to hold ready to re-kindle the fight and to provide such force of arms as the eastern reaches of Ennaris could provide. Assuming this was Grensor, then he did not want to make an enemy of the Hero.

Those thoughts took no time at all to flash through the cunning mind of the First Prophet, now that he was back on something like an even keel. He raised his fleshy arms to quiet the crowd, who had been conditioned through their lives to cheer - loudly - whenever any-one of power spoke in the Great Temple, and who were doing so now, although the vast majority were unaware of what they cheered.

"Hero Grensor," the First Prophet declaimed, "as was promised by the First Prophet long ages past, the Grokog will honour our promise to provide arms and support for our brothers under the great Hero Goroth, to the glory of Groks, the god of Ennaris."

More cheers, while Grensor withheld a grimace. They called them-selves Grokog? And would fight for Groks more than Goroth or Grensor? Fair enough, but Groks had been killed by Marjory in the engagement where Goroth had been captured. When Grensor fled the field with his few followers, including the one who would become the First Prophet of the east, Groks had lived but its link to its own realm had been sundered, weakening the Kindred's power and leaving it vulnerable. From what Grensor had been able to ascertain, Marjory had destroyed Groks with little trouble. Still, if they would fight for Groks then so be it. As long as they fielded the promised army.

"The Grokog army will prepare and follow your instructions to join with the great Hero, Goroth. But tonight, we will feast in honour of the Hero Grensor."

Cheering again. The Great Temple's feasts were hedonistic masterpieces and the people joined in enthusiastically for the most part. The food would be good, the ale and wine would flow, and various powders and liquors would be made available that allowed the people to forget their difficult, mundane and restricted lives.

The First Prophet gave a sign and a temple guard led two young women over to where he and Grensor stood.

"Chambers are ready for you. These temple acolytes will help you in any way you wish as you prepare for the feast tonight, honoured Grensor," the First Prophet said in a much quieter tone. "They have been well trained in all of the arts. Of course, if you prefer, I could arrange male company."

Grensor looked at the two women. He had his pick of women and, if he so desired, men in his own compound. From what he had seen and heard during the days and nights since he had been on the eastern side of the mountains the "arts" mentioned were likely to be of a significantly higher order than his own people could deliver. Why not?

"Thank you, First Prophet," Grensor said as he carefully stepped back into his sedan chair. "I believe that will be suitable. I look forward to joining you for the feast. In the morning, we will return to the west to continue our preparations. I will look forward to having your army join us within four tendays."

The two men nodded one to the other with differing degrees of enthusiasm and Grensor's chair was lifted and carried off to his chambers, trailed by the men of his party, the two young women and finally the four black-shrouded ones and the ghazrak. After watching them leave the courtyard the First Prophet signalled for his own carriage, which was pulled into place by one of the few hrss available to the Grokog. With a groan he took his seat and the carriage moved off, to the well-practised acclaim of the people who remained in the courtyard.

# 5. Dalresar

For the first time in his available memory, Dalresar felt satisfied. He knew that there were things in his past that he had to uncover still, no matter that glimpses had been provided in recent times. He realised now that it was not some failing of his own that he could not recall anything much before the day that Flin had driven the fever away. Ogun and Menra both had made that clear. There was some sort of barrier that had to be breached. In this, Dalresar was in a similar boat to Varna.

What he had been able to do, though, was establish - regain - a sense of himself via the extreme physical work that he had been doing with Ogun. The warmaster, an odd position for a Guardian who apparently did not take part in wars, was hard as stone, and his skills were sublime, aided by the unique attributes that the Guardians all shared, even when in physical form. Menra concentrated on hand-to-hand combat, and in this she had no peers. Dalresar absorbed it all although he was sure that all he was doing was re-establishing old skills. The movements came too easily, the exercises were too smooth, for his body to find them alien.

He knew that he was not ageing as others did. He had known for quite some time, even before it had become obvious to others. He had been told that he had a gift, perhaps more than one, which was the reason for his continued youthful appearance. Everyone suspected that his gift was for warfare, thus the reason for Ogun's assistance now. Dalresar did not doubt it, either, based on what he found himself now able to do. Every weapon Ogun threw at him, Dalresar was able to wield expertly, or master within a very short time. Every test of physicality was passed with little thought, even if they required significant exertion. His body, trim and taut as it had been, was now rock hard. Once again, it was a feeling of rightness, a return to what had been rather than something new and different, but more so.

Now he was outside the bounds of Fernis' tree and running through the Forest, at speed, footfalls even and light, moving lithely around roots, branches and small shrubs without losing pace. He was wearing light clothing, pale green in colour, for the weather was mild, but he had a long knife strapped to his right hip and tied lower down his leg, with a short sword of exquisite quality in a plain scabbard on his left. Both were gifts from Ogun. Neither inhibited him as he ran.

He scanned the surrounding Forest constantly, alert for any source of danger. After a time, he exited the boundary of the Forest of the Guardians proper and entered the surrounding woodland, running still with an easy gait, breathing slowly and evenly. If anything, his senses became more alert now that he was outside the Guardian's immediate domain. But his pace did not falter. Anyone watching would have been reminded of the smooth, graceful progress of the mountain peris with its sleek fur rippling as the taut muscles moved, always primed to spring into attack or defence if the need arose.

Dalresar stopped suddenly, a whiff of wood-smoke causing him to halt his run. Breathing easily, he stood perfectly still for a moment, watching and listening, smelling and feeling the breeze as it moved through the wood. He identified the direction from which the smoke came, and moved forward again, angling to follow the smell. He glided through the wood, making no noise, feeling for footholds where others would have snapped twigs and branches to announce their presence. He moved from tree to tree, using their bulk to mask his presence. He was downwind of whoever had the fire and decided to test himself on his approach.

He could hear them from a distance away. Loud voices, more smoke as a fire was built up inexpertly with the wrong materials. There was more noise as at least two people moved around. Dalresar realised his attempt at stealth would not be required as whoever they were would have no chance to hear anyone approaching anyway. Still, the test was for him, not them, so he continued to approach unheard, unseen, unsensed. He could see the fire through the trees now. His clothing blended into the surrounding shrubbery and undergrowth, with its dappled shade and filtered light, allowing him to get close without detection. He could make out clearly what was being said. He stopped quite still as he listened, his mood changing.

"Ha, that was a nice 'un," a rough voice announced with satisfaction, followed by a belch. "I 'aven't 'ad one as good as that for a while."

"You use 'em up too fast, Mulch. You don't leave nuthin' for the rest of us," a second voice growled.

"You 'ad the girl, didn't ya? So I 'ad the muvver. Fair's fair, I say." Mulch paused to take a long drink from a wineskin, smacking his lips in contentment. "Not my fault she didn't last long enough for ya to 'ave ya fill."

"We didn't have to do that, Mulch," a third voice said carefully. "All that does is bring people down on us."

"Ha, who's gonna do anythin', eh? No guards in these places. Jus' folks out there alone an' ripe for the pickin'. An' I aim to do the pickin'. Anyway, there's none left to tell anythin', anyway." He laughed, a heavy, guffawing sound.

Dalresar paused, listening, appalled. A roar started behind his ears but where, in the past, that roar presaged total loss of control, now it stoked the fires of rage that had ignited deep in his being. Unwonted images of a woman abused and killed, and a small child murdered, spun across his inner vision. He started forward once more. Stealth became menace to any who may have watched.

"There are plenty more aroun' 'ere'," Mulch was saying as Dalresar emerged from the wood into a small clearing, standing still and silent.

A second man gasped, causing the speaker to spin around. Four men were clustered around a fire, too large for the purpose. Smoke continued to rise, showing where they were to any who knew what to look for.

"Who are you?" Mulch demanded, tossing the wineskin aside and lurching to his feet.

Dalresar remained quiet, hands clenched, listening to the roar as it increased in volume. Only this time his senses remained his own, the images of the woman solidifying in his mind, the emotional toil building as it did so.

"Ya made the wrong call, sneakin' up on us, ya did," Mulch growled, pulling a sword from an old and worn belt scabbard. "I guess ya heard what we was sayin', yeah? Well, too bad for ya. You from 'round these parts? Then ya can die here, too."

The other three stood. Two carried swords, one a shorter blade. They separated as they slowly approached Dalresar, leaving Mulch to do the talking, as he liked to do.

"And ya might 'ave a woman of ya own aroun' 'ere, too. When we've finished with ya we'll jus' go visit wif 'er, we will," Mulch continued, waving his sword arrogantly. "An' then we'll take ya friends' wimmin and make 'em watch, like we did with the sod whose wimmin we 'ad yestidy." He laughed again, confident in four against one.

Dalresar felt the roar crash against the barrier he had built up inside, again and again, the same barrier that Ogun and Menra had sought to weaken. He trembled as that barrier was unpicked, stone by stone, piece by piece. His inner turmoil turned to anguish as memory stormed back into place, as he remembered finding Capes and their son in the small cabin built away from the main thoroughfares, all those years ago. Capes, the team member who became so much more to him, who surprised the ultimate loner. He remembered her face, the laughter even as both became sure that they were alone and that the Union ships would not be coming back. The joy when young Evian was born to them. The unadulterated pleasure he found in the family life that evolved from what had been a disaster for the team. And his thoughts cleared as he watched the four thieves, rapists and murderers approach. Emotion became ice.

"So, what's yer name so we can carve it into yer headstone when we plant yer remains? If we bother to do so, that is." Mulch laughed at what he imagined was a clever statement.

Dalresar stirred finally, the statue coming to life. With a single movement, faster that the four rogues could follow, sword and long knife were in his hand.

His action was the trigger for them to charge at him from different directions. Clay drifted to one side, cutting down one, then a second ruffian, without giving them a chance to bring their own swords into play. He turned and leapt high, somersaulting over the other two to land behind them, throwing his knife in an underhand throw as the third, the one with the knife, turned towards him. It lodged in his breast. Mulch stared, unable to believe that mere moments had elapsed and now his three companions were dead. He then realised that their target was advancing on him. Desperately Mulch swung his sword, trying to keep this threat at bay, only to have it swatted aside. He felt the bite of Dalresar's sword as it entered through his abdomen and emerged from the back, looking up to see a fierce glare on the face of his vanquisher, the last thing he would ever see.

"My name is Clay Anders," Clay said quietly, fiercely, "and I am the Champion of the Light."

# 6. Starfire

"Admiral, incoming ships detected. Five light years away, direct course, flank light speed, slowing, estimated time of arrival three minutes." Rork looked up from his console. "From the wake signature I estimate fleet size."

Bard nodded. The *Starfire* fleet had been at general quarters for some time, and the strain was beginning to show on the crew. There had been an increase in petty disputes, some fist fights between the Marine contingent - to no-one's surprise - and some errors made by crew who were tense and tired. But Bard remained confident in his ships' ability to fight and hold.

"Sound battle stations, please, Mr Rork," he said calmly. "Try to identify the incoming vessels as soon as you can."

Jord and Serra arrived on the bridge as the strident sounds of the alert died away, to be replaced by a penetrating muted tone. Jord moved to take in the current disposition of the fleet while Serra cocked an eyebrow at Bard.

"Incoming fleet, Admiral," Bard said in response to the mute query. "Not sure who just yet, but it's coming from Union space. We're at battle stations because I'm not really sure what to expect at this moment."

Serra nodded. "Good move."

"Twenty-eight vessels emerging in twenty seconds," Rork said. "One Marauder class, a few cruisers and a gaggle of smaller vessels."

"Weapons hot, target the estimated jump point. Anyone who fires without my order gets a free trip into that sun over there," Bard said.

"Aye, sir," Kiri replied, coming up behind the Admiral so quietly that he jumped.

"Kiri! More warning for an old admiral, please!" he said as his heart rate returned to normal.

The small by-play settled a few nerves among the small bridge crew. If the senior officers could make a jest, then things were probably okay.

"Emerging now," Rork said, as a series of bright flashes lit up the screen and, where there was nothing a moment ago there now was a fleet, moving slowly at a tangent to the *Starfire* fleet. "Receiving comms traffic."

"On speaker," Bard ordered.

"*Starfire*. This is *Moonbeam*. Acknowledge," said the voice that came through the speaker.

"Acknowledge *Moonbeam*. Hold for Admiral Bard," Rork replied.

Bard grimaced to Serra. "I've always thought that's a stupid name for a Marauder class dreadnought. If there's anything less like a serene moonbeam, I've yet to see it."

"Denton, this is Trip," a new voice came over the open channel.

"Trip, good to hear your voice. I do hope you're not here to do anything silly," Bard said smoothly, "given I received no notification of your coming out here."

"Nothing silly at all, Denton. The last message to Fleet HQ caused a bit of a flurry and was instrumental in unmasking a few people who had been working for the Empire. They panicked a bit and made a mistake." Trip chuckled, his delight clear over the ship-to-ship channel. "We've always thought something was wrong somewhere, and we were right, Denton. There's a clean-up happening right now. And I've been dispatched to assist."

"Well, that's good news, Trip. My tactical officer will send over instructions for your ships to position themselves in the cordon." Bard gestured to Kiri, who nodded in response, having already started to update the plot.

"Denton, your message was signed by Serra," Trip replied. "Was that a ploy?"

"No ploy, Admiral," Serra replied.

In the background, over the open channel, *Moonbeam's* AI could be heard confirming Serra's voice print. Serra glance to Bard and smiled slightly.

"Admiral Serra," Trip came back on the channel. "Admiral Trip Ghosten at your command, sir! *Moonbeam* is yours to command."

"Admiral, *Moonbeam* command systems have registered change of fleet designation for Union Second Fleet to direct command of Grand Admiral Serra." Rork glanced to the senior officers. "Accept?"

"Yes please, Mr Rork," Serra replied. "Admiral Ghosten, welcome to the party! You can expect festivities to commence some time relatively soon. We are expecting the main Empire fleet to arrive any time, commanded by Likud. Please slave your secondary command systems to *Starfire* so we can establish consistent firing solutions and zones."

"The main fleet? And Likud? In person?" Trip could almost be heard rubbing his hands together. "Boy oh boy! What does this planet have that everyone wants?"

Aware that the channel was open to the bridges of both ships, and the speed at which rumours moved around a fleet, even in the depths of space, Serra merely replied, "The future, Admiral. The future."

## 7. Escar

The walled fortress city of Escar was quiet in the early morning. The bustle of the day had yet to start, and only a few merchants had started to set up their wares in the central marketplace. The banner of Escar was flying high above the ramparts, indicating the presence of the King. From afar, the stones of the walls seemed to glow a soft gold in the early light, which was reflected in the yellow accents of the stone. Closer, the stones assumed a different form. Massive, set deep in the ground on which the city was built, the stones were huge, apparently rough-hewn but set together with exquisite skills. The battlements atop the massive walls ran completely around the city, studded with embrasures and slits where archers could be protected from attackers, and with points where hot oil could be poured over anyone silly enough to attempt to breach the walls. It looked formidable.

Escar was preparing to ride to aid the Faero as requested, but at the same time King Ensert and his advisors knew that the norther army moving around to the north-west changed the situation. A trickle of refugees had started to arrive with word of more to come. The people were from the regions further north and west, close to the wastelands, a hard land that required hard people, but these were scared and fleeing.

For the last two days the trickle of refugees had become a steady stream and then a flood, bringing with them reports of a strange and vicious, and deadly, army now laying waste to the northern regions of Escar. Stories of half-man, half-beast creatures from nightmares that could not be defeated with arrow or sword were spread by the fleeing newcomers, of flying monsters that would swoop on unsuspecting targets, of beings with dark robes who had no bodies but glided across the ground to attack and kill. King Ensert of Escar was unsure about what to believe, although from what the twin Mages had told him many of the stories were likely to be true. His new chancellor, a trusted former knight who had been with Ensert for thirty cycles, likewise was unsure, but as stories mounted from many sources it became obvious that this invader posed a significant challenge. Ensert sent a pair of scouts to the north with orders to investigate and return, not to engage. They failed to return. As did a second pair of scouts.

In Council with his key advisors, Ensert was worried. He had already put Escar on a war footing, something that was rare for the kingdom in recent memory, seeing as it boasted the strongest military presence in the northern continent, although the Clans of the grasslands would dispute that claim. Any expedition to the Citadel was delayed until this challenge was dealt with. The walled city was bursting at its seams. Gate guards, reinforced with regular soldiers and even armoured knights, were turning people who sought sanctuary away because there was no space. A shanty town was growing around the walls of the city. Slowly spreading across the plain, this shanty town hosted despair and disease. Water was in short supply outside the city walls, for the wells were all inside the walls. Refuse was not being managed effectively, if it was being managed at all, and the smell told the story of bodily waste being dumped rather than buried.

Murder and mayhem were becoming more of a factor in the city and the shanty town. Ensert had kept strict rein on lawlessness within Escar and its surrounds, but the crowding of the city and the growing tumour that was the shacks and sheds of the shanty town played into the hands of thieves and villains of all sorts. Murders were a nightly event now, and many were robbed at knife-point of their life savings, usually carried in gold or silver or precious gems. Escar was having to feed and support an increasing number of people, and the treasury, usually so well endowed, was suffering.

And still the people came from the north. And the stories of the approaching army grew.

In desperation, Ensert decided to send a troop of his knights, under the command of his cousin, Prince Enselem, to do what the scouts were unable to do. Enselem was ordered to return within a week. The troop rode from the city with pennants fluttering from lances held upright in their stirrup boots. Armour gleamed on both knights and hrss. Broadswords were strapped across the knights' backs, short swords and knives rode at hips. Five days later a single hrss returned with dried blood on its saddle and bearing heavy scratches. The people in the shanty town watched in silence as a member of the city guard rode out to capture the hrss and bring it into the city walls. The people on the walls watched just as silently as the bloody and injured hrss was taken to the main yards of the palace grounds. Dread settled on the city.

That night the exodus from Escar began, people from within the city and from the shanty town starting to trek further south. Once again a trickle became a stream and then a river, but it did not become a flood. Escar had never fallen and the people of the city did not believe it was possible. Ensert was not so sure, but maintained a positive and confident mien. Still, he was pleased to see the shanty town shrink, and ordered that it should be dismantled as far as possible. As people left the city they were replaced by those from the shanty town, reducing it in size further.

Moving against the river of people leaving Escar for locations further south was a single figure, an aged man on a nondescript hrss, wearing a brown robe hemmed in green openly for the first time in thousands of cycles. Resting on his brow was a green stone, glowing with an inner radiance. A long, gnarled staff was held in one hand, resting on a stirrup. A swirling green stone that was caught in claws at the staff's peak roiled with its own inner energy. Many of the refugees he passed stopped and stared before continuing their flight. A few called on him to turn back with a warning of danger ahead - these he thanked gravely for their kind thoughts but kept going. Those few people who remembered their stories paused and bowed as he passed, receiving a nod of acknowledgement and a request to remain safe.

As he approached the walled city he paused and took stock. The banner of Ensert floated atop the battlements of the city wall, which were fully manned with the soldiery of Escar. Trebuchets were lined up on the broad walkway inside the battlements of both the city wall and the higher palace wall. The shanty town had been reduced to a small size, and city guards were in the process of shrinking it further. Smoke rose from fires on the city walls where oil was being heated in great cauldrons. An eerie quiet arose from a city that usually bustled with energy. The noises of industry and daily happenings were dampened in a gloomy hush. Flin sighed and kneed his hrss into motion once again.

At the city gate, a pair of guards stood and crossed their halberds, denying him entry. Flin stopped his mount close to them and stared at them, his gaze one that long in the past had been known to cause young Mages to trip over themselves to get out of his way. The two guards swallowed nervously, watched curiously by the few people outside the gate, but maintained their stance.

"State your business at Escar," a guard with two stripes on his tunic sleeve said, eyeing the two stones, each swirling to a different beat. "The city is closed to visitors."

Flin nodded, and his gaze softened.

"You ready for war," he said quietly. "I am here to offer my counsel and my assistance to Ensert."

"And, er, who might you be to do that?" the guard asked, his gaze still shifting between Flin's Enchara and the staff.

A fully armoured knight ran from the gate as Flin regarded the questioner. He almost made it to the small group before Flin replied.

"I am the Archmage Drewflin, head of the Council of Guides, leader of the Council of Mages," he declared in the same quiet voice, but the Enchara flared and the Tree of Fernis glowed brightly, to gasps of shock from the watchers and the guards alike.

The knight skidded to a halt behind the crossed halberds. The knight gestured to the guards and the halberds were uncrossed. The knight knelt to Flin and then bowed. Nervously, the guards stood still, unsure at what to expect at a legend returned to life in front of them.

"Archmage," he said, "welcome to Escar. Please follow me. King Escar will be pleased to see you. Very pleased," he added.

Flin nodded and dismounted, handing the hrss' reins to one of the guards.

"Please make sure he is well looked after," Flin asked of the guard. "He has carried me a long way and quickly."

At the guard's open-mouthed nod Flin smiled. The knight stood and turned, and both knight and Mage entered Escar side by side. Flin noted the crowded conditions as he walked through the throng, which parted as news of his identity spread, many bowing or kneeling while some, recalling stories of the Mages' part in the rebellion, frowned at Flin being so honoured. He had been in Escar on a number of occasions, usually as a Teller of stories and tales from the past, but sometimes as a travelling conjurer. He knew the way to the palace but allowed the knight, who introduced himself as Sir Jonfrey, to lead the way.

At the palace gate, which were nowhere near as grand as the city gate but which was just as functional, a hurried honour guard awaited. The soldiers snapped to attention as Flin and his escort appeared. Flin grimaced.

"We're not going to have this sort of thing everywhere I go, are we Jonfrey? It will get tiresome."

Jonfrey tried to maintain a stern mien, but the ghost of a smile broke through. "The King has commanded that you be given all honours, my Lord Archmage," he replied blandly. "You wouldn't want me to get into trouble would you?"

Flin glanced at Jonfrey sourly, his expression belied by the gleam of appreciation in his eyes at the humour. "Just as long as it doesn't happen every time I'm near. It could be a problem on the field of battle."

"The field of battle?" Jonfrey stared as they continued to walk. "You intend to lead us into battle?"

"I will assist you, not lead you," Flin replied. "As much as I can do. I am not a Battle Mage, and there are very few Mages left today. But I will assist where I can."

Sir Jonfrey nodded thoughtfully. "Still, knowing the Archmage assists will lift spirits," he said. "I for one am grateful, and I know my brothers in arms will be also."

They arrived at the throne room, walking unannounced through the huge iron-banded double doors that hung open. They found Ensert amid organised chaos as maps were updated with the latest information drawn from the few refugees who still arrived occasionally, and those few scouts who returned. The King turned and saw Flin enter, and waved him over, nodding at Jonfrey in thanks. The latter bowed formally to the Archmage and withdrew, back to his guard post. Flin nodded in return before moving to stand with the King.

"Ensert," he replied.

"Flin," the King nodded. "So you finally decided it was time? I knew there was more to you, but I wasn't expecting a legendary Mage."

"Circumstances dictated it," Flin replied. "You have an army approaching. It has ghazrak in its numbers as well as northers."

"The northers are savages," Ensert said, dismissively. "Your twin Mages told me of these creatures. I don't like the sound of ghazrak. They said that they are creations of the rebel Mages. Is that true still?"

"True it is. The ghazrak were created by Goroth during the rebellion that led to the fall of Ennaris," Flin said, nodding. "Actually, mostly by Grensor at Goroth's command. Goroth's chains have dissolved and he is free once again. His minions have been creating a new army of ghazrak, probably for some time now. They've been encountered as far south as the Citadel. Probably further south, too, but I don't know that for sure. They're brutish and vicious fighters and give no quarter. And don't dismiss the northers so readily. There are many of them."

"Is Goroth with this army?" Ensert asked.

"I don't know. I doubt it, though. If he were I expect he would be making more of it. No, I think this is the first outing of his army. I expect it will be to try to wear down those who may be loyal to the Faero, trying to reduce numbers before the real thing." Flin paused. "At least, I hope so."

Ensert snorted, eyeing the Enchara glowing gently on Flin's brow. "And how many do you have on your side, old friend?"

"Not enough, if it's Mages you ask about. But the Children have returned, as you may have heard, so the Prophecy is coming to pass. I have hopes that, between us, we can hold and prevail."

"I was told also that you don't have the Battle Mage," Ensert said, reaching for a goblet of wine on the table strewn with papers.

"Indeed that is so," Flin replied, a pang stabbing him as he did so. "Marjory has been gone for some time. I don't really know the circumstances and they don't matter now. We have a war on our hands, and you are on the front lines."

They were interrupted by a page hurrying through the doors and approaching the King.

"My King," he said, eyes slightly wild, "The Captain of the Guard sent me to inform you that the wall has come alive. It has lights and has changed to a strange grey colour."

Flin grinned, and gave a sigh of relief. "Yes, the portals have come back on line. Ensert, they must be guarded at all times, for Goroth knows their secrets also. I expect you will receive a visitor shortly."

The King gave the Archmage a short glare. "You could not tell me that sooner?" He snorted slightly and turned to the page. "Tell the Captain to bring whoever comes through the portal to me, unless it's an enemy. In which case, kill it!"

"My liege, how will we know it's an enemy?" the page asked.

"It will be trying to kill you," the King growled. "Get going!"

The page packed away, turned and ran from the throne room. Ensert took a pull at his goblet and turned back to Flin.

"Do you know where this army is?" he asked shortly, war-leader of his nation once again.

"No, but I think I may know someone who does," Flin said, looking around the room. He found what he was looking for in one corner and gestured to Ensert as he started to walk towards it. "Over here."

There was a small mound of objects blocking the corner. With an almost negligent wave of his hand the pile of chairs, tapestries, scrolls and leather objects slid across the flagstone floor with a screech, watched by the occupants of the room with open mouths, Ensert included.

"You may recall," Flin said as he approached the now clear corner, "that Escar was built on the site of an ancient structure from well before the rebellion. In fact, the fortress city called Escar has had many names before your distant forefather named it Escar. The stones of the outer city were harvested from the damage wrought on the city of Aberwin, but what you know as the keep remained intact somehow. This room, which you know as the throne room, was the Council chamber for the city governor. Most of the cities had something similar, with a portal gate somewhere near by. They also had an access point." He pulled aside a tapestry to reveal a smooth piece of the wall. "And you use it like this."

Flin touched the smooth panel. A moment later the panel started to glow, changing to a dull grey colour. Ensert stared, entranced, as did the others in the room.

"Is this some of the ancients' work?" he asked breathlessly.

"It is," Flin replied and smiled. "Just remember when you say 'ancients' you include me!"

Ensert chuckled nervously in response, watching closely as Flin turned back to the panel.

"Portal, identify yourself," he commanded.

"Portal Aberwin Main," was the reply, in a male voice. "Recognise Archmage Drewflin."

"Aberwin Main, rename to Escar Main," Flin said.

"Renamed. Escar Main available."

"Escar Main, connect to the Council Assistant." Flin directed.

"Connected," Escar Main replied.

"Archmage, Council Assistant available," the voice of the Assistant stated.

"Can you determine where the army approaching Escar is?" Flin asked.

"Approximately seven endars north," the Assistant replied promptly. "Sensors have identified two hundred ghazrak and five thousand men and women, approximately. There are also three creatures that I do not have in my knowledge base, but it appears they can fly. There are eighteen entities that appear to be incorporeal."

"Shadows," Jalor said from behind Ensert. Everyone started and turned to the newcomer, who had entered the room when attention was focused on the panel and Flin.

"Ah, Jalor," Flin said smoothly. "Your timing is superb. King Ensert, may I present Vinca Jalor, general of the army of the Faero of Ennaris and one of the Children."

A murmur went around the room at the last statement. Jalor stepped closer to the King and bowed shortly. No-one thought to stop him, despite him being armed with a sword and knife.

"King Ensert," Jalor acknowledged.

"General," Ensert nodded in response. "Have you come to offer assistance?"

"Assistance with what?" Jalor asked. "Flin?" Jalor paused. "Has any-one told you you have a rock in your forehead?"

"Yes, thank you," Flin said dryly. "It's called an Enchara and is an ancient device acknowledging the position of Archmage. And the what you ask about is an army of Goroth's creatures less than a day away."

"Ghazrak?"

"And men and women and some sort of flying creature," Flin said. "Two hundred ghazrak and three of the flying things. About five thou-sand men and women from the northlands. According to the sensors."

Jalor nodded. "What are your defences like?" he asked Ensert.

"We will meet them in the field!" the King exclaimed. "I have one hundred and fifty knights as well as four hundred pikemen and infantry, plus a further fifty archers."

"Your archers should concentrate on the norther men and women. Their arrows won't get through the ghazrak's armour. I assume these flying things are a form of ghazrak, too, so don't target them either." Jalor paused and considered. "King Ensert, my purpose in coming here was to seek your assistance and support for Corm when he battles Goroth. It looks like we need the reverse first. Your knights won't last long out there. I assume they will go into battle on hrss-back?"

Ensert glowered. "We will. And what makes you think knights will not last long?"

Jalor watched the King for a moment. "Yes, I was told about that. I think it would be wise for you not to lead your force but to stay and manage the fight. As for the knights, your hrss will be targeted by the ghazrak and that will leave your heavily armoured men on foot. I've seen what that might look like in other places, but I doubt their stamina if they are accustomed to riding to short battles."

"I lead my knights," Ensert growled, to the accompanying calls of "aye" from the few knights in the room.

"Who is your heir, then?" Jalor asked the King, ignoring the monarch's glowering countenance. "We should prepare for the change of command."

Ensert was taken aback by that. "Well, I have no male heir. I have just taken a new life partner and she is not, er, we have not, well, that is..." His voice trailed away, embarrassed.

"So, no heir. And you would leave your people leaderless in what is going to be one of the most difficult periods in Ennaris' history? Well, I have one possible solution." Jalor turned to Flin. "Is that a working portal?"

Flin nodded, bemused at Jalor's matter-of-fact encounter with the strongest king of Ennaris. Jalor stayed where he stood, thinking of what he would say.

"Portal, state your designation," he said to the air.

The panel immediately responded. "Escar Main online. Recognise Flight-Colonel Vinca Jalor."

"Flight-Colonel?" Ensert asked, intrigued.

"My rank in my own military," Jalor said absently. "Escar Prime, connect to the Citadel of the Faero, please." He turned to Flin. "The others should be monitoring, just in case."

"Connected," the portal announced.

"Almin Bor?" Jalor said in query.

"Here, Jalor," came the voice of Almin Bor in response, the slightly breathless tone causing Jalor to grin. Almin Bor saw the technology as a marvel of magic, even though he had been told that it was not magic but advanced technology from Ennaris' past.

"We have a situation in Escar," Jalor said. "Change of plan. There's an army of ghazrak and northers bearing down on the city, and the available forces will be stretched. How many trained soldiers are there in the infantry that could be brought to bear? Under our new captain?"

"About nine hundred are probably ready to be tested," Almin Bor said. "The, ah, new captain remains unconvinced," he continued with evident humour.

"Unfortunate," Jalor replied, with a wry grin that Almin Bor could not see. "Please arrange for the captain and the nine hundred to deploy to Escar. And I think Corm should come through now also."

"Yes, sir," Almin Bor said. "I will have the first contingents ready to move in one hur. Corm and the captain will come through ahead of the first contingent."

"Okay, thank you. Oh, and we'll probably need the twins." Jalor said.

"Just try to stop us," Raglin's voice boomed through the link, causing Flin to chuckle and Jalor to smile.

"Wouldn't think of it," Jalor laughed. "Jalor out."

Ensert was staring from Jalor to Flin and back again.

"Would you care to explain that?" he asked of Jalor.

"I'm bringing up reinforcements," Jalor said. "I also have a new captain who is a terror in a battle but needs to learn command. No better time. Same with Corm. He needs to see warfare up close and personal before he tries to lead one. And from what I can gather, he will have to lead one in the not too distant future."

"Then this is not the final battle?" Ensert asked.

"I doubt it," Jalor said. "We have been encountering ghazrak in troops of ten and twenty, so a force of two hundred does not sound like their main force. No, I'm thinking this is a test. Hopefully it's not a feint." He walked to the table, strewn with papers and maps, and stood considering. "I need to see the field. Can I get someone to show me, please?"

Ensert gestured to one of the knights, who nodded. "Sir Kylin will escort you to what is likely to be the field of battle."

Jalor bowed once again and followed Sir Kylin from the room. Ensert glanced to Flin and raised a single eyebrow.

"Children of Ennaris, eh? The stories are coming true after all. Or was that a story, also?"

"No, that's real," Flin said in return. "Jalor is one of the Children. As a bonus he is a senior officer in the military service of his world. And wait until you see Blaine in action. The man is like no-one I have ever seen." Flin paused to consider what he had just said. "Change that. There is another who may be better. It would be interesting to see them matched."

"This Blaine is the new captain?" Ensert asked as he strolled over to one of the windows to look out over the plain in front of the city.

His gaze traced the single road that ran in a slightly meandering line as it avoided long-buried masonry from the old city that had stood here so long ago. As he was watching two figures mounted on hrss rode from the gates along the road, the only two on that long ribbon that he could see.

"Maybe. I've been away from the Citadel for some time. But I doubt that Blaine needs training to lead in war. If there was anyone born to the role it's him. Likewise Almin Bor would not need it."

"Almin Bor?" Ensert turned around in surprise. "I thought he had retired from warfare long ago."

"You know him, I see," said Flin. "Yes, he did. But his farm was sacked by the ghazrak and Almin Bor and his family were saved by Jalor, Blaine and Varna - she is the third of the Children, by the way. That was their first sight of the ghazrak and between the three of them they just, well, destroyed all ten ghazrak. Almin Bor came to the Citadel with them and was drafted into organising the army, then Corm had a rush of genius and convinced Jalor to act as general."

"He's not really all that much into deferring to kings and such, is he?" Ensert said thoughtfully.

Flin smiled. "Where he's from they don't have kings or queens. Nor Archmages! Most advanced civilisations leave kings and queens behind as they develop. It's sort of a rite of passage in a way. If this goes the way I hope it will, my friend, you may have to consider that."

"And Archmages?" Ensert asked without turning.

"Oh, there are very few of them around anywhere. But with luck, my role will change also."

Ensert watched from the window, nodding absently, as the two figures dismounted and walked back and forth over the field.

One hur later Jalor was back in the throne room, having visited the portal room on his return to the city. He was thoughtful as he entered the room, looking over the maps of the plain before turning to the portal.

"Escar Main," he said.

"Yes Flight-Colonel Jalor?" replied the portal.

"Can you show me a topographical map of the city of Escar's surrounds, and overlay it with the roads, please?"

The grey screen became a riot of colour, shades of greens and browns with waving lines showing small ridges and dips and the road running through it all.

"Now are you able to map the larger masonry pieces from the old city, those buried down to say the height of three men?"

After a pause a series of white dots appeared on the screen, mostly on the large plain but some few to the sides and back of the city. Jalor turned to Flin.

"I take it that Escar was built from the ruins at one side of the old city?"

Flin nodded. "Yes."

"And Raglin and Ragnor helped to build it?"

"I have met Raglin and Ragnor. They truly are the Twin Mages of legend?" Ensert asked, rising from where he had been sitting reading through a report.

Jalor smiled. "They are," he said. "Well?" he asked Flin.

"Yes, they did, or rather they led the rebuilding of it to repair the ravages of time. Their joint talent is for building and they are able to exert force on building materials as well as create some masterful designs." Flin looked curiously at Jalor. "Why?"

"Just trying to understand where we stand," Jalor said. "Literally, in this case."

Flin was about to ask further questions when there was a minor disturbance in the corridor outside the throne room, loud exclamations of welcome ringing out. The doors were pushed open by the guards and Corm strode into the room, outfitted in hardy clothing suited for hard riding or outdoor work, but wearing a very business-like sword and long knife, head bare and long hair held back by a single strap. Behind him came Blaine, dressed in a similar manner, broadsword strapped to his back and two long knives at his hips, and then the twins in their brown breeches and soft blue-grey shirts. Behind them, striding confidently into the throne room in full mismatched armour, except for the helmet which was held under one arm, was Helt. The others separated slightly and paused, allowing the Princess to walk to where her father stood, looking stunned, where she went down on one knee.

"My king," she said clearly, loudly.

Ensert stood staring down at the bared head of his only child. "Arise," Ensert said. "My daughter."

Helt stood and Ensert was surprised to see that she was as tall as him. "If it please my liege, I would present Ragnor and Raglin, Mages of the Council, who I believe you met some time ago," Helt said, gesturing to the twins who each gave an identical bow, "and Corm Ramesa, Faero of Ennaris." The latter nodded to Ensert but did not bow, eliciting a slight grin from the Archmage in recognition of the twins' work. "And this is Blaine," Helt finished, moving to stand alongside the Warrior, who gave a respectful bow to the king.

"King Ensert," Blaine acknowledged.

Ensert felt that he was just standing there nodding as each was introduced. The Twin Mages had been legend for ever, of course, their feats of engineering having taken on mythical dimensions with stories of them harnessing clouds to provide permanent shade for the old cities, delving deep into the ground for the right stones. Their names were a by-word for beautiful design, despite no-one having seen their handiwork for thousands of cycles. But they had been the ones to bring warnings to Ensert. He looked at Blaine with interest, the second of the Children of Ennaris, recognising the fighter as well as the attachment between him and Helt. And Corm, who Ensert recalled as a spoilt brat, doing whatever he could to avoid duty and responsibility, suddenly looked like a, well, like a Faero.

And then there was his daughter, a little taller and stronger he thought, despite the armour that to his critical eye did not fit at all. He was about to speak but Jalor beat him to it.

"Captain, do you have the troops with you?"

Ensert paused to allow Blaine to respond and was shocked when the princess replied.

"Yes, general. We have just over nine hundred ready for the field. Actually," she thought, scratching her head exactly as Ensert did when thinking on his feet, to the evident amusement of the watching Sir Kylin, "we probably have about seven fifty ready for battle and the rest need blooding. We can spread them through the ranks and give them a taste if this battle shapes up."

The king was gaping. "You're the captain?"

"Yes, my liege. Captain Anhelter, of the Army of the Faero of Ennaris," Helt replied, standing straight and staring at her father.

"But, but you're a royal princess!" Ensert spluttered, not sure if he should be outraged or proud, which indecision was made no better by Kylin laughing and other knights smiling broadly.

"And one of the best fighters Corm has," Jalor said, turning to Helt. "When they are all through the portal, make sure they get settled somewhere. Then we will work out how to blend them into the King's forces. We don't have much time. I want to have a conference here in one hur. You can already see the advance units at the far end of the plain, so I expect we'll be fighting tomorrow morning."

She nodded and, with a bow to the king, hurried out with Blaine at her side. Ensert watched them go, bemused at seeing his daughter, whom he had thought estranged since she had left Escar, in a position of such responsibility.

Jalor turned to the king. "King Ensert," he said bluntly, "can you have your officers here at the same time, please?

At Ensert's nod, Kylin mirrored the nod and walked from the room. Jalor next turned to the twins. "I have something I want to discuss with you two, also."

He led them to the portal, where the topographical map was displayed once more, and the three of them fell into earnest discussion.

Ensert felt as though things were passing him by and he turned to Flin, who was watching him with a mixture of sympathy and amusement.

"They grow up, don't they?" Flin said, then smiled broadly. "Let's let them get set for what is to come. Do you have any ale around here?"

Ensert considered for a moment and thought that probably was a good idea. Without a word he led the Archmage from the room. Flin's Enchara glowed faintly as he accompanied the king.

# 8. Clay

Clay Anders, Champion of the Light, walked purposefully through the woods. The pale, early evening light filtered through the thin canopy and gave enough light for him to continue. It would be time to halt shortly, but then he only had a short distance left to go.

He listened carefully as he moved through the trees, skirting undergrowth where it might make a sound brushing against his clothes. In the ten days since leaving the Tree, he had encountered no-one, but he knew he was being tracked, probably by a pack of ghazrak. He had never lost his old skills, he realised, but now they were far more acute, sharper, honed to a hard point. Ogun and Menra had taught him ways of fighting that he had not known before but, more importantly, Ogun had reinforced disciplines that had always been there as part of him but now were more integrated. If anyone from Clay's past as a Warrior of the Light had been told that he would be immeasurably better as a fighter, they would have been incredulous. But Clay knew that he was better now than he had ever been before.

As a result of the lift in skills, or maybe of the gifts that he was supposed to possess, he was able to sense the ghazrak from a long distance. He knew they would not catch up to him before he reached his destination, and he knew there was no-one else around to be harmed when they did catch up to him. He could have moved faster but he concentrated on maintaining a steady pace, enforcing the disciplines, reinforcing what had been buried for so long. Every so often he paused to make sure there was some sign of his passing, pointing the way to where he wanted them to go. He had in mind a place for that encounter, one that he now remembered. He thought it a fitting place.

Finally, he walked into a small clearing. A tiny cottage occupied one corner, along with a small garden that seemed to have run wild. The surrounding woods had not encroached. He half expected to see that someone had moved in, but it appeared not to be the case although, on closer view, the garden did show some signs of being tended, or harvested at least. Well, at least someone was getting some benefit. He stepped up to the single door and pushed it open. Or rather, it fell open when he pushed it. Clay caught the door before it hit the rammed dirt floor and placed it gently against one of the inside walls. He stood in the small space and looked around. Dirt and dust overlaid everything. He could see signs of animals, rodents probably, having been active in making nests, probably taking advantage of the shelter offered. Cobwebs hung from the ceiling and trailed across the home-built table and two chairs, all that they had needed. The bed was in its corner still. The straw mattress had long since collapsed and rotted away, leaving the wooden frame and slats in place. Some stains in the floor showed evidence of leaks. A small stone stove still stood in its own corner, with its own store of cobwebs.

Clay stood still, remembering at last, allowing himself to remember. Capes after a day of tending the garden sitting at the table they had made together, with tea made from their own herbs. Evian crawling around the small cottage, more a cabin really. His expression stony, Clay walked from the cottage and, with a single glance to orient, strode into the woods. He followed what had been a faint trail at one time, long ago, but which was now a trail in his memory only. He found the boulder, nestled against its brother such that a small space was created where the two met. It was not a cave by any means but, still, it was a possible point of shelter for creatures needing such. Clay knelt to examine the entrance, noting small paw and claw marks that spoke of possible occupants. He ensured there were no spiders that could cause him grief and then felt around inside the entrance, finding the small shelf and the flint kit on that shelf.

It was but a moment before he had a small fire going with twigs collected from around the boulders and then he selected one particular limb that had something like a pine cone attached to it. The cone flared as it was thrust into the flame and then settled to a steady burn, as Clay expected it would. It would last five minims or more, which should be enough. Burning brand in hand, Clay half crawled, half slithered into the opening, rising to a crouch in the larger space revealed within. It was large enough for three of four people to recline if necessary. He looked around, memories strong once again, and then dampened them down, before moving to a spot against one of the rocky walls that looked no different to any other spot. The earth was more compact than he remembered, but then, it had been forty to fifty Ennaris cycles since he had been in here, so that was not a surprise. Using the stick, he scrabbled at the surface enough to dig down a short distance, enough to uncover the handle of the utility spade he had left there. He extracted and unfolded it and then made short work of digging the rest of the hole necessary to uncover what he had come for.

He exited the small cave as the cone sputtered out, dragging after him the small container, made of an almost unbreakable material. The small image of a sunburst set into the side of the case caught the light of the small fire, causing Clay to pause once again in remembrance. And once again he pushed the memories aside as he brushed the remaining dirt from the case, examining it to see if it was as unbreakable as had been claimed. He could find no signs of damage, but when he placed his thumb over the sensor nothing happened, so he set the case aside and set to work to build the fire up a little more. After so long he had not expected the sensor to be active.

A meal of flatbread, cheese and fruit drawn from his travel pack was consumed, after which he kicked dirt over the fire to extinguish it and made his way through the dark to the cottage. Acting on memory, and almost by feel, he carefully placed the case where the moon light and the first rays of the sun would find it, allowing the inbuilt batteries to charge. He then made his way back into the woods, but in a different direction. He found the tree he was searching for, much larger than it had been, but still sturdy. With little effort Clay climbed to the first large bough, which now was broad enough to act as a form of bench. Settling himself in the crook where the trunk and bough met, he arranged himself with his back against the trunk and legs stretched along the bough and closed his eyes, trusting himself not to fall while asleep. He gave in to memories for just a moment, his thoughts haunted by images of a smiling woman and laughing child, before exerting discipline once more and entering a state half-way between sleep and doze.

He awoke at first light. He listened intently but could only hear the expected birds and smaller animals of the woods. After a light stretch in place, Clay looked up the tree, locating hand and foot holds, and then lithely clambered up to the higher branches. This particular tree had reached to the top of the canopy in the past, and with the extra growth, may now have stuck its head through and above its fellows, all of which were of a different type. Sure enough, he was able to reach a point where he could scan over the treetops, looking for signs of his trackers. In the distance, from the direction in which he had come, Clay saw a thin spiral of smoke, probably ten kilometres away. So, about three hurs, he thought, before they caught up. He clambered down again and walked to the cottage's clearing. He noted that the case was receiving the early morning sunlight and decided to have breakfast before getting to work on it.

Another brief meal was taken, again with stores from his pack provided by the Guardians. It was nothing special but was fresh and hearty. Clay stood, brushing crumbs from his hands. He repacked his travel pack, which he placed just inside the door of the cottage. Then he strode through the garden to where he had left the case, lifted it so it was upright and placed his left thumb against the sensor. A moment passed and then a slight *whirr* was heard, followed by a click. He nodded to himself, satisfied, laid the case flat again and pressed small studs on each of the two top corners, simultaneously.

The case latches released, and the case sprung open slightly. Clay paused, surprised to feel a surge of emotion as the case opened, and then pulled it open fully. Delving into the contents he pulled out item after item, placing most of them in a position to catch the sun, although some he kept close to him. A thin belt he placed on the ground after examining its many small pouches and attachment points. Finally, he reached to the bottom of the case and drew forth breeches and tunic, designed to look like clothing from Ennaris, but with two small additions. On the left collar of the tunic there was a tiny patch with an icon of the Light blazing, surrounded by a white circle and then a second red circle, the symbol of the Champion. On the left shoulder, a second patch, larger, showed a sunburst with a lightning bolt running through the centre on a diagonal. He reached to remove the patch but caught himself, considering, before pulling back. No, he would leave the crew patch in place, in honour of his former crew mates, most of whom he was sure would be dead by now, if not all.

He left the case and other items to finish charging their internal batteries and took the clothes into the cottage where he changed, leaving the clothes that Fernis had provided neatly folded on the table. They would come with him later. Then he decided to spend a few minutes tidying the cottage.

It was one hur later that he emerged, brushing dust from his hands. He walked to the array of items he had drawn from the case, checking that they were charged. Most of them had charged enough for his purpose, A couple had full charge. Only one was showing less than half charge. It had always been slower to charge, but held its charge longer, so he thought that would be okay. He picked up the belt and slung it around his hips, settling it in place, tying down the holster to his right thigh. He left the partly charged items as long as possible, taking those fully charged and adding them to loops on the belt, or secreted in small pouches sewn into his tunic. Would they be of use? Probably not, but there was no use if he did not have them. Finally, when he decided enough time had passed, he picked up the remaining items. The blaster went into his holster, sitting snug. He tried a few fast draws and was satisfied that it would not snag. The needler went on the belt where he could get it easily, and the two tiny thermal grenades he snapped into place, their magnetic clamps allowing them to sit on the belt against metal studs where he could get them easily at need.

Clay closed the case once more. He moved it to a place where it would be safe, against one wall of the cottage, and then settled down to wait for the ghazrak. It was time for the Champion to go on the offensive.

He only had to wait for an hur. He knew the ghazrak were close when all bird and animal life fell quiet. He watched from his place of concealment - three trees growing in a triangle such that a small space was created in the middle of them - as the first of the beasts crept into the opening. It sniffed and snuffled at his scent, entered the cottage and came back out again, then made a strange warble that called the rest into the clearing. Clay watched as nine more ghazrak crept from the woods, making no attempt at stealth. His gaze sharpened when a Shadow followed them, gliding from the woods into the centre of the clearing, between the garden beds which the ghazrak were trampling. The Shadow looked around the clearing and examined the cottage before its gaze came to rest on the case that Clay had left against the cottage wall and glided over to examine it. Clay almost felt its shock as it turned the case to reveal the sunburst symbol. The Shadow actually recoiled, letting the case fall as it did so. The ghazrak all turned to see what had happened.

Clay chose that moment to step into the open, hands falling to his sides. The Shadow turned from the cottage towards the ghazrak and saw Clay. It was shocked once again into immobility, and then died. The Champion swept both hands down and up. The right came up holding the blaster and the left the needler. The first blast took the Shadow through the centre of the hood. As the black robes collapsed and the ghazrak reacted to the threat, the blaster fired again and again, each blast killing one of the band. Eight ghazrak were down before the surviving two sought to counter Clay's fire. One leapt into the cottage and the other charged at the Champion. Clay holstered the blaster and dodged the swipe of the sword, which he noted still was not of great quality, before firing the needler from point blank range. The ghazrak stopped in its tracks. A tiny smouldering hole was drilled through its inbuilt armour in the centre of the chest, telling the tale. It slowly fell backwards.

Clay walked unhurriedly to the centre of the clearing, facing the door of the cottage, his blaster back in its holster. He waited, breathing easily and smoothly. Patience was not a strong suit of the ghazrak, as had been proved time and again. Sure enough, after only a few minims, the remaining ghazrak charged from the cottage, roaring a guttural challenge and brandishing its sword. Once again Clay's right hand swept the blaster from its holster and the Ghazrak died, pierced through one eye. Quiet reigned in the clearing and the surrounding wood as Clay stood and surveyed the carnage. His expression was bleak.

Another hur later the ghazrak had been piled in a second small clearing some distance away from the cottage. Their weapons were tossed onto the pile with them. The Shadow's robes were tossed on top and Clay placed two of the incendiary devices that one of the ghazrak had carried onto the pile. He stepped back and, with a fluid motion, drew the needler and fired a single shot at each incendiary. The devices exploded with a blast of heat, causing Clay to retreat to the edge of the clearing. Fire engulfed the ghazrak bodies. Its fierce heat left very little after only a few minims. Clay waited to be sure the dwindling blaze would not set fire to the surrounding wood and then turned back to the cottage.

For the rest of the day he worked to reset the door of the cottage and made running repairs to the roof. He cut several poles as he located appropriate thatching material. As the daylight faded, he selected a spot and in a single neat line erected ten of the poles, placing on top of each the burned remains of a ghazrak skull. That was grisly but, he hoped, would keep some people away, and may cause any wandering ghazrak to beat a retreat as well. With night falling he collected his rudimentary tools and his mission case and entered the cottage. He settled for a small fire and dry rations again. His food supply was almost finished, so he would have to leave the following day.

In the morning the birds were singing once again, and he could sense nothing inimical in the vicinity. Early morning light was brightening the clearing as Clay stepped from the cottage. The mission case was left in a hidden cabinet inside the cottage, but was now empty anyway. He wore the breeches and tunic from *Sunburst*, with his hooded travel cape wrapped around his shoulders. His belt carried the blaster and needler. His sword hung from the left side and the long knife from the right. With travel pack held in one hand, Clay paused to survey the scene in front of him, and stood still, allowing his senses to stretch wide. No un-expected sounds, no unexpected smells, the slight breeze only carrying the promise of rain during the day. No enemies could be sensed. He pulled the door to behind him and walked around the cottage to a tiny plot behind.

Only then did he allow himself to relax his iron discipline. He walked to the two plots, one of which was much longer than the other. Both were over-grown with weeds and thickly carpeted with wildflowers, Capes' favourites in red, blue and yellow. He dropped his pack and knelt between the two in a single motion, placing one hand palm down on each, remembering and grieving, allowing the bitter tears to flow at last. He stayed like that for a long, long time, communing with the memories of his lost family before, with a silent promise to return, he stood, slung the pack from one shoulder and turned away. With swift steps he walked past the cottage, past the line of helmet skulls standing as sentinels and through the smaller clearing where the blackened centre showed little trace of what had been burned. His face was set and his eyes were dry and hard.

The Champion set out once again.

# 9. Rocs for War

Ar-kunya sat on the rocky prominence, as he had taken to doing as day merged into night. High in the great dividing range of mountains, scraps of light lingered on the western slopes even while the east was in darkness. He enjoyed watching the light fade and then, suddenly, extinguish. He would then head back to the ledge where he and El-arwe had their eyrie, backed by a cave that ran into the mountain.

The Rocs had spent a busy time since Kunas had returned. After a period of celebration, followed by a further period of uncertainty about what the Guardian expected of the Rocs, the ruling council of the Rocs decided that, if the time for battle was approaching, the Rocs needed to be prepared. No-one remembered the old days, of course, and the knowledge handed down from generation to generation, even for the long-lived Rocs, had deteriorated. Therefore, a program was put in place to re-establish that older capability. Kunas gave them advice about older drills and practices.

Watchers from afar would have seen the great birds swooping, diving and ascending at speed, many wearing great harnesses filled with rocks to increase their stamina and load carrying ability. There were speed trials held to ensure that everyone knew who was the fastest among the Roc numbers. Formation flying was practised and in-flight signals were devised, some drawn from traditional knowledge and some devised anew to counter potential dangers or deal with situations that were thought likely to be encountered. From the ranks of the Rocs, traditional roles were resuscitated, wing leaders, squadron commanders.

It was telling, Ar-kunya thought, that all of a sudden, the Rocs, for so long maintaining numbers but not increasing markedly, had a surfeit of chicks. He questioned Kunas about that one evening.

"Are you increasing our numbers in preparation for deaths in battle?" Ar-kunya said to Kunas, as both watched the mock fights high above the mountain peaks.

"No," Kunas replied. "I'm not doing anything. It may be that my father is doing so, or it may just be destiny taking a hand."

"Your father?" Ar-kunya queried, twisting his head in shock to look at the Guardian. "Guardians have fathers?"

"Indeed we do," Kunas laughed. "Or perhaps I should say we have a parent. Depending on mood, that parent may be mother or father. The last time we spoke it was with my father."

"But," Ar-kunya started to speak and the thought better of it. "Can your, er, father actually do that for us?"

"I would say so, yes. But he usually allows peoples to get along without direct intervention. So I suspect it is destiny taking a hand."

"I have never considered destiny to be someone or something real," Ar-kunya said thoughtfully.

"Ah," Kunas replied, smiling. "But consider. The Rocs were demoralised over the long millennia since the rebellion. How else to explain the break-down in your skills, no matter how good you thought you were. And now there is increased vitality, the flights are showing pride, the crests are standing up more than when I returned. Your flocks are far more alive, more fit for their tasks than they have been for a very long time. Is there really any surprise that greater vitality is experienced elsewhere also?"

Ar-kunya considered, thinking of those surprising episodes when he and El-arwe had acted more like young flightlings than older and more experienced elders. He nodded, his great hooked beak apart in silent laughter, communing with Kunas via thought alone and sharing a rueful moment.

"Indeed," Ar-kunya said after a while, "that could be the case. There is a greater spirit amongst the Rocs, and that has translated to more partnerships being formed. It is something to remember when this is done. The Rocs must find means to ensure that we do not fall back into the ways of a death spiral."

"If you and the Mages win the coming battle, I feel you will have no fear of that," said Kunas. "The time will be when Ennaris re-establishes its place amongst the peoples of this galaxy. And the Rocs will be part of that. I can foresee great times ahead."

"For those who survive and if we win," Ar-kunya replied.

"There always is risk in these matters," Kunas nodded gently, tilting his head in a very bird-like manner to glance at the Roc leader. "But that should never cause Rocs to doubt their way. This battle will be fought by all Ennarisi, in one form or another, and each must contribute. So intimates the Prophecy, and so says logic."

Ar-kunya nodded again, thinking of times to come when the Rocs could once again be a core part of the Ennarisi. Already the peoples of the lower valleys had become accustomed to the Rocs visiting. After the initial alarm and awe at being so close to the great birds, who stood taller than a man in most cases, the villages welcomed them as of old. There were even a few children discovered with the old gift of conversing with the Rocs by mind-speech and now, far from being viewed with suspicion, these children were lauded and protected by the villagers and Rocs together.

The ancient order of the Alnar-kun has been re-instituted, a blending of Roc warriors with battle-trained gifted and highly skilled non-gifted Ennarisi, working together to form an elite fighting force. Ar-kunya and others watched them drilling with undisguised envy.

They were learning to work together. The villagers from the heights were learning to direct the Rocs onto targets with loads of rocks, and that training was ramping up. Others had been found from the isolated villages scattered amongst the peaks of the ranges who could sit atop the Rocs. They would be taught to wield the ancient, traditional crossbow and spears. Kunas had told the Rocs that a Roc and skilled rider could cause absolute havoc in an attack, and many had taken the challenge to re-establish the skill. Others had come from the other side of the continent with their own skills and battle gifts. Ar-kunya regarded their leader with undisguised awe.

Ar-kunya and the council had also instituted one of the old traditions, the sweep. Every day a flight of two Rocs was tasked with sweeping a part of Ennaris, separate to the regular patrols that were for shorter durations. Rocs could stay aloft for very long periods, flying very high indeed, their keen eyesight able to discern and identify movement far below. It was one of those sweeps, lasting two days, that brought news of the army approaching Escar. The Roc council debated what should be done and sought the advice of Kunas, who told them of the army of Goroth that approached the walled city. The Rocs were especially interested in the flying creatures. The council made its decision, and preparations were begun, training stepped up.

That decision would be put into effect on the morrow.

"Are we making the right decision?" Ar-kunya asked Kunas as the light faded.

"That is for you to decide," the Guardian responded, before relenting. "But know that I and my brothers and sisters were pleased with your decision."

Ar-kunya stood and fluffed his wings.

"Thank you, Guardian," he said formally. "I must make final preparations for the flight."

Kunas nodded as the leader of the Rocs leapt from the peak and glided to his eyrie to ensure all things were ready. For tomorrow, for the first time in thousands of cycles, the Rocs would go to war!

## 10. Likud

Likud stood on the bridge of *Qorv*, the flagship of the Empire fleets and of his armada speeding towards Ennaris. With its blunt prow and numerous weapons pods and blisters plastered to its sides, it was anything but sleek. But then, in space, it did not need to be. It was Likud's first true journey for thousands of cycles. He was angry and frustrated. Thousands of cycles had been expended to make sure that he was there when Goroth came out of stasis, as the Prophecy now said. His latest reading said that it had happened, and he was not there! He had waged war against the second great offshoot of the Ennarisi to blunt their ability to intervene. He had suborned generations of Union Fleet officers so he would know when he must strike, all the while allowing his Andorethi to be destroyed from time to time so suspicion would not be raised.

The Andorethi raised his frustration levels higher. He had turned a peaceful people into wrathful pseudo-demons who believed that the humans were the enemy because he, Likud, said they were, and yet there remained a stubborn undercurrent of resistance to that message among many, despite so much conditioning of the race.

*Qorv* was the greatest battleship the Andorethi had ever produced, Likud knew. It was not as good as the Ennarisi ships of the long past, but then, Likud had been informed that Marjory was dead, and the secrets of those ships died with the Battle Mage, she who had designed the last generation of needle fighters and the great behemoth ships that had been destroyed during the rebellion. Likud remembered Marjory fondly, however, although he was pleased that she was not around to give him trouble. She had always encouraged him to make the most of his gifts. His were not nearly as good as her own when it came to strategy and warfare, and certainly he was not in her class when it came to warfare using their gifts, but she was generous with her time, and solicitous of his feelings when he was disappointed at the outcome. He still squirmed inside when he thought of the look on her face that day when she understood that he was with Goroth as one of the rebels. Disappointment had warred with grim determination, and he knew he did not want to have to face her again. Well, she was dead, so he did not have to!

Standing on the bridge of his great ship, Likud felt invincible. He knew the Union had nothing that could stand up to this vessel, now that *Sunburst* was gone. Marjory and *Sunburst*, the two things that could have stood in his way, and both gone, although neither had actually been seen to die. A twinge of uncertainty about that was suppressed. No, they were gone, and he was on his way to take his place alongside Goroth, as in days of old. Nothing would stop that!

As though waiting for that thought, Likud's Andorethi Bridge Lieutenant approached, cautiously, diffidently. He stood to attention waiting for Likud to notice him, for to interrupt anything Likud was doing, even thinking, could see him executed. Likud deliberately made him wait, standing at attention like the lackey that he was. The Andorethi were useful tools but they lacked imagination. Of course, Likud had never given them any real leeway in their actions. Orders came through him. He had always done things that way. He recalled Marjory's advice that, by not allowing people to think independently, his subordinates would never be in a position to deal with unexpected events. Likud snorted. In this he knew that he was right, and she was wrong. Discipline was all, as he had learned during the rebellion. They had lost because of lapses in discipline, even though they were so close to victory. Marjory had maintained discipline and her dwindling forces had done what she said to the letter. And her tactics had been brilliant, unexpected, and delivered to the letter. He had learned much from that, and so did not allow deviation from his plans.

Finally, he turned to his Bridge Lieutenant and said, "You have a report?"

Likud always spoke aloud, rather than using the mind to mind speech favoured by the Andorethi, and demanded that they responded in kind. He allowed them to believe it was an affectation, a harking back to the past, but the truth was that Likud had never mastered the art of mind to mind speech, as had many of his fellow Mages.

The Bridge Lieutenant bowed low, almost convulsively. "My great lord Likud," he said with a slight tremor, "the pace of the fleet is proving to be too much for several of the smaller ships. The commanders of *Ghaz* and *Bhuta* have requested a slower speed for the fleet or themselves, or they fear their engines will overload."

Likud snarled. "They will maintain course and speed. They will remain with *Qorv*, or the commanders will explain to me, in person, why they did not. Discipline will be maintained." He turned back to look at the viewscreen in front of him, technology stolen from the humans because the Andorethi did not have the imagination to create things like that and Likud had not thought to take such plans with him when he fled Ennaris. "Is that understood?" he finished in a voice replete with menace.

"Yes, my great lord," the Bridge Lieutenant said, bowing and retreating.

Likud sighed to himself. He had to think of everything. The new engine design had also been stolen. The humans built better engines that survived punishing treatment. Unfortunately, they had to be adapted to ships that were designed for an older and less capable engine design, and there had proved to be variability in their performance and reliability. He frowned as the icons on the screen for *Ghaz* and *Bhuta* changed to an alert. The fleet was proceeding at flank speed, and he had placed these smaller vessels inside the screen of the larger ships, with the better ability of the larger ships to push the tiny bits of space debris out of the way.

Of course, he had no-one to discuss his orders with. His own Ennarisi followers had all died long ago, but he knew what he was doing.

The icons for *Ghaz* and *Bhuta* showed critical. Likud stared at the screen as both disappeared, and each of the ships in the vicinity showed alerts, with two of them rapidly moving to critical before they also disappeared. Five now showed alerts.

"My great lord," the Bridge Lieutenant appeared again, his agitation such that he did not wait to be acknowledged. "*Ghaz* and *Bhuta* have exploded. Their star engines overloaded and could not be contained at the current speed. The debris from both ships impacted on other ships of the fleet. *Bhat* and *Krut* have been destroyed as a result, and five other ships have damage. The fleet commanders are awaiting your orders, my great lord."

A tactical error, Likud thought to himself. He should have allowed the two to drop out and follow, and now he had lost four, with five more in doubt. He reviewed the losses. *Ghaz* and *Bhat* were torpedo boats, nimble and fast, designed to get in, release their torpedoes and get out. They would be missed in a pitched battle. *Krut* was a slightly larger vessel that mainly did supply duties, so was not such a loss. *Bhuta*, though, was a small version of a cruiser, and had carried weapons far greater than would have been expected of a ship its size. The five damaged vessels included the two pocket cruisers as well as a heavy cruiser and two other torpedo ships. The fleet of fifty-seven ships was now fifty-three, and five in trouble, and his offensive capabilities had been dealt a blow. But Likud could not allow weakness to show. They still had two days to go to reach Ennaris. He stared at the screen, his face stern.

"Maintain speed!" he snapped.

# 11. Battle of Escar

Jalor stood atop the battlements of the city of Escar and watched as the norther army arranged itself. It was not a huge army, as those things went elsewhere, but on the scale of Ennaris it was significant. The force of ghazrak were held to the rear, with thousands of men and women from the norther kingdoms to the front. In the midst were six siege engines, great machines designed to throw huge boulders a considerable distance, and each had a supply of boulders alongside it. That explained why it had taken so long for the army to get to the walls, a day longer than Jalor had expected. They had to bring those boulders with them, for such could not be found on the plain without digging up debris from the ancient city. From what he could see, each boulder was almost the height of a man. They would hit with enormous force. Jalor looked along the wall's length. Despite Ensert's avowed belief in their strength, the walls had never been tested over the thousands of cycles they had stood like they would be today. Jalor and Blaine had carried out a cursory examination and the latter had stated clearly that the less well constructed parts of the city wall would not hold against consistent battering, despite its size and apparent strength.

The plain was alive with jeers and roars from norther men and women. On the plain a small pavilion had been set up atop a platform, well behind the army itself. Tiny figures could be seen on top of the platform. A small contingent of figures stood near the command post as an island of discipline among the rest. Probably regular army.

Jalor was searching for the flying creatures, without luck. The ghazrak he knew, and the men and women he also understood, although the reports that reached Ensert spoke of disciplined soldiers, which these men and women were not. However, a flying monster could be a problem, let alone three of them. The city gates had been closed and as many people as could be squeezed in had been taken up into the much better constructed main keep, behind the larger, heavier gates. That left a lot still in the lower city proper, and Jalor had placed them as far from the city walls as he could get them. If the walls were breached, though, it could be a massacre.

A horn blew. Each of the six siege engines had their great throwing arms wound back, a back-breaking task for those having to wind the windlass to make it happen. Professionally, Jalor considered how he would have done that better. The designs were almost textbook medieval, but he could see the huge wooden arms bending under the strain as they were lashed into place, and knew they could break if strained the wrong way. Still, they were strong enough for the large boulders pushed from their own wheeled platforms into the buckets at the end of the arms.

"Get ready," Almin Bor called from his place in the courtyard below, which was unnecessary for those watching but the right thing to do to assure the soldiers that their officers were alert.

A second horn sounded and all six catapults released their loads with loud *twangs*. Jalor was almost mesmerised as he watched the great stones arch into the air before starting their journey back to the ground. Two of them landed short, crashing into the ground and bouncing twice before coming to a rest a short distance from the wall. Three others impacted the city wall with resounding crashes. The wall shook and groaned. Jalor watched dry-mouthed as several defenders were thrown from the wall as a result of the impacts, landing in untidy heaps on the stone passageways. The last boulder soared over the wall to land inside the city, smashing several stone and timber buildings as it landed and rolled. This section of the lower city had been emptied, so no-one should have been hurt. Jalor watched as those who had been thrown from the wall were picked up. Without being told, he knew that all of them were dead.

Men and women were shouting to each other along the wall, some to keep their own courage up, others to bolster their fellow soldiers. Some were issuing warnings, which Jalor knew were superfluous, but he also knew this was about groups of people in dire straights, doing what they could to hold firm. For himself he stood and waited, knowing the next flight of boulders would be better aimed. Sure enough, the catapults launched the next wave of boulders, with four of them crashing against the wall and two flying the wall and landing in the city. The four that hit the wall did damage, although the wall held. One part of the battlements was crushed with several injuries but, from what Jalor could see, no loss of life. The two that fell into the city did more destruction, bouncing and rolling through shops and dwellings, again empty.

Jalor looked up to see Blaine, pointing to the sky, and he looked up in turn. High above the city, Jalor could see a flying creature, which was either the largest bird he had ever seen or one of Goroth's flying ghazrak. Either way, he would have to keep an eye on it. The third wave of boulders were being prepared now, and Jalor could see they were orienting towards one section of the wall. Jalor grabbed hold of a palace page, conscripted as a runner, and pointed to where the wall was damaged.

"See that section of the wall? I want you to get down below and see what the damage is. Then tell Almin Bor that will be the target of the attack. And be careful you don't get caught if the next set of rocks hits that wall."

With a short nod the boy sped away, leaping down the steps to the courtyard below and running to the wall and then to where Almin Bor stood with Helt. The page pointed and delivered his message, listened for a moment and then started to run back to Jalor. At the same time Helt turned to her soldiers, standing nervously along one side of the courtyard, and led the way to the section of wall that the page had pointed out. She stopped them well back from the wall.

Meanwhile the third salvo of rock projectiles was launched, in two flights of three each. As Jalor thought, all of the first three were aimed at the same section of wall. Jalor saw Blaine shooing people away from that section of the wall that the rocks hit. Two of them were aimed well enough to hit the wall roughly in the same place. The third impacted close enough to weaken the wall further. The wall groaned again but held. Debris flew and several sections of the inner side of the wall collapsed, threatening to bring the parapet walkway down. The next flight of three boulders hit the same area of the wall and it shattered. The outer wall was damaged enough that the next salvo passed through the damaged area, across the inner passage - the weakness that Blaine had seen - and crashed with devastating force against the thinner inner wall. Blocks from the outer wall were flung across the passage to create further carnage. Building blocks were thrown into the courtyard where Helt had been standing and a great gap opened in the wall. With a groan the section of the walkway above the hole collapsed, creating a mound of stone blocks on both sides of the wall.

With a roar the men and women of the besieging army charged forward, waving swords and knives in the air in a manic fury, even as Jalor saw the catapults being readied again. Looking down from his section of wall, Jalor saw Helt lead her force across the mounds of rock and form up to meet the charge. Blaine called to his charges and the small force of archers stood to the parapet and loosed volley after volley of arrows at the charging men and women. There were no ghazrak amongst them, Jalor noted, and most had no armour. The lead elements of the charge faltered as the archers took their toll. Dozens were cut down in a short time but the defenders had a relatively meagre store of arrows so Blaine gave the order to take individual targets, while he turned and ran from the wall. The attackers had been diminished but still outnumbered the defenders by more than five to one.

The fourth wave of boulders sailed across the wall and landed inside the city walls, aimed so that they caused another wide wave of destruction amongst the tightly packed buildings. Many of the buildings in that section of the city were destroyed or damaged now, Jalor saw. And then the third part of the enemy's plan made itself known, as three flying monstrosities appeared over the battle ground. Helt had been joined by Blaine, Jalor saw, and they were forming up the pikemen and swordsmen when great shadows crossed the ground, accompanied by piercing shrieks. Attackers and defenders alike paused momentarily to look up, the attackers to cheer and the defenders to quail momentarily. The three were hideous. They were about twice the body length of one of the defenders, with bone-armoured chests and thickly muscled legs that ended in claws. Huge heads had razor sharp hooked beaks. Broad wings had cutting appendages, like knives, at each pinon and the leading edges of the wings looked to be sharpened and armoured also. Long tails that trailed behind in flight were spiked at the end and showing similar bony armour for part of the length. They truly were flying ghazrak.

With a yell, Jalor ducked below the stone parapet as one of the flying creatures went over, soaring along the length of the wall. Some of the defenders were not quick enough and paid the price. The wings of the creature tilted to crash into them as they stood and stared, transfixed in fear. One defending archer, bravery personified, stood and loosed arrow after arrow at the creature, none of which penetrated the armour, before being picked up and dragged high above the battle field, crying in fear. He was then dropped in front of Helt's fighters.

The other two winged ghazrak were wheeling and plunging over the walls, ensuring the archers were unable to loose any more arrows at the attackers. The defenders were being cut down without any chance to defend themselves. Jalor called the retreat and somewhere a horn sounded - one of the signallers was still alive, then, he thought. The archers ran down the steps, some of the more agile jumping through the gap in the wall-walk to land on the rock pile. Those that could do so made their way to the edge of the wall and loosed the last of their arrows, before dropping their bows and quivers and moving the join the swordsmen.

The charging northers reached Helt's line of defenders, a triple line of pikes that stretched shoulder to shoulder across the space in front of the wall breach and some distance to each side. As the wild-eyed attackers reached the line, the pikemen thrust the end of their pikes into the ground, angled upward slightly so the runners impaled themselves. There was no thought of self-preservation, however, as the first wave and then the second flung themselves at the pikes. Sheer weight of numbers of dying men and women forced the pikes to be dropped and the lines to move back. The defenders were shocked at the ferocity and single-mindedness of the attackers. Jalor reminded himself that his soldiers were not experienced professionals who had seen warfare before. The numbers were overwhelming and the defenders would be overwhelmed shortly. And then he saw the smaller force of ghazrak start to move forward, first at a trot and then a shambling run, roaring and waving their rude swords.

Jalor waved his sword in a circle around his head, hoping someone was watching in the heat of the moment. He sighed with relief as the huge gates swung open. Another horn sounded. From the castle issued the knights of Escar, a multitude of armoured men and hrss in the multi-coloured suits of armour, with pennants flying from lances as they galloped down the sloping road to the plain. Jalor looked down to see a small number of knights hold back and was relieved to recognise Ensert from the colours of the armour. The King had objected strenuously to staying behind while Sir Kylin led the knights to battle, and was only convinced when he learnt that not only would Jalor be staying back, but that his knights thought it was the right thing to do also.

The knights moved out smartly and galloped down the road in double file, to a designated point, arriving as the ghazrak were starting across a patch of the plain where there were no remnants of the old city to trip the hrss. Wheeling and kicking their heels into their hrss, the twin file now became two waves of knights charging towards the ghazrak. The latter in turn snarled and turned, raising their swords in challenge and charging towards the oncoming knights. With a mighty clash, the two came together, the smaller band of knights lowering their lances and punching through the ghazrak, leaving many dead and wounded. In their turn, several of the knights were brought down and were immediately set upon by any ghazrak in the vicinity. Armour could not protect them for long and all five of the downed knights were dead before Kylin could turn his troop for a second pass through. Stubs and shards of lances were discarded. The knights raced back towards the ghazrak with broadswords held in mailed fists. They started to lay about themselves with gusto, cutting down into the ghazrak from hrss-back. When the ghazrak started to attack the mounts, Kylin gave a shout and the knights dismounted as one, slapping their hrss across their broad rumps to move them aside, and the battle became one of knights and ghazrak on foot. Tempered swords and battle axes combated crude swords and other misshapen implements.

Jalor returned his attention to the battle between the northers and Helt's soldiers. The weight of numbers of the norther men and women were taking their toll, and the Faero's army was being pushed back. As Jalor watched, Blaine clambered through the gap and leapt down the slope, extracting the great broadsword from its back-harness as he ran. He was followed by the city guard. These were Ensert's foot soldiers, who had been kept back to intervene at just this moment. Jalor had relied on the archers and Helt's force to blunt the attack and hold the line. He had also hoped that the ghazrak would be held and used as shock troops, which is what he would have done. The counter of using the knights against the ghazrak was to try to even the ledger in terms of weaponry, while hoping the trained guards would be able to handle much more than their own weight of numbers. So far, that was working, although those winged ghazrak remained a threat.

As Blaine and the reinforcing city guard reached the battle, Helt shouted a command. The Citadel force opened slight gaps through which the fresher city soldiers charged with shields and swords in hand. With a defiant shout they surged into the ranks of the attackers. Blaine met up with Helt in the centre, wielding his broadsword as though it was a smaller sword, slashing and cutting his way through the attacking men and women, some of whom were lightly armoured, most of whom were not. Slowly the tide turned.

And then it turned back again. The winged ghazrak returned to the fray, dropping large stones into the mass of fighting men and women, not caring if they crushed attackers or defenders. Each pass opened up slight gaps and the defenders had to backtrack slightly to cover them, trying and often failing to pull injured comrades with them. There was now a steady stream of injured straggling out of the battle, and Jalor could see they would not be able to hold.

With a mental shrug, he left the wall and made his way to the gate, which was closed again. He found the twins and Flin in conversation with Corm.

"We're outnumbered and those winged creatures are starting to hurt," Jalor said bluntly. "We're going to have to do something about them."

Corm nodded, nervous sweat running from under his helm, light armour covering chest, shoulders and thighs. "I think this is where I need to take a part," he said.

"Yes, this is where the Faero comes in," Jalor said. "And the Mages."

At nods from the twins, and a grimace from Flin, Jalor led the way back to the gap in the wall, where the great blocks of masonry lay tumbled. The twins, gifted with the ability to handle rock and masonry with ease, linked hands and concentrated. For a moment nothing happened, then the first of the blocks lifted from atop the pile and was flung, passing across the defenders' lines and crashing with devastating force into the attackers' ranks. One after the other, faster and faster as the twins exercised their gift to the full, the large wall stones brought down by the collapse were picked up and thrown into the northers' lines, causing confusion and thinning numbers. They were not enough of themselves to hold back the attack, but enough to give respite to the defenders. Finally a path was cleared through the wall stones and Jalor turned to Corm, standing with his personal guard, led by Almin Bor.

"Standard bearer!" Jalor barked, and nodded as a soldier ran forward, unfurling the Faero's banner atop a lance. "Let's go!"

Jalor led the way through the gap created by the twins, who continued to toss blocks of masonry into the attacking army, although they were slower now as fatigue set in. Behind Jalor came the standard bearer. The banner of the Faero fluttered atop the lance and Corm and his guard followed close behind. Down the slope they ran, through the thinning ranks of the defenders, with cries of "Ennaris!" and "Faero" preceding them. The troops from the Citadel and the city took up the cry and pushed harder as the Faero entered the fray, swinging his sword and dodging as he had been taught, becoming caught up in the fight.

Near the gate, Ensert saw the banner of the Faero enter the fray and decided enough was enough. He had been watching his knights battle the creatures and give better than they received, but he could see that they were tiring. With a roar, Ensert charged down the slope, followed by his small guard, forming a flying wedge as they galloped across the plain and crashed through the edges of the battle with the ghazrak. Dismounting quickly, the King and his small guard began to cut down the half-men. They quickly found themselves besieged as the ghazrak concentrated on the King.

The battle had been going for only a short time but already the casualties were mounting. Bodies of knights, soldiers, northers and ghazrak littered the field, getting underfoot and causing those still battling to slip. The defenders quickly learnt that an injured ghazrak was not out of the fight, as several, even laying on the ground, continued to wield their blunt swords with deadly effect. But the effort to ensure they were dead reduced the ability of the knights to maintain the fight, and slowly they were pushed back, rallying on Ensert.

From the sky, the flying ghazrak now swooped, knocking knights from their feet where they could or dropping rocks on them, causing more than one to stagger out of formation where the ghazrak could pounce on them. The number of knights able to fight were shrinking. The twins had ceased to fling rocks while they attempted to regain strength, and Flin stood guard over them, as had been agreed with Jalor earlier. The Archmage, as he had said on many occasions, while very powerful was not a battle Mage, and did not have the gifts required to actively fight for any length of time, but as he watched the battle unfold, and could see the fortunes turn, his fury mounted.

In the midst of the fighting, Helt and Blaine stood side by side, or back to back, fighting off the seemingly inexhaustible numbers of attackers. They, like the knights, were being forced back. Flying ghazrak still dropped stones and darted in to skewer a defender with their knife-like pinons or rend with their claws or sharp beak. Blaine fought like one possessed, his broadsword creating a barrier through which no attacker could pass.

And then, disaster struck.

One of the northers thrust a pike at Blaine, who countered with a strike of his sword. While the pike was chopped in half, leaving the norther open to Helt's slicing blade, Blaine's sword shattered, leaving him without a weapon. He and Helt shared a moment of shock, which passed quickly as both rallied and the armoured Helt stepped in front of Blaine to shield him. With a snarl, the Warrior looked around but could see no weapon he could use, despite the number of casualties. He gestured several men forward and stepped back through the battle, seeking a weapon to use. He could find nothing that was not damaged already. With an oath, he ran back through the rear of the fight towards the city wall, brandishing the stub of his sword and yelling for a weapon.

Blaine turned at the top of the slope and looked over the battlefield. The knights were struggling to maintain a defensive formation now, and the armies of both the Faero and the city were straining to hold. The flying ghazrak continued to cause destruction to both defensive forces. Far in the distance, the catapults were being prepared once again, he could see. The battle was being lost!

# 12. Defender

Blaine turned towards the city wall, calling again for a sword. Frustration burned in his breast as he watched the tide of battle turn against them. He could see Jalor and Corm, with Almin Bor by their side, battling through the turmoil as they tried to reach Helt. Blaine saw, with a shiver of fear, that she was now in danger of being cut off. The knights were hard pressed and there were more who were unable to fight, or who were obviously injured, than were fit. The knights were tiring rapidly, as Blaine had expected they would once forced to fight at ground level.

Overhead the flying ghazrak were taking a toll on the defenders, causing them to have to protect themselves from aerial attack as well as fight opponents in the melee. The twins were exhausted, he knew, and Flin was acting as their protector.

Blaine snarled again, turning as someone tapped him on the arm, the remaining shard of his sword raised to strike. With a shock he saw it was an old woman, standing before him, carrying a cloth-wrapped bundle that could be nothing but a greatsword. Blaine nodded his thanks and reached for the bundle, but was blocked by the woman as she held back the bundle.

"Woman, if that's a sword I need it, now!" he growled to her.

The woman nodded serenely. "Indeed it is a sword, and it is destined for your arm, Defender!" she said formally. "Do you take on the responsibility?"

"Do I take on what responsibility?" Blaine snapped, anger at the absurdity of being offered a sword only to have to beg for it.

"Will you defend Ennaris from its enemies, first and foremost? Will you protect those who cannot defend themselves? Will you lay down your life for Ennaris?" The woman's voice was calm and unhurried, formal in tone, her gaze sharp and penetrating.

Blaine responded in some heat, "What do you think I've been doing, woman? Yes, I will defend this planet."

"Do you so swear?"

Her gaze pinned Blaine, and he felt something inside turn and quicken. He responded with equal formality, still frustrated but now recognising that here was something different. "I swear, in the name of the Light!"

"So be it!" the woman declared, somehow causing the wrappings to fall away from the sword, revealing a plain two-handed sword, burnished and gleaming with a cold light.

"So be it!" she repeated, swinging the sword with surprising dexterity for an old woman and presenting the sword to Blaine, hilt first.

"So be it!" she repeated again as he grasped the sword's hilt.

Blaine felt a surge run through him as he gripped the sword, a wash of searing heat and then icy cold that ran through his veins and reached into his very core. He did not consider it to be more than an adrenaline surge as he paused to nod to the woman who smiled for the first time, a beautiful smile that made Blaine wonder at what the young woman may have been like. Then he was turning and charging back down the slope. His exhaustion was forgotten. In fact, he felt as though he was energised anew, his steps were light and the balanced beautifully sword felt like it was an extension of himself. He swung it once or twice, marvelling at the feel as he re-entered the fray, failing to notice the shocked looks he received from his own troops.

Flin, watching from where he stood with the twins, gaped. The twins sighed as one. From high above the flash of gold caught the eye of the watcher soaring high above the conflict. She remembered the stories and was glad it was she who would take this story back to her people.

"The Defender!" the twins said in unison.

Raglin turned to Flin. "Archmage, I believe you will be required," he said, his quiet words cutting through the din of battle.

Flin frowned and said, "I'm not battle trained. That was always Marjory's role."

"As we are not," Raglin said, "but we could use our gifts. Now is your time. We will have energy enough shortly to rejoin battle, but they will need you now."

Blaine ran through the rear ranks, using the new sword to break up desperate battles where defenders were almost overcome by multiple attackers. He cut down opposition men and women alike as he went past, marvelling at how they seemed to be slightly slower than he recalled them to be only shortly before. Ahead he saw Helt, sore pressed by several attackers who were trying to move on her at once. Her armour was taking the brunt of multiple blows while she stood stolidly and returned stroke for stroke. But Blaine could see that she was tiring. The indomitable spirit was strong but physical strength was waning. With a battle roar that came from somewhere far in the past, he threw himself into the fray, cutting, slashing and parrying with dizzying skill and speed, blasting the attackers away from Helt and cutting them down without mercy.

Jalor, who was engaged in his own battle with three attackers, felt the change in the tide of battle, while not seeing what caused it. He took advantage of one of his opponents glancing away to cut him down with a swift stroke of his razor-edged sword, giving him space to shift to one side and deliver a killing blow to the side of the second, finally felling the third. Only after that did he realise he had taken several shallow cuts himself and blood was running down his arm. He took the opportunity to glance around and stopped in astonishment. He was almost too late to block a descending blow from a norther, and almost absently turned it aside and plunged his sword through the other's breast.

The cause of his astonishment was Blaine - at least, Jalor thought it was Blaine - clad in golden armour that hugged tight to his body rather than the solid plate-like armour of the knights. He was blazing like a beacon as he plunged through the ranks of the attackers, leaving death and destruction behind him. He created gaps in the attackers' ranks where none had existed before and rallied the spirits of the defenders. Jalor fought his way to the back, looking anxiously until he saw Corm, with Almin Bor by his side and surrounded by most of the Faero's guard.

Looking to the side, Jalor could see the knights were in trouble. Several if them were lying prone, while others were defending only. Their declining energy and wounds allowed them to do no more. Ensert was laying about himself with skill and power. By dint of his own prodigious efforts, he was creating mayhem in the ranks of the ghazrak, of which there were many casualties. But even as Jalor watched one of the winged ghazrak swept across the battlefield, dropping low to swing the razor sharp wing tip across the front of Ensert's armoured chest. The wing cut through the King's armour easily. Ensert staggered, although he continued to defend himself. He was obviously sorely injured. The ghazrak soared up and wheeled to start a fresh strike on the King, flinging its wings wide as it did so. Jalor watched, helplessly, as the ghazrak lined up his attack run and with powerful beats of its wings, charged back towards the battle.

A powerful surge of light, like flame, beat against the head of the Ghazrak, causing it to shriek and climb away from the attack. Jalor, astonished, saw Flin stride across the approaches to the battle-field. The Archmage's staff blazed and the Enchara on his forehead pulsed a brilliant green. Stopping between the two battles, Flin thumped his staff into the ground and stood straight, an old man no longer, blazing with power, sending surge after surge into the three ghazrak as they circled, causing them to be burnt and disoriented but not doing significant physical damage. The ghazrak appeared to realise the same as they climbed high and commenced a coordinated attack on the Archmage.

High above the battle, the watching Roc called to her fellow watcher, thrilled and astounded. A Mage! The defenders had a Mage on their side. But the thrill became a moan as she realised that the Mage was unable to seriously damage the ghazrak, only cause them inconvenience. She made a decision and sent the thought to her wing-mate, who agreed without hesitation. The Rocs wheeled into position, as they had trained for during the days since their Guardian had returned, and folded their wings close to their massive bodies.

Flin, knowing that he would be the target, stood firm as the three ghazrak oriented on him and swept forward. Bolt after bolt of fire and light was sent from his staff, splashing against the ghazrak but causing no real injury. Flin's gifts were to heal and grow, to help and assist, not to destroy. Although he knew how to cause destruction, he also knew that it would take most of his available energy. Jalor was running towards the Archmage, already knowing he would be too late. The ghazrak attacked from three sides at once, wings wide and flapping as they swept across the field. At the last moment, Jalor saw something from the corner of his eye, and then two cries echoed across the field, the battle cry of the Roc that had not been heard for thousands of cycles. The two Rocs smashed with incredible force into two of the ghazrak, both targeting the area just behind the head. The two ghazrak were dead before they hit the ground. The Rocs managed to disentangle themselves and swung wide of the battle while they built up speed and gained height again. Another ringing challenge rang out as they gained altitude.

The third ghazrak, although distracted, stayed on its course. It angled its wings as though to slice through Flin, who was still pitching bolts of light. And then Jalor, running still, was passed by Blaine, a golden blur sprinting across the field. As the third ghazrak swept its wings forward to strike Flin, Blaine leapt high and with a great two-handed blow sliced through one wing, causing the ghazrak to veer away and crash into the ground. In a flash, Blaine was on it, hacking through the remaining wing. He jumped onto the ghazrak's broad back and drove his sword through the ghazrak from back to front, withdrawing his sword as the ghazrak shuddered. To make sure, Blaine swung once more and the glowing sword sheared through the strong neck as though it was soft butter, decapitating the creature.

The remaining ghazrak, dismayed at the loss of their flying comrades, drew back and regrouped to charge the knights once more, when the ground started to shake. Both sides of the battle were staggered, but Jalor knew what was happening and gave silent thanks. He shouted to the knights to regroup and fall back, which they did, carrying their wounded as far as they could. The ghazrak started to charge once again, looking to take advantage of the confusion, when the ground heaved around them. Great blocks of masonry pushed from the earth and rose into the air. The ghazrak stopped and stared as the huge blocks drifted over where they were standing. And then the stones were dropped, crushing all but a handful of the ghazrak. More building blocks from the toppled city of old Ennaris were dropped onto the rear ranks of the norther force, and then more were forced from the ground and dropped. The few surviving ghazrak surged forward once again, to be met now by twice their number of knights and speedily dispatched.

Jalor glanced back to the hole in the wall to see the twins slowly collapse, having expended all of their remaining energy. He saw people of the city rush out to gather them up and carry them inside the walls. Turning back to the fighting, he could see that from losing the battle only a short time ago, the defenders now were on top. Those knights who remained able to fight had reached the edge of the fierce battle with the northers and were slicing through them. The armour that was only partially effective against the flying and ground-based ghazrak proved to be far more so against the poor swords, knives and farm implements of the norther men and women. Blaine was amid the melee also, his golden armour sweeping all before him.

Suddenly, almost as one, the remaining northers turned and fled, running from the field. In the distance Jalor could see the commander had already retreated and was making a dash back across the plain, surrounded by uniformed troops who had taken no part in the battle. Surprisingly, all six of the catapults had been destroyed by huge blocks from the old city. Jalor had not even noticed that the twins had dealt with them.

An eerie quiet fell over the battle field, as the exhausted defenders took stock, standing and looking at the carnage around them. There was a brief cheer from the soldiers and one of the Faero's guard bent to pick up the banner and raise it high, but celebration was muted. For most, this was their first experience of war and, while many were stunned, there were some weeping openly.

Helt turned to find Blaine striding towards her, golden armour shining. With a single motion the Warrior - Defender of Ennaris - swung the sword high and thrust it into the scabbard slung across his back. In moments, the golden armour swept back and somehow folded into the sword. They were joined by Corm and Almin Bor, who both regarded Blaine with stunned looks. Helt's gaze turned to the knights. A group of them had gathered to remove Ensert's armour. With a cry, Helt charged across the field, although her own armour held her back from achieving any speed. She reached the group as the heavy breastplate was removed. Ensert's chest had a deep and bloody score across it and his breathing was heavy and broken. Great pain was evident in his expression. Flin was but a moment behind Helt, exhausted from his efforts but moving quickly even so.

"Did we win?" the King gasped.

"Aye, my King," one of the knights replied. "At a cost, but we vanquished the enemy."

"Then it was not wasted," Ensert said, rallying his strength. "I can die in peace."

Helt dropped to her knees alongside her father, gripping one hand. "No, you cannot die," she said firmly, tears running from her eyes and down her cheeks. "Escar needs its king now more than ever."

"It is my time, daughter," Ensert said. "It is meet that a King should die in battle, fighting side by side with the Faero against the ancient enemy. I die happy at that."

"Well," Flin said, "that's very impressive and I hate to break this up but I have no intention of having you die, old fool. Helt is right. We need you and your fighting men. So, if you would all move your great chunks of metal out of the way I'll see what I can do for Ensert, and then the rest."

"Are you sure I won't die?" Ensert asked, pain twisting his face.

"Pretty much," Flin said as he bent over the King, holding out one hand.

And for the first time in the memory of all but a few, the Archmage of the Council of Mages openly practised his primary gift, that of healing. The green stone in his staff flared, as did the Enchara, and a green glow enveloped his hand, moving down to spread across Ensert's torn chest. With a gasp from the watchers and a groan from Ensert, the damage was restored, slowly knitting bone, organs, flesh and skin. The angry redness that had edged the wound faded, leaving a hairline scar as all that remained. Flin took a deep breath and the glow faded, leaving Ensert in a deep sleep and Flin looking tired. At a gesture from Flin, several knights lifted their King and bore him away. Helt remained behind as her worry for her father was assuaged.

"How many wounded do we have?" Flin asked, looking around the remaining group.

"Too many for you to do that for all of them, if that's what it took from you," Jalor said. "Almin Bor is arranging for a field hospital, so let's limit your healing to the worst of the soldiers and the knights. There are very few northers left alive for us to worry about and most of them won't live, but I want a few for questioning if possible."

Flin considered. "Can we get Almin Bor's daughter here? Her gift is to read people, and she may be able to tell us which are most in need. What we really need is an amplifier, but we have not seen one of them for long ages."

Sir Kylin took part in the discussion for the first time. "How would we know of this ampli - ample - whatever it is?"

Flin smiled tiredly. "Amplifier. It is someone who can make our efforts last longer. They often will be found where people do better at things when they are around, often without realising it. Sports, things like target practice. They also will seem to be able to calm anger, although we've never been able to work out why the two are combined."

Sir Kylin nodded. "We will search them out, if any such are here or near," he said, turning to Helt. "Your Majesty, I suggest we set out a strong guard until the wall can be rebuilt."

With a start, Helt realised that with her father badly injured, she was the Majesty being addressed. "Thank you, Sir Kylin," she said with a grimace, and then paused for a moment before continuing with a slight smile. "Are you able to take the role of General of Escar?"

It was Kylin's turn to start and stare, before nodding to the Princess. "It will be my honour, Majesty," he replied.

"Then I will leave it to you to do what needs to be done. If anyone objects let me know and I'll knock their heads together," she said, turning to glare at an audible throat-clearing from Blaine. "After I explain clearly and rationally why they should do as I command, of course."

"Of course," Sir Kylin said as he bowed and led the knights away, smiling broadly as he considered what Ensert would make of his promotion.

The small group was rocked by a sudden gust of wind, and turned as one to see two huge birds land. Flin sucked in a deep breath, this time with delight, and smiled broadly. As he approached, followed by the others, both birds dipped their heads, beaks extended to the Archmage, who reached out in turn to touch each with his free hand.

"My friends," he said, "I thank you for your timely intervention."

He stood as though listening, and then nodded. "Yes, the time is nigh."

More listening followed, then Flin smiled and gestured Jalor and Blaine forth. "Ky-rel and As-men wish to meet you," he said. "Just place your hand lightly on their beaks in greeting." He turned back to the birds. "This is Jalor and this is Blaine, two of the Children of Ennaris."

The two Rocs turned slightly to face the Warriors, and first Jalor then Blaine did as Flin instructed, gently placing one hand on each beak. Jalor nodded in greeting. Blaine had a different experience.

*Greetings Defender*, the first Roc, Ky-rel, sent to Blaine as he touched her beak.

*Greetings Defender*, As-men sent as Blaine touched his beak.

"Uh, hello," Blaine stammered.

*We rejoice to meet the Children of Ennaris, as the Prophecy tells. We will return to our people and inform them that the Rocs have once again joined with their allies.* Ky-rel's eyes appeared to spin slightly, which Blaine interpreted as high emotion. *You have need of a repeater. We will return.*

With a ruffling of feathers the two birds stalked a short distance from the group and launched into the air, their powerful wings driving them into the sky quickly. In moments they were specks in the distance.

"You could understand them?" Flin asked Blaine.

"Yes, they said they would return and that we need a repeater." Blaine said in wonder, his composure slightly awry. "I have never felt anything like that before."

Flin nodded, while Jalor frowned. Varna and Blaine both. What was in store for him?

"And they called me Defender, as though it's a name. That's what the old woman called me when she gave me the sword. What's that about?"

"Do you recall anything from your time wielding the sword? What old woman?" Flin asked.

"Not really. I seemed to have a real burst of energy and things seemed to be easier than at other times. I didn't seem to tire out as fast. And the old woman was who gave me this sword." Blaine looked from Flin to Helt and Jalor, and back to Flin.

"Defender is a title, as Dharmoney is a title," the Archmage began.

"Varna. I heard you call her Dharmoney once," Blaine interrupted.

"Indeed, although just how accurate that guess was remains to be seen," Flin rejoined. "The Defender of Ennaris is one of the roles from ancient times, and one of the Nine. To my knowledge the Defender of Ennaris has appeared twice to date, although my knowledge is incomplete. He has wielded a sword, *Genardil*, called the 'Golden Sword' for reasons I did not understand until today. It's reputed to give the right wielder supernatural speed, strength and endurance. Not limitless, but far more than normal."

Blaine considered. "So what if it is not the right wielder?"

"The bearer will die," Flin said softly. "Which you did not do."

"So this sword is the Golden Sword. It doesn't look golden."

"Blaine," Jalor said, "draw your sword."

With a quizzical look at his team leader, Blaine reached over his shoulder and drew the sword. Immediately he felt the same surge of energy, a lightness of body, enhanced vision and hearing, even enhanced smell. At the same time, he felt what he realised he had missed when he had first gripped the sword and hurried back to battle. A wave of heat followed the golden light that swept down his sword-arm across his torso and stretched both up and down, solidifying into a sheath of armour. It hugged his body but was light and flexible. And it glowed! A soft golden glow rose from the armour, from all the parts he could see. He stared at his arm, then felt his head and found that he wore a close fitting helm that was part of the armour, not a separate piece. Hands were covered by a tight mail so light and flexible that he could not feel it, and his feet were sheathed in the same material. The difference between the golden armour and what the knights wore was enormous.

"It's so light I can barely feel it," Blaine said in wonder.

Helt just stared. "How can this be?" she asked in a tight voice.

"Blaine is one of the Nine, as well as one of the Children," Flin said gently. "The Defender has been seen as a myth, forgotten by most who do not keep the old traditions alive, and made into a tall tale elsewhere. But never forget that the myths of Ennaris tend to be drawn from the reality of the past, as I have had reason to realise lately. And Ennaris' past is long and rich, no matter that it is largely forgotten."

"Which other tales are come to life?" Helt asked. "What other marvels will we see before this is done?"

"If I'm right, then there are one or two still to come," was Flin's reply. "And they will happen when they are ready to happen."

Blaine sheathed his sword with the same fluid movement as he had done before, and the golden armour retracted in a wave too fast for any to see clearly.

"Well," he said, addressing Jalor. "You have a lot of wounded to see to, while I need to figure this out. Helt, would you be prepared to assist me once you have your troops squared away?"

At her slightly uncertain nod, Blaine turned and walked away, while Helt headed towards the city gate. At the same time, Jalor's gaze was drawn to several dots in the distant sky, rapidly growing in size.

"Our friends have returned," he said, indicating with a nod the direction from which they were coming. "Looks like five of them this time."

Flin stared.

"The Rocs were one of our true allies in times of old. They have been friends to the Ennarisi for as long as we have memories. It seems their memories go back as far. But I have wounded to see to. I expect Almin Bor has managed to get things settled by now, so we had best get to it."

He appeared to be dreading what was to come.

"Flin, are you alright?" Jalor asked, concerned at the Archmage's expression.

"Me personally? Yes, I will be fine. My concern is that we only have myself to attempt to heal so many." He sighed. "Before the rebellion we had Healers across the lands and seas, with Amplifiers on hand to help when there were heavy loads, as when there were disease outbreaks, or when a pleasure ship capsized, or other episodes where there were many injuries. With only me I am concerned that some will not get care enough to survive."

Jalor nodded, watching as Ky-rel landed, her identity confirmed by the colours of her head feathers, followed by four other birds. As Jalor watched, Flin stopped to converse mind to mind with the great bird, his expression changing from close to despair to one of hope.

"Jalor, Ky-rel has brought us a Healer and three Amplifiers. They are Repeaters in the Roc tongue." He turned to look to the city, then back to Jalor. "Quickly, get Almin Bor to bring the seriously injured out here. We will need torches as it gets dark. The Rocs cannot fit into the tight spaces in the city as it has been built, or rebuilt, and we will need them to have access to the injured."

Jalor nodded and hurried to the city via the hole that had been blasted in the wall.

Then followed as strange a night as Jalor had experienced.

A steady stream of injured were carried out of the city. Soldiers were carried or helped to walk by knights and citizens. Those too young to assist, or who were injured but able to walk, or who found themselves with nothing to do as the numbers dwindled, stopped and stared, forming a crowd three and four deep. The centre of attention were the five Rocs. The enormous birds towered over the tallest men. One, Ky-rel, remained outside the hospital zone, having neither healing nor amplifying ability. The others moved through the injured, stalking from patient to patient. One of the Amplifiers stayed with each of the Archmage and the Roc Healer - Su-tek - while the third Amplifier rested. After a while, the resting Amplifier relieved one of the other two, which took a break and a welcome drink, before relieving the third. And so it went through the long night. Many people of the city were moved to tears as the first of the seriously injured soldiers, one of the Faero's army, was assisted from the table on which he had been laid too injured to move and limped from the hospital zone.

Part way through the night, Jalor saw a small girl walk hesitantly towards Ky-rel. The huge bird also followed the girl's progress. The girl stopped a short distance from Ky-rel and looked up, up, high up to the towering head with her great hooked beak. Jalor could have sworn that Ky-rel's eyes started to twirl. Ky-rel shook her feathers out before settling herself on the hard ground in front of the child and lowering her head, the two of them staring at each other. Suddenly, with no hesitation at all, the child stepped forward and placed both small hands on the huge beak. With a moan a woman pushed through the press of people and dashed to where her daughter stood, now leaning against Ky-rel. The mother stopped short, unsure of what to do.

"It's alright, mother," the small girl said, "Ky-rel says you can come and say hello, too."

Jalor started, and walked across to the small group, who were starting to become another centre of attention as people realised what was happening. He reached them as the mother, unsure whether she should move forward to join her daughter, or to try to catch her daughter up and run, took a first tentative step.

"It's okay," Jalor said, startling the mother and causing both the child and Ky-rel to turn towards him. "Ky-rel will not hurt your daughter. In fact, I believe your daughter may well have just become one of the most important people of Escar. It seems there are very few who have the gift of speaking to the Rocs."

"But, will she be hurt?" the woman asked, before realising she was speaking to the general. "My Lord," she added hurriedly.

Jalor laughed. "I'm no lord," he said, "but I thank you for the honour. I don't think Ky-rel will allow hurt to come to her. Ky-rel has agreed to you saying hello, so just step forward and place one hand on her beak. That seems to be a way for her to know you."

Still a little uncertain, the woman stretched out a tentative hand, above her daughter's head, and placed it gently against the Roc's beak. The woman's eyes grew wide and she drew closer to Ky-rel, whose eyes were spinning in what Jalor thought may have been ecstasy. After a moment the woman drew her hand away but did not step back. She turned to Jalor.

"Ky-rel asked that I tell you that the Rocs need food. What they are doing is very taxing and while they appreciate the water they will need to eat."

Jalor nodded. "I should have thought of that. Can you ask Ky-rel what they eat, please?"

She looked to Ky-rel for a moment and then replied, "They eat meat when they need to maintain strength. Small hussars and glims are what they eat in their homes, as well as grains."

"Please tell Ky-rel that I will arrange for food for all five," Jalor said, looking for a runner or page to task with taking the message for him.

"Um, sir," the woman said diffidently, "Ky-rel suggests the Archmage needs food also." She sucked in a breath as she realised what she had said. "Is that really the Archmage Drewflin, the one who fought at the rebellion's end?"

Jalor laughed easily, snagging a runner who was passing by. "Yes, that is the same Drewflin," he said, then turned to the boy. "I need you to take a message to Almin Bor. Do you know who that is?" At the boy's confident nod he continued, "Tell him the Rocs need food, small hussars or glims or something similar. He will know. Raw, I'm guessing," Jalor said, cocking one eyebrow at the mother, who nodded after a while. "Yes, raw. And something for the Archmage, too. Off you go," the last to the page who ran off towards the city walls, following a line of burning stakes that had been shoved into the ground to act as torches.

Jalor turned back to the proceedings for the injured. He was fascinated at what he saw. Flin stood, eased his back muscles with a universal gesture of stretching against a knuckle shoved into the middle of his back, and moved on to another patient, this one a knight. He stretched one hand over the knight's body in preparation, then held it firm as his hand glowed green and the glow spread. One of the Roc Amplifiers reached out a great wing and with enormous gentleness, laid the tips of the wing, a light touch of feathers, across both Flin's hand and the knight. As Flin's hand glowed, the Roc's wing glowed also, and then the wing's glow grew and stretched over the knight, staying like that for several minims before subsiding. Flin did another test and nodded. The knight was helped from the table and started to stagger away with assistance before stopping and turning back. Carefully, and none too steadily, he gave a formal bow to both Flin and Roc, before his helper took hold again and both moved through the now dwindling supply of badly wounded patients.

The Roc healer was even more efficient, possibly because he was working with a Roc Amplifier. The great bird stalked to the side of a patient, in this case a soldier who eyed the approach of the bird uneasily, despite seeing so many healed around him, and without hesitation swung one wing over the man's chest. The Amplifying Roc slid his wing so that the feathers interleaved and immediately both wings glowed a pale rose colour, which spread over the chest and down one side of the soldier's torso. After only a short time, the patient was helped up and away, unsteady but walking. The Roc stalked to the next table.

A small commotion drew Jalor's eye. An untidy procession made its way down the path from the city gate, led by Corm, now dressed plainly but with a tabard on which was the crest of the Faero. Corm was holding a large round basket, in which Jalor could see meat segments. Behind him came two other men carrying similar burdens and then two men carrying sacks that Jalor assumed held grain. Corm walked out into the field near where Ky-rel held station and placed the basket on the ground, directing the other men to place their burdens at distances from each other. Finally, he drew his knife and slashed the sides of the sacks, allowing the grain to spill out. Then he turned and walked to Ky-rel, where he bowed slightly.

"On behalf of Ennaris, and especially on behalf of the soldiers and knights who fought today, I thank you for your actions, and for your help tonight," Corm said formally.

Ky-rel gently disengaged from mother and daughter and stood to her full height, before spreading both wings very wide and somehow bowing forward so that her beak hovered in front of Corm.

"Ky-rel said that she is honoured to meet the, the," the woman paled slightly but gathered herself to continue, "the Faero of Ennaris." She looked up to see Corm smiling. "That's you?" At his nod, she said, "She wishes to know you, Corm, uh, Faero, if you are prepared to do that honour."

Corm had been reading in the archives of the palace, where he had found ancient tomes telling tales, thought at the time of writing to be tall tales and legends, of the Rocs, including tales of how to greet a Roc. Without hesitation, Corm reached out one hand and placed it on Ky-rel's beak, giving a slight bow as he did so. With a gasp, Corm slid onto one knee, eyes focused on Ky-rel. Instinctively, Jalor started to move forward but a hand on one shoulder held him back.

"Hold, general," Raglin's voice said in his ear. "He is in no danger."

"But, the others who met Rocs reacted but not like that," Jalor said, not taking his eyes from the Faero.

"Indeed. I suggest the others have demonstrated that they have a talent to speak with the Rocs, which is rare enough in itself. I suspect there may be more and we will arrange for testing. I think Corm has just found a life partner. There are tales of such from the past, special relationships forged between a Roc and a man or woman. This may be a special one, though, for Ky-rel is a warrior Roc, and from what I can see a leader of warrior Rocs."

"Do you speak with Rocs?" Jalor asked Raglin.

"Yes, both Ragnor and myself have that gift."

"Hmmpf," Jalor grumped. "It seems everyone except me can do that."

"Ah, well," Raglin said apologetically, but then chuckled lightly. "I suspect Varna will be able to do so also. All Mages seem able to converse with the Rocs."

"Of course she will," Jalor said in a long-suffering tone.

"And Helt cannot either," Raglin said.

Jalor nodded, then rethought what Raglin had said. "Varna is a Mage?"

"I'm not sure just what she is, or will be, when she returns to us. We believe she is Dharmoney, and that is a legend of legends." Raglin paused. "Dharmoney comes only when Ennaris has the greatest need, and each one who takes that role brings different things to it. The original Dharmoney, a legendary figure from long before the time when

Ennaris went to space, defended us from invasion, driving back a hostile space-faring race. We know very little about her or those events, it was so long ago. The second was almost a million cycles ago, when Ennaris was faced with destruction from a comet on a collision path with the planet. She rode a craft out to the comet and deflected its path, saving us all. There are two other instances that I know, and may be more. In each case Dharmoney saved Ennaris or the Ennarisi. But whether they were Mages or specially gifted people we cannot be sure."

Jalor considered what Raglin had told him. His thoughts were wandering even as he kept one wary eye on Corm and Ky-rel. So, Varna and Blaine were something more than normal. There were inklings about that when he considered their histories, although he really only knew service records. Varna had her psi leanings, although there was scepticism about whether that was real - not any longer as far as he was concerned. Blaine's skills had always seemed to be so far above those of anyone else, so that made sense also. Himself? Was he destined to play some sort of superhuman role? Or was he the straight guy, the planner and strategist able to get others and himself in and out of seemingly impossible situations but without any spectacular gifts? Well, time would tell.

"Corm," Jalor said, not too loudly but enough to register with the young man.

"Jalor, it's amazing! Ky-rel, I, we," Corm halted as he realised he was making no sense. "I'm not sure what happened but it seems Ky-rel and I have become some sort of partners."

"That's what has happened, Corm," Raglin confirmed. "It's rare and a great privilege, for the Rocs are and have always been highly selective. Perhaps at this time it's a clear sign." A thought struck him, and he started to turn away. "There's something I must discuss with Ragnor and Flin when he's done. I'll catch you up later."

As Raglin hurried away, Jalor said, "We need to get some planning of our own happening. This battle resulted in lots of casualties, and even the work by Flin and the Rocs won't get most of them ready for another fight in the short term. Meanwhile, the Rocs need to eat."

Corm nodded, watching as the great bird stalked away to where the baskets had been placed. She delicately nipped one of the small carcasses with her beak, lifting it and turning away from the crowds as she tore off strips of meat and swallowed it. Corm turned a slight shade of green before sighing in relief. As his colour returned to normal, the Amplifier Roc who was not on duty followed Ky-rel's lead and started to devour his meal.

"She broke the link," Corm said to Jalor. "Probably just as well. I'm not ready to take part in that just yet, I think."

Jalor smiled faintly and nodded. "I'm going to get some sleep. There's nothing I can do here and things are well in hand. And I think we need to work out what we do next. This was not anywhere near the final battle in scale and that worries me. We almost lost this one!"

Corm nodded, yawning. "I checked the portal map before coming down here with the food. I think we can plot a series of movements to catch up with most of the leaders we need to meet, assuming they want to meet us, that is."

"Good. Well, that's for tomorrow. The wounded seem to have dropped in number now and dawn is not that far away. You probably need to rest also. Hopefully, someone can explain what happens now that you and Ky-rel have established a bond, and what it may mean for the campaign that is to come."

He nodded to Corm and bowed politely to Ky-rel, who had completed her meal and was watching, before walking up the slope to the gate.

# 13. Ice People For War

Xymin was not usually a reflective sort. Right now he was quiet, thinking over events of the recent past. It had been around half a cycle since Tine had returned, saving him from the sinking floe. Actually, to be fair, she had been part of the cause of his trouble also, so in a way she was cleaning up her own mess. But Xymin did not think it politic to mention that. Tine had shown a somewhat breezy notion of responsibility in some surprising ways. Where she did not surprise was in the power she displayed, usually without thinking.

The people of the ice regions were fairly simple in their approach. They had to be to survive all this time in one of the least hospitable environments on Ennaris. They had developed their traditions and, while they had remained believers in the Guardians, in reality they had never been more than a name to invoke, occasionally part of the common expression of surprise ("By the Guardians!") or perhaps a mild curse ("For the sake of the Guardians!"). Certainly, the people of the ice did not consider the Guardians to be gods, and nothing in their lives for more generations than any of them could trace back had taught them anything except that they had to fend for themselves.

They remembered the old tales, repeated from time to time as the roving Tellers made their appearances, usually spaced well apart. It was difficult for the Tellers to make their way through the snow and ice, so they tended to arrive in Ennaris mild summer, when the snow was slightly intense less and the temperatures were a little higher, although still below freezing in the further north. Those Tellers, especially the one called Trab, had been reminding the people of the ice for a couple of generations now about the ancient history of Ennaris, and the role of such figures as the Faero. The Prophecy had been discussed over and over, and it had been stressed that it would be the duty of every Ennarisi to provide whatever help they could. The Prophecy, which was obscure in some things, was clear in that there would be some sort of conflict, bringing together the forces of the former Mage Goroth with those led by the Faero.

Tine, on her return, had made it clear that she expected the people of the ice to take part. Xymin grinned ruefully when he recalled the discussions he had on his return from first meeting Tine. He had gathered the people of his village and described what had happened to him. Of course, they did not believe him, and Xergis had made it clear that he would not be convinced by mere words. And why should they believe him? He was pretty sure that, if it had happened to someone else, he would not have believed either. Therefore, he was not overly put out about it. But Tine was! She appeared in the meeting hall like a spring storm, a thunderclap announcing her presence, after which she roundly berated Xergis and, to prove she was who she said she was, made him disappear and re-appear on the top of the ice mount a short distance from the village. By the time he had made his way back to the meeting hall he was almost blue - Tine had not bothered to give him the usual outer fur garments before transporting him.

Still, the demonstration had been effective. Xymin was believed by most, although some who were not there remained unbelievers, and had then moved from village to village across the ice wastes, telling his tale and bringing the word of Tine. In a short time, he found himself with followers, which had not been his intention, but it allowed him to reach more people faster, for the ice people existed in surprising numbers but were scattered in small communities far and wide. A system of communication was established. The Tinetings, as they called themselves, found that Tine somehow had gifted them extra endurance, resistance to the cold and enhanced senses in most ways. Their physical strength was greater, which allowed them to push through the deeper snows to make their appointed rounds. As a side benefit, the Tinetings had made several rescues because they were able to reach places and withstand conditions that others could not. They were able to maintain searches where others had to stop, and they were able to see more clearly when the ice glare was at its harshest.

Those abilities, and the growing affinity of the ice people for Tine, led to more people becoming Tinetings, and thus inheriting those additional capabilities. These were not gifted Ennarisi, exactly, but Tine had a purpose in extending the existing strengths and limiting the reach of the weaknesses of the people of the ice. And then Trab returned, appearing at one of the regular meeting places where several communities came together from time to time. Xymin was not present at the time, but Trab was welcomed by the people of the ice and was intrigued by the Tinetings. He told of the return of the Mages, of the Archmage and the Children of Ennaris. He told that Goroth had been released from his confinement and of the ghazrak, the creatures created by Goroth's minion Grensor as superior warriors. And he revealed himself to be Trabor, one of the Mages of ancient history, and asked for the people of the ice to join in preparations for the battles to come. He told of the defence of Escar that had just occurred, and of the Rocs. The imaginations of the people of the ice were fired, none more so that the Tinetings.

But Xymin was troubled when Trabor's words were repeated to him, and he sought out Tine.

"Why is it," he asked, "that there needs to be such a battle? The Guardians have returned, according to Trabor and evidenced by your own presence, and you are so much more powerful than any Ennarisi, even a powerful Mage like Goroth. Why can you not just destroy him and his followers."

Tine smiled grimly. "My Xymin, many of us wish we could do so," she replied. "However, we are constrained, forbidden to do so. We must allow the people of Ennaris to make their own way. We are permitted to protect the planet, and will do so as well as we can. We are not gods, remember, nor do we wish to rule. So, we must assist the people of

Ennaris to make their own decisions, and to prepare for the events that will unfold."

"And do you know how those events will unfold, and what the outcome will be?"

"No and no. We must trust to you and the other Ennarisi to make the right choices and to fight for your own world. We do not have fore-knowledge of the outcomes, although we have a greater understanding of possible consequences than you may do. For you have lost much knowledge since the rebellion."

"But," Xymin asked with some perplexity, "if you are permitted to protect Ennaris then why did the destruction happen?"

Tine sighed. "We did the best we could do, and lost three of our number in doing so."

"Three Guardians died?" Xymin was shocked.

"Yes. They gave their all for Ennaris, joining with the Archmage and Battle Mage to save as much as could be saved." Tine frowned as she remembered. "Most of us were injured or exhausted following that and could not halt many of the things that followed. Thus, the devastation happened and the land was changed irreversibly. And then, the Prophecy told us to leave or risk even greater damage and possibly the destruction of the planet. So most of us did leave, while the ones who remained continued to make repairs, such as they could."

Xymin thought for a long time, while Tine watched him. He worked through his thoughts in a systematic way, one thought following the next in a logical pathway. Finally, he nodded.

"Then you are preparing us, the Tinetings, for our part in the battle. That is why we have been granted deeper perceptions, more powerful senses than the normal. It is why we can withstand the cold better than others, and why our reflexes are faster." It was statement more than question, but he waited for Tine's response.

"It is that and more. It is my desire to see the people of the ice play their part, should that be required. But also in preparation for the times to come once this battle is done. For Ennaris will then be part of the greater galaxy once again, and the people of Ennaris must be made ready. There are many threats outside of this world."

"I understand," Xymin said thoughtfully. "And yet the people of the ice are not warriors. Of warfare we know nothing, of fighting we know less. Were we to seek battle against these foes I fear your Tinetings will fall before we cause any damage."

"Which is why I have asked someone to assist you to learn how to fight against these foes in your own way, using your own skills and this harsh land," Tine said, turning to a figure who had appeared behind her. "Xymin, this is Ogun, and he will teach you and the Tinetings how to assist the Faero in your own ways."

Xymin saw a tall, serious-visaged and imperious individual, wearing a long mail coat with plate armour located in strategic locations and paying no mind to the cold at all. His head was bare and his blonde hair was worn shoulder length and parted in the centre. Strapped to his back was a long sword and attached to his belt was a knife almost as long as a sword itself. Balancing the knife was a war-hammer, attached by a thong to the belt on his other side. Xymin was unable to see how a single man could carry that much weight and remain upright, let along move. But, of course, Xymin recognised the name of Ogun and so bowed low before the Guardian.

"Well met, Xymin," Ogun thundered in a voice to make Xymin wince, advancing to clap Tine's first acolyte firmly on the back such that he was sent sprawling. As Xymin picked himself up Ogun declared, "Let us see about turning you ice people into a fighting force, for the evil must visit you at some stage and you need to be prepared. War is coming, my friend."

Tine directed a withering look to Ogun. "What are you doing?" she demanded. "Are you trying to frighten them to death, deafen them or just kill them before they need to face the ghazrak?"

Ogun grinned and replied in a slightly more normal tone, although still loud. "Ah, Tine, allow me my little pleasures. I have assisted Dharmoney and the Champion, but they merely needed us to guide them to their own discoveries. We were there when the Archmage received his Enchara at last. I was watching as the Defender was made known. But this will be the first time in thousands of cycles that I can teach our children what they need to know." The grin turned fierce, almost a snarl. "And I *will* teach them how to deal with those misbegotten creatures and defeat Goroth and Likud, especially Likud who caused our Ennaris to be so damaged, once and for all."

# 14. Champion

Varna sat quietly, meditating. She was in a small glade that she particularly enjoyed, deep in the Forest. A small stream wound through the trees to create a pool before continuing its journey through the Forest of the Guardians. Above her head, small birds chittered and argued, fluttered from branch to branch, preened their feathers and eyed the ground, alert for any chance of getting a worm or two. Occasional *plops* from the pool told of small water creatures breaking the surface and diving back into the shallow depths. Varna could feel two tiny vole-type creatures gambolling outside the entrance to their tunnel while the mother watched on. She was alert for danger, but was not alarmed by Varna's presence.

Varna no longer suffered from the debilitating headaches and extreme lethargy that had afflicted her when she first arrived on Ennaris. She could now sort the different mental images she received. She had learnt to separate them and could push aside those she did not want to deal with, or that were merely noise. When she wanted to do so, she could now expand her senses and examine her surroundings with a level of detail that she had never imagined was possible. What was more, she now understood what she was seeing. She understood what the colours meant in the auras displayed by all living things - or most, rather, given the ghazrak appeared to have no aura but, rather, exhibited a black *lack* of colour. But then, there were those odd flashes of under-colours.

Eresh was not completely satisfied with her. There still remained the last, intractable blockage to get through. Varna now knew that she had suffered a traumatic event when she was very young caused by the circumstances of her mother's death. Intellectually, at least, she knew that she could not be blamed for that, and she felt that she had accepted it. Still, she was unable to let go of the sense of guilt that she could have done something different, or perhaps should not have done what she did. Her panic had resulted in her mother dying, as well as the men who had broken into their home. No matter what Eresh and Balgor tried to tell her, she could not forget that. Were they going to do anything other than steal? Did they just panic when Varna's mother caught them doing so, and might they have done nothing more than flee if given the chance? Had Varna's own panicked reaction as a young child doomed them all when it was not necessary? Had there been other times when her panic had caused damage to others? How could she be sure that it would not happen again and again? The possibility of that outcome filled her with fear, which caused the insecurities engendered by her recent torture to flare forth once more.

Was the Warrior a fake after all? She turned that over in her mind. She reviewed her own history, of which she now had a much better understanding. She considered the endorsements that she had received from Jalor and Blaine, now her fellow team members, and others whose opinions she trusted. The conversation with Rashi when she was in the sick bay on *Antilles* gave her reassurance. Her record before the Mastic mission where Wensor had betrayed her was good. Very good, in fact. On Ennaris she had won the regard and trust of several Guardians, and Varna doubted that such regard was handed out easily. No, she decided, the Warrior was no fake.

Take that line of thought further. On Ennaris she had been singled out for several gifts. The Guardians were sure that she had significant power lying behind the blockage. These very powerful beings seemed to believe that she was, or would be, worthy of that power and wanted her to achieve its release. That meant a lot to Varna. It took significant deep thinking time but she finally accepted that her gifts were a positive part of her. This was despite the heavy feeling of guilt that remained.

Varna tried repeatedly to release the blockage but could not do so. However, while she was frustrated and irritated at her failure, her innate strength came to the fore and she continued to strive towards success, working with Eresh, Menra and others or on her own. She was determined to get past this problem, for she was sure that she had a significant role to play on Ennaris. She held no belief in predestined outcomes but she was coming to believe that she had been placed on Ennaris by something or someone for a reason. Could it be to leverage her gifts to make a difference. Perhaps she could use her powers to bring those who preyed on others to change their ways and become members of society once again. Could her purpose be to do that for Goroth and his followers and thus end this war before it caused even more death and destruction?

In their last session Eresh had been clear. Varna had learned all that she could in the Tree. The Forest had given her nurture and a sense of calm. It was up to Varna to take that final step, to break out of what Eresh assured her was a self-imposed limitation. Events were continuing through the world of Ennaris that she needed to be prepared for. A battle had been fought in the plain of Escar which resulted in Blaine somehow being revealed to be one of the heroes of legends. The Faero had taken part also and, where the people of Escar had been somewhat inclined to support him in the battles to come, they now were fervent supporters. And it seemed Corm had become attached to one of the great Rocs, who Varna wanted to meet.

Balgor stayed close but gave her room. He deliberately did not intervene in her sessions with Eresh or Menra, and was content to be a support when her frustrations spilled over. Their intimacy grew more intense, though, and without realising it Varna found an anchor, while the Guardian was astonished to find that he also had a new foundation, and one that terrified him like nothing had done for so long. For he knew that he would not be able to protect Varna from everything that was to come, whatever that would be.

It was while starting the day with a light snack - fruits, nuts, grains and cereals that were more earthy than she was accustomed to and yet had a taste that grew on her - that Varna decided she had been there long enough and had to face Ennaris again. She waited until Fernis joined her, as he did each day, before broaching the subject.

"Fernis, I feel that I need to leave here. I've learned so much, and I feel that I understand Ennaris now in a way I never dreamed possible, but I have friends and a mission to continue. Two missions, I guess," she said, thinking of the original mission and her new one on behalf of the Ennarisi. At Fernis' nod she continued, "How much longer do I need to stay before I am ready?"

"You've been ready for quite a time now," Fernis replied in his deep voice, smiling gently. "It's been you holding yourself here, your own need for certainty that has stopped you from going back out there. We've only been waiting for you to make the decision."

"But Eresh has continued to drill me and keeps trying to break though the block. Does that mean she's done so?"

"Oh, the drilling was to keep you occupied, and also to make sure that you continued to exercise your gifts. That will remain important for a short while, but you have everything you need now." He held up a cautioning finger. "However, that does not mean that you realise everything you can do. The blockage remains. Your gifts are ... unusual, I think would be the best word, and you will discover them as you need to do."

"Unusual?" Varna frowned. "Unusual how?"

"Unusual in that we have been unable to identify their boundaries," Fernis said. "None of us can gauge just how deep your gifts run. That in itself is unusual. Add into the mix the fact that your genetic make-up is far purer than anyone on Ennaris and we are not really sure what that may mean."

"Far purer? How can my blood be purer than anyone on Ennaris. By definition, they are Ennarisi!"

"Yes, but changes have occurred over the long ages, and even the Ennarisi have drifted slightly. You don't share those drifts."

"So I'm a throwback, via Earth? That sounds unlikely to me."

"Oh, I agree. It's so unlikely that we double-checked and then checked again. But it's true, nonetheless. And because of that we decided to send one of our number to Earth, but Odruf held against it until the state of affairs here is settled, so we will wait. Guardians know how to wait, although our patience grows thin at times." Fernis chuckled. "Kula was all for just jumping over there and running tests on a few thousand people, just to see what we could find."

Varna's puzzled gaze caused Fernis to chuckle again.

"Kula is one of us you have yet to meet. He's a little impetuous at times."

Varna's gaze narrowed. "Do you think there are others who may display gifts among humans?"

"Oh, we're pretty sure that's the case. Earth may not allow the gifts to become clear, for some reason that may have to do with atmospherics, or even simple things like trace minerals in your soils, where Ennaris does not have the same effect. But we think it's possible." Fernis caught something in Varna's gaze. "Why do you ask that question?"

"Because you have several thousand humans just out there," Varna said, pointing vaguely towards the sky.

Fernis stared for a moment and then laughed. "By all that's precious, none of us thought of that. Brilliant minds, eh?" His gaze became slightly unfocused. "Kula says he will join us shortly?"

With a small flash Kula appeared, his bodily image that of a tall, muscular, blonde-haired Slavic stereotype, with an open and friendly face, sporting a smile and wearing something that approximated a Roman toga, including the sandals.

"Kula, meet Varna," Fernis said.

With a broad grin Kula gripped her arm half way up, meaning she did likewise.

"You requested my presence?" Kula asked of Fernis.

"You recall we discussed testing humans to see if there were others with potential for gifts?"

Kula nodded. "Yes. I would like to see if there is any chance. I expect there will be, given what we've seen with Varna and her colleagues, but we can wait. Odruf is correct that we should allow the present events to conclude first." He shrugged. "As long as Goroth does not win, of course."

"We can never be too sure about that. It's possible that he is the one spoken of in the Prophecy, even though his methods are abhorrent to us. However, Varna has suggested a possibility that none of us so highly intelligent beings thought of," Fernis said wryly.

"Oh?"

Fernis shrugged and gestured to Varna.

"Why do you need to go to Earth to see if there are other gifted humans? There's a whole fleet of us in orbit around Ennaris."

Kula stared at Varna, mouth gaping, a rumble starting deep in his being that became a long low laugh.

"Oh my! I don't think I'm going to live that down," Kula said as he regained composure. "Of course there's a sample of the Earth children nearby."

"Something else," Fernis said, considering, watching Varna as he spoke. "There's a second group as well."

Kula thought, and then nodded. "The Andorethi, yes, we should test them also. Goroth has muddied the water, from what I have been able to see of those he has on Ennaris already. Or rather, Likud has done so in continuance of Goroth's policy. But we should test them also."

"Shadows?" Varna asked, face paling. "But they're the enemy!"

"Maybe, maybe not," Fernis said carefully. "The Guardians will protect Ennaris, as we have done for longer than you can imagine. And we must consider the different children of the Ennarisi. The Andorethi were subject to change in much the same way as Earth dwellers were, although via different means. They were assisted to civilisation as your people were, less judiciously perhaps. But it remains likely that genetics were altered. Where would the material come from?"

"From the Ennarisi," Varna replied. "Even though they have different physical bodies, you think they may have some of the same genetic heritage?"

"I think it remains a possibility," Kula replied. "Many Andorethi do have corporeal bodies still, although Likud has destroyed many in his quest to create a non-corporeal warrior race. I'll look into it and consider what to do. I'll consult with our brothers and sisters and make a decision after that." He smiled to Varna. "You have my thanks, little sister," he said and vanished, with another pop.

"Little sister?" Varna asked Fernis.

"He gets a little sentimental at times," Fernis replied. "And you need to think about leaving us for a while. I'm sure you will return and you will always be welcome. The Tree knows you and will welcome you whenever you need succour. And know that the Guardians will watch over you and help you as far as we can."

"But you remain limited in what you can do," Varna nodded.

"Indeed, although we may have some wriggle room from time to time," Fernis said rising. "Your pack is ready, and a store of foodstuffs has been prepared for you. You will have a travelling companion, one who has also found his path once more."

"Dalresar?"

"He approaches now."

Varna nodded and stood. "I think I'll go say hello, and then we can see when we leave."

She left the small room, making her way to the point where she emerged into the dappled shade under the tree's great boughs. Not a door, but not anything else she could describe either. When she turned back the huge trunk was smooth and unbroken, but she knew where she could return to its embrace. She smiled to herself and turned to see a figure emerge from the Forest and make his way toward her. She frowned slightly, for while she recognised her travel companion he had a lighter tread, a more open visage and yet a shadow was evident on his spirit. She turned her sight on him and was astonished to see his aura flare into brilliant silver, fluctuating and shifting.

She moved forward to greet him and faced a further surprise as he dropped his travel pack and then removed his travel cloak, revealing dark tunic and breeches, the former with the badge of *Sunburst* and the insignia of the Champion. Hanging from a utility belt strapped around his waist were blaster and needler, and an array of objects, some that Varna did not recognise. Varna stared for a moment before standing to attention and saluting crisply.

"Champion!" she said in a voice laden with emotion.

Clay shook his head. "No, you never need salute me, Varna," he said, nevertheless returning her salute with a casualness she would not have believed him possible of not long ago.

"So it was you I could see in those pictures!" Varna said, more for something to say than any other reason, given it was obviously the case.

Clay merely nodded. He had worked through all of his emotions, had grieved anew and had taken some form of revenge by destroying the party of ghazrak.

"Who was the other figure I saw you supporting? After the blitz mine - that's what it was, I assume?"

Clay paused. "Yes, it was a blitz. She was Capes. She was injured and unable to walk."

"What happened to her?" Varna asked, sensing a change in the big man in front of her.

"She died," he said flatly. "She was murdered by a group of men who tried to rob our small hut, even though we had nothing. And our son was murdered, also. I came upon them as they were leaving, and took care of three of them, but the fourth managed to knock me out and got away."

"Oh," Varna said in a high voice, more a sigh of regret and sorrow. "I'm so sorry, Clay. But how did you come to be with Flin?"

"I don't really know. I now recall coming to and finding Capes and Evian dead and burying them behind the hut. But I'm not sure what happened then. I'm guessing some sort of post-traumatic event. Eresh and Ogun think it may have been an attempt to forget, or perhaps it was physical. But I do know that I ended up wandering and was taken on by a farmer who put me to work with his scroffers and other farm animals. That he was a slaver I didn't know at the time, and didn't care, truth be told. I must have been there for only a short time before Flin came along and took me to live with another farmer. I still don't really remember that. It may come back to me in time, but there's no real hurry for that. He obviously saw something. A little later he returned and took me away with him, teaching me the stories and tales, and some sleight of hand. I was pretty good at that."

"Flin said you were with him for almost forty cycles, our years near enough. But during that time, you also helped him with intelligence gathering and other things, I take it." Varna made it a statement, and Clay merely nodded in agreement. "Which explains how you were with the Faero at the time he was injured?"

"Yes. Flin expected something to happen based on the Prophecy, and he'd already worked out that the Faero was likely to be involved. He made sure that I was positioned with Intika. Luckily I'd retained enough of my weapons knowledge to be useful from time to time. It wasn't enough to save Intika, though. Nor could we get to Flin fast enough."

"But that doesn't explain how you escaped from a blitz mine! I thought they had a complete kill zone. How did you keep that patch intact."

For the first time Clay smiled, even if only slightly. "As Champion no-one questioned or even checked what I took on missions, so I grabbed a few mines and a new form of personal shield the Grand Admiral was developing. It was the shield that protected us, although we took a battering."

"A shield? On a planetary mission?" Varna looked askance at Clay.

"Yes, of course. You take what advantage you can, especially as Champion, when you have more lee-way. I bet your team brought some stuff that's hard to explain to the Ennarisi?" He chuckled at her discomfiture. "Like arrows that don't shatter against armoured ghazrak? A bow that drives those arrows further and faster than anything locally? How about a battle staff that telescopes both ways?"

"Well, we thought those things could be hidden or explained away. But we brought no power weapons with us, or any other stuff like that. Or clothes with ship emblems," she said pointedly, glancing at his tunic's ship patch.

"There was something off about the mission, so I packed a few extras," Clay said. "I'd like to go back and ask the Grand Admiral a few things, just to see if I guessed right."

"Well, the good news is that you may be able to ask her yourself," Varna said. "But don't expect any sort of straight answer."

At Clay's questioning look Varna explained about *Starfire* finding the Grand Admiral's ship drifting in space with Serra in stasis after the loss of *Sunburst*. The loss of the battleship was sad news to Clay but the survival of Serra brought a smile to his face.

"I have some thoughts about that," he said. "Did you know that she designed *Sunburst*? Did you know that about every fifty to a hundred years for the last three or four hundred years, maybe more, there was a leap forward in Union military technology, usually driven by a woman who rose rapidly through whatever ranks there were at the time? And there are no pictures of the women responsible?"

"So?" Varna asked, puzzled.

"I just find it interesting," Clay said mildly. "I believe she may be able to tell me how that came about. She was also a student of the Union military history, or at least could talk about it with great knowledge."

"Well, as I said, you may be able to ask her if we get through this mission. We were here to find you and any other survivors, but that has morphed now that we find Shadows embedded here. It seems Goroth is the enemy for now, and I was just preparing to move out."

Clay nodded. "Yes, although I think you may find that Goroth has been our enemy for a long time," he said. "Let me pay my respects to Fernis and the others and we can head off."

# 15. Jalor on the Steppes

Jalor had been busy. After dealing with the aftermath of the attack on Escar and assuring himself that King Ensert would recover fully from his encounter with the flying ghazrak, he returned to the Citadel with Blaine and the twins. Helt remained behind to assist with the recovery, having become a celebrity as well as their Princess. Corm remained for another couple of days before returning to the Citadel, with Ky-rel returning to her eyrie.

The Escar city walls were being repaired and were being enhanced with great platforms where the Rocs could land, should they ever visit. The imaginations of the people of Escar had been fired by the intervention of the great birds in the battle, and they were acclaimed as heroes. Helt, on behalf of her father, decreed that every Escari city or town should have Roc platforms constructed, and stores of suitable foodstuffs were to be available at any time, should a Roc be in need. In the taverns, songs ranging from bad to execrable in Jalor's opinion told of the battle and the part played by the Faero, the Rocs and the shining warrior. Ensert had formalised his support of the Faero, but his force of knights had also taken a battering and would take time to recover in number as well as health.

For his part, Jalor had a better idea as to what could be faced when the full might of Goroth's army was brought to bear. He assumed that it would be many times larger than what was presented at Escar. He knew it would be a deadly battle and he had to come up with new and better tactics. And reinforcements, because the number of soldiers available had proved to be almost inadequate, and only by dint of Almin Bor's training and the terrible tactics employed by Goroth's army - not Goroth himself, Flin had assured Jalor - had they prevailed. Goroth would have used much better tactics and his battle gifts, Flin had told Jalor. So, Jalor had started to prepare for his next trip seeking allies. Three tendays after the events at Escar, Jalor stepped into the Citadel's portal.

The steppes were east of Escar. A great sweep of mostly level, grassy land stretched from the fertile south of the northern continent to the broken lands below the mountains that walled in the northern twin kingdoms. A very wide, apparently sluggish river separated the steppes from the lands to their south. Despite its sluggish appearance, the river had a strong current, strong enough to carry away those foolish enough to try to swim its breadth or to cross via the light-weight canoes and row-boats that were used for fishing and harvesting edible water plants. The two points where crossings could be made were at points where the river bent around considerable obstructions, so the current was reduced slightly in power. At those points, flat-bottomed ferries were drawn across the river by hand or draft hrss winding a great rope around a capstan. So much had Jalor learned from the Citadel's portal AI.

The people of the grassy steppes were enigmatic to most. The Mages had seen the evolution from groups of broken and dishevelled refugees fleeing the rebellion's devastation, utterly unprepared for life outside the great cities and the civilised life of Ennaris, to a hardy, very independent tribal society. They called themselves the Clans, while the Mages knew them of old as the Pelar. They were self-contained, although comfortable when dealing with the inhabitants of the small and rudimentary cities that grew out of the rebellion's destruction.

Over the first several hundred cycles after the fall of civilisation, the Pelar developed customs and rituals suited to their own existence. Fixed abodes were not known to the Pelar. They travelled as the seasons demanded, pushing their herds of hrss and wool bearing sanbors across the expanses of grass from waterhole to waterhole, pitching their tents where they stopped. Fiercely loyal to their tribe or clan, and bound by a code of honour that they developed as a foundation to their way of life, the Pelar were formidable fighters from hrss-back, wielding short bows and arrows and wicked curved swords. Legend told that they had been helped long in the past by Mages, and the Council Assistant and twins confirmed that several interventions had occurred to help the Pelar.

In general, the Pelar tribes raided other tribes to test their skills, with no quarter given. But when threats were made to the Pelar they came together, shrugged off tribal enmities and selected a war leader. That had happened many times in the past, but it had not been required for three or four generations now, not since they had seen off a threat from Ensert's great-grandfather, whose knights had proved to be poorly matched against the highly mobile Pelar. A strained peace had held since then.

Jalor regarded the map displayed on the portal monitor. Two portal gates were shown in the steppes. From what he could tell from the map, there was literally nothing near either of them. There were no cities, no villages, no defined roads. According to the twins, a regular gathering of the Pelar was to be held at one of three traditional locations, two of which were located close to the portal gates, while the third was a point that formed a rough triangle. They rotated around those meeting grounds so all of the tribes could have a convenient locale once every three gatherings. The twins did not know which meeting ground was to be used, so the plan was to go through each of the gates and hope that it was not the third location.

King Ensert had offered an escort of knights, which Jalor had declined politely, given the uncertain history between the Escari and the Pelar. In a slight change of plan, Corm would remain behind to continue the rebuild and extension of the army, ably supported by Almin Bor. Jalor would be accompanied by the twin Mages and a small troop of the Faero's guards, the latter mainly to show the Faero's standard. The Pelar had been strong supporters of Faeros from far in the past, but they had not been visited by any Faero, or invited to the Citadel, for many generations.

Preparations made, Jalor activated the portal gate and stepped through. He found himself in a large chamber with wall lights coming on as he exited the portal gate. He waited while Ragnor, Raglin and the guard followed and then deactivated the portal gate. He looked around with interest, examining the floor mural and the wall illustrations, some faded and others vivid in their colours. No cities were displayed. Rather, there were views of the grasslands with some showing a riot of colour, others dull greens and greys. Others again showed images of long and low buildings with fanciful spires and tall trees. All shared the common attribute of broad vistas, looking into distances that seemed not to end, merging into misty horizons.

"The steppes were here for a long time as pasture land," Ragnor said to Jalor, pointing to an image of a set of low buildings. "And there were several permanent settlements. They were abandoned when the water failed after the rebellion, which is what forced the people to wander. When they were joined by city refugees there was a huge problem. Many died during that time. Crops failed, and there were only a few crops that were suited to the grass plains even before that time. Those who could make it out of the steppes did so. Those who could not escape changed from the peaceful tenderers of hrss and sanbors and feed crops and over time became very hard. But they also became resourceful and uncompromising. Honour is very strongly valued and a person without honour is shunned."

Jalor nodded. Ragnor took the lead and walked towards a section of wall that had the outline of two doors, closed fast, etched in it. As the Mage approached, the centre line cracked open and, with nearly identical groans, the pair of doors swung outward, revealing a small portico. Jalor followed Ragnor, with Raglin and the small guard following him. They stood in the portico. Four steps led down to a broad flagstone courtyard, ringed by low walls. Opposite the portal's doors was a large break in the wall and Jalor made his way to that point, looking over the vast stretch of long grass blowing in the light breeze. The grasses varied in colour between pale green, grey and brown and extended to the horizon in all directions. The land appeared to be featureless from his vantage point, although he knew there were gullies and hilly mounds scattered across the land, with waterholes available to those who knew how to read the land. But there were no people in view. No tents or corrals. Just grass bending and waving in all directions that he looked. He bent and scratched his hand across the top of the ground, to find it rock hard and bone dry. The air also was dry. Humidity was almost non-existent, he thought. Anyone on foot and not knowing where they could find water would not last long. Even though the temperature was not severely hot, the sun beat down and enhanced the dryness. Jalor walked back to the portico.

"Can we be sure they won't be here?" he asked the twins. "I'd hate to leave only to find they arrived the day after."

"By my calculations the gather should have started a couple of days ago," Raglin said. "And they usually keep to their timetable for these gathers. They're too important to the tribes as a whole."

"So, we go to the next one, then," Jalor said, walking back through the open doorway and heading towards the portal screen. He was followed by the rest of the troop and the doors groaned closed once again, leaving no more than their outlines.

With a gesture Jalor brought the screen online, directed it to display the nearest portals and pointed to the other steppe gate. The portal gate flared and turned grey, and Jalor led the way through. Because of the portals, little time had been wasted, he thought, by trying the two gates in sequence. The second was slightly closer to where the third site was, and if they had to cross the steppes this would be their starting point.

This portal building, built in a similar manner to the first, also showed similar scenes, although the buildings here had more trees and there were bodies of open water included in several of the images. Some fields showed obvious signs of intensive farming.

"This area had more water?" Jalor asked Ragnor.

The latter nodded. "Yes, this region was where the food stocks for people and animals were farmed. Grains and cereals. Mostly for the animals, I must say. With the gates it was easy to move harvested crops to other parts of Ennaris, so we had very specialised farming. Apart from some grains, most of what this part of the steppes grew went to feed the herds."

"Which was not so good when the portals failed," Jalor guessed, to matching grimaces and short nods from both twins.

Jalor looked around and spied the double doors, located in the same spot as those of the first portal. He walked towards them and was gratified when they cracked open and swung back. A slight shower of dust fell from the roof line as they did so. The same sort of portico with a similar courtyard revealed themselves as he exited the doorway. And the same vista presented itself, long waving grass for as far as they eye could see. Only this time there were three hrss standing head down and chewing on the hardy grass a short distance from the courtyard opening, and three men who jumped from where they were sitting on the low wall, staring as Jalor made his appearance.

The guard followed hard on Jalor's heels. When he saw the three men, the sergeant gave a curt gesture and the soldiers formed a line in front of Jalor. The twins regarded the three men with interest, as did Jalor. All three wore slightly baggy and comfortable-looking trousers of a uniform neutral grey-brown. The legs were cinched at the ankles to fit inside the tops of soft brown leather boots. Baggy shirts of the same neutral colour, gathered at the wrists, had drawstrings holding a broad V together at the neck. All three wore broad-brimmed hats. Thin leather straps ran under the men's chins and held the hats onto their heads. Each wore a short sword and at least one long knife, although Jalor would have sworn there were others not visible.

The three showed no concern at facing the guard. Each wore a serious face, but there seemed to be relief more than anything else. The centre man took three steps forward, putting himself within reach of the guard's swords and bowed, arms spread wide.

"In the name of the Clans of the Pelar, I welcome you. My name is Horint and I am first acolyte to Lak. My Lady bid me to meet you and escort you to the gather." He bowed once again, as did the other two.

Jalor nodded to the sergeant, who ordered the guard to stand easy, and then made his way between guardsmen to where Horint stood. The twins followed, eager to meet this man who spoke of a Guardian as though he had first hand experience with her.

"Horint, I am Vinca Jalor, general for the Faero." Jalor paused. "Why did Lak send her first acolyte to meet us?"

"She said that the Clans would have to decide whether to assist or not when the time came to face the greatest evil, and that one would come who will lead the way. She said that the one is of the Prophecy, and the Prophecy is of the one." Horint smiled slightly. "I have learnt not to doubt Lak. Are you the one?"

"I'm not sure of that. According to the Archmage I am one of the Children of Ennaris mentioned in the Prophecy." Jalor shrugged. "But whether that is the one you're seeking or not, I'm not sure."

"Archmage? There is an Archmage once again?" Horint looked from Jalor to the twins, who had come up behind him. "And the Children of Ennaris have returned? Have the Mages returned, also?"

"Indeed the Archmage has been appointed," Ragnor said. "But we never left."

"Horint, I present to you the twin Mages, Ragnor and Raglin."

Horint stared, as did the two men who stood behind him. "The Twin Mages of legend?"

"I am Ragnor," said that twin before pointing to his brother, "and this is Raglin. We're not legends but we are Mages. On behalf of the Archmage Drewflin, we offer greetings."

"Drewflin? *The* Drewflin? The leader of the final defence?" Horint and his friends were overwhelmed. This was not what they expected.

"Are we far from the gather?" Jalor asked, to bring things back on track.

"We will travel five nights," Horint said, "but you cannot go on foot. And we have only our own hrss."

Jalor nodded, turning and gesturing to the sergeant. In a few seconds the guard had retreated through the portal gate once again.

"They will bring our own mounts back with them," Jalor explained.

"They are inside this structure?" Horint asked, looking askance at Jalor.

"No. This is called a portal gate and it's from the time before the fall," Ragnor said. "By using the portal we can move across large distances. The guardsmen have returned to the Citadel of the Faero to retrieve the hrss we left there, in case we needed to make a journey."

Horint nodded, although he did not truly understand. "I think there will be much to discuss at the gather," he said.

Jalor agreed, but just what the outcome would be he was not sure. He hoped, given Lak's intervention, that the Clans - not tribes as the twins had referred to them on occasion - would join with the Faero. But if not then he needed them to be neutral.

# 16. Flin and the Old Woman

Archmage Drewflin looked out over the plain of Escar. He was troubled by something but could not put his finger on just what it was. He had learned over a life that had seen its fair share of trouble not to ignore those feelings. Instinct often was merely a way of dealing with unconscious thought patterns that led to something of significance.

Far in the distance, he could see the knights drilling, galloping to and fro across the plain practising things knights practised. He smiled to himself. At the height of Ennaris' civilisation metal armour was not something anyone considered. He wondered how Escar had ended up with heavy armoured fighters where others continued to rely on smaller and lighter body armour. He knew that it had happened quite quickly so that within a short time Escar society had changed based on the needs and growing traditions of the use of heavy armour, and consequently the breeding of hrss that could support riders wearing such a weight of metal. Still, here they were and they could be of use although, as the recent battle had shown, they had limitations.

Flin turned as Ensert, King of Escar, entered the room, now showing no signs of the near fatal injury he had suffered not long before. The King joined Flin at the window.

"You have new knights, I see," Flin said by way of greeting.

"Yes, and some good ones, too," Ensert replied. "They learn quickly, but will not be ready for some time yet. They need to build muscle and endurance still, but they have been training with sword and long knife since they were young."

Flin nodded. "And have you heard from the Princess?"

"Only that she has returned to teaching Corm's soldiers how to fight," Ensert said with a scowl.

"You continue to object to her playing her role?" Flin asked quietly, carefully not looking at the King.

"She is a royal princess, not some sort of common soldier," Ensert growled, then sighed. "But she did do well in the battle."

Flin now turned to look at Ensert, a slight smile playing across his lips and an eyebrow quirked in mock query.

"Okay, okay," Ensert said, pride breaking through, "she did very well. I hadn't realised she'd become so accomplished."

"Well, she has had some additional training from Blaine, but most of it she had already," Flin said. "Her troops do look to her, though. She's turned into a leader, which is as much a surprise to her as anyone."

"She always wanted to take part in the knights' training," Ensert said. "Even though I objected and forbade it, I know some of them gave her lessons."

Flin nodded, continuing to watch the knights in their practice.

"But that armour!" Ensert grimaced. "It doesn't fit her well at all. If she's going to be acting the part she may as well look the part."

"I believe that's being taken care of," Flin said. "Have you told her of your pride in her accomplishments?"

"She knows," Ensert said gruffly.

"I'm not sure she does," Flin replied. "I believe a mark of your favour would be welcomed."

Ensert merely stared out the window, not seeing anything. He remembered a daughter growing up without a mother, living in a society where the strength of arms was valued. He then recalled the same daughter, clad in ill-fitting armour and leading her soldiers - the Faero's soldiers - in defence of her home city.

"Aye," he said pensively. "Something is needed, to show Escar that she has my favour if nothing else."

Flin nodded. "I must be away," he said. "I have things to attend to before rejoining Corm."

"I thought as much," Ensert smiled grimly. "This is your time coming, my friend. The Archmage who defeated Goroth! You get the chance to finish the job."

"It was not me who defeated Goroth," Flin replied soberly. "I'm no warrior and my gifts are not those of battle. I'm easily exhausted should I use them for such. It was Marjory and her battle Mages who held against the forces of Goroth."

"And Marjory is no longer with you," Ensert nodded. "Still, the Prophecy allows us a good chance at victory. I have been told of the Golden Warrior. Surely that gives hope."

"Hope, yes. But Blaine, the Defender, is not sufficient alone. Each of the Nine has a role to play and no single one can render victory certain. We don't yet have the Nine."

"Where do you go?" Ensert asked. "I ask through curiosity, nothing more."

"I've been feeling a pull towards the south-east," Flin replied. "There's something there that I need to see or do. But I'm not sure what that may be."

"So you'll head south-east and trust to luck?"

"I doubt that luck will play a part," Flin said ruefully. "There are forces at work here that are guiding us towards a final decision. Goroth's bindings have failed, and some of the old ways are returned. Ennaris was a true leader in the galaxy, amongst all of the stars you see when you look into the sky at night. Some of that remains and we cannot let Goroth get his hands on it."

Ensert again nodded.

"I miss my Marjory," Flin said quietly. "She had a way of making the complex seem simple. And she was the power behind us."

"And she was your life mate," Ensert said, smiling as Flin started. "My friend, do not for one moment believe you have hidden your feelings from those of us who've known you for some time. Every time you talk of her your memories are written in your face. We just did not realise to what extent those feelings were real instead of the skills of a gifted Teller."

Flin merely nodded, not daring to remember too much. "You are, of course, correct. We were paired long before Goroth was a threat. Were she here today, Goroth would quail."

"But she's not, so we must trust to ourselves and the Children of Ennaris." Ensert turned. "I have a kingdom to run and a city to repair. I'll see you before you leave?"

"I'll be leaving this day," Flin said. "Ky-rel will be here soon to assist me."

"The Roc!" Ensert replied, staying his exit for a moment. "Never did I believe they were real!"

"And that they remember promises of old," Flin said with a smile. "And they saved many lives."

"They will never be forgotten again," Ensert said. "This I guarantee. We have already built one of the platforms, so there's a place for them to land. Escar will welcome them today and for as long as this city exists."

It was late morning when Ky-rel arrived, accompanied by a second Roc, Tu-pol, a huge dun-coloured bird with brilliant green and blue plumage atop his head and around his feet. Both Rocs landed on the platform that had been newly built, watched with interest and no small sense of pride by the men and women who had constructed the landing stage. The small child who had greeted Ky-rel and her mother also met them, the mother turning to pass onto the watching workers the Rocs' thanks for such a splendid platform. After a drink from an enormous bowl through which water cycled continuously to keep it fresh, the birds fluffed their wings and settled to wait.

Flin hurried up the steps to the platform after bidding farewell to Ensert, and promising to return in the short term. As he made it to the platform, Ky-rel sent greetings and introduced Tu-pol, who bowed deeply to the Archmage, wings spread wide, the breadth of which amazed the watchers. Flin returned the greetings.

"So, Ky-rel, are you or Tu-pol giving me the honour of carrying me to where I need to go?" Flin asked, aloud, so the watchers could hear and understand the respect with which he addressed the Rocs.

*It will be my honour to carry the Archmage*, Tu-pol sent to Flin.

*I must attend to Corm at the Citadel*, Ky-rel sent. *Tu-pol is flight second to the Arragat.*

"Flight second of the battle wing?" Flin paused. "That makes you the equal of a captain of the Faero guard, I believe."

*In the days of old, perhaps*, Tu-pol replied. *We will see what the days to come will bring. Are you ready, Archmage? And whence do we go?*

"Ready," Flin said. "Ky-rel, would you please let Corm know that I will be with him in a short while, perhaps half a ten-day? There is something I feel I must attend to first."

*Indeed I shall*, Ky-rel replied.

She launched after a brief mental touch with the child and mother. Tu-pol crouched to allow Flin to grasp hold of a strap that extended from a harness over the middle of the bird's broad back, clear of the wings, and scramble atop.

"It has been long since I have flown with a Roc," Flin said. "Please let me know if I cause discomfort."

*Thank you, Archmage*, Tu-pol replied, and Flin caught a hint of suppressed humour. *Likewise, this is a new harness, made from the old designs, so we are not too sure how they will work. We thought the Archmage would make a suitable tester for it.*

Flin was laughing as Tu-pol, after a similar brief touch to child and mother, spread his great wings and with a mighty beat launched straight up, as though to test the harness immediately. The down-draught scattered scraps of leather and twine across the platform, causing the watchers to catch hold of hats and cloaks as they fluttered around. Flin, having had some experience with Rocs in the past, had a tight grip and sat straight and high on the Roc's back as the powerful wings bore them aloft.

*In which direction are we heading, Archmage,* Tu-pol asked once they were high enough to circle the city.

"I have no clear location, Tu-pol," Flin said apologetically, "but I know it will be east and south. As we get closer I will be able to provide you with a clearer destination. There seems to be someone I need to see."

*As you wish,* Tu-pol sent, wheeling and straightening on a south-east bearing before adding speed.

Far below, across the great walled city of Escar, work that had paused while almost everyone watched the huge birds land and take off once again resumed. Children and adults alike wondered what it must be like to ride one of those great birds, like in the old tales that had started to be told again. Another legend come to life.

As they flew, arrowing across Ennaris at speed, Flin took the opportunity to survey the land. This was the first time for thousands of cycles that he could see Ennaris from the air with his own eyes, and the last time he had been in an atmospheric shuttle and so could see little. He knew that the land had changed from images the Council Assistant had shown him before the technology was partially blocked, but now he could see the extent, at least in this part of the planet. Escar was built on the ruins of what had been a centre of trade and leisure. The trade had been catered for by a large spaceport that was the source of the large plain in front of the city, as well as the tall administrative buildings that had all been destroyed. The leisure was catered for by a range of outdoor activities ranging from river rafts through the nearby rapids to climbing up and over the moderately high peaks that were behind the city and hikes through what had been beautiful forests. Now, even thousands of cycles after the rebellion, the change brought a tear to Flin's eye. The city was gone, of course, as was the spaceport, but so too were the peaks, having been partially destroyed by the energy weapons unleashed by Goroth's forces. The forests were mostly recovered but would never be the same again, for the climate had been altered following the geographic upheaval, and the river had changed course and become little more than a wide stream, winding its way through gullies and across flats, remaking its bed as best it could on its way to the new sea between the two continents.

Flin's reflections were interrupted by a renewed sense of purpose, as he felt the tug once again. He sent a change of course to Tu-pol, who veered slightly. Several minor course changes later and Flin knew they were close. In the time Tu-pol had carried him aloft, they had travelled the equivalent of at least one tenday of travel by road, even with hrss to aid them, and possibly closer to two. In the distance Flin could see the forest change character, with shorter trees further apart, and they were of different varieties. Occasionally there was a straight, tall tree with broad fan-type fronds that properly belonged closer to the tropical middle of Ennaris, and at other times there were patches of shorter, scrubby growth where trees had once been cleared.

Finally, Tu-pol could make out a large, cleared area in front of a grass-covered hill, bare of tree-life, rising to the heights of the surrounding trees. An enormous stone monolith was partly buried in the hill, with the top rounded like a gigantic egg. He sent a view of it to Flin, who in turn sharpened his gaze and asked Tu-pol to land in front of the monolith where there was a small cottage, looking like it would fall down at any moment. With a flare of his wings, Tu-pol landed a short distance from the cottage and allowed Flin to alight. Flin, frowning slightly, nodded to the Roc and walked towards the rickety door of the cottage. There was something odd about this place, not just the fact that something had drawn Flin here over a large distance. He could not put his finger on just what it was, but ... something ...

Stopping on the small stone stoop, Flin rapped on the door post for fear that he might knock the door off its makeshift hinges - which were leather straps, he saw on closer inspection. That was not not unusual for the more remote parts of Ennaris, he knew, and the cottage looked like it had weathered many a storm.

He waited patiently and his patience was rewarded as he was considering rapping again. From within he could hear a shuffling step and the door finally was pulled open. Framed in the doorway was a wizened old woman, straggly white hair poking out from a bonnet of indeterminate colour and vintage, with a gnarled stick acting as a walking cane. She looked at Flin through rheumy eyes, almost milky white, set in a mass of wrinkles. She was wearing a number of mismatched, faded and worn items of clothes that looked like old scarves over a long skirt or dress that had once been red with a faded blue tunic and a green-brown over-jacket of some loosely woven material. From her stooped position she looked up at Flin and smiled a gap-toothed smile. Flin returned her stare, feeling that he knew this woman but was unable to place her.

"And who might you be?" she asked by way of welcome, in a scratchy voice.

"Good day," Flin replied politely. "I am Drewflin. For some reason I have been drawn to your door, and I would like to know why."

"The why is because I called to you," she replied. "Just Drewflin, eh? Then why are you wandering around with that green stone stuck to your forehead?"

Flin smiled. "Yes, well, I am Archmage Drewflin, then."

"There was a Drewflin once, a long time ago. Just a young feller. Found himself with a bunch of other youngers fighting off Goroth and his ilk. Made a pretty good fist of it, I heard."

Flin's smile faded. "That was me, yes. But much of the true fighting was done by others. My gifts, and those of many of the Mages who remained at that time, did not include warfare at that time, and still don't."

"Well, Archmage Drewflin of the heroes of Ennaris, come in and take a seat." The old woman shuffled aside and back, then turned and made her way into the tiny cottage.

"Heroes of Ennaris?" Drewflin asked as he followed her, pausing as the door swung shut behind him. "I have not heard us called that for a very long time. Many believe we caused the fall and the suffering that resulted."

"Well, that's true up to a point," the old woman said, pointing with her stick to a stool. "You could have just let that fool Goroth do whatever he wanted and saved everyone all that trouble. But it would have found them in the end, anyway."

"That decision had been taken by others much more experienced than I was at the time," Flin said, looking around at the cottage and noting that there was much more room than he expected to find. "You speak as though you knew some from that time."

"I know many people," the old woman said, as she hobbled to the hearth where a kettle was sitting over the open flames. "I now know you, for example, and you were there. And I have met the twins from time to time."

She found two battered metal mugs and poured into each a thick, black liquid from the kettle, its handle held with the aid of a bundle of rags, before setting the kettle back in its place. She carried one to Flin and handed it to him by the handle, so he had to gingerly grasp the rim and quickly grab hold of the handle with his other hand when she let go. A careful sniff showed it to be tea. His eyebrows lifted as he inhaled its aroma.

"Hyborian green tea!" Flin said in wonder. "Where did you get this? The Hyborian plantations were destroyed during the rebellion and are now at the bottom of the inland sea."

"Oh, I manage to find and keep things for a while," the old woman said, gesturing around the cottage.

Flin looked around. There was all manner of things on shelves, piled in drifts on the floor, hanging from hooks attached to walls and roof beams, sitting on the single table that he could see. From where he sat, he could see a stuffed hooter bird, whose eyes seemed to stare at him disconcertingly. It sat on top of a set of scrolls, which were crushed and torn. In one corner, there was what looked like a set of armour and, hanging from one arm of the armour, a basket full of dried flowers. Mounds of material that may have been clothes were piled alongside bundles of herbs, which rested against kindling and a small wood supply. Everywhere he looked there was something. Almost the only clear space was in front of a closed door at the back of the cottage which, Flin thought, must be against the huge rock.

"Indeed," Flin said neutrally. "And why did you call me here?"

"Maybe I wanted to know what is happening in the world," she said, a small smile quirking her withered lips.

"Maybe," Flin nodded, "and maybe you already know much?"

"Oh, I know that the Prophecy is at hand, and that the Guardians finally decided to return. I know that the Children are on Ennaris and Goroth has been freed from his captivity. He returns to the north and seeks to join with Grensor, the fool who decided to attack Escar and did such a poor job." She shook her head at the follies of some men.

"So, that was Grensor at the back of the field who fled. And it has been Grensor who has been experimenting as they did of old. The ghazrak were abominations that I thought had been dealt with, and then we found ourselves against flying ghazrak. I expect there will be more now that Goroth has returned."

"That was the norther general who ran off, not Grensor. And yes, you can expect more of those things. Grensor didn't have the touch of Goroth in his black arts, though, so his ghazrak are stupid. Vicious, but stupid, just like Grensor. Oh, and you should be aware that Likud will join them soon." She watched Flin as she dropped that news.

He sighed. "Goroth is bad enough. Likud has little imagination, but he would have made a full Battle Mage with a little more training, and the two of them will make it very hard. Are you aware of any others?"

"No," the old woman replied, "they're all that are left. Four went with Likud but all have perished in the cycles since. Likewise, Grensor had two others, but they did not survive very long."

"So, old woman who seems to know so much," Flin said, taking a sip of the tea and savouring a taste he had not had for what seemed like forever, "who are you?"

"Oh, that's not important," she dissembled. "You will not recognise my name. I am not a Guardian, to answer that question, and most of them are not truly aware of my existence, although Odruf and Fernis are. They always took far more notice of happenings than others. I think Balgor does, too. He's a shrewd one." She took a sip of her own tea before continuing. "What of the Faero? I know that Intika has passed to his reward. I always had time for him."

Flin understood the implication that she had known the previous Faero and just nodded. "His son, Corm, has assumed the mantle of Faero. He's done well so far and is surprising many. He took part in the defence of Escar and is building his army for the battles to come. He knows it will be fought out by the Mages as much as the non-gifted, but he means to be at the front."

"He's a good boy," the old woman said, eyes turned inward. "His father didn't know how to look after him and allowed him to run wild."

"He's had some good teachers since his father's death," said Flin. "Ragnor and Raglin, along with Balgor, have been bringing him up to speed on the history and other things."

"Balgor helping? The trickster, as many think of him? It's good he's returned also."

"Balgor never left," Flin said. "He stayed to protect the Citadel and the Faeronar."

"The wall!" the old woman muttered to herself.

Flin smiled again. "The wall," he confirmed.

"I always wondered why it never weakened over all those cycles. Even though it was built by the twins, it should have in the time since the rebellion." She frowned. "What of the Children?"

"Well, the Children are from a planet they call Earth," Flin began.

"Ordoreth," the old woman nodded. "It had to be, for Likud ruled Andoreth."

"Yes. Blaine has been revealed as the Defender," Flin said, watching the woman carefully but she only nodded, unsurprised, "and Varna seems to be Dharmoney."

"Seems to be?" asked the woman, to which Flin shrugged. "And the third?"

"I think Varna will prove to be the one. The third is Jalor, who led them to Ennaris. His role is yet to be made clear." Flin took a mouthful of tea, surprised to find he had finished the mug. "I feel that I must be moving on, I'm afraid. I'm sure you didn't call me here to exchange gossip," he said pointedly.

"Always in a hurry, you young people," the old woman said. "Well, I have something for you to take with you. It will be needed in times to come. Follow."

She stood and hobbled to the door at the back of the cottage, pulled it open and passed through. Flin followed obediently. He was stunned to see a large room where he expected to find the rock. He had known he was speaking to someone of power, and this confirmed it. Still, he could not understand who she might be. He looked around. The room was occupied by a single rack of shelves and little else. The shelves stood to the height of a tall man, and there were five shelves in all. Flin was astounded to see a disparate array of items sitting on them - knives that resembled those used by the men in the far northern ice wastes, a stone thrower like those used in the desert to the south, swords of different styles and types, small cauldrons, cups and bowls, bracelets and at the bottom, a dark cloth-wrapped parcel that could only be a sheathed sword.

The woman moved to the shelves, Flin at her side. His restless eyes latched onto an ornament. He started and reached for the ornament, only to find his hand swatted away.

"That's not for you," the woman said.

"It's an Aldenthrush," Flin said, wondering. "Marjory wore one like it."

"Indeed, it is," she replied. "But this is not Marjory's. This is for someone else. No, this is for you."

The old woman reached to the top shelf and pulled down a staff, with a white stone embedded among clasps at the top. The staff itself was a mass of spirals and whorls engraved down its length. Flin gasped in recognition.

"It is your time very soon, my friend. This is yours to hold for now."

Flin took the staff carefully, sighing sadly. "I'm not a Battle Mage," he said. "This is Marjory's staff."

"I know," she replied, "but know that you hold it in trust for the one who will wield it when the Prophecy is fulfilled. You are not destined to be the war leader, no matter how skilled you may be in the other arts."

Flin reacted with shock at her words. "There will be another?"

"If all goes well, the war leader will find you at the time required. Meanwhile, use the staff as you need, for you are worthy." The old woman sighed and looked pointedly to the door. "It's time for you to be on your way. I'm weary and there remains much to be done before I can rest."

Flin looked quizzically at her but, realising he would get no more, he merely nodded and followed her from the room. Once again, the door closed behind him without assistance. Flin picked up his travel pack and walked to the door.

"Who are you?" he asked gently, looking at the woman directly.

For a moment the old hag was replaced by another face and the rheumy eyes became sharp and clear. It was a face that Flin recognised from the battle at Escar, before the flesh sagged once again.

"You gave Blaine the Golden Sword!" Flin breathed.

"As I have given you the staff of the Battle Mage," she said. "The world moves towards the point of decision, Archmage Drewflin. The final battle will not be fought by the lower Ennarisi clashing one against the other. Oh, that must happen, of course, it always seems to be required. But the gifts bequeathed to each side of the battle by the Guardians will be the keys. The Prophecy is almost in place and misses but a few elements. The time is close. Be ready!"

Flin stared at her for a long moment, then nodded shortly and walked through the cottage door, spying Tu-pol at his ease some distance from the cottage. The great bird rose and strutted towards Flin, stopping abruptly as the old woman appeared on the threshold. Trembling suddenly, the Roc spread his wings as wide as possible and bowed so low that its great breast feathers brushed the grass. He held the pose as the woman walked past Flin and approached him. She laid a hand on the great head, above the hooked beak and between the eyes. Flin felt a surge of some form of power that he could not identify, and the woman stepped back. Tu-pol rose once again. His forehead now was marked with the Tree, exactly as was Flin's Enchara, and it glowed in a similar manner.

Flin was astonished, and the words of one of the more obscure parts of the Prophecy now came clear.

"'*And the Tree will take flight and will bear the Light*'," Flin muttered to himself. "But who or what is the Light?"

The old woman stopped as she retraced her steps and smiled slightly. "You know the answer to that already. You just have to believe."

She entered the cottage and the door closed, while Flin readied himself with Tu-pol. The great bird was somewhat subdued and watched the cottage as though expecting something to happen, but when nothing did, he spread his wings, took a few steps and launched into the air. Gaining height rapidly, Tu-pol and Flin flew in a spiral above the clearing. They had reached a height where they could see the woods stretching out to each side when, with a mighty crash, the cottage disappeared, along with the rocky monolith and the clearing, and the woods were now unbroken. There was nothing to suggest anything had been there at all.

# 17. Rocs Prepare

The flight of Rocs wheeled in the clear sky, every one of them in the exact right position, wing-tips separated by the tiniest margin and yet never touching. They rode the thermals, making minute adjustments to stay in formation. Seven Rocs, their feathers of all colours shining in the bright light, reached their designated position and with one mind tipped over and folded their enormous wings tight against their huge bodies. Each bird stretched out its neck so that they resembled nothing so much as a set of blunt wedges dropping out of the blue vastness. Almost vertically they dropped, their streamlined bodies cutting through the air and reducing the amount of drag that one would imagine such a large creature would experience. Seven thunderbolts headed towards the ground and Ar-kunya held his breath.

No matter how many times he watched the warrior wings practice, the Roc leader could not help but feel a thrill of fear for his fellow Rocs. No warrior himself, Ar-kunya was in awe of the feats of these Rocs, fearless in the face of the possible death they expected to face in the near future. Kunas had been spending more time with Ar-kunya and the Wing Commander, and the latter had projected distinct feelings of pride and satisfaction, as too had the other Rocs.

Ar-kunya thought back to the recent time when Ky-rel and As-men had reported that they had left their assigned patrol to assist the Archmage - an Archmage! - and other Mages to defeat the hated ghazrak, including winged ghazrak. In doing so, the Rocs had also been on hand to witness the attack of the Defender! Wonder of wonders! The first time in memory of any of the living Rocs that they had fought in a battle with their old allies, and against their old enemy at that, and were there to witness history made! And then Ky-rel had sought and been granted the services of Tu-brel, the best healer of the Rocs, and three Repeaters to aid the Archmage in healing the wounded. Tu-brel had returned full of praise for the Repeaters and brimming with satisfaction, preening his feathers unconsciously as he told of helping Archmage Drewflin - the legendary Drewflin lived still! - to heal many of the Ennarisi warriors.

And Ky-rel had bonded with the Faero of Ennaris! The Wing Commander had tried to make it sound matter of fact, but his crown had lifted and he was almost dancing as he told of the feeling of bonding with the Faero. Ar-kunya was both elated and envious, as were all of the Rocs. The list of volunteers for future patrols was long now, and the warrior wings practised endlessly. Patrols now were dispatched morning and afternoon. Every one of them hoped to find their life mate, as the old tales and the Rocs' own racial memory told them. And each of them wanted to have a chance to fight against those who had destroyed the Ennaris of legend and story.

The flight snapped open their great wings as one and the seven members split apart to take their own targets, each of them hitting the target dead centre. Of course, static targets made for easy testing, but they were only a part of the training that the Rocs had ramped up dramatically since the events at Escar. Kunas had expressed both satisfaction and pleasure at Ky-rel's actions in taking his patrol into battle, especially when he understood that in doing so they had saved the Faero and destroyed the winged ghazrak. Ar-kunya, and all of the Rocs, had been surprised by the fierce reaction of Kunas, although on reflection the Roc leader was less surprised. The Guardian had told them how he and his flight-mates were held back from taking an active part in protecting the Ennarisi and could only directly protect the planet itself. They must take part in events using their proxies. Thus, Kunas celebrated the Rocs' achievements.

Ar-kunya watched as the training flight wheeled away from their targets, clearing the site. Their wings pumping urgently as they made a dash for height, straining to gain height as fast as possible in case their adversaries managed to get above them. As they reached the desired height the patrol reformed and dashed away in formation, crossing above the next flight as it entered the practice field. Once again, Arkunya watched as the flight flew to its launch point and once again, as one, the Roc warriors folded their wings in close and commenced their plummet towards the ground.

Yes, the Rocs would be ready to play their part!

## 18. Incoming

"Captain, incoming," Rork said.

"Where and when, Mr Rork?" Jord asked calmly.

"Quadrant four, in about 5 minutes," Rork said, equally calm. "A large wake can be detected. I would hazard a guess and say quite a large number of ships."

"So, Likud makes his appearance," Jord said. "Kiri, call the admirals to the bridge please. Rork, let the fleets know we will have visitors, although I'm betting they're aware."

"Aye, sir. *Moonbeam* has gone to general quarters," Rork said.

"Well, that seems like a good idea. Sound general quarters, please, Kiri. Fleet wide."

The two admirals arrived on the bridge a minute later, both immediately looking at the monitor to see what had changed. Rork displayed the incoming wake and both nodded.

"Took his time getting here," Admiral Denton Bard said as he took his accustomed command seat. "Status, Captain?"

"Both fleets are at general quarters, Admiral," Jord replied.

"Very well. Rork, any idea about numbers?"

"No Admiral, but there will be quite a few," Rork said, eyes glued to his monitors. "They should come out of hyper-space in one minute. The Empire ships have started to change position."

"Admiral, do we enter the pattern?" Bard asked of Serra, receiving a simple nod in return. "All ships, execute pattern Amber."

That minute crept past, and the small number of Empire ships that had been holding station at a safe distance from *Starfire* and *Moonbeam* continued to manoeuvre. Now the Union fleets started their own movements. The capital ships moved further apart and took wide-spread positions. The smaller destroyers and gunships clustered behind them. The fleets' fighters launched, and half immediately moved to flank speed from their position behind the capital ships, moving away from the scene of imminent action and taking a location whereby they could engage with different attack vectors.

With a brief flash the area of empty space indicated by Rork became filled with ships. The one to catch the eye was *Qorv*, Likud's own flagship and the largest ship of the Empire fleet. It was heavily armoured, blunt-nosed and squat in profile, and it projected raw power. To each side were two battle cruisers, each larger than Union cruisers but appearing smaller than they actually were when arraigned alongside *Qorv*. A further twenty destroyers ranged out in a crescent, although three of them seemed to be listing, and behind them came a flotilla of smaller vessels. As they came out of hyper-space one of the smaller craft exploded, sending large shards of metal across the fleet, at least some of which caused damage to other ships.

"Admiral, a ship has separated from *Qorv*," Rork called out. "Looks like a shuttle of some sort, but with some real weapons. It's on course for the planet."

"Likud," Serra breathed, eyes like flint.

"Yes, as you expected Admiral. Likely landing place, Mr Rork?" Bard asked.

"Northern continent, somewhere north of that big grassy area," said Rork. "Enemy ships are powering weapons, sirs."

"*Moonbeam*, weapons free," Bard said, his message immediately relayed.

"*Moonbeam* and her cruisers are firing, Admiral," Kiri said. "Energy weapons only. Targeting the smaller vessels as planned before they get into formation. *Qorv* is firing, as are the cruisers. Targeting *Moonbeam*."

"She can take it for a while," Bard said. "*Starfire*, target the destroyers. Fire!"

Space lit up as the fleets exchanged energy fire. The Empire fleet adopted their doctrine of attacking the larger vessels, while the Union plan called for the smaller vessels to be removed from the board as quickly as possible.

Serra considered the situation. With Likud on the planet things were ramping up. Was it time yet?

Grensor groaned as he pushed himself out of the hard cot and staggered to his feet. He was able to walk, of course, but not with anything approaching his old steadiness of gait. He made it to the small cabinet against the wall of the shack where a pitcher of water, drawn from deep under the parched land, awaited him. He wedged himself against the cabinet and poured a small amount of water into the bowl set alongside the pitcher. He splashed some up and over his head, trying and failing to reduce the heat, that constant heat.

Ablutions completed, such as they were, Grensor staggered across the room and donned his tattered robe. Once it had been a deep brown colour but was now a dirty and dingy grey. Absently he fingered the remainder of the robe's sleeve fringe, which previously had been a vibrant red but now was the same dirty grey. His memory wandered back, as it often did of late, to the days of the Council when he had been a scientist and healer, working to assist people to regain the use of limbs that, even with the advances made in medicine, still became damaged for any number of reasons. It was Grensor who had built on the advances made by many others through the long ages of Ennaris' history and successfully developed methods to implant laboratory-grown organs using genes sourced from different creatures. There were other advances that made possible much more sustainable food stocks, although by then many in Ennaris had ceased to eat animal flesh and relied on scientific advances to provide their food based on plant matter. And he helped to develop the techniques that were used for better creating adequate plant food supplies also. He had been well-regarded then.

It was those skills that Goroth had sought out and corrupted, although Grensor had been a willing partner at the time. His philosophy had long been different to many on the Council, and he found a leader and mentor in the senior Mage. When his own skills and techniques were paired to Goroth's increasing use of the dark arts, those long known but also long forbidden aspects of certain more advanced gifts, one of the results had been the ghazrak, the army of choice by Goroth during the rebellion. In his blinkered drive to perfect those techniques, Grensor had fallen into Goroth's wider schemes, enthusiastically and with full commitment, failing to see what was actually happening until too late. When the rebellion was brought to an end, Grensor had already escaped to the blasted lands, now a harsh and unforgiving wilderness between what had been the delights of Aberwin and the icy north. Of course, the destruction had not been Grensor's fault, but he had been part of the cabal that brought it about.

*I must be getting old*, he thought. Well, it was about time. By his calculations he was around a hundred and eighty-five thousand cycles old - one stopped counting at a hundred thousand. He had spent many cycles, centuries, in space or visiting other worlds. The things he saw! However, he had spent almost all of the time since the end of the rebellion in this same wasteland. It was forever hot and dusty, and utterly without any form of civilisation to speak of. Worse, for so long he only had the northers, the remnants of Goroth's Ennarisi followers, to keep him company after Wentgar and Hylvor died. Wentgar died of shame, he still believed, after seeing what they had done to Ennaris. Hylvor, ever unstable to some extent, finally went mad and threw herself into the lava flows that wended their ways under parts of the wasteland. Why, Grensor still did not know but then, with Hylvor the *why* sometimes did not matter. Both had been gone for a long time, leaving Grensor with the remnants of Goroth's more rabid followers.

The northers, which was a name given the unruly, undisciplined and vicious descendants of the rebels, lived any way they could. For a long time, Grensor had largely ignored them and they had fallen into practices of such barbarity that, when he finally stuck his head up again from the deep depression that he had been in for a thousand cycles, he could do little but effect minor change. Of course, that was too little and far too late. In truth, he admitted ruefully, he had let himself decline physically. The blood workings gave a short, sharp boost but one paid a price afterwards. Grensor was paying that price now. He doubted that he had the innate energy to reverse the decline.

Now it was starting all over again and Grensor was both excited and very weary. For some time, Goroth had been able to reach through the bindings imposed on him, enough so that Grensor had started to experiment in earnest once again. He had never really stopped his work to build a better ghazrak, of course. That had been a matter of pride more than urgency, especially as the period of Goroth's imprisonment stretched into thousands of cycles. Now, however, while still using the northers as the base, and with the crude equipment that he could build in the absence of true technology, helped by gifted northers who could produce something like a power source, he had reinvigorated his work to develop better ghazrak. He did not have as strong a grasp of the dark arts as Goroth, but his memory was sharp and he had succeeded to a significant extent, aided by forced advice from several Kindred at times.

The new breed of ghazrak was better armoured than the old, at least above the waist, and was stronger. The innate viciousness of the northers added a concentrated malevolence to the mix now. He had needed to add some form of control to stop the ghazraks' rampages among the northers that the early batches had indulged in whenever they lost control, which was often. Of course, they did not stop at violence, for that was merely the prelude to slaughter. Grensor realised that if he did not change the mix somehow then he would have no northers left at some stage. However, the changes were uneven and throwbacks were common. It was the throwbacks that he sent on the scouting and disruption missions, hoping they would be killed even as they caused fear and damage. Lately, many had been.

Grensor knew of the changes that were happening. He knew that the Faero had been replaced by his son, an untried and largely dissolute youth. He also knew that, supposedly, the Children had returned. He had been gifted Andorethi by Likud on several occasions, as well as information about when the Children would arrive. It had been a little over fifty cycles ago when he had first sent the Andorethi, whose weapons seemed to be immune to the technology ban for some reason, to kill the new arrivals. Almost the entire available force had taken part and Grensor had been dismayed when they had all been destroyed by some form of device operated by the one they called the Champion. But the party of Children had been destroyed.

Now Likud was returning to Ennaris. In the immediate aftermath of the rebellion Grensor had not been aware that Likud had escaped the devastation until the first Andorethi appeared, and he was astonished to find that he was not the only one left. The last message he had received via the Andorethi said that Likud was planning on returning to Ennaris in time to take part in the final resolution, as forecast by the Prophecy.

Grensor also knew when Goroth's stasis bindings were loosed and then failed, again as foretold. That was only a very recent event, and Goroth had yet to put in an appearance, but that would not take long. Of course, there were no working portals in the wasteland so he would have to come across the land somehow. But Grensor knew he would come. While on one hand he looked forward to seeing Goroth again, in another sense Grensor was not sure he wanted to do so. He had been spending too long remembering what had been, what was lost. Did they have what it would take to succeed this time?

Grensor had heard the chime as the Enchara was placed on the Archmage - Drewflin, he assumed, had finally been recognised - but he also knew that Marjory had perished. At least, that was what the remaining Mages believed and Grensor had been able to find no trace of the Battle Mage over the last few hundred cycles, so he believed it. That was a shame but also a relief. Truth be told, he had always held Marjory in high regard. She was the final reason for the failure of the rebellion, and had proved herself to be one of the greatest Battle Mages in Ennaris' history. What she had achieved Grensor still could not credit, even though he knew that it had happened. Not only had she protected large stretches of the planet, but she had destroyed their weapons and then captured Goroth. If they had to restart the fight, then not having her leading the Council forces would tilt things toward the rebels - for Grensor still thought of himself and them as rebels - and despite wanting to take Ennaris by whatever means necessary, occasional guilt at the last outcome still pushed through his thoughts.

If only he could take himself back, he thought, and deny Goroth, a lot of what had happened may not have happened. Regrets were of no use, though. Now he had to see this through, and he would not be too unhappy if he did not survive it.

He heard the commotion or, rather, he sensed it before it started. The clamour from outside his shack rose like a wave. With a grunt he thrust himself towards the door, pulled it open and staggered to the opening. Across the dusty expanse, he could see the ghazrak approaching a craft that had landed amid a cloud of rusty, red-brown dust. But they did not attack. Rather, a path was made through them and Grensor saw a tall figure approach. It was only when he removed his flight helmet that Grensor recognised him.

Likud!

## 20. Jalor and the Pelar

The encampment was large, very large. Each of the several Clans of the Pelar had constructed a hub from enormous tents, and each hub was the centre for the Clan at the gather. From the slight rise on which they stood, Jalor was able to see seven such hub tents, each surrounded by a myriad smaller tents, differing little between them beyond splashes of colour and, as he found later, the patterns of those splashes. The colours did not cluster by Clan, either, so the tent city looked like a riot of different colour splashes on top of a beige base.

Surrounding all were pens holding various animals. Many hrss were evident, as expected, but also tough and hardy wool-bearing sanbors and nimble-footed lombors that were lean rather than fat, as Jalor had seen in the villages closer to the Citadel. The pens were widely separated, and each was patrolled. Jalor recalled Ragnor telling him that the Clans practised their skills by stealing hrss, sanbors and lombors from other Clans, which sporadically led to fighting. While the gather was, supposedly, a time where all such conflicts were forbidden, obviously no-one was taking chances.

In the centre of the mass of tents was a large open area, roughly oval in shape. Horint pointed it out to Jalor as the meeting place, where the main business was conducted and where the key entertainments took place.

Through it all flowed the clansmen, wearing similar garb to Horint and his friends, all with a flowing walk as though they glided across the ground. Most wore their headgear open, while some wore it not at all. All appeared to go armed, the universal protection being a short, curved sword and a knife. Of the latter, there were differences in that some were long and straight while others were short and curved. All were business-like.

The five days had passed rapidly, the troop riding at an easy pace so their hrss were not strained. Horint had shown how to locate the small amounts of water that was in this grassland, mostly by recognising slight differences in the grasses, even their colours. He had proved to be good company, telling Jalor and the twins of his experience with Lak since her return and how she had decreed that the Clans must reinvigorate their training for war in preparation for the battle to come. Jalor hoped that meant that the Clans would be more inclined to join Corm's army and follow him into battle, but Horint cautioned him.

"The Clans are proud," he said, "and do not forget that the Faero has not maintained the contact that was promised. They also do not forget that the last clansmen who visited the Citadel was imprisoned and treated poorly."

"When was that?" Jalor asked, not having been made aware of such a happening.

"Five generations past," Horint said seriously, then smiled slyly. "The Clans have long memories."

Now they stood and looked over the gather, and Jalor was impressed at the number of Clan people that he could see. Still, for the size of the grassland, they were small in number, which made sense.
Jalor turned back to where the Faero's troops stood, allowing their mounts to take their ease and chew on the tough grass.

"Mount up," he said shortly, walking to his own hrss where its reins were held by the sergeant. "Double file."

The troops formed a short column with two per row and Jalor and the sergeant at the front. The twins trailed the troop. The hrss stood patiently, tails swishing to brush away the flies that had become insistent. No matter where he went in the galaxy, Jalor thought, there were flies, of one form or another. The Ennarisi version were as persistent as anywhere else.

"Unfurl the banner," Jalor ordered, and the trooper behind the sergeant released the loop that held the banner in a tight furl and shook it out, placing its shaft in his boot stirrup and gripping the shaft half-way up.

Jalor nodded to Horint, who was watching from one side, and the acolyte turned his mount. He met up with his two companions and led the way down the rise. Jalor and the small column fell in behind them, allowing a slight gap to open. The Faeronar, aware that they were on show, sat straight in their saddles, eyes ahead, one hand resting on sheathed sword hilt. Through the tent city they wove, attracting a larger following as they moved closer to the oval at the centre. Jalor could hear muttered words and could see clansmen pointing at the banner but did not trouble himself to make out the words. He already knew there would be some who supported the Faero and others who did not, or who did not care. That was why he was here.

By the time they reached the oval, they had acquired a sizable escort, accompanied by a swelling noise. All movement ceased on the oval as they emerged from among the tents onto the oval proper. Jalor, using his peripheral vision more than anything, noted that its size was about half a kilometre long, maybe a bit more, and about two-thirds that wide. There were the unmistakable tracks of many hrss running round the periphery. The grass was trampled flat in a broad swathe, sure signs of races or tests of skill. Horint led the way towards one end where a pavilion had been set up. A small fire burned in a cleared space to one side. Under the pavilion, which was little more than a large piece of cloth held up by tent poles, were five men and two women. All seven reclined on large cushions scattered around overlapping rugs. All seven watched with wary eyes.

Horint stopped in front of the pavilion, his companions moving off to each side and melting into the watching crowd. Jalor and the small column of troops halted behind Horint and sat upright and still on their hrss. The twins, likewise, remained mounted. Jalor nodded politely to the seven and dismounted, allowing the reins to fall to the ground, hoping the hrss would stay true to its training and remain in its place. In this place of supreme hrss riders and trainers, he hoped to demonstrate some control over the creatures. One of the women flowed upright, moving forward to where Horint waited. She was tall and middle-aged. The hair beneath her head-dress was a dark brown laced by grey, but she looked lean and hard-muscled.

"Who have you brought to this gather, Horint? And why? You know gathers are for the Clans only!" Her voice held an accusatory tone, but also some interest.

"I am aware, Hartik," Horint said respectfully. "This is Jalor, general of the Faero's army. He has come to ask the council for aid."

"He is not of the Clans," one of the reclining men said, without heat. "They should not be here."

"I met them at the house of the gate, Urtol," Horint continued, "as Lak requested. And brought them here, also at Lak's request."

"The gate?" Hartik queried. "Why meet there? That is already on Clan land, so they had already trespassed."

"No, they had not left the gate yard," Horint replied, and waited.

"They passed through the gate?" Hartik asked, eyebrow raised in surprise. "Such has not happened for a very long time. How do you know they did so?"

"Since the fall of our world," Horint said with a nod, "and I know because I was waiting for them, and they exited the house of the gate. While I was talking with Jalor and his friends, they brought their hrss through the gate also."

"Who are you to know how to use the travel gates?" Hartik demanded of Jalor.

"I am Vinca Jalor, general to Corm Ramesa, Faero of Ennaris," Jalor said quietly. "I have come to seek your support in the coming war with Goroth."

"Corm is Faero?" Hartik asked, receiving a nod from Jalor in reply. "And what talk is this of Goroth? He is a tale told to children, a figure to excite fear in the weak-minded. Goroth, if he ever existed, was killed by the Mages, who have also perished."

"Not quite," Jalor said calmly. "The Mages remain, only a few of them admittedly, but still, they seek to protect Ennaris. And Goroth was not killed but was locked away in a chamber made by the Mages and their ancient technologies. That technology has failed, as the Prophecy foretold. You do recall the Prophecy in the grasslands?"

Hartik nodded, while one of the men sneered.

"The Prophecy," he laughed. "Another tale for the weak. We of the Clans have no need of the Prophecy, nor do we have to aid the Faero, who has not seen fit to speak with the Clans as he was warranted to do."

Horint glanced to Jalor and his lips quirked in a tiny smile, as though to remind Jalor of his warnings.

"No matter what you choose to believe," Jalor replied evenly, "the Prophecy is coming to pass. The bindings on Goroth have loosed and he is free once again. The forces of the old evil are returned. The ghazrak walk the land and fly through the air. The Defender has been revealed. And the Children of Ennaris have returned."

"Ghazrak that fly?" Hartik asked, aghast. "We have had dealings with the ghazrak at the northern borders of the grasslands, and we have found them to be very difficult to kill, even using our hrss. If they fly also, the difficulties may be made much more."

"Tales again," the sneering one said. "The Defender is legend only. And the Children do not exist."

"To the contrary, Travol," Horint responded, refusing to be baited. "The Children are real, as Lak has said. Jalor is one of them."

Jalor glanced at Horint, surprised that he was aware of that. But then, he thought, if Horint did speak with Lak she would certainly know about the Children.

Travol stared at Jalor, anger suffusing his face. With a swift motion he stood and walked from the pavilion to stand in front of the Warrior. They were of a height, although Travol was leaner than Jalor.

"You do not look like a saviour of Ennaris," he sneered, looking Jalor up and down, seeking to insult the visitor.

Behind him Jalor could hear the troopers shifting in their saddles and Jalor held up one hand. The soldiers quieted.

"Be careful who you seek to insult, Clansman," Jalor said quietly. "My men have just come from defending Escar from attack by hundreds of ghazrak and thousands of northers. They have been blooded in battle such as you have not known and will not take kindly to insults. They fought with the Defender, they watched as the great Rocs fought against the winged ghazrak and prevailed. They fought as their comrades died. They watched as the Archmage and the Roc healers combined to save life after life following the battle." All sounds had died away as the Clans listened. "While the knights and Faeronar fought the ancient evil that has arisen again, you complain of not being visited. While the Mages strive to hold back the evil, you recline and take your leisure. While the Faeronar hold back those forces as of old, you hold to your refusal to believe. Take care, Clansman, for the evil is real and is coming. And insults will not stop them."

The quiet was marred only by the distant sounds of beasts moving, stamping hooves and the occasional bird call. The Clans were silent, staring at Jalor. He did not speak for a long time, allowing time for Travol to squirm under the accusatory glares of many. Finally, Jalor lifted his voice again, speaking clearly so all could hear.

"Know this, people of the Clans of the grasslands. I am Vinca Jalor of the Union of Sentient Planets. I do not come from this world of Ennaris, but I am one of the Children of Ennaris, for my home world was seeded by Ennaris of old. At the request of the Faero, Corm Ramesa, I am general of his army and will lead his forces into battle against the forces of Goroth. He is not a legend or a myth but a Mage of power, who had been held in strong chains by the Mages of the Council from the past. Those chains have weakened and fallen. Goroth walks Ennaris once again. The Mages of the Council once again seek to oppose Goroth and his minions, while allies of old have returned. The great Rocs joined with the knights of Escar and the army of the Faero of Ennaris to defeat Goroth's preliminary thrust."

He walked away from the escort, away from the pavilion, deliberately ignoring the seven who had reclined on soft cushions. He addressed the gather directly, knowing that this was a risk, but also knowing it was one he needed to take. The Clans were direct people and would appreciate direct speech.

"I call on the Clans to join with the Faero to defeat Goroth. I call on the Clans to join with the Children of Ennaris, with the Defender of Ennaris, with the knights of Escar, with the Rocs of Ennaris. I call on the Clans to end this evil of the ghazrak and the northers once and for all, for the alternative is a terrible one. And I pledge my own life should that be required to make this happen, as I have pledged it already to Corm, the Faero, and to the Guardians of Ennaris."

Silence reigned once again as the people of the different Clans looked to each other in wonder. They had heard many tales of the rebellion and the fall of Ennaris into mayhem, and of how the Children of Ennaris would return to lead the people of Ennaris into the future and save them from the darkness that would arise once again. Even the sceptics were impressed, and the Clan leaders stayed still, all but Travol, who stirred and turned to watch the effect of Jalor's words on the listeners. Finally, he could not hold back.

"You have said nothing, man of the Faeronar. Anyone can stand there and say those things. Anyone can call themselves one of the Children of Ennaris. Yes, we have heard the stories, the tales that have started to be told again only recently as tales of the past, where before they were told as children's tales. You expect the Clans to pack up and leave the grasslands to fight some war against a myth? No, I say! As the leader of the Clan of Nal-bar I say no! I will not allow my people to be destroyed." He was breathing hard, passion suffusing every fibre as he shouted. "The Clans are not the plaything of the Faero."

"And yet," came the quiet voice of Horint, "this man has the favour of Lak."

The simple statement shattered Travol's argument. The Clans had only had a Guardian amongst them for a short time, but it had been a time of great growth for them as she had made herself known to each of the Clans, always with Horint and his fellow acolytes in attendance to make it clear that they were her attendants and spokespeople. She had told them of the past, of the rebellion and the origins of their own people amongst the destruction and despair from that time. She had instructed them in new ways of doing things that were already paying dividends. Old, lost knowledge was being used again. New medicines had already helped to heal sicknesses that killed the people of the Clans for as long as they could recall. She had told them of places where they could locate raw materials for simple things like new dies, additions to the simple fabrics they wove from specific types of grass-type plants that made them hardier and blocked the force of the sun better. Lak had brought them a tall man named Ogun who was giving instruction in how to fight better as mounted forces, how to handle their weapons better to make them even more of a formidable force from hrss-back.

Now Horint drew on that position to place Jalor within the boundaries of their Guardian. Travol's eyes grew wide at the acolyte's intercession. He saw the effect on his people. For a long time Travol had been counselling patience, had sought to hold back the Clans from joining with any other Ennarisi. He had been the sceptic, downplayed the evil of the ghazrak even as they raided the northern Clans, and always talked of the benefits of holding their own counsel without others interfering. He had his adherents within his Clan, all of whom made the same arguments, although without the same passion and fire.

Travol leapt to his feet and stared at Horint. Hatred lent his countenance a terrible cast. With a cry he launched himself at Jalor, whose back was turned to the pavilion, drawing his curved sword as he did so. Too late Jalor realised what was happening. The gasps and cries from the Clans as Travol charged at Jalor with sword raised rose loud into the air. Jalor had only turned part way, was reaching for his own sword as Travol swung his sword in an arc to cut through Jalor from shoulder down when Jalor was shoved from his feet. Travol completed his swing through the air where Jalor had stood a moment before, only to find a resolute sergeant of the Faero's guard drive the sharp metal point of a spear through his side. Travol collapsed, shuddering and kicking slightly. Those actions faded to the stillness of death after only a few moments. His razor-sharp sword, dropped from nerveless fingers, brushed Jalor's arm as it fell, slicing through the tunic easily and scoring his skin.

Shaken from his close call, Jalor forced himself to his feet. The guards ringed him and the twins stood with staffs ablaze. He ignored the astonished shouts of the Clans people and did not acknowledge the slight injury. Nodding to the sergeant, and then gesturing to the guards who had taken up a defensive position around him to stand easy, he regarded Travol for a moment. On an inspiration, he bent and searched through Travol's garments. A small pouch was unearthed, and Jalor pursed his lips, knowing what it would contain. He opened the drawstring and tipped out the red gold coins. A ripple of consternation rolled across the open meeting ground, and the news of what had been found was transmitted rapidly to those who had not had a clear view. With cold eyes, Jalor turned back to the pavilion, where all were now standing.

"Do the Clans prefer to stand with the northers and Goroth?" Jalor said, pointing to the red gold coins. "Is this why the Clans do not wish to honour promises of the past? Is this your price for forsaking your fellow Ennarisi?"

Hartik walked to where Travol's body lay. The coins that lay in an untidy pile by his side proved his guilt. Hartik looked at Jalor and then the twins, whose staffs continued to shine out. She turned back.

"This is not the Clans' way. We do not attack men who come in peace. We do not attack the Faero's messenger and general. Where are Travol's supporters? Where are those who strutted with Travol?" she shouted in fury. "Find them and bring them to the council."

Horint glanced from Hartik to Jalor and then the twins, giving a shallow bow before saying, "Would you care to join the acolytes for some refreshments while Hartik clears this up?"

Jalor assented and, with the twins and the troop following, he trailed after Horint. The twins' staff were extinguished. A large tent, larger than Jalor thought would be needed for three acolytes, was their destination and Horint held the tent flap open, gesturing Jalor, the twins and the soldiers inside. Within, the tent was a light and airy chamber with scattered cushions on mats. Several women and men stood as they entered, many more than three.

"The acolytes of Lak," Horint said, gesturing with his arm around the tent. "Our numbers vary but most are here." He gestured to a woman, standing amongst the others with a slight smile playing across her face. "And this is Lak," Horint said quietly.

Jalor, startled, recovered and made a formal bow to the Guardian, as did the twins. The sergeant and the other soldiers immediately dropped to one knee, head bowed. None had ever been in the presence of a Guardian, even though they now knew that Balgor had been at the Citadel for long ages.

"Arise, men of the Faero," Lak said in a voice at once warm and calm. "I bid you welcome. I trust you took no harm from your encounter with Travol?"

"Only a scratch," Jalor said evenly. "I didn't expect to find a Guardian here. Nor did I expect to unmask a traitor. Were you aware of Travol's contact with the northers?"

"We were aware that someone was dealing with them, but not whom," Horint replied. "Lak suggested that, by introducing you, the guilty party or parties may make themselves known. It seems to have worked."

"As long as Travol was the only one," Jalor agreed.

"Meanwhile, please make yourself comfortable," Lak said, "while your wound is looked after. The Clans will have things to discuss after the events that have occurred, but I think you have achieved your aims."

"My thanks," Jalor replied, removing his sword-belt and nodding to the soldiers.

All followed suit with alacrity, receiving mugs of ale and invitations to mingle with the acolytes. The twins made their way to where Lak stood, as conversation resumed.

Outside the tent Hartik convened an emergency Council, with Travol's place taken by a hastily elected successor, one who openly demonstrated that she had no red gold. Inside the tent Jalor, the twins and the soldiers, on their best behaviour without being ordered, enjoyed the company of Lak and her acolytes.

# 21. Goroth Returns

The tall, finely-robed figure emerged from the thick dust swirling around the small homestead. This was a hard land and the people who inhabited it were just as hard. If they were not, they perished. The animals they kept in small enclosures and untidy barns were tough, wiry of muscle and as hard as the land and the people. The few crops that survived in this land likewise were hardy and, inevitably, stringy with most of their vitality hidden beneath the surface. Getting at those vital bits was difficult, but it produced a plain food that was nutritious. It took a special type to live in this wild country, in an almost forgotten corner of Ennaris where the northern edge of the steppes met the lower edge of the tall range behind which was the broken country of the twin kingdoms, and both joined to the harsh foothills of the eastern range that split the northern continent.

Accustomed to the harshness of the land, resolute and stoic in how they lived their lives, the inhabitants were intimidated by little that the land could throw at them. Still, the homesteader was shocked that someone would be walking across that wilderness. The homesteader waited on the porch of his home, sitting on an old rocker that had seen much better days, chewing on a stalk of tough, bitter plains grass. His eyes followed the progress of the stranger, noting the care with which he placed his feet and the slight uncertainty evident in his movements as the strong wind swirled, lifting the dust and throwing it up in curling whirls.

The stranger arrived at the path leading to the homestead. He pursed his lips at what he saw. A ramshackle building stood in a dusty yard. In his memory there should have been a small garden that ran around a large and rambling but stylish villa in locations such as this. Soft green grass should have stood between a smart fence and the garden fronting the villa. Instead, there was the dust and a rough path marked through it to the porch where the man sat. The stranger walked up slowly, carefully. He had wrapped his head in some sort of material, leaving little but slits for his eyes to see through, and he held his hands within the folds of the robe's sleeves. Reaching the porch, feeling the wind drop away in the partial protection of the building, he extended his long and fine-fingered hands from the sleeves and, reaching up, loosened the head wrappings.

A strong face was revealed, with deep set dark eyes that appeared to glitter. An aquiline nose above a sharp mouth combined with his spare, almost thin, face to give a harsh appearance, but his skin was not such that had lived in this climate for any length of time. Rather, it was burnt and rubbed raw, probably from the wind-driven sand and dust, and his eyes were rimmed with red where they were irritated by the same sand and dust. The robe, a deep grey in colour, was rimmed with blue and extended to his feet, which were shod with brown boots that had known better days only recently. When the robe was allowed to open the tunic and trousers were the same grey. The materials were unfamiliar to the homesteader, who had lived with simple materials for his whole life. Obviously, they were of high quality, robe and clothes and boots. The head wrappings, if he was not mistaken, were also of a fine material with which he was not familiar.

The homesteader gestured for the newcomer to take a seat in a second chair and, with a singular economy of movement, reached down to uncover a pail sitting by his side. He extracted a simple metal mug and dipped it into the pail's contents - hard-won water - and handed it without comment to the stranger. The latter took it gratefully, nodding his thanks, and took first a tentative sip, then a second and then a longer draught, draining the mug. The homesteader nodded to the pail and the stranger dipped the mug once again, after which the homesteader covered the pail again before too much sand was blown in.

"Not many people we see walkin' in these parts," the homesteader said in a slow drawl once the stranger had taken a pull at his second cup of water. "That's a tolerable hard means of getting' from here to there."

The stranger started to reply and then had to stop, clearing his throat a couple of times. When he did speak his voice was scratchy, possibly from the effects of the wind and dust, possibly from not being used for some time.

"It was not my choice to be afoot," he said, words precise and even. "And I thank you for your generosity with the water."

The homesteader nodded. "Out aroun' here people need to look out for each other," he said. "Any of us would do the same, but you're welcome none the less."

"This is a hard land," the stranger said after another small drink. "Once this was a lush and fertile part of the planet."

The homesteader snorted. "Once maybe, but if that were the case it was long ago. My family has had this place for many lifetimes and there are no family stories of it being' anything but hard, scrabble land. We make the best we can but even that's failin' now. Legends told by the Tellers, when they bother to come this way, talk of grass and water and trees, but that was before the fall."

The stranger nodded sadly. "So, it was this fall that caused this land to become such as it is?"

"So they say," the homesteader replied. "Me, I never knew anythin' other. Family story tells of a well that gave water to a garden, but the hole in the back of the house just gives up dust now, mostly."

"It looks like this was a place of comfort once," the stranger said, looking at the part of the house he could see with appreciation. "A basic construction but one that could have had comfort."

"Most places hereabouts are similar, some bigger, some smaller," the homesteader replied. "All are old, and no new ones have been built for generations. Most are empty now, with the people headin' away from the Wild." He gestured to the parched and battered land which the porch faced and from which the stranger had emerged. "It seems to be reachin' out for us." He fell quiet as both considered the Wild.

"I have been out of touch for a time," the stranger said after a period of companionable silence. "Are you able to tell me anything of events around Ennaris?"

The homesteader laughed quietly. "Well, we don't get much news aroun' here, and what we do get is pretty old. The Tellers have been talkin' about the old days, back when the Mages were runnin' aroun' and doin' their thing. They've been tellin' the stories of the Prophecy, child's tales really, of things gettin' better with the return of the Children of Ennaris and how Goroth is comin' back to destroy everythin' again." He snorted. "Child's tales! Ghosts and ghoulies! If there were a Goroth he's dead and done, and the Mages have done little to make things better up aroun' here. The Children had better be careful, too, because this land is hard on young'uns."

"Old tales indeed," the stranger said, eyes glittering. "Do people not believe in the stories of the days before the fall?"

"Those days were thousands of cycles ago," the homesteader said, stroking his scraggly grey beard. "Even if they happened, it were so long ago that no-one can recall clearly, now can they?"

"There may be some who can," the stranger said, his expression held steady despite the shock felt at the man's words. "Thousands of cycles ago? Yes, that would explain the state of the land. And what do the rumours say of the Mages and the Guides?"

The homesteader looked sideways at the stranger. "You ask questions you should already know how to answer," he said, getting a shrug in return. "The Mages are gone. Stories are that the Guardians have returned, but I don't believe that, neither. If there were Guardians, they should have taken better care of us, shouldn't they?"

"I am far from my home," the stranger said, "farther than you would credit. I am not aware of the stories you tell here, but I am interested in hearing them and of events. Even though they are out of date. It passes the time. Have there been strange happenings that may have caused the old stories to be told again, for example?"

"Well, I don't reckon you're goin' anywhere at the moment," the old homesteader said, looking out as the wind continued to gather force. "This is goin' to blow for a few days. So, you may as well rest here awhile. I don't have much but you're welcome to share. I guess we can trade stories for a bit."

The stranger nodded, sitting back in his chair and staring out into the Wild, as his host called it. The sheer bitterness of the land astounded and repelled him. The changes wrought were massive, even though the overall shape of the land was similar enough. He almost wept for the lost beauty, and his memories took him back to a time that remained recent to him.

The stranger stayed for six days with the homesteader. Stories were exchanged. The stranger knew many tales of the great days of Ennaris and was happy to tell them. He told with bitterness of the rebellion against the confines of the Council of Mages, of how the rebels had felt impelled to fight against boundaries that they knew were imposed purely because of tradition and uncertainty. He told of wonders of the age, of machines that were able to fly the skies, to soar far above the land, of journeys to other worlds and efforts to lift and guide other creatures to the benefit of civilisation. The old homesteader's imagination, never strong, was unable to make a lot of sense of much that he said, but he became caught up in stories of the Mages and their deeds, of how the Guides and Mages would help crops to grow. The stranger would tell his stories and then look sadly out onto the blasted land in front of the homestead.

At times he told stories of the rebellion, of how both sides had caused great destruction to the advanced civilisation that had been Ennaris. Strangely, he had no stories of the aftermath of the rebellion, or of the after-effects. All of that seemed to be new. At times, he seemed to be in distress at what he encountered as he looked out from the porch.

In return, the homesteader told him what he could of recent events, as passed on by the Tellers. None had been seen for nearly half a cycle, but the stories were of the evil growing anew, of the Faero dying and his successor being but a lad, of strangers who were said to be the Children fighting against the creatures of the evil. The stories were of the Prophecy coming true, of Goroth and his minions walking the land again, of the return of the Mages to help to protect Ennaris. The old man poo-poo'd the tales but the stranger listened avidly, asking questions about where this evil was, what sort of creatures of evil were they. The homesteader was unable to answer, merely that they were misshapen beasts, half men and half some other creature, and that they came from the distant Wild. He would point towards the left, behind the cottage as he said this. He told of the general shape of Ennaris and of the different lands, but his information was limited in scope and told at third or fourth hand. His education had been poor and of little value beyond how to scrabble a living from this hard land, and he could pass on little. But the stranger took what he could.

There came the day when the winds died down to a persistent breeze, which the old homesteader told the stranger was normal, and the dust settled. After taking his relative ease, the stranger was feeling much better and declared that it was time for him to take his leave. He could feel that his energy levels were rising rapidly. He walked to the well at the back of the house. He stood at the lip and stared into the depths, where there was nought but dust on most days.

"I owe you my thanks," he said, as he stared down into the hole. "And I offer you my apologies for the changes you and your forebears have had to endure. I continue to believe the struggle was and is necessary, but I regret the outcomes."

The homesteader was unsure what was meant, so he merely murmured something. He watched the stranger uncertainly. Even after spending several days with him, he had no clear idea as to who he was or even where he came from, and the strangeness had never gone away. It was as though this man was seeing the country for the first time, which was very odd. His thoughts were disturbed by a sudden shaking. It felt like it was relatively minor, but it was something out of the ordinary. From the well came a plume of dust, swirling up and out, causing both men to back up slightly. The stranger nodded in satisfaction.

"Tell your friends to beware, for the danger will return, and there can be no guarantees of safety. But, for now, I leave you with this, as thanks for taking me in and providing me with food and shelter, even though you know nothing of me."

The stranger bent to pick up a stone and tossed it down the well. After a few seconds both men clearly heard the splash as the stone met water. The homesteader was stunned and stared at the well, then at the stranger, then at the well once again.

"How did you ... what did ...," the homesteader stammered, then, "Who are you to do this?"

The stranger walked from the well, turning at the corner of the house. "Remember that this" - he gestured around - "was not what was intended, no matter what may be said. But the cause was and remains a just one." He paused once again, then nodded to himself as if making a decision. "I am Goroth! And I have indeed returned!"

Turning again, he walked back into the Wild from which he had come.

# 22. Meilani Gro Tillek

Meilani Gro Tillek was in a pensive mood. She was a woman of immense resilience, as she had to be. Her job was a difficult one, she reflected, and that was being very conservative.

She found herself alone much - almost all - of the time, and every so often she found that to be hard, because she liked being around people. Of course, she had volunteered for this duty. She had known that it would be difficult, that she would have to leave her home, her few remaining friends. She had no family, so that made it an easier decision, but she had been a very social person far in the past with many friends. Most of them had died before she was confronted with the task, making here choice easier again. She had left all of the rest behind when she agreed to take on this task.

Did she have regrets? Yes, of course she did. As time passed those regrets multiplied, compounded. She was old, as Ennarisi counted age, very old. Everyone she knew from her youth and early adulthood were long dead. When she saw herself in a reflection she was shocked at the deep wrinkles that lined her face, at the sagging flesh. But, much worse than her own aged appearance, she had been forced to watch as the remnants of her people were destroyed by aggressive warlords who seemed to face few consequences. Some of them suffered in the end, of course, because these petty warlords grew enemies fast and lived relatively short lives, by and large. She took some comfort in that.

But she had seen the cycle repeat and repeat and repeat. Her white-hot anger when her own people succumbed had been replaced over time by an icy determination that she would survive to represent them when the evil fell. The time was coming. She knew it deep in her being, could feel it, could feel the paths of time moving to what she hoped would be the victory of right over evil.

She knew the Prophesy, of course. Stupid thing! She knew who wrote it, and who inspired it, but she hated prophesies. A prophesy that seemed to change every time you read it was infuriating. She knew the Prophesy forwards and backwards, referred to it constantly. Luckily, she had been blessed with a gift that allowed her to *feel* what she needed to do. She was not sure if she had that gift before she volunteered, or if it came after.

In the old days she would have been a Seeker, one who located things, one who could see through layers of lies, untruths and obfuscations to see to the very nub of things. These days were different. The old gifts seemed to have disappeared, although Meilani knew they had gone underground. Many with gifts had been killed over the years by fools who acted from fear of the unknown before they thought. Many had lived their lives without revealing that they had any form of gift.

But the gifts had started to reappear, and for that Meilani was thankful. Grensor had tried to stamp them out, and failed. It could be too late to try again, she thought, although the old Mage might try. But the situation had changed. The Children walked Ennaris. At last! After such a long time! The Prophesy said the Children would bring the Ennarisi together. Already they were doing that, at times without realising that they did so. Bit by bit, piece by piece, the Children were establishing the conditions for Goroth, the embodiment of the old evil and now released to the world again, to be confronted.

The Guardians had returned. It had been such a relief when she felt the first of them return. She knew that Odruf and Fernis had remained, and she had consulted with them on occasion. They knew of her task and gave her support when she needed it. There had been echoes for the whole time since the rebellion's end, almost as though others had stayed. Drewflin told her that Balgor had remained, too. Could there have been others? Perhaps. Her gifts may have picked up others or they may merely have been those echoes. That the Prophesy caused them to leave was a source of great frustration to Meilani as, she was sure, it was to them.

The Guardians' complete belief in the Prophesy brought it sharply into focus for Meilani. Prophesies were the stuff of fiction stories and charlatans, usually, but the Guardians not only heard this one, but they acted almost precipitously on it. Which side did the Guardians take? They were to safeguard Ennaris, of course, but more than that they were to safeguard the Ennarisi and the other peoples of the galaxy. They were not permitted to act unless there was danger of destruction of the planet or the people, so they may have to stand aside and allow Goroth his victory if that was how the cards fell, as long as Ennaris and its people survived.

She had more leeway in that. The Prophesy did not say which side of the battle would prove to be victorious, but it did call for a united Ennaris to stand with the Nine. She was playing her part in bringing the Nine to light. Across many long cycles she had sought out the artefacts that would be needed by the Nine. Some of them were objects of deep legend and others were of more recent times that had been produced for the purpose. She had worked to ensure that the right people were given the right information at the right time. By and large that was proceeding as expected.

The loss of so many Mages during and after the rebellion had been a shock, of course, and the survivors' decision to withdraw from the Ennarisi for long periods was a disappointment. She understood why that decision had been made but she would have made a different decision. Of course, she was not a Mage who took the long view but a warrior, born and bred. She had led her squadron of fighter craft to oppose Goroth's suborned forces. Ennaris had lost at least one generation of talented spacers when both sides destroyed each other. She thought back to those days more frequently of late, as she felt her time coming to an end.

Meilani had found herself stranded on Ennaris with her squadron destroyed. She relived that episode frequently. How had she been the only survivor, with her mother ship also destroyed? How had she been able to pilot a near powerless and heavily damaged fighter through the debris of the battlefield and the atmosphere of Ennaris to make a successful landing, leaving her fighter in pieces but herself intact and healthy? True, she had been rated among the best pilots of the Ralnar-kun, the elite battle wing of the premier fleet, but there had been better pilots that succumbed to the battle.

She made a hard landing that day and scrambled away from the fighter, dragging her injured leg behind her. She tried and failed repeatedly to contact her mother ship. Around her the land was shaking, groaning, tearing itself apart in the aftermath of the battle in which she had been engaged. The damage was bad, of that she was well aware. Even while fighting for control of her fighter as it careered towards the surface, she had seen the ocean flooding into the huge inland valley that had been the heartland of Ennaris, the centre of its civilisation. A heavy haze had spread across the whole planet as enormous quantities of dust and minute particles were lifted into the atmosphere. That would have devastating outcomes for the people, she knew.

Then, even while trying and failing to understand fully what was happening, she had been approached by Odruf, although she was not to know that immediately. All she knew was that a tall man with long dark hair had walked up to her wearing nondescript clothes.

"Squadron Leader Meilani Gro Tillek," he said in the calm, evenly modulated voice that she would come to know well. "Have you taken any injury?"

"My leg," Meilani muttered. "I'm not sure what I've done to it, but it's pretty bad."

"We can help with that," Odruf replied.

"Can you tell me what's happening?" Meilani asked as she worked herself to a sitting position. "I've lost contact with my ship."

"The battle is over," Odruf said in an even voice.

"Did we win?" Meilani asked, wincing from the pain.

"There are no winners," Odruf replied sadly. "However, Goroth and his forces have been defeated."

"So we did win," Meilani sighed. "The fleet? I was with the Premier Fleet."

"None of the fleets survived," Odruf told her as gently as possible.

Meilani was stunned. None?

"That's impossible," she replied, shocked.

"Nevertheless, it's true."

"We had nearly forty fleets, thousands of ships, hundreds of thousands of spacers when the rebellion started," Meilani objected. "I know we had conflict within and between the fleets but how can we have lost them all."

"Fleet stability was one of the first casualties. As you know very well, every fleet had internal conflict. Many ships were destroyed to deny one side or the other the use of those ships, usually as mutinies took hold. In every fleet there were suborned ships that turned their guns on loyal ships. By the time that was resolved there were very few whole fleets left. The Premier Fleet was alone in remaining largely intact. Until the recent battle."

"Am I the only survivor?" Meilani asked in a whisper, dreading the response.

"No, there are others, but not many. Many are injured, of course, and scattered around Ennaris. The greater majority were lost, however."

"What sort of damage has been done to the planet?" Meilani thought to ask after a further moment of stunned silence.

"It's significant and will continue for some time yet, I'm afraid," Odruf replied. "Many have died already as the western ocean broke into the inner valleys. Land slides have claimed many. Every city has been destroyed utterly. I fear many more will die."

Oddly, Meilani accepted that this man knew these things, even though the battle was very recent.

"What about the Mages?"

"Most of the Mages perished," Odruf said. "The few that remain must recover their strength following the battle with Goroth."

"What can we do?" Meilani breathed.

Odruf heard her. "We must endure," he said evenly. "Most of Ennaris' technology resources have been destroyed and the people have been thrown back on their own resilience. Many will be tested and found wanting."

"We can build fresh tech," Meilani retorted.

"No, for an interdict has been placed on advanced technology for some time to come," Odruf replied.

"What? Why? And who could do that?" Meilani shifted her injured leg angrily as she spoke, sucking in a sudden breath as fresh pain exploded through her.

"The only remaining technology is advanced weaponry," Odruf explained. "The ban on advanced technology will ensure that those weapons cannot be used. As to who could do that? I did."

"You? Who are you to do such a thing," Meilani snorted.

"I am Odruf," the Guardian replied in a quiet voice.

"Odruf?" Meilani replied sceptically. "Really? I've always thought the Guardians are myths."

"Oh no," Odruf replied easily. "We have been here for most of the history of the peoples of Ennaris. We pulled back from direct contact as the Ennarisi were able to make their own way in this universe. We don't need to be seen or felt to do our jobs, although my brothers and sisters are making some reinforcements to their chosen groups of the Ennarisi as we speak."

"If you are a Guardian then you have more power in your little finger than the greatest Mages. Why don't you fix things?" Meilani demanded, incensed.

"Our task has been to safeguard this planet as much as its people," Odruf replied. "This we have done, as far as we were able. All of us are injured. Three of us died in holding back the worst of the damage. We gave freely of our strength when the Battle Mage required it, and we accepted the backlash. But we have little strength left. We are not all-powerful. We do not have the strength to make the ban selective, for example. Inevitably, some bits will slip through the ban, but to hold it I had to make it widespread."

"But you'll get that strength back and be able to help then?" Meilani asked, before she realised what Odruf had said. "Three Guardians died?" she whispered, horrified.

"It will take many long cycles to recover from our injuries. However, most of us must leave Ennaris or risk greater catastrophe." Odruf paused, as a frown creased his forehead, the first sign of perturbation that he had evinced. "And before you ask, I don't know why that is the case, just that it is. But with so few of us to maintain the ban I had to make it complete."

"But some of you are staying?" Meilani asked in a small voice.

Myths or legends, true or false, the *idea* of the Guardians had been the most deep-rooted concept in Ennaris for ... ever! Now that Meilani knew they were real and had to leave, she found the idea shattering.

"I will be staying," Odruf replied.

"As will I," another voice said as a second tall man walked up to the pair, looking to Odruf. "You want my help?"

"Indeed," Odruf replied. "Squadron Leader Meilani Gro Tillek, this is Fernis. Meilani has a badly injured leg to be attended to. You're much better at that than me."

Meilani stared. Fernis? A second Guardian?

"Ah, of course," Fernis agreed in a deep voice.

He knelt by Meilani's side, and stared at her damaged leg for a moment. Then he held one hand over the leg. A green glow grew rapidly from his hand and engulfed the injured portion of her leg.

"This will hurt a touch," Fernis said conversationally as the glow intensified.

Meilani gasped as a fresh wave of pain swept over her, but it rapidly faded. She watched, astonished, as broken bones re-knit and damaged muscles and tendons were repaired. She had seen Mage and Guide healers work on injured people, of course, supplementing the medical technology used by the Ennarisi medics, but had never needed to have such treatment.

It was then that awe took over. She, Meilani Gro Tillek, was being tended to by two Guardians! In the midst of Ennaris' worst crisis - she could not think of a worse one - two of these powerful beings cared for her. And both, according to Odruf, had been badly injured and so would be suffering.

Fernis sat back on his heels, obviously spent. He pushed himself to his feet and stooped to help Meilani to do likewise. Uncertainly, she looked at the two Guardians, for some reason surprised that she was very nearly as tall as they were.

"I thank you Guardian," Meilani said formally, carefully giving a bow. "But why have two Guardians thought to assist me at this time?"

"A good question," Fernis agreed, "and one for Odruf. I must get back to other things, but I look forward to speaking with you again, Meilani. The others are leaving," he said as an aside to Odruf. "I'm bolstering them before they go. I'll need your help soon."

Odruf merely nodded as Fernis disappeared without ceremony, while Meilani struggled to bring her scattered thoughts and emotions under control. She had always been able to remain or re-establish calm, but was surprised that she could do so this time.

"There's something else, isn't there?" she asked Odruf. "You want me to do something, right? Why do you need me?"

"There are some tasks that must be done by the Ennarisi," Odruf replied, nodding. "This is one of those tasks. Your gifts suggest that you are the right person. I am asking you to put aside your military career to assist us in the greater fight to protect Ennaris."

"I thought you said the battle is over," Meilani replied.

"This one is, yes," Odruf replied. "However, Goroth has been confined, not destroyed. At a time in the future he will return and there's much to do in preparation for that time. What I'm asking of you is much greater than taking part in a space battle. In any event, there is no space force any more."

Anguish washed over Meilani once again and it was a few minims before she could reply.

"So what would I have to do?" Meilani asked with a touch of asperity. "I'm a flyer, a fighter. How are those gifts of use to you?"

"Ah, those are your skills," Odruf replied, "but your *gifts* are what we want."

"My gifts have been tested and are at a low level," Meilani said dismissively.

"You were not tested correctly," Odruf replied. "You are a Seeker and your skills will grow stronger as they are exercised. You also have lesser gifts that will become evident as time passes."

"How much time?" Meilani asked suspiciously.

"I have no sense of that," Odruf replied. "It will be as long as it needs to be. If it helps, there is a Prophesy that gives some indication of what may happen. You will have your own copy."

Meilani considered that statement. A prophesy?

"Who wrote the Prophesy?" she asked.

"Ah," Odruf said, embarrassed, "I did."

"You?" Meilani asked, intrigued.

"I was not aware of it," Odruf replied defensively, apologetically. "It seems I wrote down the Prophesy over many cycles. It seems to be a true foretelling so far, accurately predicting the rebellion and the immediate aftermath. It has been left for the others to find."

"Why can't you just give it to them?"

"As far as they know I died," Odruf replied. "They knew me as a Mage named Halfgar, you see. I set the block on advanced technology and made it seem that I overstretched my powers in doing so. My Prophesy also warns that most Guardians must leave Ennaris or risk the destruction of both its people and the planet itself."

"So, what do I have to do?" Meilani asked, accepting a charge that she did not understand.

When Odruf told her, time seemed to stop.

Meilani sighed. Those events had occurred such a long time ago, and she had been left alone, largely, to fulfil her role. She allowed a moment of self-pity to run through her before snorting and pushing it away. *She* was the one who had been tasked to do what must be done. It was *her* task to prepare the way for the Nine, and that task she had worked on for more cycles than almost anyone on Ennaris could imagine.

And she would continue for as long as was necessary.

For better or for worse, she had accepted the charge, and she would see it through. She could do no less. She was Meilani Gro Tillek, formerly Squadron Leader of the Ralnar-kun of the Premier Fleet of Ennaris. But for now, as she had been for more than five thousand cycles, she was Dharmoney!

# 23. Waslit Prepare

Credar looked up. The jungle canopy stretched as far as she could see, which was not that far. The dense jungle resisted all efforts to see through it. The canopy was high, at least ten times the height of a tall person from the ground, and that was only the first layer. Credar knew that above that were another two layers. The huge trees, with trunks that measured in girth further than two men could reach fingertips to fingertips, were spaced well apart. Between them grew a riot of broad-leafed and broad-fronded bushes and shrubs of all sizes, such that the floor of the jungle, which itself was deep and lush from the rotting matter falling onto it from above, was difficult to penetrate on foot.

What Credar could not see, but that she now knew was there, was a platform that stretched between three of the enormous trees, between the lower and middle layers of canopy. This was the living platform of the Waslit, the short, dark-skinned inhabitants of the jungle whose origins stretched far back into the depths of Ennaris' history to a little after the rebellion. Some of the legends spoke of the Waslit existing long before then, but Credar put little credence in that. Of course, there were no records available to tell the truth so the legends could be correct. But still, Credar did not believe it.

What she did know, though, was that the Waslit were incredible at blending into the jungle, of not being seen until they wanted to be seen. They restricted themselves to blowpipes and wicked short, curved knives, although Credar had also seen javelins in several places. Credar had seen several demonstrations of the effectiveness of the blow-pipes and knew a half-trained Waslit could hit what he or she aimed at almost every time. A fully trained warrior never missed. Their darts could reach out and hit reliably at up to forty paces. That did not seem very far but, realistically, the chances of needing to send a dart further than that was remote in the jungle, for there were few open spaces larger than that. Even the two main paths through the jungle saw few places that size, let alone larger, given the way the paths meandered. And the poisons with which the Waslit tipped their darts were lethal, varying only in the length of time that passed before death intervened. There were other poisons that incapacitated enemies but, from what Credar could find out, they were used for hunting more than warfare. The Waslit had the quite logical approach that war meant you wanted to kill your enemies, so why use the lesser poisons.

The spears with which she and her friends had been captured were not a primary weapon, she had found. In fact, they were none too expert at handling them and were astonished when Emdur and Maxnil, who had some training at spear-play, showed them the different ways of holding, throwing and fighting with the spears. Of course, logic showed up here, also. Why, Emdur was asked by a puzzled Waslit warrior, would you use a spear if you could hit your enemy with a dart instead? Emdur struggled to answer. The javelins appeared to be used for sport, with Waslit young and old, female and male, testing themselves in a small number of cleared spaces deep in the jungle.

It had become clear that the only reason the four of them had survived was because the corrupted priests had demanded live sacrifices so they could practice their disgusting so-called worship. Of course, in general the Waslit did not allow themselves to be seen. Despite the priests' attempts to re-introduce it, cannibalism had not been taken up again, so the Waslit merely made sure jungle visitors were passing through and not likely to cause trouble. If they did seek to cause trouble, they would not leave the jungle. Credar, Emdur and the others had been shaken to realise that they had been shadowed since they had entered the jungle proper.

Credar finally found what she sought, a set of marks in the tree's trunk that pointed to the location of the ladder, itself well disguised. Carefully, she pulled herself up the trunk of the tree until she was able to put one foot onto a rung, after which she climbed rapidly. Recent practice had added to her natural agility to make it a simple task. Still, she had to be careful not to place her hands or feet on any of the crawlers that might be on the ladder. She also had to ensure that she did not miss the signs of the often poisonous slithers that sometimes used the ladders as roosts.

She pushed through the lower canopy and found herself in a different world. Here, the light was more of a bright twilight than the gloomier twilight that existed at ground level. She reached the platform, which was slung from the layer of thick branches further up and firmly attached to the tree trunk. Its uneven shape reflected the varying lengths of the materials from which it was constructed. Oddly, these were planks, seemingly sawed from the trunks of fallen trees. The Waslit had yet to establish sufficient trust in her to tell her how that was done.

Scattered around the platform were a number of Waslit, male and female, all wearing the same breech-cloth and nothing else. At first Credar had been shocked, while Emdur, Ester and Maxnil had been appreciative, even if just as surprised. Again, logic prevailed. Within a short time, Credar realised that the jungle, while warm, rarely became unbearably hot, but nor did it ever seem to become very cool, let alone cold. It did become very humid, however. Given the way the Waslit lived, surviving from a range of foods harvested from the trees themselves, and occasionally from the jungle floor - usually the animals that lived in the jungle - and with no hierarchy to speak of nor the need to differentiate between social strata via clothing, there was little need for clothes. Even the breech-cloth was not for modesty for, as Credar had found the first night she spent among them as a guest rather than a captive, they had no qualms about being seen naked. Indeed, they were surprised when Credar had declined to disrobe and even more surprised when she declined the sexual advances of several of the men and women. It seemed they did not practice any form of monogamy and were not shy about being seen while performing sexual acts. No, the breech-cloths - logic again - were because they did not want their most sensitive parts to be injured.

Now, of course, Credar was seen as one of them, even if she maintained her odd customs. But Likki had made Credar and her friends her own, so that was that - they were accepted. And somehow, all of the tribes knew who they were, and they were greeted as friends and favoured ones when they ventured to explore the jungle. But where they had come to find and remove treasure before, they now were seeking to understand both Likki and the Waslit more.

Credar, Emdur and the two former handlers, Ester and Maxnil, had spent several tendays with the Waslit. During that time, they had received a lot of information from the Waslit elders, who were charged with telling the stories. But what they learned was unlikely to be the complete truth. For example, the stories told of the Waslit having lived in a grand city, with buildings higher than the tallest forest giants, and that they had flown through the air on some sort of fanciful carts without any hrss to pull them. The stories also told of the Mages and Guides who had tried to help during the destruction of the rebellion, and the loss of most of them during the time. Unlike what Credar knew of the history of Ennaris, the Waslit did not blame the Mages for the destruction, nor did they blame the Guardians. Rather, they blamed Goroth and believed absolutely that he was not a myth.

The newcomers also received instruction from Likki about the fall of civilisation, the role of Goroth - so, he truly was real! - and the events that led to Ennaris being in the state it now was. Likki told of the Guardians having to leave Ennaris or risk what the Prophecy described as an unspecified catastrophe, and how they had to wait until the Children of Ennaris returned, which had happened. Indeed, these Children seemed to be from another world, far away in the same galaxy, which was a new concept in itself. Credar, and her people who dwelt on the fringes of the jungle, had little knowledge passed down to them of such things, even though many of them were, in fact, in part descendants of the Waslit also. Likki described the different parts of Ennaris, with the different people, and how those people would have to come together to support the Faero. Credar had heard of the Faero, of course, but what she had been taught was not exactly the same as what Likki taught. Rather than being a despot who wanted to rule all of Ennaris for himself, Likki described the Faero as Ennaris' best hope for lasting peace and certainly not someone who wanted to make himself a king.

All in all, after four tendays the four treasure-seekers were thoroughly confused. They were learning much, and were taking part in many Waslit activities. When Emdur, Ester and Maxnil were tasked with taking Likki's message to the two cities edging the jungle, they went willingly. Their enthusiasm had been fired by Likki herself and they saw a chance to play a role in the coming events. Credar herself, while surprised at how the three men had fallen into Likki's plans so readily, found herself tasked with taking the same message to the tribes of Waslit and, to her own amazement, she had also agreed wholeheartedly. Likki, it seemed, could be very persuasive.

And so here she was, on a platform with the tenth tribe that she had visited. Far from finding it a difficult task, she found that the tribes had their own traditions and were awaiting the call. They had received instruction from wandering Tellers - or the same wandering Teller for over a thousand cycles, which Credar thought to dismiss before she recalled that most of what she had dismissed so far was true - and so were aware that the Prophecy said that all of the people of Ennaris would have to battle the resurgent evil. Interestingly, the Waslit, using their own brand of logic, realised that not everyone would take the side of the Faero, and were prepared for that eventuality. They had laid plans, with typical Waslit ingenuity and, as she moved around the tribes as Likki's messenger, Credar found herself coordinating the tribes. A planning council would be held at the old temple - purely because it was central, not because of its history of sacrifice or pseudo-worship - and that would take place that night.

But the planning was merely to make sure that everyone knew their roles, for the Waslit had been primed and ready for centuries. And Credar, watching the men and women of the jungle make themselves ready, was stunned that she was expected to play a central part as Likki's emissary, for the Waslit tradition told that one would come from the Guardian and that she would guide the Waslit.

And so it was that Waslit from each tribe met in conclave at the old temple, somehow cleansed of all signs of the priests and their atrocities, and cleared of the encroaching jungle, with ten stones arranged around the clearing where a representative of each tribe could sit, none of them taking precedence over any other. And at the conclave Credar found messages that Emdur, Ester and Maxnil hoped to have some of the militia to join with the Waslit in supporting the Faero in his battle against Goroth's evil. The decision to be made seemed to be so black and white, Credar thought, where she had lived her life with many shades of grey. She was shocked that her own city had an undercurrent of faith in Likki, and that she had never been aware of it. She had thought that she was more advanced in her thinking than the many who continued in the traditions of the past. Now she found that she had been deluded, and the old ways had been correct. The shock was profound!

But even more shocking was that the tribes, and somehow the Waslit of the cities, accepted her as Likki's anointed representative and leader of the war party. And so decisions were taken, promises given and plans made, and Credar found herself agreeing to lead the Waslit to war.

Late that night, as Credar sought a private place where she could cry, for she had held back her tears of fear - no, terror - for many days, she was visited by Likki herself. The Guardian stood quietly for a short time, watching her as she wept bitter tears before making herself known. And then she had comforted Credar, sharing some of her own warmth and compassion, and steeling Credar for what must come. She touched the core of Credar and brought forth the hidden strength that Likki had seen from the first. Credar found that, after all, she was ready for her task.

And so it was that, two days after the council meeting, the Waslit, the dwellers in the steamy jungles who once had been among the best and gentlest of the Guides of Ennaris, who had been forgotten by many Ennarisi but who never forgot their own traditions, gathered in the deepest part of the jungle. From hidden stores were brought out ancient tunics and cloaks made from material that had survived all the cycles since the rebellion, many marked with the Tree of Fernis, others with the Hammer of Ogun and myriad others, and more recent weapons that Credar had not realised existed. And the Waslit gathered their mounts, mounts that terrified Credar when she saw them, and prepared for war.

# 24. Varna

Relaxed! That was what she felt, just relaxed. Varna reclined against the fallen tree trunk that marked the boundary of a small clearing and allowed her mind to probe her surroundings. There were no threats that she could identify. There were, however, many of the small creatures of the land that she now recognised. As usual when she allowed her awareness to roam, she had gathered a small coterie of birds of many sorts. Many of those that occupied the branches above her or that were perched in the trees around the clearing were content, for reasons she still could not fathom, just to be with her. Others told her all sorts of things that she could not follow - most birds had very short attention spans and most of their concerns were with food, nesting and more food. She let the chattering slide past her.

The trees here were different. Following a joint suggestion from Fernis and Balgor that they could assist Corm's efforts to win over allies by visiting the northern continent's coastal region, where the seafarers had started to develop gifts reminiscent of those of old, Varna and Clay had been directed to a portal in an ancient site where, Balgor said, a small city had once stood. The portal was active and, between them, they had deciphered how to get the information required. They had emerged from the portal gate not far from a small town that had succeeded a farming city from before the rebellion. Farming and hunting appeared to form the major industries of that town, and they decided to stop off and see what it had to offer. Clay was in the town now, getting a feel for it, as he said. Now that he had his memories back, his sense of mission had also re-asserted itself, and his native caution likewise.

Varna did not mind. She enjoyed being able to let her mind slide free and roam. Her perceptions had increased dramatically, even though she knew there remained something blocking her from full realisation of her strength. She was ignoring that for now, trying to avoid what she knew she would have to deal with. The fact was that she continued to feel responsible for the deaths of her mother and those thieves, and she was afraid that she had caused them to do what they did, somehow. Paradoxically, she also accepted what the Guardians had told her, that her reaction had been both natural and blameless. It was the fear of using her powers without adequate control that continued to give her pause, even though Fernis assured her that her control was flawless.

Perhaps the people at the academy had been right, perhaps she had been using her gifts, even if unconsciously and certainly without control, to effect change to her advantage. Uncomfortably, she remembered her reaction when Falar had accused her of cheating via her psi abilities. She also knew that she had witnessed atrocities on her missions that were not reconciled with her own view, but she also felt that if she was able to harness her powers then she should be able to make these people into better people. Too many people saw good and evil as sharply delineated qualities, and Varna had always believed that every person combined elements of both - it was balance, and she now believed that she could affect that balance using her new-found gifts.

Her thoughts had wandered to the exact place she did not want them to go, and without volition she had drawn her consciousness back as she considered the pros and cons of her beliefs. She failed to notice the creatures of the wood quieten, nor the warnings of the chittering birds, who became quieter and stopped calling. It was the complete lack of sound that finally penetrated to her, and she came out of her semi-trance with a start just as she felt a sharp pain in her left arm. Looking down she was surprised to see a dart sticking from her arm. She pulled it out as fast as she could. It was something she recalled seeing before, but she was unable to recall where, and her mind was slipping. Desperately she tried to stave off the numbness that was creeping over her, and the fogginess taking over her mind, but she failed. The last thing she saw, before darkness claimed her, was the vague shape of a person leaning over her.

Varna awoke slowly. She struggled towards consciousness. She felt like her mind was trapped in some sort of heavy syrup and she fought to break through. Slowly, the feeling faded and she was able to consider opening her eyes. At least she did not have the blinding headaches that often accompanied this feeling in the past, she thought. Then she remembered that she had not had any sort of attack for quite some time. She had not even experienced the fuzziness since being with Fernis and the other Guardians. Finally, after forcing herself to find a calm centre, she recalled the dart and the impression of someone standing over her as she fell into unconsciousness. So, not the planet impinging on her once again. She had been drugged, deliberately.

She could feel bindings on her hands and feet - wrists and ankles, really. Testing each carefully, she found they were ties of some form of coarse material rather than rope, but she was firmly bound even so. She realised that she was upright with arms and legs spread. She tried to push her senses out but could not get far. The effects of the drug, perhaps. What she *could* discover was that she was naked, although her Aldenthrush remained around her neck. Carefully, trying to do so without moving any more than she may have done inadvertently so far, Varna opened her eyes to a slit. She was in a single room, long and relatively narrow. Across from her was a wall that held a rack of instruments - her mind reeled slightly as she realised that they were tools for torture. There was a range of knives of different shape, from very thin needles to broad flat blades, some with hooks, others with curves and waves. There were clamps and various lengths of chain. In the centre was a scythe with a shorter handle than any she had seen in agricultural communities. Several lengths of rope were hanging from hooks, and there were a number of sacks also hanging from hooks.

"Ah, awake at last," said a voice from one side with immense satisfaction oozing through the tone.

Varna gave up trying to feign unconsciousness and opened her eyes fully. She took in more of the room - a rude pallet at one end with tumbled bedclothes, a small table with a single stool and the remains of a meal, a single door at the end opposite to the pallet, a small window with the shutters closed alongside the door and a second above the pallet. A flickering but bright light came from two lamps burning brightly, one on the table and the other hanging from a hook on the facing wall. The place gave the impression of having been occupied for some time.

Looking down and then left and right Varna confirmed that she was naked. Not only that, the ties to both wrists and ankles were of a tough sacking material, twisted before being applied so that it was as good a binding as many ropes. She knew that she did not have the physical strength to break free. She was strapped to some sort of large round frame, a wagon wheel or another sort of structure that had been propped against one of the long walls. A brief struggle against the bindings, which also served to try to shift the frame, told her that it was attached to the wall. Looking further she could see that there were stains running from beneath her to the door, dark brown stains as though blood had been spilt and not quite washed off. She struggled to hold her fear down, to control her breathing and force a clear head.

"Wh..." - she started and had to clear her throat to proceed, her voice scratchy still - "where am I and who are you?"

"Ah, both good questions. I shall answer them for you in due course. I have to admit that I never expected to get this good fortune, having you drop into my lap, as it were."

The man, for man it was, walked from one side and towards the rack of instruments. He wore a long robe, which had started life as white in colour but now was dirty and stained. Patches of pale almost-white warred with browns, greys and reds - blood again, Varna thought. He stopped at the rack and spent a moment running his hands across the handles of several of the knives lovingly, almost as though caressing them.

"You may wonder why you in particular represent good fortune," he said, still not turned her way. "Well, you and your friends caused me and my friends quite a lot of trouble, not to mention pain, some time ago. Do you recall?"

Varna thought back through the events since landing.

"Great Mirden," she said. "You were one of the thugs intending to kill those women?" She deliberately loaded her voice with disdain, making the word 'thugs' a deeper insult.

"Yes, Great Mirden," he replied. "I am Ortas, and I am the sole remaining priest of Likki, and you interrupted our sacred rites. Not only that, but you also caused the deaths of my fellow priests. I alone escaped. But I was able to gather the high priest's instruments of worship and bring them to this place where I could start again."

"You are no priest," Varna sneered, trying to make him lose his temper and perhaps make a mistake that she could use. She struggled to open her senses, but could only do so fractionally, probably because of the drugs. "Likki does not value blood sacrifice, as you well know. None of the Guardians would do so."

"You have met Guardians, then?" Ortas asked, his manner almost nonchalant.

"I have," Varna retorted, wondering if that was the right thing to say, and then realising it was not.

"Excellent, then you are even more suited to the task," he said, almost purring, still fingering the range of knives. "I have been trying to get Likki to take note of my efforts and have not had success as yet. The women of this place have not been the right type, perhaps, or Likki's sight remains on the jungles and I need something more to get her attention. It may be that you will be the one. And I do owe you for what you did."

He turned and faced her for the first time, and Varna saw a feverish light in his eyes. A long scar ran from above his left eye, across the bridge of his nose and then across the right cheek, obviously the result of a sword or knife. He lifted one hand to touch the scar.

"My physical wounds heal," he said quietly, "but the damage to my spirit remains. Your death will allow me to heal in spirit, as well as serving to bring my efforts to the notice of the great god Likki."

Varna was worried. He seemed to be too calm and collected. She was not getting the response she wanted. She tried to extend her senses once again and thought she could get slightly further than before. Time, she needed time so she could get a better understanding of this man. This could be her chance to turn someone from the dark using her gifts, to do what she could not do in the past, to see if she could make that change. She made her breathing calm, slowed the beat of her heart, as she had been taught long ago and as had been reinforced by the disciplines of her recent teaching.

"How does death show Likki anything?" she asked. "Tell me that. Why do you think Likki needs or wants the deaths of women? She is a woman, herself."

"It's not for me to question the Guardian," Ortas said with a sneer. "My great task is to continue my quest to be noticed by her, to be rewarded for my dedication, even though my brethren have been destroyed."

"Your brethren were destroyed because they were abhorrent to Likki, because what they and you have done is not what is right." Another push saw her get a first glimpse of Ortas' aura, the faintest hint only. The drug was wearing off rapidly. "You will never succeed in achieving your goals. But then," she continued as another thought came to her, "it's not really Likki for whom you do this, is it?"

Ortas finally selected a tool from the rack, a quirt with leather strips hanging from a leathern mount, which was attached to a long, flexible length of wood or heavy reed. With a smile, he turned to Varna and looked her up and down, his gaze resting on her breasts before moving down her torso. He was smiling, but the malice revealed in that smile shook Varna. She had to be able to reach him, to remove whatever was causing this, to stop him from continuing this vile activity to herself and other women.

He stepped close to the frame to which she was bound and gently rubbed the head of the quirt between her breasts, up and down in a rhythmic motion. He was breathing faster and there was a strange light in his eyes.

"Why should I not get enjoyment at the same time as I sacrifice to my god?" he said, slightly breathlessly. "You deserve to suffer, and suffering releases the energy for Likki to savour." Unconsciously, he licked his lips, with the quirt moving faster.

Varna held her nerve, although she was not sure how much longer she could do so. She pushed once again and was rewarded with a mental "pop", as her extra sight came into focus. She turned that sight onto Ortas' aura and was shocked at the roiling blacks that shot through the grey. She had convinced herself that people could not be evil without pause, but that they could be brought back to a more balanced state. She was unable to discern a redeemable element of Ortas' aura. She decided to keep trying, though.

"So, what do you plan to do? Rape me and then kill me?" She pushed as much disdain into her voice as she could, trying to make him angry enough that she could better affect his emotions.

"Rape you?" he said in disgust. "Why would I want to rape such as you? You are an unclean woman. You are the cause of suffering for all men. You do not deserve to live, and nor do you deserve to die without pain." He struck one breast with the quirt and Varna could not suppress the cry of pain, which caused Ortas to grin, a small grunt of satisfaction emerging.

"You enjoy inflicting pain?" Varna asked, as she tried to find an entry to his aura, some way to make a change, like she had been able to do with the far simpler birds and animals. But they were clean and clear, simple creatures who were not good or evil, but just living in the wilds and surviving the best they could. She suddenly realised that this man may truly be evil.

"Your pain makes me feel alive," Ortas panted, striking once again with the quirt quickly to each breast. "Often did I tell Leortas that the only way to deal with your kind is to make you suffer, and then suffer again. Only then can we take our own pleasure as well as make Likki pleased." He tittered, a brittle high-pitched sound that horrified Varna through the waves of pain.

"So," she gasped through her pain, "it *is* about your own twisted pleasure more than Likki. But you can stop. I can help you to stop."

"Yes, alright then," he shouted, losing a measure of control as his own excitement mounted, "I enjoy it. I love to feel the waves of pain and despair. I revel in your kind's desperation as you suffer. I have mastered many ways of making you suffer, and you will taste of them all. Why should I stop? Who is there to stop me here? You? You are a woman only. You do not have the men with you who attacked our ceremony of cleansing. Your death will release me for a time." He lifted the quirt and struck again and again, raising welts on Varna's naked skin. He deliberately worked the quirt up and down her torso.

Varna was aghast, in agony from the torture being handed out as well as her inability to find any way to make a change to this man's aura. He was experiencing pleasure that was almost sexual in its nature, as he increased the rate of striking, the leather strips adding to the pain.

Finally, he stopped, breathing heavily and gasping small, inarticulate sounds. In fact, she realised, it *was* sexual release. Varna forced herself to breathe through her pain, to regain as much control as she could. She had suffered torture before, but never for this purpose, although Wensor had wanted to cause her pain and suffering. Her certainty, built up unconsciously over years of guilt and brought into focus by Eresh recently, was that people were not intrinsically evil and that, somehow, she had caused the men who attacked and killed her mother to go further than they meant. Now that certainty broke down. Balgor had told her that there truly were evil beings, and that message had been reinforced by the other Guardians and resisted by Varna. Ortas' aura was swirling, blacks and greys moving continuously but in an ordered pattern. She realised that he appeared deranged but that, even in his pain-pleasure passion, he continued to act to a plan, to his own twisted version of logic. This was not someone she could reach!

Ortas dropped the quirt and reached back to the array of torture instruments. He lifted a knife, with a wicked curved blade as long as his forearm, and brandished it. His eyes were slightly wild as he balanced the knife in one hand, experimentally swiping it back and forth and then practising stabbing motions. Varna tried once again, although she was sure now that it was useless.

"Ortas, you can still let me go and I will help you. I will help you to give up this evil. Please," she pleaded, tears running down her face, "I have too much to do to help to save Ennaris from Goroth and the ghazrak. You must stop."

He only smiled, pityingly, as he worked through his practice again. "You think I believe all of that? There is no Goroth and never was. All of those myths were merely means of control. The priests of Likki are not fools. We know it is we who control our fates and not the Guardians." He chuckled, back to a chilling state of calm after the sexual frenzy of the beating. He showed her the long, curved knife. "This is a *bantura*, the ceremonial knife of the jungle tribes. With this they would cut out the hearts of their enemies and eat them, before consuming their enemies' flesh. The priests brought back the ceremony for our followers, but of course we sought out foul women for our sacrifices. And we have improved it.

"First, I will cut off your breasts, foul objects of desire that lead men astray. Then I will cut through to your heart and remove it, and you will live long enough to see it beating in my hand." He closed his eyes as a wave of rapture swept through him. "And then you die, and I will consume your offering to Likki."

Varna's revulsion was almost physical. She struggled to remain calm, but then she recalled again Balgor telling her that evil did exist and that she was destined to confront it in all of its forms. Here she was presented with proof that he and the others were right. She could not help those who preferred their evil. She allowed the combination of rage and fear to sweep through her. The rage came from finding that she could not affect change in this person. The fear was less of dying but more of not playing her part in the battle she knew to be coming, of failing in her duty. The struggle had consumed her, she now realised, and had held her back, but if she was to be the one who was needed, she had to accept that she could not reach everyone. There was one final attempt to reach Ortas.

"Ortas, give up and let me help you," she said once last time. "You will not defeat me. I am Dharmoney!" She struggled to hold out one bound hand toward Ortas.

"No, you are not. You cannot be. Dharmoney is a myth, nothing more." Ortas was shouting, fear and panic running through him. "I am the priest of Likki, the last priest of Likki. My Guardian will come and save me."

And Varna's final block shattered. With a thought her bindings fell away and she stepped from the frame to which Ortas had bound her. Ortas stared, convinced that his eyes were playing tricks.

"No, she will not," Varna said, in a voice of deep sorrow, "for you are not worthy of her love and attention. It was Likki who drove you from the jungle, it was Likki who banished you from her sight forever." Varna, Dharmoney-to-come, did not know how she knew that, but know it she did.

Ortas snatched up a second long knife and, with an inarticulate cry, leapt at the naked woman in front of him, seeking to stab her and cut her at the same time. His eyes were wide. Spittle leaked from one corner of his mouth. Dharmoney-to-come stood perfectly still, arm extended. A single shaft of white, brilliant light shot from the palm of her hand. That hand had been extended a moment before to save Ortas but now it was used to destroy him. Ortas ... ceased to be.

It was a few heartbeats before Varna lowered her arm. A sound in the end of the room where the door now stood open caused her to turn her head. Clay stood perfectly still, staring at the tableau.

Dharmoney-to-come looked back, at ease at being naked under his gaze. Clay walked carefully across the room, picking up Varna's clothes from the pile where Ortas had dropped them, and handed them to her.

"Varna," he said with a shallow bow. "Let us leave here."

With a shudder, Varna drooped and would have fallen had Clay not stepped in to hold her upright, clasping her lightly around her waist. A moment later she nodded and he released his hold. As she dressed, Clay turned to look around the cabin, eyes narrowing as he took note of the instruments of torture, the stains on the floor, the framework that had held Varna in place. He had seen the welts up and down her body, across her chest. She winced as she drew on her breeches but when he started forward held him off with a brief smile and shake of her head. The two walked to the door where Clay had left both packs and left the cabin.

Varna stopped to look back at the cabin in the centre of a small field.

"This cannot happen again," she said to Clay. "No-one can make use of this place."

Once again, she lifted her hand and a ball of Mage fire erupted, held in place by her will. With a thought, she threw the Mage fire into the cabin. The rack of torture instruments was destroyed first. All knives, swords, needles and pincers, as well as the whips, chains and quirts, and other tools of the twisted behaviours of the priests, were destroyed, followed by the cabin as a whole. Within moments, the Mage fire consumed it entirely, leaving a pile of embers glowing and smoking in the field.

Without a backward glance Varna led the way from the field. They had somewhere to be.

# 25. Reunion

It was a further two tendays of hard travel, pushing himself through the wilderness, using his gifts to locate protection and sustenance. Water was hard to find and, on several occasions, he resorted to tapping the underground water sources, even though they took great energy. It was not one of his primary gifts, after all, and so he had to exert much more effort than he would have otherwise. He continued on his way, weaving through the parched, dusty and wind-swept land, heading for he knew not what but knowing it was in this direction. He knew what it *had* been, but not what to expect now.

He was unsure if it was wise to leave the homesteader alive, but Goroth did not believe himself to be a murderer, although many things he had done had led to death and destruction. He was shocked at the state of Ennaris, and shocked even more that the Mages and Guardians had allowed things to become as bad as they did. Although he thought back to conversations he had with the homesteader. The Guardians were said to have returned, which indicated that they had been away. Perhaps the Guardians had been banished from Ennaris for some reason. Was that in the Prophecy? He would have to check it. The Prophecy was not something he had first-hand knowledge of, for it had been discovered in the last days of the rebellion, and then he was in stasis. For some time, he had been able to sense the world as the stasis slowly failed under his assault, although he had no real sense of time passing. Thousands of cycles had passed! He found that to be astounding and unsettling. Moreover, his memories of the land were as though they were yesterday not thousands of cycles ago.

So, Ennaris had not been guided by the Guardians for a very long time, and they had mythical status. That left the Guides and Mages. From the same conversations he gathered that they had the same mythical status. Which meant there were very few of them left, or for some reason they had withdrawn also. And they had returned around the same time his stasis prison failed or more likely slightly before. Coincidence? He did not believe in coincidences. No, this may be part of a grander strategy somewhere. More likely, though, an alarm of some nature had told of his imprisonment coming to an end, and so the Mages had come out of hiding. He would have to understand that much more.

He was a tenday into his journey from the homestead when he saw a glittering object fall through the atmosphere and speed far overhead in the same general direction as he was making. Likud? He hoped so. So, technology was not dead. Why then had civilisation moved backward so far? The state of the homestead, and the fortunes of the home-steader, had been far removed from what his memories told him should be there. Those memories were, after all, only a few tendays old after having been locked in stasis for such a time. The land through which he moved had been lush and green, bearing many varied fruits and plants, tended by the people with their Guides and machines. None of the weapon discharges had impacted on this region, which was one reason why he had selected it for his base - there were no cities of note in this region, although there had been multiple settlements from the ice down through this fertile land and across the grasslands further south. His rare touches of Ennaris from behind the stasis curtain had not prepared him for this grim reality.

The homesteader had mentioned ghazrak! So Grensor remained, perhaps, or one or more of his students. Grensor, the sometime re-luctant rebel, but one whose love of experimenting and whose drive to discover new knowledge had pushed him beyond the cares and concerns about ethics, and thus he was ripe to fall under Goroth's influence. Grensor had been with him on Andoreth and had assisted him to lift the intelligences that had been found there many cycles earlier from a simple life-form to a useful tool. His work had been instrumental in developing the course of that civilisation, and Goroth had seized on his disillusionment with the Council to win over his skills. The ghazrak of the rebellion had been a blunt instrument, nothing more than a force of shock troops, but it had taken many resources to defeat them, which was the point. Vicious, single-minded, deadly, but with no internal volition or ambition, it had been a triumph of science. Aided, of course, by Goroth's uses of the dark arts, skills that he had passed onto Grensor and Likud as his trusted lieutenants, although the latter showed little skills in that regard. It would be interesting to see what had become of both. Seeing as the land was not over-run by ghazrak he assumed that Grensor had not continued his work unabated, which was probably just as well. After all, the intention was not to destroy the planet when they started, but to rid themselves of the limitations placed on them by the small-minded, fearful members of the Council of Mages.

He could feel himself becoming angry, for that time was still recent to his memory, and his fury mounted as he continued to trudge through the wilderness. He had succeeded in his efforts to break down his prison walls. He was out of stasis and prepared to start afresh. And this time, the outcome would be different.

Grensor and Likud had reunited like the old colleagues they were. Each was suspicious of the other, disinclined towards great trust, and wary of both intent and capability. Grensor was old in look and manner, but Likud was not fooled by that. His old sparring partner could wield the white and black arts with skill, and even with the passing of time he was not about to make the mistake of believing that those skills were gone. Especially with the newer generation of ghazrak that appeared to have both a sharper edge to them, literally in the case of the wings of the airborne creatures, and some small amount of tactical intelligence. They appeared to be devoted to Grensor, which was another consideration. Likud was not sure if he expected more than that or not.

Grensor, on the other hand, dealt with Likud in a seemingly open manner, showing him around the base that had changed significantly from what they had built prior to the rebellion. The indirect effects of the rebellion had resulted in this whole region being decimated. Grensor's old laboratories and workshops, with the highly toxic materials he used in his work, had added their own destructive layers to the region, including seeping into most of the water sources. Much of the land had died.

The former rebel base had suffered similarly and had been rebuilt only partially from what materials were available. The formerly beautiful landscape now was a blasted wilderness and only the vicious survived, which Grensor thought was somehow poetic, given the cause. He had watched as Likud tried and failed to come to grips with the state of Ennaris.

Grensor described the extent of the destruction that had been caused during their frequent discussions. The extent of the changes they had wrought by their indiscriminate use of the advanced weaponry on the planet and from space stunned Likud. He had never had much imagination, and his skills were more useful for destruction, anyway, but even he struggled to make sense of what had occurred. At the same time, however, he started to imagine how he could rain down similar terror on his current enemies, the Union. He was interested in the effects of the weaponry, for he had not really seen it in action. Certainly, the long-term effects had been hidden from him after he fled the scene of the battle where Goroth had been subdued and captured. He was impressed! *Qorv* could do that to Union worlds, he thought pensively as he took in the environmental devastation that now surrounded him.

Likud told of how he had built his empire following his flight from Ennaris, leveraging his god-like status on that world. He had continued his own experiments with the Andorethi from time to time but his skills were never those of Grensor, and most of those experiments had failed, often disastrously. One thing his manipulations and policies had produced, though, was a race of beings with disturbingly little ability to think for themselves, with a small number of exceptions that were useful up to a point, but distasteful beyond that point.

The old rebel Mage - Grensor's regrets formed again and were stamped down, ruthlessly he liked to imagine - could understand why his erstwhile fellow rebel had failed in his attempts to manipulate the Andorethi genome effectively, for it took not just science and the arts but some imagination and intuition. Likewise, he was not surprised when Likud complained that his creations lacked the ability to think for themselves - from what he understood from Likud he had effectively bred that trait out of them, with only a few arising every so often. When that happened, most of them were destroyed for fear that they may rise against him. Even his vessel was a poor copy of those of Ennaris at its height, substituting blunt design and brute force for the organic lines, agility and striking prowess for which the Ennarisi vessels had been known.

The northers, brought up on a steady stream of tales, some of them even true, about the rebellion and the key players in it, treated Likud as a form of demigod, which soothed him somewhat. It was, after all, how he had been treated on Andoreth. But the northers were poor substitutes for the sorts of intelligence that Likud recalled from the times of the rebellion. Their culture had been shattered, but Likud saw only failure. When Grensor provided details of the extreme destruction caused by the rebellion, and the numbers who died over the thousands of cycles as the land settled into its new configuration, Likud only saw a people who had failed to hold fast, and in doing so had caused their own destruction.

The two had never been friends. What they had in common was allegiance to Goroth, but for different reasons. Grensor had been protected by Goroth and provided with the means to continue his search for forbidden knowledge. The two Mages had performed great deeds, Grensor thought, before being forced down the path of rebellion. Likud saw Goroth as his battle leader, one who valued Likud's natural gifts and who had encouraged him in his exercise of those gifts. Each saw his role to be Goroth's second. Each saw the other as a rival for that role.

Therefore, for the tenday after Likud arrived the two maintained a form of stand-off. Both knew that Goroth had been freed and were content to await his arrival.

After two tendays of trudging through the wilderness Goroth felt that he must be close to the location of their old base. True, for him it had been but a few tendays since being there, but the changes to the landscape in the actual time that had passed rendered it difficult to be sure. And, of course, he had been using shuttles then rather than walking, and the shape of the land was less important when dropping at high speed through the atmosphere. Still, the shape of the large bowl was familiar, along with the small hills that covered the floor of the bowl, even if the lush vegetation of memory was gone. He stood on the rim of the surrounding ridge long enough for someone to see him, if there were anyone to see, and then commenced the descent from ridge to floor.

It was when he reached the floor of the bowl that he finally had evidence of life. As he passed a scrubby bush a short, scrawny man dressed in ragged grey clothes jumped out brandishing a poorly made spear at him and yelling something unintelligible. Goroth stopped and waited, and the man repeated his challenge.

"Stop wa'r y'ar an' drop, ya' me bait now," he said, holding the spear such that its point was pointed in Goroth's direction but wavered from side to side. The man obviously was drunk.

Goroth stared at his challenger, who joined his spear in weaving from side to side, suddenly overbalancing completely and dropping his spear as he keeled over. The scrawny man was asleep almost immediately. Goroth pursed his lips and shook his head, hoping this was not an example of his army. He recommenced his approach to the camp that he could now see. A series of low buildings occupied the space between three low hills. He knew that the main base was underground, but the state of the camp matched what he had seen of Ennaris so far.

His next challenge came as he was half-way across the floor of the bowl. This one was more serious, and Goroth found himself surrounded by a troop of ten ghazrak, spears held level and rock steady. Goroth stood still, watchful but calm.

"Who you?" one of the ghazrak grunted, who Goroth assumed must be the squad leader from the fact that he had some sort of armband of a ragged green colour, where the others did not.

"I am Goroth," he said quietly.

The lead ghazrak snarled, a feral animal sound. "Goroth great leader," he said, looking Goroth up and down. "You no look great."

Goroth regarded the ghazrak team leader for a moment, turning slightly to make eye contact with several others, all suspicious and obviously ready to kill him. He smiled grimly.

"You want proof, do you?" he said, quietly and evenly.

A flare of black erupted from Goroth's forehead, revealing for a moment the damaged black stone suspended there, and the lead Ghazrak was nothing but a pile of rags and poorly made weapons. Goroth stood still, feeling the effects of using that particular war-gift. He remained undernourished, even though the homesteader had shared his food with him, and the energy drain was more than he expected. But he held himself tall and straight, although not nearly as tall as the ghazrak.

With a moan, the ghazrak dropped their spears and knelt as one, intoning "Endara" repeatedly, "Master" in the ancient tongue of the summonsed ones. Goroth allowed several repetitions before he stepped from among the ghazrak and continued to walk. He walked carefully now to make sure that none of his sudden weakness showed. The ghazrak regained their feet and followed him, making a ragged group. Others joined them, seemingly from nowhere, and each was told a single word as they challenged - "Endara". Goroth's odd entourage grew as he approached the buildings and the ghazrak started to chant "Endara" as they followed. By the time he reached the first of the low buildings - shacks in reality - the chant had become a guttural roar from the throats of over a thousand ghazrak, with more streaming from holes in the hills to join in.

The door of the middle shack was flung open and Grensor walked out, slightly unsteady in his begrimed robe, followed by Likud dressed in shiny black leather knee boots, black breeches and black shirt. The three rebels stopped a short distance apart and stared at each other for a moment. Finally, Grensor stepped forward and held out his right arm, which Goroth gripped tightly and released. Likud followed suit.

"I had expected you some time ago," Grensor said, his voice gravelly, before turning to the ghazrak and shouting, "Stop that! Endara will need rest and then will come around."

The chanting died and the ghazrak turned away, melting away as fast as they had arrived. The few northers who had joined them shrugged and wandered off also.

Goroth watched and shrugged. "I had no form of transport from where I found myself," he said. "When I finally made the stasis let go, I was transported to the edge of some sort of wilderness, without any real way to orient myself. This is not the Ennaris I recall."

"No," growled Grensor, "but this is the Ennaris we made." He waved an arm around. "We wondered what the effect of those energy weapons would be on a planet. Well, we found out. Look around you!"

Likud gestured to the shack. "Let's go in. It's no use standing out here. We'll just get more parched, and you look like you need to rest."

"Yes, I need to gather my strength once again. And you can bring me up to date with what has happened over - how long?"

"Five thousand cycles," Grensor said bitterly. "It has been five thousand cycles since the rebellion was defeated."

"Five thousand cycles," Goroth repeated in wonder at confirmation of that duration. "Yes, I need to be brought up to date."

Three days later Goroth felt that he had a better picture. Grensor had described the horrors faced by the people of Ennaris, some in considerable detail, caused by the results of the use of space-borne energy weapons and the attempts to block those uses. Goroth mourned for the civilisation that was lost, for the people that were destroyed, and the suffering that was engendered, but he refused to take all responsibility. Likud, who had always been more confident in his weapons skills than may have been supported by the facts, was in no doubt that he had not made any sort of error in his weapon settings. He declared that the destruction that ensued was caused by Marjory and her blocks. For Likud, as much as Goroth, this was the first time seeing the state of Ennaris. Unlike Goroth, Likud had flown over part of the planet, and he described the inland sea that was where the main cities had once been.

That, of course, had been where he had deployed the planetary energy weapons, and supplemented them by a bombardment from the orbiting warship they had commandeered. While Likud was absolutely convinced that his calibrations were correct, Goroth had his doubts. He clearly recalled the multiple weapons discharging, blanketing the small target area, but because of his combination of gifts he also was aware of the energy leaking through the layers of the planetary crust. However, he had been concentrating on negating Marjory's efforts to destroy the war machines, barely fending off such concentrated waves of destructive potential that he never thought any one person could wield. He only had to close his eyes to see once again the magnificent sight - he was honest enough to acknowledge that - of Marjory floating above the target area by force of will. She was the only Battle Mage to master wielding her gift whilst levitating. While doing so, she held a shield in place against the impacts of the weapons, hair streaming out behind her from the wind generated by the interplay of forces that were never meant to come together, and then pushed back. Goroth had been confident that he had her in stalemate, and the result would then have been undoubted as the secondary weapons would produce the desired result, but he had known fear as she pushed back, expanding her shields and then starting to throw bolts of Mage fire into the weapons teams.

But it was when she meshed with the second order Mages and drew on their powers that she changed the battle. The extra energy allowed her to destroy the secondary weapons platforms, although Goroth was sure it resulted in the deaths of a number of second order Mages. The main weapons were having an effect still, of course, but still she held. Goroth was a student of Ennaris' military history and had examined the records of the few Mages who had been acclaimed as great Battle Mages. None of them stood against Marjory for strength and skill, from what he saw that day. And then Marjory was joined by Drewflin, without doubt the most powerful of the Mages Ennaris had seen, but one whose gifts were for creation not destruction. However, Marjory had been able to meld their disparate natures. And combined they could not be withstood. But now Marjory was gone, although Grensor did not know how, and so the threat was diminished. The remaining Mages were few and of lower order skills when it came to battle. Drewflin remained and was Archmage now, and the twins and Trabor were not weak, but nor were any of them battle trained. So Goroth was more confident that there would be no repeat.

He had taken a look at what Grensor had done with the newest batch of ghazrak. They were still all male - for some reason, Grensor had never been able to make the changes work on women - and their propensities for violence were barely tempered by new constraints put on them by Grensor. It was the less restrained ones that Grensor had released to cause mayhem amongst the Ennarisi. Most appeared to have been killed, although Grensor thought there remained several troops at large. It was the more disciplined form that he had sent to attack Escar with a small part of the norther army. Goroth growled to himself at that. Attacking Escar had been a mistake and using the winged ghazrak in that battle had been a larger mistake. Drewflin was aware now of what he faced, and would know that there would be many more to deal with when the final battle began. So, his opponents were alerted to their dangers.

Then there were the Children of Ennaris and what Grensor called the 'Golden warrior'. Goroth snorted. He had never been a true believer in all of the Ennarisi legends. The idea of a magical suit of armour amused him but he dismissed it. It would be easy enough to manufacture close-fitting armour and give it a golden glow. That they used armour at all was amusing although, without the advanced weapons of Ennaris at the time of the rebellion, good armour could be quite effective against those weapons that were now available. Of course, it could even be that they had discovered someone with one of the old gifts which, if Grensor's spies were correct, had started to re-appear. Some of those gifts were cosmetic and could easily have been used to make metal armour shine like gold. The old personal shields were more efficient and far more effective but they were lacking now after the block against any advanced technology. And that had held for five thousand cycles!

Once again, Goroth felt that jarring sense of dislocation between the world he had last seen only a few tendays ago in his own reckoning and the current state. During the stasis, he had been able to make out some small events, and somehow Likud had managed to work through the bindings to reach his consciousness using some form of gift of the Andorethi. But the sense of extensive time passing had not been part of the experience. So many of the plans that he had half-made in that peculiar greyness of mind were dashed because of the technology block. He had visited the old weapons store beneath Grensor's compound only to find that the components had deteriorated over the thousands of cycles, which made the ghazrak all the more important.

Likud did not feel that they would miss those weapons. He had, he believed, the most powerful fleet in the galaxy, and it was facing off against the Union fleet overhead. The latter were from Ordoreth, which seemed to have made great leaps in the technology of space travel and weaponry in recent times. Likud did not believe they would be much of an obstacle. Once that was dealt with, he believed, those weapons could be turned on the planet if necessary. Goroth remained slightly unsure of the grip that Likud had on sanity, but he had been a faithful lieutenant for a very long time and had caused the Andorethi to advance and take their place amongst the powers of the galaxy successfully. Still, he remained all too prepared to risk destroying Ennaris entirely, as he had been willing to do during the rebellion. Goroth made another mental note to remain aware of Likud.

There remained much to do and his plans had taken a change of direction after coming to grips with the state of Ennaris, but Goroth was pleased with the situation. He had an army of ghazrak to build further - and to destroy later, he had to remember, for they would cause greater problems once he had won Ennaris. His primary opponents had been decimated of their key talents. The block on technology meant that the Faero and his allies were unable to maintain their store of weapons either, and most of them had been destroyed anyway. And, he was assured by Grensor, an army was being raised in the east that would join that of the northern kingdoms. All told, he was in a good position, he thought. His own gifts were ... recharging ... and he needed more rest before he would be ready to face Drewflin and his few Mages, but that would not take longer than the building of the army. And for that he had plenty of northers available. Grensor had managed to get some of the cloning equipment to work again, somehow getting past the blockage using gifted northers for power, but lately some old power sources had regenerated. The technology block had been lifted, and perhaps some of the old weapons could be made to function again, and he had the time to see to that possibility.

Goroth smiled to himself. His nascent plan had been to spend several cycles to rebuild a power base. Plans had to be flexible, he knew, and the circumstances he found demanded a lot of flexibility. A little more time, he thought, just a little more time and he would finish what he started.

# 26. Marjory Summoned

On the bridge of *Starfire,* all was quiet. The senior staff were sitting in their command chairs watching the status board as the enemy fleet stood off. The newcomers floated in space with the bloodied and battered survivors of the original Empire fleet.

Rork straightened sharply in his console chair.

"Sir," he called urgently. "Incoming energy bolt from the planet."

"Where, Mr Rork?" Jord asked quietly, glancing at both Bard and Serra to see reactions. Admiral Bard was watching the monitor intently as the streak that was rising from the planet now showed a trace directed straight at *Starfire.* "Sound battle stations, please, Mr Rork. Colonel Kiri to the bridge, please."

"No, belay battle stations, Captain," said Serra, standing and moving towards the large main screen, watching the streak slow and become a ball of energy, continuing to move toward *Starfire* slowly but surely.

Kiri hustled onto the bridge and stood, baffled, as she saw little activity despite the urgent summons she had received. She moved to her command station, noted the ship was at the now normal heightened alert posture but no more than that and relaxed slightly.

The energy ball approached the ship and disappeared from the screen.

"No matter what happens from now," Serra said crisply so the entire bridge staff could hear, "no one interferes. No matter what!" she repeated.

Bard and Jord shared a glance, neither fully understanding what was occurring, but both trusted in the Grand Admiral implicitly. Kiri shot a quizzical look at Rork, who shrugged and turned back towards Serra.

In the middle of the bridge a coruscating twist of bright lights appeared, spinning and weaving. Individual lights darted across the bridge to hover over or in front of each member of the team, then spun back to the centre where the lights slowly merged to form a ball of bright light, too bright for any but Serra to watch. Brighter still it became until, with a flash the light was extinguished and, in its place, stood a being, wreathed in a glowing golden nimbus. Of human or Ennarisi appearance, he stood tall and imperious while all regarded him with awe, including Serra, but for her own reasons.

"Halfgar!" she breathed, ignoring all else and staring at the figure who had appeared.

The nimbus winked out and Halfgar grinned.

"Hello, my child. You're looking well." He smiled genially.

"I saw you die. I watched your life fade out," Serra said brokenly, tears appearing and slowly running unheeded down her cheeks. "How is this possible?"

"You saw what you saw, child," said Halfgar gently. "But we Guardians are a little hard to kill like that, although we did lose some. It takes somewhat more for that to happen. But I had accomplished all I could at that time. I felt that I had to leave you to handle the next part yourselves."

"You're a Guardian?" she was incredulous. "All that time?"

He nodded, smiling again. "I am Odruf," he said quietly.

Serra slowly folded herself to one knee, head bowed. The cabin crew stared as their Grand Admiral offered her obeisance to this strange man, but they did not move to follow, frozen as they were.

"Arise my child," said Odruf softly. "You never need to treat us as gods. You never did need to."

Serra stood upright once more, still staring at Odruf as though entranced. She shook herself, mentally and physically, the action acting as a release. Now she smiled through the tears that continued to run down her face.

"So, what brings you here?" she asked. "Something to do with two fleets crowding space hereabouts, I imagine."

"Oh, your crew seems to be able to handle them, from what I could see. No, I came for you." He paused, and a grin of anticipation tugged at the corners of his mouth. "It's time for you to return to Ennaris and take up the battle once again."

Serra frowned. "Has the situation deteriorated badly?" she asked worriedly.

"The situation is where it needs to be," said Odruf mysteriously. "The Three have returned and the Champion has been found. The final battle is at hand. The Guardians cannot take an active role, although we will limit the field of battle. This is for the Ennarisi to determine. Goroth is regaining his strength and the Archmage prepares to do battle with him."

"Drewflin is planning on fighting Goroth? He'll be annihilated!" Serra gasped. "How much time do I have?"

"Very little, I'm afraid. Already the armies have fought the initial skirmishes. They have not yet reached the final ground, though."

Serra turned to look around the bridge. She took in the stunned expressions of her crew, the worry etching frowns on both Bard and Jord, neither of whom understood why but both realising that she was leaving them.

"Denton, Jord, it seems I must go, at least for a while. You will hold that fleet off, if you please. And if they make a move, take them out!"

Bard nodded briefly. "Yes, Admiral. We are, however, lacking in the defence part, if you remember. Two-thirds of our fighters were lost when *Nova* and *Quasar* had their hangar bays targeted and heavily damaged."

"Yes, but you just do what you can."

Odruf interjected mildly. "Not that I am interfering, you understand," he said, "but the interdiction against technology on the moon base has been lifted." He glanced innocently at Serra.

"When did that happen?" Serra asked suspiciously.

"A very short time ago," Odruf responded blandly.

"That whole thing about causing technology to fail was you? You made sure Ennaris' technology could not be used? Why?" Serra was becoming incensed. "We needed those technological capabilities. People were dying."

"No, you did not need them, and you needed to have this time without them for Ennaris to regenerate. Had we not halted your use of technology you would have destroyed the remaining parts of Ennaris, and that we could not have. That we *could* stop."

Serra swallowed her anger and nodded shortly, bringing her roiling emotions under control with an effort. "Very well. I will need time to arrange that."

"You have not the time." Odruf turned to Bard. "Admiral Bard, you will find coordinates have been entered to your computer. At that location you will find replacements for your damaged warships, including one that will require a command crew. You should find the controls somewhat familiar." He smiled wryly at Serra.

"Well, when I designed them, I had to use something to guide me, so I used the stingers as a template." She paused and her lips twisted. "Okay, so I stole the design entirely. But Denton," and she turned to Bard, "warn the crews that these ships are much more powerful and manoeuvrable than the ones they're accustomed to. And the control systems are far more advanced."

"Admiral," Bard said mildly, "the design for our fighters is over three hundred years old. And you designed them?"

"I did, yes." Serra smiled and she turned to Odruf. "A couple of other things. Computer, register battle-field promotions. High Admiral Denton Bard, Fleet Admiral Blair Jord, effective immediately."

Both stared at her, then nodded in recognition of the honour.

"Don't thank me too much. Denton, that makes you ranking Admiral of the fleet. Use the rank well, my friend."

"Until you get back, Admiral," Bard stated.

"Oh, I think I'm about to retire. I've done what I needed to do, and it seems I'm called back. One last thing that may help. *Fendaristil*," the Admiral said.

"Awaiting orders, Battle Mage," the voice of *Fendaristil* replied.

"Clear to launch, weapons free."

"All weapons, Battle Mage?"

"All weapons," Serra confirmed. "Take control of all nearstations."

"Confirmed all weapons free," *Fendaristil* replied. "Activating nearstations. Designating targets. Nearstations report online. Nearstation Six reports tracking established. Fire control solutions are online. *Fendaristil* launching. Battle Mage, may the hunting be good and the enemy worthy."

"And the victory sweet," Serra replied to the ritual warrior farewell.

The stunned crew just watched and took it all in. On the main screen a new series of icons popped up as Ennaris' nearstations dropped their cloaks and made their presence known. Ennaris' home system came alive with signals. Rork just shook his head as the changes were registered.

"The nearstations are local to Ennaris," Serra explained. "The farstations are scattered throughout the space that Ennaris once claimed. Escantil Control!"

"Escantil Control online," a fresh voice replied.

"Designate Ordorethi craft to be Ennaris allies. Designate Andorethi craft as hostile. All farstations are weapons free on my authority."

"Instructions sent, Battle Mage. Farstation 351 reports a battle fought between Andorethi and Ordorethi fleets in sector one-nine-four. The Andorethi fleet was destroyed with two vessels escaping. The Ordorethi fleet sustained losses or damage to almost one-third of its vessels. The remaining vessels are on course towards Ennaris."

"Understood," Serra replied.

"*Fendaristil* is not just an Admiral's private vessel, then?" Bard asked mildly.

"*Fendaristil* was the first of a new generation of pocket destroyers. He is the only complete vessel of the class to date," Serra explained. "He will do what is needed when it is needed."

She smiled and the smile took in the entire bridge crew.

"I have enjoyed the last few centuries," she said wistfully. "Okay Halfgar, do your worst."

"Oh, not that bad, I think. But you can't go like that. You need to change back." And he negligently waved a hand.

Serra was enveloped in the golden nimbus which faded after a few seconds. The bridge crew stared. In the place of the Grand Admiral stood a taller, imperious looking woman, slimmer than Serra, fuller of figure, clothed in rich black breeches of an unknown material with a close-fitting black shirt, black leather boots burnished to gleam in the artificial light and a short cape of the same material as the breeches, trimmed in a deep red. Her hair was brushed back and gleamed as it fell down her back, and a chain of gold encircled the top of her head such that a brilliant deep silver jewel sat in the centre of her forehead. A ripple of awe ran through the watching crew.

"Behold," Odruf intoned quietly, "the greatest Battle Mage of Ennaris. Marjory, who fought and defeated Goroth and his minions, who led the defence of Ennaris for the long cycles - years to you."

He nodded once more as he looked around the bridge. "You and your forebears have been honoured by the aid of one of the greatest of the galaxy. And now it is time to depart, for Ennaris has need of her leaders."

The brilliant light flared once more and when it cleared Odruf and Serra - Marjory - were gone.

Bard stared at the spot for a few more seconds then sighed.

"Well, I knew she was special but that was a little more than I could have imagined. Okay," he glanced around, "is everyone good?"

Nods all around.

"Good. Mr Rork, are those coordinates on your screen?"

"Yes, Admiral," Rork replied. "I've alerted the *Nova* and *Quasar* to get their crews over here on shuttles, those that were not here already. I've alerted the fighter commander to prepare for escorts of both to the moon. The course is plotted already - not my doing - and the moon now shows on our scans." He shook his head. "One man could do all of that? He could stop the technology from working, block ours? Amazing!"

"Not a man in our usual definition, I think," said Bard reflectively. "Well done, Mr Rork. Let me know when the shuttles are on their way. Keep an eye out for that approaching fleet. Colonel Kiri, battle stations, if you please."

The fleet prepared for battle.

## 27. Andira

Tu-pol deposited Flin at the entrance to the Council Chamber. He thanked the great bird and bade him to wait for his return. On receiving Tu-pol's assent, he strode towards the cliff face, the hidden entrance appearing as he approached, and then disappearing again after he entered.

The Chamber was ablaze with light. All the monitors were active, showing different parts of Ennaris with a full range of details, from the topographical display that Jalor had viewed to a deeper geophysical scan and a composite display showing the weather in different parts of the planet. Another monitor showed the portals, colour coded to show which were still active. Finally, a monitor concentrated on the hazy, feature-less area north of the steppes, where sensors were lacking and portals did not operate. Flin paused to regard this monitor and frowned.

"Who requested this view?" he asked the room.

"I did," a voice replied as a man walked into the room, followed tentatively by a young woman. He was above middle height, with fine features and hands that showed signs of hard work. His garb of utilitarian breeches, a loose linen shirt and soft leather boots was complemented by a dark brown cloak, edged in deep purple. Short sandy hair was held back by a band of silver-coloured metal, with a purple stone blazing in the centre of his forehead. The woman wore similar breeches and a red blouse, laced up at the front but hanging loose. Her feet were clad in soft moccasins. Her long dark brown hair hung loose below her shoulders, and she looked nervous.

"Trabor!" Flin said. "I was wondering where you were."

"Archmage," Trabor said, with a grin and a slight bow. "It's good to have that finalised. This is Andira. I found her in the south and asked her to join me."

"Andira," Flin acknowledged, smiling to the young woman. "You must be special for Trabor to bring you to this place." He arched an eyebrow towards Trabor, who smiled and nodded.

"Andira, this is Archmage Drewflin, head of the Council of Mages since the rebellion."

Andira bowed awkwardly, eyes wide, her face showing her surprise at finding herself in the presence of the Archmage. She trembled visibly.

"Please, you have no need to fear or to be nervous here, child," Flin said in his most soothing voice.

"Ah, well," Trabor said, "you need to understand that where Andira comes from Grensor has had Tellers visit for a while. So, the people there seem to think that you eat people with gifts, so that your own powers grow." Trabor stood and watched as Flin's countenance changed from peaceful intent to thunder and outrage.

"What?" he said shortly. "And they believe that rubbish?"

"Well, when that's what you're taught for the last two hundred or so cycles, I guess it sinks in. Luckily Andira had heard the stories from when the twins were down that way some time ago, so she was fairly sure that Grensor's Tellers were false." Trabor paused, staring at Flin meaningfully. "Archmage, Andira is more than three hundred cycles old."

Flin's face lost the thunder and was wreathed in smiles. "Over three hundred? But that's wonderful!" He turned to the woman.

"She had to keep moving from place to place so her continued youth didn't cause problems," Trabor added. "From my initial tests I think Andira may be one of yours as a secondary gift. Plants seem to like her."

Flin nodded, his smile broadening. "You like plants?" he asked. "And you are able to make them bloom, or help trees to heal?"

"Sometimes," Andira said quietly. "At other times I can see where the land is damaged and make it better. But there are times when I'm unable to see or do anything of use."

"That happens, especially when you come into your gifts without assistance, as you have done," Flin replied, nodding. "I think we can help you to understand your gifts better. Once we get past Goroth and his friends, I know someone who I think will enjoy spending some time with you."

"Goroth and friends?" Trabor queried.

"Goroth walks Ennaris once again, Trabor, and I suspect he has joined with Grensor in the northern wastes."

"The sensors tracked a shuttle of some sort coming through the atmosphere. It was lost in the same area." Trabor nodded towards the monitors. "That was a few days ago now."

"That may be Likud," Flin said. "From what Jalor and Blaine told me he's been ruling the planet of Andoreth since fleeing Ennaris after the rebellion. I would expect him to return when Goroth broke free from the stasis in which he was bound."

"So, we have Goroth, Grensor and Likud back together. We always thought that it must have been Grensor behind the ghazrak that have been used so far." Trabor nodded to himself. "At least we know Likud has little real imagination, but he was always vicious. I don't doubt that the extreme damage was his doing rather than Goroth's, although we can't be completely certain."

"And we faced winged ghazrak at Escar," Flin told Tabor. "Huge creatures with armour and razor-sharp wing edges. Be wary if you ever encounter one."

"My gifts don't exactly extend to fighting ghazrak and succeeding," Trabor remarked. "So, my primary tactic may be to run."

Flin smiled, remembering a young engineering and metalworking Mage standing shoulder to shoulder with Marjory and himself as they fought to hold back the devastating attacks by the rebels, never flinching even though they were badly outmatched and reliant on Marjory's skills and power.

"Be that as it may, and while I have enjoyed meeting you, Andira, I must leave you in Trabor's care for a short while," Flin said, casting a smile to the young woman.

"Before you do, Archmage," Trabor said, "you also need to hear what she just told me. Using her primary gift."

Flin raised an eyebrow and turned to Andira. "Important?"

"I think so, Archmage," she stammered. "I'm feeling strange tremors even though the ground is not shaking. It's as though someone or some-thing is battering at the door of a room and making the walls shake."

Flin raised an eyebrow. "Well, that certainly is odd. But it could be that your own gifts having awakened are causing you to feel odd things."

"I don't believe so, lord," she replied diffidently. "It's happening a long way away."

"A long way away?"

"In that direction," she said, pointing towards one wall.

"In that direction," Flin said flatly, turning to look at Trabor, stand-ing with a self-satisfied grin on his face. "She can feel perturbations from a distance and know the direction."

"Yes, I think sensing demons may be her primary gift," Trabor said smugly.

"And you were planning on telling me, when?"

"Oh, about now," Trabor replied, but his grin faded. "Andira, tell the Archmage how the tremors make you feel."

"Um, well, they feel kind of like some sort of slimy thing is trying to get through the wall. It feels like real evil, but I don't know how to explain it. Like when a bully is trying to make you suffer because you're different, and you just know that if she can get to you really bad things will happen." Andira shrugged slightly. "But I know it's in that direction and it's a long way away. Oh, and I think there's someone trying to help whoever or whatever it is to break through, sort of like trying to lift the bar from the wrong side of the door, and trying over and over again."

Trabor was startled. "That part is new," he said, thinking hard.

He and Flin glanced at each other at the same time, realisation striking both.

"Oh, no," Flin said. "Not now." He wheeled and faced the largest monitor, showing the display of portals. "Assistant, please show the portal gates in an arc of fifteen degrees south-west of the Chamber, all the way to the ocean's edge."

A wedge appeared on the screen. The point of the wedge was the portal located in the lower levels of the Council Chamber. The wedge stretched across nearly half the north continent to the western coast. Caught in the area covered by the wedge were four active portal gates.

"What towns or cities are near the gates covered by the area displayed?" Flin asked.

"There are three towns in that region and the small city of Bamlak," the Assistant replied.

Flin pondered a moment before continuing. "Have the sensors picked up any strange happenings, any odd energy readings, or underground shifts near any of the towns or the city?"

There was a brief pause as the Assistant queried the sensors at each location. Then, the quiet, calm voice of the Assistant said, "Yes, Archmage. Near the town of Bamjur, at sensor location seventy-six, there were several minor spikes of unknown energy, slowly getting stronger but with no risk of damage to the surrounding area."

Flin closed his eyes and cursed softly. "Damn! I must go there. Andira, I'm afraid you will be coming with me. You can trace demons, and I think that is what we will face when we get to Bamjur."

"She can, Flin," Trabor confirmed. "And she'd been to the site after she tracked them."

Flin looked appreciatively at the scared woman.

"Ah," he said. "Brave."

"More demons?" Andira asked Trabor.

"Yes," Flin answered instead of Trabor. "I think the tremors were the demon trying to break through having been summoned by someone who doesn't know what he or she is doing. The energy spikes are caused by that idiot gathering power and trying repeatedly. I need to stop it, and I need you to show me the way when we get there." He turned to Trabor. "While we're gone, would you be able to do a sweep and see whether we have other issues? Anything we need to worry about? We're heading for some form of confrontation and need to know as much as we can."

Trabor merely nodded, then reached out to grip Andira's shoulder. "You will be safe with the Archmage," he said confidently to the young woman, who was visibly trembling at the thought of confronting a demon. "He's the most powerful Mage in Ennaris' history and has fought demons before."

"But not alone," Flin muttered. "Assistant, set the portal to Resgalar and open it when we arrive in the portal chamber, please. Come Andira, we have work to do. Oh, and Trabor, there's a Roc out the front waiting for me. His name is Tu-pol. Would you mind letting him know what is going on? Tell him I will return shortly, please."

Flin resettled his travel pack on his back, having not had the chance to remove it, and strode from the room, followed by an apprehensive Andira, who glanced back to where Trabor stood with a stunned expression.

*A Roc,* Trabor thought to himself, as he forced himself to move. *Where did he get a Roc?*

# 28. Farstation 291

The four Empire heavy cruisers sped on course towards a distant point, as they had been ordered to do by Likud. All ships had been given the order and, of course, all responded immediately. Defined patrols were abandoned. In one case a nascent insurrection in one of the Empire's client systems was allowed to continue. The commander of the heavy cruiser *Nakti* even took on board all Empire soldiers from the system, leaving the insurrection to be handled by the administrative staff.

The four ships had come together near a well-known way point, one of several locations in Empire space where anomalies had been mapped. While they formed navigation hazards, those anomalies proved to be remarkably consistent in their position, as though deliberately positioned. Therefore, they were used as navigation aids, even while being given a wide berth.

The four were under the command of Commander Sertesbritisha, a veteran of the frontier districts. He had earned distinction in several fields of conflict, but he had always wanted to be one who brought aid to Likud. It would, he believed, provide him with great benefits while advancing the goals of the Empire, a cause he believed in deeply. His heavy cruiser, *Prekchu*, was a further cause of pride. He was the first of his sub-clan to command a heavy cruiser.

Sertesbritisha held command of the four vessel fleet by virtue of time on rank, even if his was only slightly greater than Frelistishar, commanding the *Denta*. He relished the opportunity to command near peers, and sent order after order to the other ships, as well as reminders of their duty and what happened to ship commanders and their senior staff if Likud's orders were not followed. This he had learned from an early commander who he had served under and he felt it was highly motivational.

Therefore, the four ships sped on their way as a unit, with *Qrusk* on point, as befitted the most junior commander. They were days away from reaching the coordinates provided to them, even at full light speed, and they were approaching another of the known anomalies, where they would drop to sub-light speed, check and change course, and continue on the next leg.

Farstation 291 was quiescent. It was in its designated position where it could monitor the nearby systems. Farstation 291 was one of the earlier farstations launched, but it had been upgraded many times to maintain its capabilities as the farstation design evolved. It resembled a large cylinder with protruding superstructures holding communication and weapon systems at both ends. Around its centre was a band of hard-points where vessels could dock. No vessels had docked there for many, many cycles.

Several hundred cycles earlier it had followed an order by the Battle Mage, Marjory nar Drewflin, to cloak. The station AI, considering what may cause such an order after such a long time without contact, decided that it indicated a heightened risk status. Working through its procedures, first established four hundred millennia before, it cycled through its defensive and offensive weapons, progressively recycling them and replacing them with the most recent designs available to the station. In doing so it almost exhausted its available materials, but it had ample fuel to perform the tasks.

Farstation 291 had been monitoring four Andorethi vessels moving towards its location at what must be maximum speed. No attempt was being made at stealthy running, for this location was deep inside the Andorethi Empire's boundaries and their commander would feel safe. Farstation 291 monitored a flurry of signals passing between the vessels, allowing it to maintain a close track of their course. It noted its log, as it had done many times before and, as a matter of course, prepared attacking and defensive plans, also as it had done many time before. Half of the missile tubes were loaded but the missiles were not armed. The energy and plasma cannons were partly charged. Defensive systems entered a watch cycle.

The four ships were well outside weapons range but approaching fast when Farstation 291 received a message from Escantil Control, on the authority of the Battle Mage. Andorethi vessels were to be considered hostile. Immediately, even while authenticating the message, Farstation 291 moved to alert status and reworked the targeting solutions for the oncoming ships. With the message authenticated, Farstation 291 directed its weapons systems to load all missile tubes, armed the missiles and rapid-charged the cannons. It calculated an optimal firing solution and waited.

Commander Sertesbritisha leaned back in his commander's harness, satisfied. The fleet was at sub-light speed while navigation officers set the course for the next leg. He had issued his latest round of motivational orders and decided that he would take some sustenance once the small fleet had rounded the anomaly.

Suddenly, alarms blared. Startled, Sertesbritisha fell into his command routine, opening his telepathic senses to receive the flood of information presented by his subordinates. A vessel had de-cloaked near the anomaly. No, not a vessel, it was some sort of space station. Where did it come from? How did it exist so close to the anomaly?

The station was targeting each of the four heavy cruisers. None of them were at ready stations, for they transited safe space and it was well known that nothing could challenge them within their own space. Defensive shields were always available, however, and Sertesbritisha directed them to be raised at full power even as fresh alarms sounded. He ordered battle stations and swung around to view the tactical screen. A shiver of fear passed through him involuntarily as he realised that the station had launched a wave of missiles, and they were much faster than any that the Empire had. As he watched the missiles disappeared only to re-appear much closer moments later. The missiles had micro-jumped! Energy weapons at both ends of the station unleashed a barrage of energy bolts that sped across the rapidly reducing distance between station and ships. Belatedly, Sertesbritisha thought to order a change of course as a second wave of missiles was launched by the station.

The Empire ships started to change course while maintaining full speed. This had the effect of disturbing the defensive weapons' aim and response, while it seemed to have no effect on the missiles. Some of the energy blasts missed, but others impacted on shields with far greater force than was the usual case when dealing with the human ships. Strange balls of plasma followed the energy blasts, seeming to expand and twist as they crossed the distance, Again, several of them missed their targets, but others hit. The effect was immediate. Large swathes of shield emitters failed where the plasma impacted on ships.

Finally, the Empire ships launched their own heavy missiles in re-taliation and began to fire their own energy cannons. It was, however, too late. *Qrusk*, on point, tried to turn to protect its now unshielded flank but was too slow. Four missiles slammed into the large ship and punched through the outer skin, exploding with devastating effect. Gaping gashes were opened to space and plumes of debris were ejected. Sertesbritisha watched in disbelief as other missiles followed the first four and drove into the ship before exploding deep within. Even as *Qrusk* shuddered from the forces unleashed, the other three ships faced their own fates.

The remaining missiles of the first wave separated to target individual ships. Flying through the shield gaps created by the strange plasma balls, some missiles impacted the blunt, thickly armoured sides of the ships, punching through the armour to explode and create fissures in the plate armour. Others angled towards the rear of the ships and drove into the large engine nacelles. Farstation 291 had examined many Empire vessels over the long centuries since this race had taken to space and had de-termined that a major weakness existed around the engines. Its plan of attack acted on that determination.

*Qrusk* exploded. At the same time, one after the other, the remaining cruisers' engines were seriously damaged. They maintained pace only because of inertia, but all remaining shields were destroyed. Sertesbritisha felt helpless. His defensive weapons, lasers and blasters and railguns layered along the sides of his cruiser, were unable to track and target the incoming missiles, such was their speed and manoeuvrability once they emerged from their micro-jumps. The missiles jinked and rolled as they careered through the defensive barrage put up by the three ships. Only one incoming missile succumbed as it flew through a small curtain of railgun pellets.

*Nakti* was torn apart when seven missiles aimed at it tore through the damaged armour and exploded deep within the ship. *Denta* managed to twist away from the path of the missiles aimed at it, despite its main engines being badly damaged, but the missiles adjusted. Unfortunately, in turning as it did *Denta* also left its stern vulnerable and two missiles flew into the huge engines. As the brace of missiles exploded, *Denta* appeared to expand and then fall back into shape, only to suffer secondary explosions as fuel and munitions stores exploded. *Denta* somehow remained intact, mostly, but was dead in space and tumbling uncontrollably.

*Prekchu* was hit by six first wave missiles and five second wave missiles. Sertesbritisha found himself unable to give any orders, motivational or otherwise, as he watched in morbid fascination graphics of most of the missiles impacting in a neat line along the flank of his ship. Two of the first wave dived to the stern and delivered their payload to the engine nacelles, while the first of the second wave was aimed at the command bridge. Sertesbritisha and his bridge crew were dead before *Prekchu* gave a mighty belch of flame and broke into five pieces.

Farstation 291 noted the action in its log. It sent a coded message to Escantil Control reporting the engagement and the result. It devoted a portion of its vast processing capability to track the expanding debris field that continued on its way. Several additional farstations had been along that vector before they had been ordered into stealth mode.

Although they were quite far away, Farstation 291 linked to them and provided the relevant information. It reasoned that, having been authorised to engage the hostile forces then the need for communication blackout was past.

Finally, Farstation 291 sent a request to Escantil Control seeking resupply when possible. Given that it had been isolated for thousands of cycles, the station AI also reasoned that resupply may take some time. Accordingly, it tasked its maintenance drones to exhaust the remaining stores of materials and restock as many weapons as could be manufactured. The drones then were tasked with launching as miners to the nearest asteroid belt where known stores of raw materials were available.

Farstation 291 returned to its watch status.

# 29. Marjory Returns

Odruf, known to the Guides and Mages across untold ages as the forever aged Mage Halfgar, watched as Marjory took in the land to which she had been brought. She recognised the desert of the southern continent and even knew the location, the Oasis of Morrig. She had been here, oh, it must have been two thousand cycles earlier. Long before that, the sand had extended far past its previous boundaries and the people of the fields that had bordered the desert found they had nowhere they could go. Those who had not starved to death, or fallen victim to the diseases that could not be contained by the few remaining Guides and Mages, had started on their transformation to the hard, arid people of the desert.

In a short time, the desert had spread across the southern continent, creating a barrier against all those who were not prepared adequately. In fact, many who were experienced and prepared failed to conquer the shifting sands. Farmlands, orchards, small stands of forest, were all decimated. Plant life withered and died as the water retreated and the harsh heat of the twin suns sucked all available moisture from the land. The sand expanded, eating up the farms, chewing through the orchards, reducing the stands of timber to dried-out husks which in turn collapsed in on themselves and added their dust to the advancing sand. Little greenery survived. The Oasis of Morrig had the sole remaining stand of old timber in the new desert, trees of a hue and form that now existed nowhere else on Ennaris. Perhaps some trace of Morrig's power remained to protect these trees, although Marjory preferred to believe that it was the result of Drewflin's work to save at least this one remaining memory of what Ennaris had been, for the Archmage - only a Mage until very recently - who was so uncertain about what he should do as a whole but so sure of what he could do in parts, spent many a tenday here adding his healing strength to the Oasis and its surrounds, including that stand of trees.

The harsh glare of the sun brought Marjory back to herself, and she looked at Odruf.

"Why have you brought me here, Halfgar, er, I mean Odruf?" she asked. "I expected to be delivered to Drewflin so we can start to fight back."

"The Archmage is occupied by something right now," Odruf said, "and you may find that Morrig has something for you to do before she commits her people. At least, so she told me." He smiled. "I doubt that it will be onerous. She was one who wanted to return and smite Goroth without mercy, even while knowing that we cannot play such a direct role."

"Morrig," Marjory said. "Legend says that she and Ogun were the Guardians who helped to fight off the Asgrengar all that time ago. How is it that you could intervene then but cannot now?"

"Well, first, that was a battle for Ennaris against external forces. But mostly it was because the Asgrengar were from another universe and should not have been here. We sent them back, although many died during the fight for Ennaris and during their return."

"Another universe? The Asgrengar resembled us in many ways, from the old reports I read. Yet you say they were from another universe?" Marjory frowned and a thought intruded. "The Kindred, too?"

"Indeed," Odruf nodded. "The Kindred are also from a different universe. Morrig and Ogun are the ones who looked forward to your return. Ogun has been helping others to find their way, while Morrig's return was slightly later than most and she has been shaping the desert people in preparation."

"I recall when this was a small desert and the Vale of Morrig was lush and green," Marjory mused. "Now it's the Oasis of Morrig and is the last bastion of the asberry tree." She turned to look at the stand of timber at the far end of the Oasis. "Drewflin loved those trees."

"So he did, and so it is," Odruf replied. "And I must leave you here now, for I must be elsewhere. Morrig will come shortly." He faded out of sight.

Marjory sighed to herself. To be dumped out here was frustrating. For so long, she had been looking forward to seeing Drewflin, to being with him, he who was her heart and soul. She knew the Guardians would do nothing idly, so she was confident that this was for a good purpose, but that did little to lessen the ... frustration. She glanced at the shrine, built like a pavilion with its sides pulled down, and then decided to walk down to the stand of timber. She went past the tall, waving trees with fronds atop that looked very like Earth's coconut palms, but without the coconuts, noting that there were fresh shoots in most of the tree bases. Perhaps Morrig's return was having an effect already.

The shade under the trees came as a cool relief. Dressed as she was, in the dark clothes of a Battle Mage that had been designed for more temperate climes, the heat seemed to multiply in its effect. Marjory sought out the centre of the grove. She walked between the straight and tall trees, with gnarled brown bark that was grooved and rough to the feel. She was looking for their tree, knowing how silly that was after two thousand cycles. She rested one hand against the bark of one tree, thinking back to when Drewflin had shown her how to feel the life flowing through the tree. This was the living force that he then fed, amplified and reinforced, drawing from her own resources when he flagged, for the effort was immense. He was seeking to save the species, not just repair a tree, and it seemed to work, with this grove as evidence.

She found it! Just as she was turning away, and from the corner of her eye, one tree seemed to jump into focus, almost as though it was waving its arms at her. She stared, astonished, for on the tree, still preserved after all this time, was the print of a large hand. This was where Drewflin had pushed his healing energy into the grove, through this tree. They only noticed the hand print when he had pulled back and recovered from the expenditure of so much power. Marjory recalled that he was aghast at having marked the tree to that extent, and he was unable to repair it, to remove that mark. She mused at how such things just happened. She was aware that the Hand Tree was talked about long after but had no idea it was the same tree that Drewflin had used as his conduit. How had it survived all this time?

She stood by the tree for some time more, communing with its spirit perhaps, or maybe just recalling a time when they had thought they might still be able to repair the damage. Marjory smiled sadly. It was not too much after that when Deris had lost hope and poured her whole being into a final act of sacrifice, giving all of her life force to ensure the creeping sands would go no further south. She remembered the twins' anguish at her loss, for they had been jointly paired with Deris after the rebellion, the three coming together in an unusual tripling. She wondered how the twins were faring now and hoped they had not lost their hope. At times, hope was all they had left. It may be that the time for hope had come.

Marjory walked from the shade of the grove and into the harsh and bright sunshine again. She noted with amusement that she had company, several watchers who were trying hard not to be seen. They would have succeeded in staying hidden from many, but not from her. Marjory was trained to notice the tiny things, but she also included in her gifts the unusual one of being aware when someone was watching her. She had no idea how it worked, but now just accepted that it did. So, when that feeling came on her, she tightened her focus and studied her surroundings carefully. The smallest indications were there - the tiny shift of sand at the top of the dune overlooking the pavilion, the pale smudge that might have been the top of someone's head-wrap. She saw and did nothing overt to show that she had seen them. After all, she was in their land, and they would want to know who had arrived without notice and whether she was a threat.

Marjory was walking towards the pavilion, intending to wait in the shade for Morrig's arrival, when she felt an odd presence. No, it was more a force that was pushing and then pulling against her with irresistible power. A wave of despair washed over her, followed by pure rage, and more, and then the outpouring of anguish from one of stupendous power. And she recognised that power even as she was drawn into it and swept along on its currents.

# 30. Blaine and Helt

Blaine looked across the Citadel Guards' common room. Several of the guardsmen were playing a card game that he had never been able to fathom, no matter how many times the rules were explained to him. There seemed to be so many variants and the rules seemed to change at whim, so that he just gave up and watched as others played.

In a corner by the window, the whip-thin Sergeant Antrel was ensconced in a lounge chair reading what Blaine was sure would be a book of poems. Books were very expensive on Ennaris, and rare. Antrel had joined the Faero's guard some time before Escar and had proved to be a revelation to most of the guards and soldiers. He carried a rapier made for him to an ancient design and practised a style of fighting that emphasised agility and speed. In fact, he now had a cadre of guards who he was training in those techniques. Middling tall, dapper of style and with a sharp wit, Antrel reminded Blaine of the old stories of the musketeers, except on Ennaris they had no muskets, thankfully.

In another corner a tall, wide and heavily muscled giant occupied another lounge, this one designed for two normal people, although he took up the entire seating space. Ahtax Kar was from the deep south of Ennaris' southern continent. To hear him speak, one would think he was slow-witted, which was very wrong. In addition, Ahtax Kar was a force of nature when roused. He had joined the Faero's guard after Escar, when the fame of that defence had spread and caused recruitment to spike, and already the giant had amassed a following for his feats of strength and endurance. Blaine was looking forward to seeing him in action, although the man's armour was made up of mismatched bits and pieces battered to try to cover as many vulnerable parts as possible. That needed work, Blaine thought.

Speaking of armour, in another corner, this one closest to Blaine, Helt - the Princess Anhelter, as she had been revealed to be during the defence of her home city of Escar - was trying and failing to patch her armour. She had been in the thick of the action in Escar and the armour had taken several hard knocks that had shifted some of the plates. It was never a good fit. Given that her father had not wanted his daughter to become a warrior in the first place, she had begged, borrowed and ultimately stolen the suit of armour when she rode away from the city several years before, earning a reputation as a hot-headed, hard-drinking and hard-fighting warrior. Blaine had come into her life at a point where she could have become a laughing stock and a liability to the Faero. Instead, she found someone to provide a guiding hand. The close intimacy that had grown up between them had been a surprise to Blaine, who was a veteran of many planetary missions for the Warriors of the Light from which he had emerged with no emotional attachments. However, close association with the Warrior had showed Helt what she could be. Consequently, she had led the Faero's guard during the defence of Escar, winning approbation from all, including from her father, the King. But she still had that old armour, and it would not do.

Blaine stood, setting aside the reports he had been reading idly and walked over to Helt, touching her lightly on one shoulder.

"Helt, that old armour won't come back, you know," he said evenly, "at least, not without being completely reworked."

She nodded morosely. "I know. It's almost unwearable at the moment and I can't get the straps to sit right. I had that new smith, Protis, give it a few whacks with his hammer, but he thinks the metal is too old and brittle and may shatter if he tries too much."

Blaine nodded. "Well, perhaps you can learn how Antrel fights and do without the armour," he said, baiting her and waiting for the explosion to come.

The card game stopped as the players all turned to watch the reaction. They expected a shouting match at least, perhaps a fist fight between Helt and Blaine, which would be something to see. They were disappointed.

"Maybe," she said in despair, running one hand through sandy hair that was cut short. "If I used this in battle it's just as likely to seize up as anything else. I'd be helpless. Worse, I might not be able to swing a sword well enough."

Blaine considered for a moment. "How about we go on a little journey, you and me. There's someone I think you should meet."

"A journey? Like a holiday? I haven't had a holiday for a long time," she said wistfully. "But I need to get this pile of junk in some sort of order."

"Not quite a holiday, although I think you'll like the village," Blaine replied. "Leave the armour. You won't need it where we're going. At least I hope you won't."

Helt looked up at Blaine, suspicious of his motives. He had something in mind, and it was not just getting her alone. She sighed. But the armour was not going to be fixed. She might be able to get it done by her father's smiths but even they would find it difficult without rebuilding it. Setting aside the set of greaves that she had been working on, Helt rose easily and nodded.

"Okay, I guess I can take a break. Do I pack light?"

Blaine nodded. "For a couple of days, I would guess. Pack your sword though."

Helt just stared at him for a moment then said, "I always pack my sword."

Blaine just grinned as he turned away to get his own pack ready. "I'll let Almin Bor know we'll be away for a few days and meet you back at the main steps in a little bit."

A short time later, after a brief discussion with Almin Bor, now appointed Over-Captain of the Faero's guard, Blaine met Helt at the steps of the administration building. In most cities it would be deemed a palace but, because the Faero was not a king, it had never been called that. However, it was the largest building in the Citadel and housed the Faero and his small personal retinue, as well as the offices of his Chancellor and senior staff and sleeping quarters for several people, including Jalor and Blaine. With a nod Blaine led the way up the steps and into the building, along the long corridors and through the nondescript door that led down to the portal chamber. Long disused until recently, the portal now was lit up by a means that Helt could not fathom, although Blaine seemed quite comfortable. Blaine walked to the portal and quietly gave it an instruction. The gateway flared and settled into a uniform grey colour. Without a word, the two walked through the portal.

Helt looked around. They emerged in what looked like a cave at the end of a long corridor that appeared to be hewn from rock. Only by close inspection could it be seen that the walls were not natural but had been made of a material that Helt could not recognise.

"Good day, Blaine," a voice said from somewhere.

Helt started before realising that it was a portal speaking. And it recognised Blaine, she thought.

"Senasarra," Blaine said in greeting. "I see the repairs to your gateway have been made. It looks very good."

"Thank you," the portal that had become accustomed to being called Senasarra replied, and Helt was sure she heard satisfaction in that voice. "It took some time but appears to have been completed satisfactorily. Of course, we had to make do with more basic materials but Hunder has followed my directions to the letter to manufacture replacements."

"Speaking of Hunder," Blaine continued, "did you pass on my message?"

"I did," Senasarra responded. "He has already produced the requisite plates and shaped them as per your request. I believe he is holding them in his workshop."

"Excellent," Blaine said. "Senasarra, this is Helt. Helt, say hello to Senasarra."

"Well met, Princess," Senasarra said warmly. "I am at your command, as directed by Jalor and Blaine."

Helt was taken aback slightly. "Hello, er, Senasarra," she said, glancing at Blaine in query.

"We decided that you should have the command codes also," Blaine explained.

"Command codes?"

"Oh, old habits. I meant that you should also be in a position of authority. Usually, the portals were used by Mages and Guides of old, and they use voice prints for authorisation. You've been included as one of very few non-Mages able to use the portals. Almin Bor has been given access similarly." Blaine started to walk down the corridor. "Senasarra, have your sensors picked up anything to worry us?"

"Nothing, Blaine. One question, if I may. The sword you carry has an odd signature. May I ask where you got it?"

"An old woman gave it to me during the battle of Escar," Blaine replied. "It seems I'm something called the Golden Warrior."

"Ah, Defender," Senasarra said, its voice adopting a notably respectful tone. "Then the sword is Genardil. It has been long since Genardil was seen."

"Genardil? The sword has a name?" Blaine stopped and turned to look at the portal.

"Yes, it does," Senasarra replied. "It has somewhat mythical origins, supposedly made from the core of a fallen meteorite and imbued as it was forged with the talents of five of the greatest ever metalworking Mages of Ennaris in the days before Ennarisi trod other planets. It is reputed to deliver great strength and endurance to the bearer, and to provide protection, although how is not revealed in the Council archives."

"I'll show you one day," Blaine said, dryly. "Meanwhile, we need to see Hunder. Has he shown you any of the material yet?"

"Samples only, of course, but the quality is good, using the processes I recommended. I believe you will be pleased."

"Very good. We expect to be here for a couple of days, so I'll return to check a few things with you during that time. Helt will need time to get used to it anyway."

"Well, I'm not going anywhere, so drop in whenever you wish," Senasarra said with a touch of humour, and not for the first time Blaine found himself wondering about just how advanced the Ennaris AI was.

Helt was feeling left out and bewildered, which was not a good combination for the impetuous warrior.

"What was that all about?" she asked as she followed Blaine from the corridor leading onto the hillside that held the portal. "And I thought these portal things were some sort of machine. You were carrying on a conversation with it."

"Well," Blaine said as he blinked to get accustomed to the suns' glare on exiting the corridor, "as to what we are doing, you'll have to wait a bit. As for Senasarra, that's difficult to explain. It's what is called artificial intelligence, a machine so advanced that it can think almost like you and me. But because it's a machine it doesn't forget - well, unless it's damaged. Ennaris seems to have a network of these sensor stations and portals all over the planet, as you know, but they all link back to a central, um, brain, I guess you could say."

"That's hard to believe," Helt said, "even though I have heard you and Jalor talking to them."

"And Flin and the twins," Blaine reminded her. "Once we get through all of this, you and the rest of Ennaris will have to become accustomed to a lot of new and strange things. For some it will be very hard, and for others it will be a great release. But for better or for worse, Ennaris will change. The key is what position Ennaris will take. Anyway, first things first. We need to make sure we're there to see it, and that's why you're here."

They entered the small town of Manis Reach via the back trail, the same one Jalor and Blaine had taken to search out the Oracle only to find the portal. Blaine led the way to the same tavern, which he visited each time he came to the town, and found Edmas swabbing down the wooden tables.

"Blaine!" Edmas exclaimed as the two walked into view. "I was wondering when you would turn up again. Hunder has been expecting you."

"Hello Edmas," Blaine replied. "We've been busy, so it's been difficult to get away."

"So we hear." Edmas chuckled. "We heard tales of the battle of Escar against Goroth and how you beat him. And some fanciful thing called the Golden Warrior who won the whole battle single-handedly. You can tell us the tale properly tonight." She eyed Blaine's companion with interest.

Helt snorted and Blaine coloured slightly in embarrassment, which interested Edmas even more.

"Some of the stories are exaggerated," Blaine said, "and it wasn't Goroth leading the enemy. But it was enough to know we will have a fight on our hands sometime soon. This," he continued, turning to indicate Helt, "is my friend, Helt."

Edmas' eyes opened wide as she looked at the tall woman wearing warrior garb with a large sword strapped to her back and she dropped into an awkward curtsy. "Princess," she gasped.

"No, no, no," Helt said, grasping Edmas' hand and drawing her back to her feet. "It's Helt except when I'm in Escar, and I'm nothing more than a captain of the Faero's guard."

Edmas looked at her sceptically. "Yes, my lady," she said, causing Helt to quirk her lips in frustration and Blaine to grin widely at her chagrin, "but captain of the Faero's guard is not something to be sneezed at, either."

"Do you have a room we can use for a couple of nights, Edmas?" Blaine asked. "We will be working with Hunder quite a bit so won't be around during the day."

"One room?" Edmas asked with exaggerated innocence.

"One room," Helt confirmed, inwardly squirming as Edmas stared at her, surprisingly relieved when the other woman nodded in approval.

"Ah, and we need to see Hunder now," Blaine said quickly as the two women shared a conspiratorial smile. "We'll be back for something to eat after that."

He beat a hasty retreat, almost dragging Helt along with him as he made his way to Hunder's workshop, eager to see what he had produced. The changes surprised him, but then he realised that to do what Senasarra would have required meant changes were needed. The smithy was much larger, and Blaine could see that he had punched through the wall to occupy the building alongside him which, Blaine recalled, had been empty. The furnace was now twice the size and there were smaller furnaces to each side, so the blast of heat as they approached the entrance to the smithy was intense. An array of new tools, made of steel rather than iron, hung from a large harness spread along one wall, and a great roller was suspended above a table where the tabletop was a series of smaller rollers. There were casting moulds scattered around the workshop, some empty, others full of cooling metal or other materials. In one corner, two young men were hammering on metal billets, iron hammers clanging against the metal held to an anvil in the time-honoured way of smiths, while in another corner Hunder was examining a piece of shaped metal that he had just removed from a mould.

"Yo, Hunder," Blaine called, lifting his voice to a parade-ground bellow to get over the clamour of the hammers.

The two young smiths did not stop their hammering, but Hunder looked around and his face wreathed in smiles when he saw Blaine standing at the entrance. Like Edmas, his interested glance went to Helt, but it returned to Blaine quickly. He placed the moulded piece carefully on a worktable and made his way through the workshop. He greeted Blaine with a hand grip that would have caused other men to collapse writhing on the ground before clapping him on the back with enough force to shove Blaine forward a step and expel all breath.

"Blaine," he thundered, "it's about time you got here. I was thinking you had forgotten. And this must be Helt," he said, turning before Blaine could respond. "Princess, it is an honour," he said, bowing from the waist with surprising elegance in a man of such a huge size.

"Just Helt, thank you Hunder. It's my pleasure to meet you, although I have no idea why I'm here," Helt replied, with a meaningful look at Blaine.

"Hello, my friend," Blaine said as he regained his breath. "Do you have to do that?"

"You're the only one who I *can* do that to and who is likely to stand up afterwards," Hunder said with a broad grin. "Come, let me show you what we have so far."

He led the way across the workshop to a large cleared area at the back, reaching for a pile of shaped pieces made of a metal that Helt did not recognise.

"This is what Senasarra has had me making for you," Hunder said, holding up one piece, a breastplate, and looking at Helt's figure critically. The warrior coloured before realising that there was nothing more than professional interest in his appraising stare. "It looks like it should do," the smith continued, speaking to Helt. "Senasarra called it *inmithas*, and apparently, it's an alloy that was invented long ago. Senasarra says this will be the strongest armour of any on Ennaris. It should withstand almost any sort of strike, although you may get shaken up."

"This is for me?" Helt asked, astonished.

"Yes, Blaine asked me to make this for you and to get Senasarra to show me how to make it with the right alloy. It's taken a long time, but I think I have it. Senasarra was happy with the samples I showed him."

Hunder handed the breastplate to Helt and reached for another piece. The warrior was amazed at how light the piece of armour was, being accustomed to plates of heavy metal that was worked into a basic shape. She turned it around, only belatedly noticing the two shallow mounds to accommodate her breasts. She coloured as she looked at it, turning to stare at Blaine, who smiled and shrugged.

"There's no point you wearing armour designed for a man," he said wryly, "so I had Hunder make a set for a woman. The size should be okay."

"And how do you know the size is right?" Helt asked indignantly, continuing to stare at the contours of the cast and polished alloy.

Blaine laughed. "One of the things I found from the portals is that they carry measurements of the people they transport, probably as part of their algorithms to ensure you're put back together again. I was able to isolate yours and pass them to Hunder."

"Senasarra helped me to make sense of what Blaine sent to me," Hunder said with a satisfied nod. "And I've made the mould exactly to that size, allowing for cushioning and such beneath it. You must try it on to make sure."

Helt looked down at the shirt she was wearing and then looked back at both men. And waited.

"Ah, perhaps you can go behind this," Hunder said, blushing slightly as Blaine grinned.

Hunder draped a blanket over a line stretched between two posts, making a somewhat more private space, and the two men waited while Helt took the breastplate and back-plate into the area. Within a short time, she returned. The two plates were fitted to perfection, ready for the shoulder and arm pieces to be added, which Hunder proceeded to do. The usual leather straps used for Escar's knights had been replaced by a flexible membrane. Once Hunder was finished fitting and making minor adjustments, Helt stretched and tried experimental turns and movements.

"Hunder, this is marvellous," she said, eyes wide open. "It's so light and the fit is perfect. I can feel the armour moving but it doesn't rub against me anywhere."

"Senasarra also mentioned an undergarment that Blaine was looking to have made for you," Hunder said in response, feeling pleased at Helt's reaction. "It will be thin enough to wear under the armour but will act as the padding also."

"Oh?" Helt looked to Blaine.

"That's waiting for you at the tavern," Blaine replied. "I wanted to see how this went first, and the undergarment Hunder mentions may take some getting used to. It is somewhat more, um, modern than most Ennarisi will be comfortable with, I'm thinking. But it will suit the armour perfectly."

Helt stared at Blaine for a while, then turned back to Hunder. "How do we deal with the lower parts of the armour? And hands and feet?"

"Oh, the lower torso is done also, and the leg pieces will be completed tonight. They've been cast already." Hunder considered his next words. "The feet and hands will be very different to the heavy style of armour that you've used before, though. They're from a different material that Senasarra had me make, like a sort of chain mail but far more flexible." He reached into a wooden box against which he was standing and from it pulled a pair of gloves. "This is one pair, but I'm planning on making more for you, and for others. The process is quick once it's set up. Again, the sizes were provided by Blaine, so I expect they will fit well."

Helt took the gloves from Hunder and marvelled at their near weightlessness. She pulled the right-hand glove on and it fit her exactly. She wiggled her fingers and flexed her wrist and felt no discomfort or restriction of movement. By contrast, her heavy armoured gauntlets were cumbersome and did not wrap around the hand completely. She pulled the glove off again and placed it on the workbench. In a single fluid movement, she pulled her sword free and smashed the edge against the glove, stepping up to see the result. The glove showed no marks and was completely intact.

"If someone were to do that to you, you would likely have some broken bones," Hunder said, "but you would not lose your hand or fingers."

"Can you make whole chain mail sets from this?" Helt asked.

"Yes, but for now I'm concentrating on hands and feet," Hunder replied. "Blaine set the priorities. Once we have you outfitted properly, I'll work with others."

"I can think of about two hundred knights and knight-trainees who would gladly be your next customers," Helt said seriously.

"Well, we can worry about that later. Meanwhile, get yourself out of that and let me finish off the leg pieces and you can try the whole thing tomorrow." Hunder smiled. "I'm amazed at this material, Blaine. I've made some extra pieces, and I thought you might take this with you when you leave."

Hunder reached behind the bench to retrieve a large almost rectangular object, covered by a cloth. He placed it upright on the workbench and removed the cloth, revealing a shield, shaped like a flattened oval, with a small boss in the centre. The edges were raised slightly. The shield was coloured bright red, and centred on the shield was the Faero's personal insignia surrounded by a thick white border.

Blaine looked at the shield, and then nodded thoughtfully. "Hunder, this is wonderful work," Blaine said, while Helt stared. "Corm is not an expert swordsman, and this will provide the additional protection he needs."

Blaine picked up the shield, its weight almost nothing to hold, and smiled. "My friend, your skills will be renowned throughout Ennaris and, I think, beyond."

Hunder blushed but was obviously pleased. "Oh, the credit goes to Senasarra. He gave me the design and the formula for the materials, as well as advice on how to make it work. All I did was follow the instructions."

"It takes skill to follow those instructions, and then to make the changes needed to make a device like this," Blaine replied. "This is true craft work, and I'm sure Corm will be grateful."

"Grateful? Corm will be overjoyed," Helt said. "I'm going to take this off now and then you can show me the other things you have made. You did say you had some other pieces?"

"Yes, I've experimented with other bits and pieces," Hunder said, as Helt moved behind the blanket screen again. He re-wrapped the shield and pulled a second wooden box from under the workbench. "These are a little more normal."

Helt and Blaine spent some time with Hunder, examining the array of small tools he had made, including the inevitable ploughshares, before leaving him to finish Helt's leg-pieces. Helt walked back to the tavern as though on a cloud. She had never had someone provide anything of this nature for her before and, once again, she looked at the man walking beside her with fresh eyes. Blaine always seemed so calm, and rarely expressed feelings, but his regard for her, and for many others who he met, never ceased to amaze her. Defender, he had been called, and most people thought of that as a warrior protector, but Helt was starting to feel that it may have a far greater meaning.

The evening was spent in the tavern. Helt could see the regard and affection with which Blaine was held in the town. It appeared that he had been a frequent visitor after the initial one with Jalor, and he had become an adopted son of sorts. Helt was regaled with stories of his attempts to wield a hoe. She laughed with the group when Blaine's efforts at threshing one of the grain crops were described, complete with the children of the town competing to see how many grains they could extract from his hair and clothes. The story of Blaine staring down a trio of bandits only a tenday before was told, as was his efforts of strength alongside Hunder when a barn collapsed on a farm and the two men held up the collapsed side so those trapped inside could be rescued. Through it all Blaine remained good-humoured, laughing at his own mistakes and obviously enjoying being ribbed by the villagers.

In their turn, the villagers adopted Helt without question. Some of them knew her as a royal princess, but not all. There were several sideways glances at her by townspeople, but she recognised that it was by people who cared for Blaine and wanted to be sure of her fitness to be with him, for it was obvious to all that they were paired. The fact that her sword was as big as Blaine's was a source of discussion and some quite ribald amusement that coloured Helt's face. She enjoyed herself that night more than any she could recall.

The following morning, after a good breakfast, Blaine and Helt returned to Hunder's workshop for the final fitting of her armour. The leg pieces and boots were every bit as perfect for Helt as the breast and back pieces had been. And she received a further surprise when Blaine handed her the sack he had carried from the tavern, from which she pulled what seemed to be two garments, some sort of breeches and a shirt. When she pulled them on behind the screen, she initially refused to step out but finally, at Blaine's cajoling, and with tentative steps, she did so. The two garments fitted like a second skin, so tightly that her full figure was clearly on view. The two apprentices gaped and Hunder smiled appreciatively, causing Helt's face to cloud.

Blaine stopped her from storming back by the simple expedient of grabbing her arm and spinning her around so he could see the overall fit. All he did was nod, satisfied, while Hunder glared at the apprentices who rapidly went back to work, stealing glances at the corner where the fitting was carrying on.

"This seems like an odd thing," Blaine said to Helt, who remained uncomfortable, "but you will find these garments will be well suited to wearing under the armour. Senasarra delved through the archives and came up with these, which are like what we have in the Union when we use full body armour. The material is light and very flexible, made of material that could be sourced from the southern continent and treated using techniques lost to Ennaris before now. But it will act as padding when you need it and will also absorb some of the strike force should you get hit hard. It's very close fitting for that purpose, and so is made to very exact measurements, which means someone else may not be able to wear the set made for you."

Hunder started to hand the armour pieces to Helt and, with a couple of stumbles she donned the whole suit. Hunder showed her how the pieces went together, both the upper items she had worn the day before and the newer lower garments. Fully kitted out, Helt stood in the silver burnished suit of armour in the workshop and experimentally moved arms and legs and then twisted and bent, all without apparent discomfort. Finally, Hunder reached under the workbench and retrieved a helmet, open at the face, and handed it to Helt. Worked into the sides of the helmet were her personal devices, the crest of Escar and the sigil of the Princess. With tears forming, Helt lifted the helmet into place, settling it and feeling the pieces of *inmithas* mail hanging below the helmet as neck protection. Hunder fussed a little to make sure all pieces fit correctly and then attached the face-piece, lifting it to sit above the face opening and then lowering it to sit into grooves in the helmet designed for the purpose. Helt now was encased in this strange, ultra lightweight material from Ennaris' past.

Hunder stood back to inspect his work and nodded, a broad smile of satisfaction and pride breaking out across his leathery face. Blaine merely nodded, but there was a gleam to his eye. The two apprentices momentarily stopped what they were doing to gape once again, before returning to their work hammering at a piece of metal. Helt walked across the workshop and back, working arms and legs, continuing to twist and turn, flexing wrists, ankles, hands and feet. She stopped in front of Hunder and pushed her faceplate up. Her eyes were shining bright, and she reached forward and planted a firm kiss on Hunder's cheek before turning to Blaine.

"Good," Blaine said simply, "very good. Hunder, you are both an artist and a master craftsman."

"It feels like nothing I've ever felt before. No armour can be this light and protect the wearer, can it?" Helt asked Blaine uncertainly.

"Well, you saw the test yesterday. I guess we need to do a proper test now," Blaine replied with a sly grin. "Let's see how it works."

"What, here?" Helt asked.

"I'd say in the main square. There's room there and no-one will mind. What say you, Hunder?"

"Aye, the square is the ideal place. You'll have an audience, lass, but you'll have to get used to people seeing you in that suit sometime, so it may as well be now." Hunder nodded to himself as he spoke.

With some misgivings, Helt followed the two men from the workshop and the three made their way to the main square of the village. The two apprentices shared a look and as one pushed their unfinished pieces into the forge and followed. Several villagers stared as Helt walked past, the armour's rounded curves causing astonished comments. A small crowd gathered to watch, without knowing what they would see.

Helt stood in the centre of the square, her sword now strapped to the back of the armour, and glared at Blaine, who just stood and grinned as the villagers gathered, commenting and pointing. A couple of good-humoured jests were raised, one of which caused Helt's face to colour, but then she gritted her teeth and growled at Blaine.

"Okay, so you have your sideshow," she muttered, "so what next."

"Let's see how this armour works for you," Blaine said, reaching back to draw his own sword, the normal one.

Tentatively, and then with growing confidence, he tapped the armour with his sword, slowly making the strokes harder, walking around Helt so he could strike her in different spots. A final bat with the flat of his sword on her backside caused the crowd to laugh and Helt's eyes to smoulder.

"Finished?" she growled.

"Yes, seems okay," Blaine replied blandly, although with laughing eyes. "How about you?"

"I think it needs to be exercised," she said through gritted teeth, drawing her own sword and making experimental swings to ensure her arms retained free movement.

Satisfied, she clapped the faceplate down and in a single movement charged at Blaine. The latter, expecting just such a move from Helt, laughed as he met her blows and turned them aside. The villagers had seen Blaine practising moves during previous visits, but had never seen him display his prowess before. Now, Helt moved from practice strokes into a flurry of the more advanced techniques that Blaine had been teaching her, and the villagers were treated to a display of swordplay such as none had ever seen. Back and forth the two combatants moved,

Helt's huge sword moving in dazzling arcs, twisting and turning as though a living thing. Blaine, defending and then attacking in turn, but without the benefit of armour, shifted and moved, swung and twisted, never staying in the one spot for more than a few seconds at a time. The square rang with the clash of the swords and the combatants moved back and forth across the flagstones fluidly, almost as though dancing.

Finally, the two drew apart, as with a single thought, and the battle ceased. Helt threw up the faceplate, laughing with delight, drawing deep breaths. Blaine merely stood and watched, a tiny smile catching the edges of his mouth.

"It's so light and easy to wear," she said in delight. "I feel that I can fight forever in this."

The crowd, stunned to silence at the spectacle they had just witnessed, broke into voice and swarmed onto the square, small crowds gathering around both warriors. Standing at the back of the crowd, Hunder smiled broadly, relieved and pleased at his handiwork.

# 31. Champion and Dharmoney

"There's a small town coming up," Varna said.

"Oh?" Clay glanced to where his travel companion walked easily by his side.

Clay and Varna were on the road to the north-west region of the northern continent. Fernis had told them that this region, further north than they were, had been attacked by the norther army before it attacked Escar. Many were killed, several towns and villages laid waste. Varna's lips compressed as she thought about it. Ogun was convinced that it was for nothing more than to raise fear and thus influence forces that could oppose Goroth to stay at home, which showed a poor grasp of the current state of Ennaris.

"I can feel that there are people clustered there," Varna explained. "I'm not sure how to describe it but different things seem to be opening up now."

"Well, it's not far from full dark. I'm thinking we stay out of town tonight," Clay replied after an answering nod.

"Suits me," Varna replied. "But I think I need to see what I can do. I've always been able to read people. Let's see what else I can do."

Clay snorted as he led the way from the road.

"I think the question is more likely to be what you can't do."

They found a suitable camp site and Clay set about clearing an array of stones, twigs and other debris from their selected spot. The site was ideal for them to remain out of site, being shielded from view on three sides and protected on the fourth by a stream. Nor was he worried about anyone creeping up on them with his and Varna's enhanced capabilities.

Varna dropped her pack, hooked her staff to her belt and started her walk into the town. She was eager to see if she could discern any extra powers, anything that may help with the mission. In theory, this blockage removal could open significant possibilities. She thought of her ... destruction ... of Ortas without flinching. She accepted now that there could be truly evil beings - not always human or Ennaris, of course - but she felt compelled to consider whether individuals could be brought back. She considered that position. It was in some ways the same as applying a compulsion, which was what Grensor was thought to have done during the rebellion. That was one path she did not want to tread! Perhaps she could work to identify those beings who wanted to change but needed help in doing so. How would she do that? Would she need to seek permission? She turned it over in her thoughts as she walked.

Clay set a small fire, just enough to ward off the slight chill that would be felt a little later. Their bedrolls would provide enough warmth while they slept, but it was always cheery to have a fire. He paused every so often to let his senses run wide as he continued to work. With the fire dancing on the small sticks he fed it, Clay started to clean his weapons. They probably did not need it but he had the chance so why not? Still, he kept his senses scanning for any change that may mean danger.

Suddenly, he was aware of a presence, someone approaching. That person had not been there a moment earlier. Clay would wager that such was the case. There was no noise, nothing to indicate that clay was not alone. Clay had no sense of danger. He continued to clean his weapons, completing his needler and reaching for the blaster.

"It's getting dark," Clay said without turning.

"There's sufficient light," a female voice said, with an inflexion that suggested she was smiling.

Clay stood and turned in one motion. Facing him at a comfortable distance was an old woman, standing at Clay's height and wearing what looked to be a collection of old scarves atop a nondescript tunic. Her face was heavily lined and her eyes were rheumy. At least, that was Clay's initial reaction but, on second glance, maybe not. The old woman now stared at Clay with a sharp gaze, as though looking into his very soul.

"Greetings Clay Anders, Champion of the Light for the Union of Sentient Planets," she said with a gentle smile. "Child of Ennaris, although not one of the Three."

Clay nodded, bemused but not worried. In naming him as she did, this old woman demonstrated that she knew his human name, that he was not from Ennaris and that he had a role different to the others.

"Would you care to share my fire?" Clay asked finally. "And do you have a name?"

"Thank you," the old woman replied with another smile. "That would be lovely. And yes, I do have a name. I am Meilani."

She moved closer to the fire and, as Clay started to hold out a hand to help her to sit, lithely folded herself into a seated position. Her eyes seemed to sparkle in the firelight that was taking over from the daylight, as though revealing a mischievous nature. He sat also, so that his weapons were between them. He held the blaster still.

"I congratulate you on the restoration of your memories," Meilani said, "and offer condolences on your remembered loss. Your family were taken from you in an untimely fashion, as were many families of Ennaris across the cycles since the rebellion."

"Thank you," Clay replied, feeling the pang of loss that he stamped down to concentrate on this mysterious woman. "What brings you out here?"

"Why you do, of course," the old woman replied. "Events move in the direction that they must, and you will be integral to them. And I felt the need of some company for a short time. It gets lonely sometimes."

As Clay nodded again - he was doing that a lot, he thought - Meilani idly reached across and picked up the needler. She turned it so that she could examine it more easily, hefted it in her right hand as though testing its weight, and finally nodded at though in approval. Clay made no move to retrieve the needler, noting that at no time did it point towards him.

"Very nice," Meilani said. "It has a good weight and balance. Powered from the suns?"

"And the moons," Clay replied. "It can use both. The suns provide more concentrated charging, of course."

"Of course," Meilani agreed. "What is its range?"

"Ah, this one is built to my own specification," Clay said easily. "It has a range of around fifty metres in my measurement, so the distance of twenty to twenty-five tall men laid end on end."

"Very good," Meilani nodded.

"It will last for more than a hundred shots," Clay continued. "Very useful."

"I imagine so," Meilani replied. "Light, well balanced, easy to charge, with a good range and ample firing rate."

Meilani deftly flicked the safety off and swung around. Without pause, she fired four shots at a fallen tree that had a series of small branches sticking up from the horizontal trunk. She hit four of the branches, the first marginally off centre.

"It pulls..." Clay started.

"Slightly to the left," Meilani finished for him. "Yes, I noticed that. It's a good weapon. Seems to have good power delivery. The beam is a little tight for my liking, but I can see this being useful."

"Ah," Clay replied, working hard to reconcile the sight of this very aged Ennarisi woman handling modern weaponry as though born to it. "This may be more to your liking then."

He handed Meilani the blaster, receiving the needler in return. Again, she examined it for weight and balance, examining the gun with interest.

"Yes, this seems to have a better feel in the hand," she said.

Once again she aimed at the tree trunk and fired four blasts. The surface of the fallen trunk exploded, large chunks of wood flying into the surrounding night. In contrast to the quiet sizzle of the needler as it almost surgically removed the small branches, the blaster sent sharp reports across the landscape as it destroyed the trunk.

"Much better," Meilani said with a grin that told Clay that he was in the presence, somehow, of a pure warrior.

She hefted the blaster one last time before pushing the safety on and handing it back to Clay with a sigh.

"Ah well," Meilani muttered, "play time is over."

She stood once again, a smooth action that should not have been possible for one of her age. Clay stood to join her. For a moment they looked at each other in the dim light of the fire. Meilani gave an enigmatic smile before allowing the wrinkles to dominate again.

"Clay Anders," she began in a more formal tone to what she had used before, "will you battle those who mean ill to those weaker than them with all your skill and might?"

Clay felt a chill run through him. Ogun told him that there would be times when he would know that turning points were at hand, when he had a choice that would change him and his future irrevocably, and that he would recognise those times in his own way. He had felt this same chill when he had been asked to take the mantle of Champion of the Light. That was a turning point for him. This felt like another. And it was an easy question, for this was what he felt he had done as a Warrior of the Light and Champion, and recent events on Ennaris showed the depths to which some of power were willing to go.

"Yes," he replied quietly, "I will."

"Will you protect Ennaris and her people from those who would do evil, even if it means the loss of your own life?"

Another easy question. Ennaris felt like home to Clay. This was where he had formed a family. This was where his family was buried. This planet and these people were now part of his being.

"Yes, I will," he repeated.

Meilani smiled as though in sympathy, as though she understood his reasons and empathised with them. Perhaps she did, Clay thought.

"Will you extend your protection to all if so called to do so?"

That question caused Clay to pause. The words seemed so simple, but could mean so much. "To all" may or may not have boundaries set by context, inherent knowledge or language limitations. Clay felt that none of them applied here, for Meilani struck him as a being of clarity of vision. She would not misspeak. But he was the Champion of the Light and he took that role very seriously.

"Yes, I will," he repeated once again.

The old woman smiled again, a beautiful smile that lifted Clay's spirit even as a second chill ran through his being.

"I name you Champion of Ennaris," Meilani said in a strong voice. "As Ennaris will be the light of this galaxy once again, so I also name you Champion of this galaxy and this universe. No," she continued as Clay started, "that does not mean the Ennarisi will conquer all others, but I foresee that they will guide many to the right path." She nodded, as though to herself and shrugged as she said, almost as a throw-away explanation, "The One gifted me with a measure of foresight to help with my task."

She reached into a pack that Clay had not noticed her wearing, rummaged around for a moment and extracted a chain with a small bird ornament. Clay recognised it as the same as the one Varna wore when she stood naked before Ortas.

"Varna has one of those," he said.

"She does," Meilani agreed. "As do others. This is an Aldenthrush. While those who wear it may not understand it, this is a symbol of particular favour of The One. Wear this at all times close to your skin. It will offer additional protection in times of extreme need."

She handed the chain to Clay.

"The One?" Clay asked as he lifted the chain over his head and settled the Aldenthrush beneath his tunic so it rested against the skin of his chest.

He was surprised by a sudden flash of light that came from the pendant. Meilani merely smiled.

"The One guides the Guardians," the old woman replied. "The One is to the Guardians and their people as the Guardians are to the Ennarisi, only more so by a long way."

Clay held still as he considered that. The One - the name indicated a single being - was so much more advanced than the Guardians, which was mind boggling. And she referred to the Guardians and their people, so were there more of them? What could that mean going forward? And Meilani spoke as though she represented this superior being.

"And you are the emissary of The One?"

"At times, and at other times I help Odruf and the Guardians. I have some leeway that they don't have."

"But you are not one of the Guardians?"

"Oh no," Meilani demurred. "I am of Ennaris. The Guardians hail from a far galaxy, one of the earliest to be born. The Toree, the people from which Ennaris' Guardians are drawn, were the first people of this universe. Truth to tell, I believe The One has a soft spot for them, but don't ever say I said that."

"I'll keep that in mind," Clay smiled.

"Well, I've enjoyed our chat, but I must depart," Meilani said. "Varna approaches and it would be better if we did not meet yet. Keep what we have discussed to yourself, Clay."

Clay smiled and bowed to the old-seeming woman, who turned and walked into the rough and broken terrain. Despite his best efforts to follow her progress, she was lost to Clay's sight and senses almost immediately.

Not long after, Varna walked into the camp, carrying a small sack that she placed near the small fire.

"Some fresh fruit," she announced. "I thought it might make a nice dessert. Anything happen while I was away? I thought I could hear something from this direction."

"Nothing of note," Clay replied easily. "Just an opportunity to think about a few things, make a few connections. Recent events have been a little overwhelming. I think I'm clearer on my role than I was."

Varna nodded as she settled by the fire and held out her hands to the heat. The visit to the town had been a good idea. She had been able to use her greatly enhanced perceptions to read people, and to get a view of what they were like here. There were no great insights, but she found it much easier to slip into the right mindset. There were many things she still needed to understand, of course. She could use some extra clarity herself, she thought, despite the gains made with Fernis and the others.

# 32. Umber

"Umber probably still is a relatively small town," Raglin said as the twin Mages walked with Jalor and a troop of guards towards the portal room, all wearing cold-weather clothes. "They liked to think of it as a city. I assume they still do. In the mountains that's probably fair enough. Even before the rebellion, most people up there lived in small villages located where they could run their stock on meadows and where they could get protection from the elements."

"These are the highest mountains on Ennaris," Ragnor continued, "and conditions can become pretty extreme. The villages are not on the peaks, of course, but in the valleys. Umber is in a valley, too, near the site of Abroshar, which is where the portal is located. So we'll have a walk to Umber."

"Abroshar was destroyed, I take it?" Jalor asked as they pushed through the heavy door.

"Yes," Raglin said sadly, "although it had little strategic importance, so it was targeted later than most. It was mostly a recreational city, with people visiting for various snow sports or to test themselves on climbing. A number of reflection centres were maintained in the mountains, secluded places were people could go to, um, recharge, I guess you could say. Unfortunately, because it seemed to have avoided the attacks that destroyed the other cities, it became a refuge of sorts."

"Which meant that when it was destroyed the loss of life was much higher than it might have been at other times," Ragnor said as he picked up the story again. "Those not in the city at the time were left alone with inadequate supplies and no way down from the mountains. The

Rocs flew resupply missions for a while, but ultimately were unable to do much as our ability to restock food or anything else failed quickly. And then the Rocs disappeared."

"That sounds horrific," Jalor said as the group entered the portal room. "Did they all die?"

Raglin shook his head. "Not all, but many did. Those who survived had the small herds that could be used for food. Mistakes were made, of course, but enough people survived to maintain the villages. Several new places were built at the old retreat sites, so they could start with at least some shelter. There was some small-scale grain farms, and some artisans who made objects aimed at tourists. They became important when the mountain people had to fend for themselves, of course. Umber itself grew larger because it was on a key crossroad used by the villagers to exchange goods."

"Have any of you visited Umber?" Jalor asked.

"Yes, but a long time ago," Ragnor replied. "We did twice and I'm sure Trabor has a few times. I don't think the others did, though. There were some dealings with settlements lower down the mountains, so they were not completely isolated for the entire time. Then the one pass into the whole area collapsed during a shake to the point where we were unable to restore it. That was around two thousand cycles ago."

"How were you received?"

"If things haven't changed there will be a certain lack of trust in Mages," Raglin replied. "We were blamed for the damage and loss of life. There was no real differentiation between Council or rebel Mages. We did some work to help them to survive better, but it was of small impact, I feel. There are long memories of the destruction that ensued and who was responsible."

"Okay, so more ill feeling to get past. Any chance we run into ghazrak or some of Goroth's crowd there?"

"It's unlikely but you never know. In many ways Umber is strategically insignificant today as Abroshar was in the past." Ragnor paused and considered.

"Wonderful! So why are we doing this again?"

"Because we need all of Ennaris to join the effort, at least so says the Prophesy. Umber represents a group that often is forgotten, but today there are many thousands living in the high reaches and valleys. There is a second reason, though. Trabor suspects that the easterners may be under the sway of Goroth. At least that's his interpretation based on tales he picked up about parties of easterners being found dead in the high passes with amulets of Groks. If that's the case, then these peaks may well be used as an avenue by them to get into the fight, assuming there's some way to summon them."

Jalor nodded as Raglin activated the portal and selected their destination.

The small group emerged from the portal in a room similar to those experienced in the visit to the Clans. The mosaic floor showed scenes of mountain vistas or ski fields, climbing groups pictured part-way up a cliff-face. One image showed the main square of the old city of Abroshar, as Raglin told the group while he examined the map displayed on the portal's screen. The walls carried other scenes of the city.

Abroshar had characteristics similar to other cities pictured in the portal gate rooms. The buildings were not as tall as some others but graceful spires were linked by paths that appeared to float above bustling promenades and squares. Tall trees abounded around the squares, with deep green foliage offsetting the muted colours of the buildings and pavements. It was the promenades and squares that caught Jalor's attention. Other portal images that he had seen of Ennarisi cities lacked people. In these images, finely rendered even though presented via mosaic, the Ennarisi were shown to be relatively slender as a rule and wore a mix of robes or long shirts and tight-fitting leggings or loose trousers. It was not, Jalor thought, any different to what he had seen on Ennaris during the course of this mission. He said as much to the twins.

"Oh yes, of course," Ragnor replied. "What you see has been the common dress for many millennia. There is little need for more, except in a few areas such as the icy far north or the desert. Abroshar was not a strategic city, but it was an Ennarisi city, so it had its own micro-climate controlled so that its citizens could walk around without discomfort."

"Its own micro-climate?" Jalor queried. "All Ennarisi cities had climate control?"

"Indeed, yes," Ragnor enthused. "We developed our weather controllers over thousands of cycles. At first they were used to protect food crops from inclement weather but long before the rebellion the cities' weather was managed. Our citizens were quite comfortable. Using the portals or the air and land-based rapid transport systems, we could move from city to city and within the cities in comfort. In part, that's what made the fall so devastating."

Jalor nodded. "People who knew nothing but comfort were forced to deal with harsh conditions, uncertain weather patterns and a complete lack of services."

"Yes," Raglin said bleakly, as Ragnor's enthusiasm faded to sorrow. "Even the ones who had more difficult lives by choice were unprepared. To bring us back to our task, those who lived in these mountains were made as comfortable as anyone on Ennaris. The adventurers who went into the wilder parts knew they had those comforts to return to."

Jalor nodded again, trying to put himself in the shoes of a highly privileged people, with so much done for them, who where suddenly thrown on their own resources. The result would have been disastrous, on top of the apocalyptic destruction of their planet and the resultant deaths of so many. Another thought came to him, one that he had meant to ask on several occasions.

"You said there were artisans who practised old ways. Where was your heavy industry? You must have had a strong manufacturing sector to provide all of these comforts, building materials and the whole range of goods. I expect that these centres were destroyed during the rebellion but none of the portal images show heavy industry."

"No, they were all off-planet," Ragnor said, looking around at the images on walls and floors. "We mined the asteroids or planets with no life forms and all processing was done either close to the mines or in orbital facilities."

"Those orbitals were destroyed during the last battle," Raglin took up the story, "although we think that was accidental. There were so many damaged ships and debris drifting in all directions that we think the orbital stations were victims of collision. To the best of our knowledge none survived, and we do still have functioning space-based monitors."

"So no means to keep making stuff, either," Jalor mused.

"No," Raglin continued. "There was nearly nothing left."

A moment passed as each considered what had happened. The guards were scattered around the room, examining the images shown.

"Well, we won't get far standing here," Jalor said. "Let's get moving."

Confidently he walked towards the doors but they remained closed. A faint whine told of a mechanism trying to work and failing. Jalor tried again, stepping back and then forward again, but the doors remained in place.

"Abroshar portal, are the doors to this gate room functional?" Jalor asked.

"The doors report no failure, Flight-Colonel," the portal replied. "However, there is significant pressure on them that may be holding them in place."

"Rock fall, perhaps," Raglin replied.

Ragnor nodded, walking to the doors and holding both hands against against them on each side of the centre line. He concentrated for a time before turning back.

"Yes, there's a lot of rock on the other side. We should be able to shift it, though."

The twins took position in front of the doors and stood quite still. Having seen what they could do during the battle of Escar, Jalor was confident that they would clear the blockage quickly. After only three or four minutes by Jalor's estimation, one door shifted slightly before both opened in a series of jerky movements. The group was confronted by a wall of fallen rock. The twins remained in their places. Jalor could hear what sounded like rocks being thrown aside, which continued for a further ten minutes or so. The twins stepped back in unison.

Jalor and the guards stared as the pile of large, jagged rocks seemed to collapse in on themselves from the top. A trickle of rock dust fell through the small gaps between the rocks. The trickle became a flood as the lower rocks lost their internal cohesion. Finally, after only a short time, a large mound of rock dust stood before the portal gate room beneath a rough arch of rock, roughly ten metres in depth by Jalor's estimate. Raglin held his concentration while Ragnor made as series of small gestures, as though spreading something out. The rock dust swirled into a short column and then separated in two. The rock dust swirled across the walls and ceiling of the arch, forming a smooth surface that solidified as Jalor and the guards watched, astonished.

The two Mages relaxed, shaking themselves to relieve tight muscles. Ragnor stepped into the newly formed passageway and examined their handiwork, while Raglin turned to the watching group.

"This will hold well enough for now, I think. We'll come back and finish the job so that it's safe for anyone using the portal gate. That can wait for a while, though."

"It's solid," Ragnor reported, "It may not survive a shake though, so care will be needed. But for now it's good."

Jalor nodded, impressed but trying to take it in stride.

"Do you know the way to Umber?" he asked of the twins.

"Abroshar Portal, show a map of this area and the location of Umber," Raglin said.

The portal screen configured to show a map of the area, with a town clearly marked on it. A path was drawn from the town to a diamond icon that Jalor assumed represented the portal gate room.

The map was checked and then Ragnor led the way from the portal gate room. The small group walked through the archway and into a tumbled ruin. The map may have pointed the way to the town, but the remains of the destroyed city made any sort of direct path impossible.

The thousands of cycles since Abroshar was destroyed had done nothing to hide the devastation that had occurred. Twisted and melted metal had rusted but the remains of beams and spars emerged from piles of rubble in every direction. A vague path may have been a thoroughfare once, but now it was merely a means of skirting the mounds of debris.

The twin Mages looked around themselves as they walked, taking in the destruction.

"It's worse than I remembered," Raglin said sombrely. "Immediately after Abroshar was destroyed, we came here on two Rocs to see what we could do to help. There was very little left then. Almost no people remained alive in the city. A lot of it was vaporised, of course. The weapons used were horrific. We helped the survivors to build a few sheds and huts in a nearby protected valley using some of the debris and were able to build a well to provide water, but could do little else. That became the core of Umber over time."

"We couldn't stay," Ragnor continued quietly. "The Rocs were anxious to return to their eyries to see if their mates survived. Many Rocs had been killed also and we believed that the whole race had fallen below their ability to breed enough fledglings to survive, especially when we saw none of them after such a short time. In that, I'm glad to say, we were wrong. And we knew the Archmage would have need of as many Mages as possible, even if only to provide extra power for the fighters."

"General," the guard sergeant said, "we have a watcher or two. In front and about thirty degrees to the right. Behind the base of the broken column."

Jalor nodded, slowly turning as though surveying the area. He saw no movement from the spot the sergeant pointed out, but had no doubt there was one or more people watching.

"Well, let's see what happens if we put on a show," Jalor said. "Form the guard up. Break out the standard."

"Yes, sir," the sergeant replied, turning to his guards troop. "You heard the general. Form up, by twos. Standard-bearer to the front. Unfurl the banner. Stand at ease."

A few moments of bustling activity soon saw the guard lined in twos with the standard-bearer at their head holding the pole bearing the standard of the Faero. All stood at parade rest with their small shields held in a relaxed pose and hands on swords. Jalor nodded.

"Let's go," Jalor said. "We'll aim to go past that column."

Jalor led the way followed by the Mages with the guard following close behind. When the winding path took them close by the column base Jalor called a halt again. He looked around, as though examining landmarks.

"You may as well come out," Jalor said conversationally. "We know you're there and I'd like to speak with you. You will come to no harm."

Jalor waited. The guard sergeant made a faint gesture to the two guards at the rear who broke away and circled around mounds of debris to come on the watchers from behind. A short time later, two men walked from behind the ruined column followed by the two guards with swords drawn. As the four reached Jalor, the guards sheathed their swords but held position behind the two watchers.

"Good day," Jalor said conversationally, "my name is Vinca Jalor. I am general of the army of the Faero. I assume you live in Umber? Can you lead us to your city?"

The two men looked to each other. One, a shorter man with ruddy complexion, coarse round features and thinning dark hair, shrugged. His companion, leaner and taller than the first by half a head but still shorter than any of Jalor's party, with narrow features dominated by a long, thin nose and unruly red hair, just nodded.

"Well, general," the first said in a slightly nasal voice, "I guess we don' have no choice. Don' know who or what this ferro is though, nor nothin' 'bout any army. An' how'd you get here anyway? Where from?"

Jalor nodded and smiled easily, even as his heart sank. Not to know who the Faero was indicated a complete lack of knowledge of Ennaris' history. That was logical in a way, given that Umber had been isolated in the high mountains for generations, but that the twins knew of the city and the people and that the Mages had visited it several times had raised hopes that he would be able to garner additional support. That hope seemed destined to be dashed.

"We will explain all of that once we have met your leaders," Jalor replied. "You do have a leader, don't you?"

"Well, yer, we do," the shorter man said. "Jerrod's the Noll of Umber and the area 'roun' about. I guess we c'n take yer to see 'im."

"Thank you," Jalor smiled again. "What are your names?"

"I be Karox," said the first man pointing to himself first and then his companion, "an' he be Vellis."

"Well Karox, Vellis, please lead the way," Jalor said. "Is Umber far?"

"No," Karox nodded, "will take 'roun' 'alf an 'ur."

The city of Umber proved to be a compact settlement that Jalor would have called a large town in many places. Constructed almost completely of stone, the city had no wall but was built between a natural steep-sided depression spanned by a stone bridge and a stony cliff that reached high above it. Individual structures were built side by side, with many sharing walls in common with neighbours. Narrow paved streets wound through the city, as though the buildings came before the paving.

The twins were gazing with interest at everything they saw, quietly discussing different aspects of the city or its buildings. Jalor, likewise, looked at Umber with interest and uncertainty. On one hand, he was fascinated at seeing this city that had been so completely isolated from the rest of Ennaris for such a long time. On the other hand, his hopes and expectations for any level of support that may be forthcoming from Umber were evaporating.

The residents of Umber stared curiously at the strangers as Karox and Vellis led them through the narrow, winding streets. A small procession formed, trailing behind the guards. By the time they reached a small paved square that Karox informed Jalor was where the administrative centre of Umber would be found, there were almost a hundred people following them.

In the middle of the square was a low stone structure, with no windows and a stone tile roof. A single heavy timber door allowed access. Standing in front of the building was a stone-sided well with square timber beams supporting a handle from which a rope extended into the depths of the well.

The twins stared at the building before sharing an amused smile. Jalor was about to ask what they found so fascinating when the door was flung open and a man exited the building. He was taken aback at the crowd descending on him and stopped abruptly. Karox and Vellis also stopped, followed by Jalor and the twins. The guards contingent did likewise but adopted a parade rest stance.

"Karox? Vellis? What's this? Who are these people?" the man demanded.

"Jerrod," Karox replied, nodding. "We foun' these people in th'old ruins. This one," pointing to Jalor, "says he's a general of someone called Ferro. He wanted to talk with yer."

"Someone called Ferro? Do you mean *the* Faero? And why do you want to talk with me?" Jerrod demanded.

"My name is Vinca Jalor," Jalor said. "I am General of the army of the Faero of Ennaris. We are seeking out any who can assist us when we confront Goroth and his allies, as the Prophesy of Halfgar tells us to do."

Jerrod was perplexed.

"What army? The only Prophesy I know about is one that stories tell us about? And that's for children."

Jalor nodded to himself, his suspicions mostly confirmed, although Jerrod knew of the Faero. Maybe the Mages had made it this far in the past, but this isolated group was missing knowledge that had been spread through the rest of Ennaris in more recent times.

"This may be difficult to believe," Jalor said, aware of a growing crowd, "but there is a Prophesy that has so far proven to be accurate. It may be the one you were told as children. It tells of the return of Goroth, the rebel Mage who caused the great destruction of Ennaris thousands of cycles ago. The Prophesy tells that the people of Ennaris must join together to oppose him or risk falling under his control. That resistance will be led by the Faero of Ennaris."

Jerrod stared.

"It's just stories. Why come here with your tales? And how did you come here, anyway?"

"We came through a portal gate," Jalor explained. "That is a piece of the old technology that has come awake once again. And we came because Umber represents a section of Ennaris who should be part of the fight against Goroth."

"What's a portal gate?" Jerrod asked, seizing on one part of Jalor's response.

"It's like a gate that can take you to different parts of Ennaris," Jalor replied.

"What? Like magic?" Jerrod asked sceptically.

"It may look like magic, but it's not. It is, however, from the time before the rebellion and the destruction that the rebels wrought on Ennaris," Jalor said, continuing to stress that the destruction was caused by rebels.

"That destruction was caused by the Mages, that much we know," Karox chimed in.

"It was caused by *rebel* Mages, who were opposed by the loyal Mages as well as loyal people from everywhere," Jalor replied.

"And between them they ruined everything," Jerrod said bitterly, and Jalor was surprised at a murmur that passed through the watching crowd.

"That was a consequence, yes," Jalor said. "Believe it or not, had the loyal Mages not done what they did it may have been worse. Goroth and his followers were trying to destroy all of Ennaris."

"So where're these Mages now, then?" Karox asked to another murmur.

"There are very few Mages left," Jalor replied. "Most died opposing the rebels, and many of the rest died trying to repair the damage caused.

No new Mages have been found since then. The few remaining prepare to meet Goroth once again."

"Well, why 'aven't they come here to help us?" Karox demanded.

"They did," Jalor said. "Do you have old tales of two Mages providing aid in the days immediately after the disaster happened?"

"The old stories say somethin' 'bout that," Jerrod conceded. "They built th'initial shelter for the people here, but then they left us to our own efforts."

"They were needed elsewhere," Jalor nodded. "The damage and loss of life was great and widespread. And then they were unable to get back here to do anything else to help your people".

"Old Anbella said that the Mages weren't ta blame," a voice piped up from the crowd.

"Old Anbella was crazy," another voice said, to a mixture of laughter and objections. "She told my da that she were 'ere when th'old city was destroyed. Ha!"

The two Mages glanced to each other.

"Where is Anbella now?" Raglin asked.

"She died about forty cycles back," Jerrod answered. "She knew the old tales, back from when we had wandering Tellers come to Umber. She said we needed to know what happened and why."

"She use' ta sit at the back and just listen to 'em, she tol' me once," an older man said into the quiet that followed Jerrod's statement.

"She sounds like a wise person," Raglin replied. "How did she die?"

Jerrod looked uncomfortable, and more murmurs rolled around the assembled crowd.

"A buildin' fell on 'er durin' a shake," Karox said.

"She saved me mam an' 'er mam," a woman said defiantly. "I'll say it even if you won't. She stood in the middle o' th'old meetin' hall an' held the roof up with 'er mind while everyone got out but she couldn' get out 'erself."

Raglin sighed while Ragnor shook his head.

"She used her gifts to save your people, and may have used more strength than she could afford," Ragnor said quietly. "There is no shame in that, either for her or for you."

"Gifts?" Vellis chimed in uncertainly. "Why call it that? Some o' th'old ones use' ta talk about 'how they was scared o' her and 'ow they made fun o' her. 'Ow can they be gifts?"

"And yet still she was prepared to give her life to save others," Raglin commented. "I would say that makes her a special person. Gifts are neither good or evil. But they might be wielded by good people or bad people. Anbella sounds like a good one."

Jalor nodded his agreement, while he wondered what to do.

"She use' ta keep the well runnin'," an elderly woman said. "Said it were blocked because the water moved. She use' ta move the rocks aroun' and get th' water runnin' again."

"She moved the rocks?" Raglin asked.

"So she said," the old woman replied with a firm nod. "Said she weren't as good with that so couldn' do it right, though."

"I never knew that," Jerrod said. "Th'old well don't run now, anyhow. Now we have ta get water from the spring. Long walk."

"This well?" Raglin asked, moving to stand by the stone well.

"Yer," Jerrod confirmed. "Story was this well were made by the Mages after th'old city collapsed. That were a long time fer a well to last."

"It was built to last," Raglin replied absently, staring into the depths.

"Well?" Ragnor asked.

"Yes, there has been a build up of fallen rock in the subterranean water course," Raglin replied, still gazing into the well. "Probably caused by shakes over the cycles. The water probably changed course to compensate but moved away from the base of the well."

"Can you do anything about it?" Ragnor asked.

The crowd was watching curiously at this strange exchange. Jerrod opened his mouth as though to speak, but thought better of it and joined the crowd in watching. Jalor merely stood with a faint smile as the twin Mages ignored the fact that they had an audience.

"I think so," Raglin asked. "Give me a moment."

The crowd gasped as Raglin's Mage stone flared into life on his forehead as he concentrated. From the well came a prolonged grinding sound and a puff of dust, followed by a pop. Raglin stood back, blinking slightly as his concentration dropped. The Mage stone's light faded.

"That should do it," he said conversationally.

"What - what did you do, er, um, master Mage?" Jerrod asked hesitantly.

"Oh, I moved the water channel back to where it was. Trabor can do that sort of thing much better than me. It should be fine for a while, but we should come back and do a better job when all this is over," Raglin said easily. "Assuming we win, of course."

"Jerrod, allow me to introduce you to my companions," Jalor said into the silence that ensued following Raglin's statement. "These are the twin Mages, Raglin and Ragnor" - the twins nodded as they were introduced - "and this is Troop Leader Mastin and a contingent of the Faero's Guard."

Jerrod and the people of Umber ignored Mastin and his troop and just stared at the twins.

"The, the twin Mages?" Jerrod stammered.

"That's what we've been called," Ragnor replied. "We apologise for not returning sooner but there were greater needs elsewhere. And then all paths to Umber were destroyed and, well, we couldn't get here."

Jalor allowed the moment to stretch out as the people of Umber continued to stare open-mouthed at the twins.

"Your stories, the ones you were told when young, the ones that Anbella listened to and repeated for you," Jalor continued, "were to make sure you did not forget what had happened and what remained to be done. That time is now. We are asking for your aid as members of the Faero's army as we prepare to battle Goroth once again."

Quiet reigned. The assembled people turned to Jerrod, their elected leader. He, in turn, looked from the twins to Jalor.

"We have no warriors," Jerrod finally replied. "We have had no need. And the young who are inclined to take up arms left a short time ago."

"Where did they go?" Raglin asked.

Silence again, as though the residents of Umber were wary of revealing secrets. Watching Jerrod, Jalor thought that he was torn.

"We were sworn to secrecy," he finally said, almost as a sigh.

"He's the Faero's general, and they're the legendary twin Mages," the old woman who had spoken for Anbella said. "Anbella would tell ya t'speak."

Jerrod looked from face to face, seeing opposing emotions reflected. He had been sworn to secrecy, but that was to protect the young ones from the enemies. The one who swore him to secrecy said that they would play their part to protect Ennaris. He never said who the enemy was. Surely the Faero or his general would not be that enemy? But the Mages caused the death and destruction long ago, so were they the enemy?

Jalor watched the play of thoughts run across Jerrod's face. He considered just returning to the Citadel and accepting this waste of time, but there was a niggle that was making itself felt.

"Who swore you to secrecy?" Jalor asked.

"I don' know his name," Jerrod said. "He came with ... the others ... and spoke for them."

"What did he look like?"

Jerrod considered again before speaking. "He was tall an' lean, with black hair, real black. 'Twere strange. He wore a simple robe with sandals but the cold had no effect on him."

Jalor nodded. He glanced to the twins, both of whom nodded to him, as though with shared understanding.

"What did he say?" Jalor asked. "Do you recall his words?"

Jerrod nodded, as though to himself. "I do. This was his third time visitin' with us. The first time he wanted us to spread the word through the villages of Umber that fighters were needed. He never said who was th'enemy. He left us with tests to be done and said he'd be back to choose. Things like walkin' on thin edges an' standin' at the big drops without scarin'. He came back with two others. The ones who wanted to fight had to ... er ... talk with th'others."

"And not everyone could talk with these others?" Ragnor asked.

"No," Jerrod shook his head to add meaning.

"So they could not be selected, could they?"

"No, master Mage," Jerrod replied. "But they could go with the fighters if they wanted. To help them, he said. They all went."

"And the third time?" Jalor rejoined the discussion.

"He came back with the others and they took the young ones with 'em," Jerrod said quietly, as though with dread.

"How did they get here?" Jalor asked.

Silence. No-one said anything. The assembled townspeople avoided looking at anyone.

"Did they fly?"

Jerrod started, giving Jalor the answer.

"How many Rocs came?"

"They were wonderful," a middle-aged woman said. "So big!"

That opened the flood-gates.

"So many colours!"

"Their eyes ... they seemed to spin and twirl!"

The townspeople all provided their own additions to the descriptions of the Rocs. Jalor allowed them to have their say, nodding and smiling. Finally, the excited comments died down. Several of the townspeople looked to each other with a grimace. The secret was no more.

"And they were seeking fighters, you say?" Raglin said into the quiet.

Jerrod merely nodded, receiving an answering nod from Raglin.

"We believe the dark-haired man was Kunas," Raglin continued quietly. "He is one of the returned Guardians."

Mouths opened in shock as Raglin's statement took effect. Jalor realised that the crowd had grown greatly, and amazed looks were everywhere. None of them, it seems, had considered that the strange man might be a mythical Guardian.

"Guardian?" Jerrod breathed.

"Yes," Jalor said. "But why did they need your people?"

"For th'Alnar-kun," a young voice piped up.

"What?" Raglin asked, spinning to look at the small boy who had spoken.

The boy shrank back against a woman who wrapped a protective arm around him and all attention swung to him. Raglin made no movement but held out one hand.

"Have no fear," the Mage said gently. "Who told you about the Alnar-kun?"

The boy looked to the woman - his mother, Jalor assumed - who nodded.

"It were Ny-kar," the boy said. "He took Jellis with him."

"And you could speak with Ny-kar?" Raglin asked, glancing to a smiling Ragnor.

"Yes," the boy said in a small voice.

"What is your name, child?"

The boy stayed quiet, gripping the woman's skirt tightly.

"This be Dellor," the woman said. "Jellis be his cousin."

"Jerrod, Dellor is very important," Raglin said. "Those who can speak with Rocs are few in today's Ennaris."

"Some of the towns are building structures for them to land on," Jerrod said. "I been think' we should that 'ere."

"The Faero has ordered the same for the Citadel, as has the King of Escar for his city and towns," Raglin said. "It will be a good idea. We can return and assist you in the task once our job is done."

"What is the Alnar-kun?" Jalor asked.

"It is the elite warrior group among the Rocs," Ragnor chimed in. "Roc warriors are joined with men and women to form fighting pairs. Traditionally, they were among the most feared warrior groups. Tell me, did any of your fighters display any gifts?"

"No, of course not," Jerrod said.

"Or none that you are aware of," Ragnor said with a slight edge. "As I said, gifts are neither good or bad, they just are. They should not be feared, but should be celebrated."

Jerrod merely nodded.

"So the Rocs we have seen are the warrior wings, but there is a more elite group?" Jalor asked, surprised.

"I assume they will have to be trained, and I expect Kunas will help there," Ragnor replied. "But yes, traditionally the Alnar-kun were the best the Rocs had."

"Usually they were paired with battle gifted," Raglin said. "Not full Mages, necessarily, but they had strong gifts."

"So we may have allies drawn from Umber after all," Jalor said, glancing to Jerrod.

"So it seems," Raglin agreed.

"Then I don't believe we have any further need to remain here," Jalor said. "Jerrod, if you would come with us to the portal we can show you how you can communicate with us, or at least leave us a message. Should there be any who wish to join with the Faero's army then send a message to me. They will be welcome."

# 33. Goroth Prepares

Grensor was furious. Not only had Goroth continued to criticise his decision to have General Morsen attack Escar, but Likud was dismissive of the benefit provided by the ghazrak. There had been some problems with the newer batches, assuredly, but nothing a quick reset would not solve. Grensor had even worked out a way to make use of parts of the batch that did not work out. So far, he had more than a thousand ghazrak, and they were more efficient fighting machines than ever.

He still was unable to breed or design into most of them any sort of coherent and consistent decision-making capability - and if he truly was honest with himself the breeding part always resulted in dead females rather than a new generation of ghazrak - but Likud's Andorethi were tailor-made for controlled decision-making and Grensor had been experimenting with making the Andorethi more amenable to his control and more able to control the ghazrak. The Andorethi seemed to have a natural ability to delve into the psyches of the ghazrak and take control. The problem was that Likud had bred out of the Andorethi almost everything required for independent thought, which explained, Grensor thought wryly, why Likud had not been able to defeat his enemies. Even now, he was instructing them on what to do with the battle fleet rather than having someone there who could decide for themselves. It was a curious outcome for Likud, but entirely in keeping with his views on accepting orders.

And that was another thing. Likud believed that he had stepped into the second-in-command spot and that Grensor would do whatever he, Likud, wanted. That was not Grensor's idea at all. If anything, Likud should be third in line not second. Goroth appeared not to care one way or the other, which grated. Was it not Grensor who had held fast, on Ennaris, rather than fleeing? Was it not Grensor who had devised ways to create new forms of ghazrak that rivalled the Rocs in the air. True, they had not passed their first test against the Rocs, but Grensor had seen where he went wrong, and the new lot would be much improved. They were more heavily armoured now, which meant they had to have greater wing spans and greater muscle mass, but that had been accomplished. And that was not to mention the ghazrak of the sea! These truly formidable beasts would destroy any shipping on Ennaris today, and the Faero almost certainly had to use ships to get some of his forces into place.

But none of this was considered of great enough value! The Escar attack allowed Grensor to observe how his forces worked, how the northers and ghazrak could be used, how they handled the knights or the infantry. The attack was almost a success, after all, only defeated because of the Rocs and that golden fighter who seemed to be everywhere. Probably there were more than one. Grensor had a tickle of awareness at the back of his mind that told him he should know more about that fighter, but he pushed it aside in his anger. The attack had also showed that Drewflin had not developed true offensive weapons, and none of the others had them either, which is why they had to throw stones. There were no such weapons underneath the grasses of the steppes, which was where Grensor had planned to engage the Faero's army.

Goroth wanted to make his attack in no more than four tendays time, but Grensor would not have enough ghazrak available at that time. Goroth wanted two thousand, but he would get around three—quarters of that, probably a few less. Not only that, but Goroth wanted to attack in multiple directions at the one time. The main body of the attack would be via the steppes, which was what Grensor expected, so that was good, but the other thrusts would be problematic. Ghazrak had not been tested in extreme cold. He knew that the small band he had sent to the desert to wreak havoc had not survived. He assumed that was because of the heat of the desert. So there seemed to be some sort of operating temperature constraints that he had yet to fathom.

Likud was disparaging to Grensor when he objected to the time frames and was dismissive of the problems encountered. Grensor ground his teeth when he thought about the conversation.

"Grensor's creations cannot be ready in time? Well, my Andorethi will be in place at the right time. Already they have taken up positions to confront the Union fleet and at the right time *Qorv* will deploy its primary weapon and disrupt their tactics entirely." Likud puffed out his chest as he spoke.

"But you have to tell them what to do all of the time," Grensor replied with a smirk. "How can you be sure that this will happen if you're not there?"

"They will do as they are instructed," Likud growled, "because if they don't then they don't survive. My monitors will make sure of that."

"Monitors?" Goroth asked idly.

"The monitors make sure my instructions are followed. If they're not, then the chain of command is initiated, and the successors *do* follow orders."

"And what of the one who did not?" Goroth was interested despite himself.

"They're dead and dealt with, along with their families," Likud snarled. "I find it an effective means of ensuring obedience."

Grensor had sighed. "So not only do you remove those who think, you also remove the families of those who think, thereby ensuring the ability to think is not passed down to the next generation."

"There are always throw-backs," Likud shrugged, his voice harsh still, "but the monitors are effective and stamp them out when they try anything."

Goroth had looked to Grensor and grimaced. "How are you progressing at developing Andorethi who can control the ghazrak?"

"The control part is easy. It's what they had naturally," Grensor had replied. "It's the decision-making that is failing, and I can see why. There's almost nothing to work with."

"Well. From what I can see the current batch of ghazrak are uncontrollable when they're let loose, so we need some form of control, or I can't rely on them in battle. I need them as shock troops, but I also need some of them in reserve to send in if needed." Goroth thought for a moment. "Can we bring one of the Kindred in to control them?"

Grensor had paled. "The Kindred? Why would we want to do that. If it gets loose there'll be nothing left for us to rule!"

"But you can control it, can't you?" Goroth had said. "You told us you've been growing stronger in your interactions with them."

Likud snorted. "Talk, all talk! Just what I expected of you, Grensor. You talk and do nothing. Even the much-vaunted ghazrak can't be as effective as they should be."

Grensor rose to the bait. "I can handle one of the Kindred without any trouble," he shot back. "But don't blame me if it mistakes your Andorethi for food."

"Enough," Goroth said quietly. "I need both of you to play your part in this. I need as many ghazrak as you can make, and I need the Mages to be occupied in defence. How do we deal with the Rocs?"

"I will have at least twenty flying ghazrak, improved, for them," Grensor replied. "For some reason they seem to be more independent, possibly because of the root stock I used."

"We will have to move on time," Goroth said. "We will use all the northers, and I've been made aware that the desert people from the south are moving also. It seems they've sat still long enough to find a war leader. I want them to find the battle already over when they get here."

"They'll have to come by sea," Grensor said, "and I have a surprise for them, too."

"Let me guess, fish with teeth!" Likud said derisively.

"Something like that," Grensor retorted. "I'll release them shortly."

"As long as they make sure those boats don't get there," Goroth replied, giving Grensor a searching look. "We can't have any more mistakes."

Mistakes! Grensor snarled to himself in frustration and anger. He made no mistakes. It was not his fault that Goroth had been caught during the rebellion, nor was it his fault that the imprisonment had lasted so long. In fact, that was entirely down to Goroth and Likud and their decision to try to destroy Ennaris. In Goroth's case, it came because of trusting in Likud. In the latter's case, it was because of his nature to kill and destroy. To hear him talk, you would think that he had been wildly successful with his Andorethi, where in fact it seemed to Grensor that Likud had come close to destroying what he remembered as a people who had been close to achieving the goals of an advanced civilisation by themselves.

From Grensor's view, it was likely that Likud had corrupted if not destroyed that once proud and independent people. And that was what he wanted to do with Ennaris. Remove any hint of the people having any sort of will of their own. They were merely to do the bidding of Likud. Where Goroth had failed because his intentions were not supported by enough of the Ennarisi, Likud appeared to fail because he deliberately drove out of his subjects the ability to think, to act without his direct instructions. There was no way that the Andorethi would be able to destroy the opposing fleet, if the latter had even a small amount of skill and at least equal force. And Grensor thought that would be the case.

Once again, a measure of regret raised its head, unlooked for. Grensor stared at nothing as he travelled back through the decisions that caused him to arrive at the current juncture. One poor decision after another, and now here he was, caught in the jaws of a trap of his own making. He had created the ghazrak with Goroth, those creatures who had been the cause of so much pain, suffering and destruction during the rebellion, and thus put himself beyond the ability to be redeemed. And now here he was again, creating even more fierce creatures, and all because ... Well, he could not really say why. Nor could he explain why he was going to invoke one of the Kindred and unleash the ghazrak of air and sea. It was now just a factor of keeping going and hoping it was all worthwhile.

Goroth was just as dissatisfied as Grensor. However, where Grensor had lived through the thousands of cycles since the rebellion's failure and had grown discontented and angry, Goroth had existed in a sort of frozen daze and had only been aware of the passage of time for a very short period. Once he had realised how long he had been imprisoned, and that Grensor had been free for that entire time, he expected to find a ready-made army of ghazrak that were much improved on what they had created for the rebellion. Instead, what he found was an old man wallowing in self-pity who seemingly had spent his time in a funk of self-delusion and a vague form of research. In fact, almost nothing had been done, nothing achieved.

Oh, Goroth admitted that Grensor had ensured there was a supply of raw material for his ghazrak by retaining the loyalty of the northern people. And, from what he had been told, the people on the eastern side of the great mountain range that divided east from west had been groomed to provide support using historical grievances against the Faero and Guides. And Grensor had developed ghazrak for both air and sea, although Goroth had yet to see them in action.

But the fool had shown his hand by attacking that city. Escar was its name, Goroth recalled, and it had been built on the ruins of Aberwin. And in doing so he had caused the Rocs to play a part and thus renew their ages-old alliance with the Faero and other Ennarisi. That could be a disaster! Goroth had never seen the Rocs at war, even during the re-bellion, but the legends of old told of a warrior race, and the stories told during the rebellion by Goroth's own people showed that should they be angered they were formidable indeed. Just how the northers were de-feated at Escar Goroth was not sure, but from what he heard there were several Mages involved, and that would have to be considered. Still, it was obvious that Marjory was not one of them, so perhaps the rumours of her death were true. Goroth could not imagine Drewflin fighting a battle, given his lack of offensive gifts, without Marjory by his side. They were, he recalled with a twist of the lips, inseparable. But without her, the other Mages would be lost.

For a moment Goroth paused. For him, of course, it was but a short time since Marjory had opposed him and Likud and defeated them. How? He was not sure, but he could feel clearly the fear that had shot through him as he realised that they were being overwhelmed by her power. Never had he felt such power pushing back. She had not only held them but then had increased the pressure so that Goroth had to defend. The end was but a matter of time then. He remembered her eyes, blazing as she levitated and then *walked* towards them through the air, with her long hair blowing back by the forces that had been unleashed. Her will held at bay Likud's attack with the most advanced weaponry Ennaris had developed, and Likud tended to attack using massive power rather than finesse, but she had walked *through* it, creating a shield that expelled the forces into space to destroy Goroth's last loyal fleet, constantly adjusting her shield until she had it just right, so that finally it cut through *Scaliba*, the great battleship they had in orbit.

When the last field generator, powered by a quantum power unit, had failed Goroth found himself facing her almost alone, for Likud had fled already. He remembered she flicked a lance of power through the others, leaving him without support. He had felt his death reaching for him, only to find her held back by Drewflin, for a reason that he still did not understand. Then, between them, they had managed to bind him. The rebellion ended then, of course, and he knew nothing more, for his binding was a stasis chamber. He never did find out where that was located, not that he cared now that he had broken out. And now she was gone. He was able to admit that he had been terrified when he found himself facing her. She was a Battle Mage such as Ennaris had not had for a long time, perhaps never before. They tended to be quite prepared to end battles very permanently, especially when arrayed against those who had caused such destruction. He knew that, as it was part of his early training also.

For a moment he felt supremely weary, and the weight of guilt pressed on him unexpectedly. Never had he intended to destroy Ennaris, and yet, that was what he ended up trying to do. Never had he intended to destroy the civilisation that had shone brightest in the galaxy, and yet, that is what he and Likud had done. All he wanted was to be acknowledged as a leader of the Council and to take Ennaris in a direction more suited to its place in the galaxy. He also dreamed of being a true Battle Mage in his own right. Instead, he found that he was not considered to be a leader, and he was but a shadow of a Battle Mage such as Marjory. His supporters had all been disaffected, especially after they were recalled from both Andoreth and Ordoreth and disciplined. He growled unconsciously. The memory was still raw enough to rankle. After all, he had done nothing truly wrong, nor had most of his team. True, some of them had set themselves up as powers of the planet, and the Andorethi and Ordorethi had worshipped some of them as gods in their early development, but that would not have continued and was harmless. As the civilisations developed, the ideas of gods would fall away naturally. He had even encouraged the religious developments that arose. The results, he believed, had been that the peoples of both worlds had developed much faster than they would have otherwise.

But the Council had seen fit to condemn the whole team. As leader of the team, he had borne the brunt of the blame. He frowned. As though his was the only team to have done that! He was sure he remembered others doing the same although, uncomfortably, he could also recall them being disciplined. Somehow the Council always knew, and he had never discovered how. The review team had reached Andoreth only after the Council had been warned, which meant it must have been one of his team, but still he was unable to work out who that might have been.

Grensor? Maybe, although he doubted it. Grensor had gravitated to Goroth because of his own disciplinary troubles after it was found that he was experimenting with creating new life forms on a planet whose name Goroth could not recall. He remembered that Grensor had made the discovery that the Andorethi could call on what they now knew as the Kindred and had shown Goroth how to make contact. He had come to recognise that the Kindred could provide him with knowledge outside the usual paths of the Mages. Grensor had created the first batch of ghazrak using the techniques gleaned, adapted by his own unusually detailed knowledge of genetic engineering. That knowledge was unusual because, despite their advances, most Ennarisi relied on either technology or their gifts. Grensor, however, relied on his incredible memory for genetic sequences and his ability to make significant changes using nothing more than ingenuity and very basic tools. That and the ability to call on the Kindred for assistance, which required control such that Goroth doubted anyone else could do, other than himself. Certainly, Likud could not. He was erratic at the best of times and tight discipline was needed to control the Kindred.

Could it have been Likud? The warrior Mage had been involved in some of the design work for Ennaris' weapons long before Marjory was raised to a Mage. She had surpassed him within a few cycles and then left him far behind. Likud had never accepted the fact that Marjory was superior in skill to him, although he could not even fathom how some of her later technology functioned. But no, Likud stood to lose as much as Goroth. He was one of the ones who had taken Andorethi females as concubines, and many of them, Goroth recalled, over the more than four hundred cycles they were on Andoreth. He also was one who revelled in being a god and relished his self-appointed role as the lord over all the Andorethi.

Grensor's experiments on the Andorethi caused some of them to become more spirit than corporeal. Before that, they had been flesh and blood, with the ability - the gift - of being able to shift into a non-corporeal state. It had been not long after that failure by Grensor that the Council had recalled them. It seemed that Likud had continued that work without thinking through the result. Now, from what Likud said, many if not most Andorethi were non-corporeal from a young age and the population was in decline.

Goroth shook his head, driving away both memory and the sudden uncertainty that afflicted him as he thought of the various failures that had led to the rebellion, his own and those of others. The task remained. He had to clear out the remaining Mages or he would not be able to re-establish himself as a leader of Ennaris. *The* leader of Ennaris, he thought. If that meant more Ennarisi had to die, then so be it. Having been the cause of so many deaths, he would not shy away from more. In fact, Grensor's ghazrak had already caused more deaths, as had the norther army, and there would be many more to come.

So, he would delay for a short time longer so Grensor could try for another batch of ghazrak, and then he would launch his attack, draw Drewflin and the other Mages into a conflict and deal with them all at the one time. Halfgar, that old fool, had made some sort of Prophecy that this would be the final battle. He had been reading Grensor's copy and could not tell just what the Prophesy was saying. It clearly foretold a final battle, casting Goroth as an evil force, he thought with an un-conscious snarl.

So bet it! The final battle it would be. Goroth would rule after this final battle. Then he would extend that rule through the galaxy, taking his rightful place amongst the stars, as once he had dreamed. He had only Grensor and Likud of all the Mages from the past, plus a few northers who had shown gifts for warfare and a motley force of ghazrak and northers, those descendants of a once proud people who had lived in the northern part of Ennaris before joining him in the rebellion. Grensor promised additional forces from the eastern reaches. But the real battle would be fought between the Mages.

Time! He needed time, but it was time he may not have. He had to ensure that Drewflin did not have enough time, too. He had to make his attack before his enemies were set even if he was not fully ready. That would be the balance he needed - how long could he wait before letting Grensor's creatures loose? How long before Drewflin's reinforcements from the south came up? Could Grensor's sea creatures give him the edge there? Time! It all came down to time.

from the south came up? Could Grensor's sea creatures give him the edge there? Time! It all came down to time.

# 34. Maf and the Alnar-kun

The rocky high reaches of the huge mountain range that divided west from east glittered in a dusting of snow. Drifts of deeper snow piled up in small hollows and behind larger stones, while the constant breeze swept the huge, slanted rocks almost clear. Far below there was the green of meadows scattered through the mountains and hardy grasses and shrubs clung to various nooks and crannies, but at the heights the colours mostly were greys, browns and whites.

Maf found the sight entrancing. Hel-nor perched beside him, enjoying Maf's sense of wonder at the sight that he had known for so long that it was common-place. This was not Maf's first visit to these heights. It had become his place to sit and contemplate. The sense of space that opened in front of him and below him gave the recently acclaimed Mage of the Hides a fresh perspective on the world, *his* world. For he had been named Protector, a fabled character in Ennaris' legends for those who took note of such things. Maf was one who did.

He and his chosen band had been with the Alnar-kun for some time now. It had been a time filled with intense activity. The day after the old woman had given him the staff of a Mage of Ennaris, which had been the same day when he was introduced to Hel-nor, the Roc had departed with a promise to return. Maf's job was to select those with suitable gifts to join him and Hel-nor to form the renewed Alnar-kun, the old name for the force of Rocs who flew with Mages and Guides versed in war skills.

This Maf did after Lexis' sending. Many of those chosen had been trained by him, and all were skilled in battle gifts to some extent. Most had been rescued by Maf and others in relatively recent times. He and some others had provided a refuge for them, a place for them to be safe while learning how to control and develop their gifts without causing harm to others. They were taught as much as Maf could teach them, although he knew that he had much to learn still. Still, there were no others, so it was his task as the oldest and the most skilled.

Of the group selected by Maf, Hel-nor would conduct his own assessment, seeking out those who could converse with the Rocs, for that was necessary.

It was a tenday after the battle against the bandits when Maf led his charges away from the Hides, as agreed with Hel-nor. The leave-taking was poignant, for some of the recruits had formed attachments. None opted to remain behind, however. In a field nearby they waited. Not long after, one of the recruits pointed into the distance. An array of dark spots high in the sky became two flights of Rocs, led by Hel-nor. Mouths gaped as the great birds swooped down to land in a flurry of backwash, dust and grass.

Hel-nor made his selections. Twenty were chosen, and Hel-nor observed to Maf that he could have chosen several more. However, he had berths for the twenty only. The remainder returned to the Hides, disappointed but determined to perform their own roles. Maf and the chosen recruits were instructed by their Rocs in how to mount to the birds' backs, how to grasp the harness straps so they did not harm themselves when the Rocs launched and how to sit once mounted. That took some time but, once Hel-nor was satisfied that Rocs and riders were sufficiently prepared for a first flight, the twenty-one Roc and rider pairs took to the skies. Those not chosen returned to the Hides.

It was a leisurely and awe-filled first flight. The recruits had never been so high, had never had a chance to see as much of Ennaris at one time and from such a perspective. Many of them had tears in their eyes when they landed for the night. They had flown across the north-western part of the northern continent, a place where they had spent all of their lives, but never had they seen it laid out below them. Small villages swept past, surrounded by fields and orchards. At one stage they flew over a small town that had been destroyed by fire, the result of the norther army's raid into the area, according to Hel-nor.

For Maf, the short flight had hardened his intent to protect this land, the land of his parents and his friends of the distant past. He knew he had power. For a long time he had considered that, with the Mages gone, he may be the most powerful person on Ennaris. Even though the old gifts appeared to be returning in greater numbers than he had seen in past times, none that he had seen had reached his raw power levels.

During that first flight he had communed with Hel-nor, who had told him of the happenings that the Rocs knew about. The tales were interesting to Maf and he learned much about the peoples and lands of Ennaris that he had not known. But it was when Hel-nor described how the Rocs had aided a Mage at Escar that Maf received a shock. A Mage? A Mage had fought at Escar? And the Defender had been seen? Maf reeled, missing any further information that Hel-nor gave about the aftermath of the battle. The Roc realised that his rider was badly perturbed and fell silent in Maf's mind while the shock was worked through.

That night Maf apologised to Hel-nor.

"I've spent all this time believing no Mages survived the rebellion," he said. "Knowing at least one exists gives some hope."

"When we roost you may get more information," Hel-nor replied. "There is one who has much more knowledge than I."

Maf merely nodded, before settling beside Hel-nor and looking around the large area where twenty-one Rocs and riders had settled. This was on the western edge of the grasslands, where the grasses were greener and more supple than they were further east. Several of the Rocs took he opportunity to hunt while the recruits made a meal of the supplies each carried. The recruits were exhausted, Maf included. It had been an emotional day, filled with amazement and thrills, as well as unaccustomed physical exertion. It was not long after the suns had set that the recruits were asleep.

Dawn saw them preparing for the long flight to the eyrie.

"Hel-nor tells me that today we will fly higher and faster than yesterday," Maf announced to his charges.

"Higher and faster?" Kelfrith, one of the younger recruits asked.

Amusement emanated from each of the Rocs. They were looking forward to giving their riders a demonstration of what riding a Roc could be, although care was needed yet.

"Apparently so," Maf replied, smiling wryly. "Make sure you're strapped in tight."

The flight was wild for the new riders. Hel-nor launched first. His powerful wing strokes pushed Maf back in his harness such that he had to grip harder, and propelled Roc and rider rapidly to a sufficient height that Maf could see quite a distance across the grass. The rest, seeing Maf's experience, gripped the harness straps as tightly as possible. From the height, Maf could see how the Rocs had arranged themselves in their two flight groups, spaced apart. On Hel-nor's signal, all twenty Rocs launched as one, climbing nearly vertically into the sky. Hel-nor flew in a wide circle, waiting for the Rocs to join up, which they did quickly, settling into their two wings of ten.

A further circle was flown for the riders to settle themselves and then all Rocs reported ready. Hel-nor broke from the circle, banking hard before straightening on their course. Twenty Rocs followed as though on a string. The Rocs accelerated, lifting higher into the morning sky. As the Rocs arrowed towards their eyrie Maf received a wash of elation from Hel-nor and the other Rocs, followed by fierce determination. This was the first flight of the Alnar-kun in many long generations. They would play their part!

The eyrie was like nothing any of the recruits had seen before. Not that they knew what to expect, of course, but the broad landings fronting deep caves in which the Rocs lived, with the dramatic view of peaks both above and below them marching into the distance, stunned and awed them. The long drop from the eyrie into the steep mountain valleys was sobering, telling them all that they were in a very different world to their own. They had been informed that the only access to the eyrie was by air, but none of them could imagine the reality that they met.

The recruits were welcomed by Ar-kunya and El-arwe. Standing on the speaking stone in the meeting place Ar-kunya offered his greetings and welcomed them to the Rocs' home and to the Alnar-kun. The depth of feelings shared with Maf and his chosen team surprised them all, and told them just how important their presence was to the Rocs. A further surprise awaited them when Ar-kunya finished speaking. A large, jet black Roc standing in front of the speaking stone seemed to blur and was replaced by a tall man with jet black hair. The recruits all stared wide-eyed at the change. The Rocs stared with interest, never having seen Kunas outside the appearance of a Roc.

"I also welcome you," the man said. "I am Kunas. I will assist you to learn your roles."

The newcomers were stunned to be in the presence of a Guardian. Maf took the lead and dropped to one knee, head bowed, followed unevenly by the rest.

"Please stand," Kunas said. "I thank you for the honour but you have no need. We'll be working together and that will get in the way."

"Now," El-arwe broadcast into the sudden silence, "it is time to settle our Alnar-kun riders into their own eyrie. We have some friends who will guide you to your places, which were the perches of our riders in ages past. We hope they will suffice for now. They will assist you to prepare food. We will reconvene in the morning when your training will begin."

A small group of people who had been standing unseen in the shadows came forward and gestured them to follow. After a bow to Kunas and the Roc leaders, Maf led the recruits after their guides down a steep path to their accommodation, which proved to be surprisingly spacious and comfortable.

Training commenced the next day following an early breakfast. The same people who had guided them to their accommodations the evening before were introduced afresh as the Rocs' riggers. They showed the newcomers how to put the harnesses onto the Rocs and how to remove them, which the recruits had to do repeatedly. There was an in-depth explanation about what happened to a Roc if a harness was poorly fitted, and how to determine if that was the case.

This was followed by an introduction to their weapons, at which point a second group joined them.

"These are our second group of recruits," Kunas said to Maf and his group, before opening his arms to include all in his next words. "Again, I welcome you all to the Alnar-kun. You will be divided into four battle wings, the traditional number for the Alnar-kun. Hel-nor is the wing commander of the Alnar-kun. Maf will be joint leader, a role that I believe you are well suited to play." Kunas waited while the second group all turned to regard Maf. "Maf," Kunas continued, "has been named Protector of Ennaris by Dharmoney."

Kunas waved his hand and the stone centred on Maf's forehead shone out, a wave of silver and green bathing the scene. Those from the Hides knew of Maf's new title, of course, but the mention of Dharmoney, an equally legendary figure from Ennaris' mythology, caused them to wonder anew. The second group looked like they were overwhelmed.

"Maf and his friends are battle-gifted," said Kunas, "but we will deepen that skill during our training. The rest of you demonstrated facility in other aspects of the work of the Alnar-kun. You are all on equal footing, however, and both groups will be blended into the four wings. I asked Menra to help with your training. She will teach you how to use the weapons you will use. These are weapons from far in the past, but suitable to today. I asked Ogun to help the battle-gifted to improve their skills."

On cue, two more figures appeared, to stand beside Kunas. Rocs and Ennarisi all bowed before the newly arrived Guardians, before standing upright again.

"Ah," Ogun said with relish, "I'm going to enjoy this."

"Indeed," Menra added. "I thank our brother Kunas for the opportunity to help rebuild the Alnar-kun."

"Now," Kunas said, "let's begin. Maf, you and I will work on your control of your staff."

There followed a period of intensive training for Rocs and riders. The riders were taught by Menra how to load and shoot the crossbow, an ancient weapon that replaced the power weapons used before and during the rebellion. They also were taught hand to hand fighting with short, extremely sharp knives, and how to hold and throw a short javelin, also provided by Menra. Finally, each was outfitted with thin, razor-edged swords. Maf, of course, had his own twin swords.

Ogun took charge of the battle gifted, drilling them mercilessly in how to best use their gifts. Each of the Hides recruits were assessed by Ogun and then given their own training regimes. For some, this involved little more than a deepening of the training they had undertaken with Maf. For others, however, Ogun extracted depths of gift that had not been realised before.

Maf took part in the lessons with Ogun, learning much about how to assess gifts in others as well as how to impart the learning required. He was gratified to note how Hertik, one who Maf thought should have exhibited strong gifts but who had never done so, proved to be adept at hurling spears of energy. This, Ogun said in an aside to Maf, was a rare battle gift, for most could only shape and hurl balls. Restab, another whose strength of gifts had proven elusive, was found by Menra to have shield skills that would rival many Mages of the pre-rebellion times.

Maf found Kunas to be a master of harnessing the energies of the Mage and using them to activate and work with the artefacts. He was surprised that the stone that had centred itself on his forehead could be a weapon as much as a focusing tool, which had been his understanding.

"The stone does assist with focus," Kunas told the Mage of the Hides, "but it also enhances the skill of the wielder. In the case of the battle-trained Mage it becomes another avenue for your power to be wielded, to be projected."

Maf's staff remained Kunas' focus, however. This, the symbol of a Mage through Ennaris' long, long history, Maf found was tied into its wielder's own power and became an extension of that power. Once acclimated together, the Battle Mage's staff could perform tasks independent of its wielder.

"The greatest Battle Mages all used staffs and stones to multiply their own presence," Kunas explained. "Most could not. Only the most skilled can do so, for it uses the wielder's own will to guide its actions. You need to be able to separate threads of your will. Many are unable to do so. For them the staff remains a focusing tool alone."

Maf, therefore, found that his lessons changed from learning how to wield his staff and stone, which he learned quickly, to learning and practising how to split his willpower into threads with their own targets and goals. He found these sessions frustrating, for he repeatedly failed to create multiple threads of willpower. Kunas remained patient, reassuring Maf that he had the necessary capability.

Finally, Kunas drew Maf into a merging of minds. *Here*, he told Maf, *I will show you how a true Battle Mage performed this task. This is Marjory in the last battle of the rebellion.* Maf's breath caught as he saw the legendary Battle Mage stand with only a few companions as an enormous stream of energy crashed through the planet's atmosphere to impact on a shield created by Marjory. Maf *saw* the Mage's willpower hold that broad energy beam despite threatening to buckle under the onslaught. The destructive power spilled into the planet's crust as Marjory was unable to exert enough control to avoid it. But she steadied, pushing herself upright from a half-crouch by the strength of her determination and then pushed into the air itself and advanced towards the enemy. He watched as she split her will into two threads, creating a second shield to gather much of the energy and reflect it back into space, and then each of those threads of willpower split again to create four shields that now captured the energy discharge and shaped it into a much more narrow beam that back sped into the upper atmosphere.

Maf watched open-mouthed as Drewflin and others stepped forward to merge their powers with the Battle Mage. New threads appeared as Marjory drew into her working the powers of her companions, freely given, and those of the remaining rebel Mages which were not as freely given. Her staff how floated free and it created a spear of energy that also blasted into space. The silver stone, blazing on Marjory's forehead, added its own thread of power to the meld. Finally, from a vantage point high above, Kunas showed the return energy beam striking and defeating the shields of the huge rebel ship. The beam tore through the vessel. The attacking beam cut off abruptly as the power circuits were destroyed, and the ship careered into the atmosphere.

Kunas switched his view back to those on the ground. The Council Mages lay in untidy heaps, whether dead or badly hurt Maf could not tell. Goroth and the rebel Mages were decimated likewise. Overhead, the great ship streamed from on high, passing far overhead on its way to crash into the western ocean, which would add a fresh layer of devastation along the shoreline.

Kunas ended his viewing and waited while Maf processed what he had seen. Kunas understood what it meant to Maf to see those two Mages, both young in Mage terms at the time of the rebellion but astonishingly proficient in their control over and command of their powers. Finally, the Guardian spoke.

"That will be seen as one of the greatest acts by Mages in Ennaris' history. Their readiness to sacrifice their own lives to protect Ennaris is beyond compare. Did you see how Marjory divided her very willpower to address different demands? How she not only divided her powers, which most Mages of strength can do, but divided the *intent* of those threads. Even at the last, with Drewflin's aid she made one last division to confine Goroth. The power in that act alone was enormous, for Goroth is a trained Battle Mage of above average power."

"I never dreamed that she could be that powerful," Maf replied in a whisper, shocked and amazed at watching the deaths of the Mages on both sides. "How many others could have done what she did?"

"She was not alone in the delivery of that power, remember," Kunas said, "and the Guardians played a part in bolstering her and absorbing the energy that spilled into the planet. But I can tell you without doubt that there has never been a Mage of Ennaris who could have done that before her. More importantly, did you see how she divided the threads, how she directed them with her own threads of willpower?"

"I believe so," Maf replied, returning to his usual calm state, outwardly at least. "I need to consider what I've seen and then try again."

The following day, Maf tried and failed to create two threads of willpower. On the following day he tried and failed again, but felt a potential that was just out of reach. On the third day, however, he succeeded, in dramatic fashion.

Several members of the Alnar-kun visited a small town in the mountains called Jellarstig, which was home to several of the riders. It was not their first visit, and they were welcomed by the people of the town. A platform was being raised to support the Rocs when they visited. The platform would overlook a deep slash through the mountain, and would provide an ideal launching point for the Rocs. The Rocs landed a distance away from the town and the riders walked in to provide assistance and to see what progress was being made. The platform was well advanced, with large timber supports stretching a short distance out from the cliff edge. A group of townspeople toiled to build a frame on top of the large supports. Timber boards would be placed on the frame.

The riders joined in with a will and good progress was made. It was during the afternoon that a shake was felt, causing those on the platform to retreat to the safety of the village itself. However, four townspeople who were working against the furthest edge were forced to cling to the timbers as they shook. A loud *crack* rang out as the shake ended. Aghast, the watchers saw one of the huge supports shatter. The framing timbers that rested on it were thrown into the abyss below, along with the four workers.

The watching townspeople screamed in dismay. Maf, however, even as the timber was failing, leapt onto one of the stable supports. With his Mage stone shining brightly, he reached out with his will to hold the four. He could only get two. Desperately, Maf started to draw those two back to the cliff edge and without pause set a second intent to capture the third and then another to reach further down into the depths of the deep mountain slash and grab the fourth. Straining to support all four, Maf held out one arm imperiously and his staff sped across the distance from where it had been placed, flaring into silver and green life as it did. Maf took hold of the staff and a solid beam speared out to engulf the fourth man, the one who had fallen furthest.

As the people watched, awe-struck at what they were seeing, Maf held his arms wide. He hands glowed with a silver nimbus from the power being exerted as the three were lifted and, one after the other, gently deposited on the grassy sward that separated the edge of the town from the cliff edge. Maf's Mage stone settled to a muted glow and he lowered his arms. The staff's stone, however, continued to blaze as it held the fourth. A cry rang out and Hel-nor sped over the heads of the watching throng and dropped into the deep gorge. He re-appeared a short time later, grasping the fourth man in his huge, strong talons. Maf's staff blazed for several moments longer, as though in triumph, before its light also dropped to a muted gleam. Hel-nor hovered above the grass while several riders dashed to relieve him of his burden before he lifted away again. Maf used the staff to steady himself for another moment before he carefully made his way to the cliff edge. Reaction was setting in, both from the unusual exertion and the realisation of what he had accomplished.

The townspeople surged around Maf when he reached solid ground, some offering support and others celebrating what he had done. No further work was done on the platform that day. The four were shaken badly. One had a broken arm and all had some scrapes and bruises. As a result, the townspeople were treated to a demonstration of Maf's other major skill as, with hands glowing a bright green, he set the broken bone and strengthened it, then healed the scrapes and bruises.

That night, after a delayed return to the eyrie, Maf found himself with Kunas. Around them the Rocs and riders were discussing the events of the day. Kunas was in his Roc guise, and the Guardian was pleased.

"I congratulate you, Protector," the Guardian said formally, before humour broke through. "It would be better to learn these things more easily, would it not?"

"It would," Maf agreed, tired.

"Your strength will grow rapidly now that you understand how to do what you did," Kunas replied. "The training of the Alnar-kun is almost complete. From here on, you will be perfecting skills in preparation for their use. You will be ready to join with others to oppose Goroth and his forces."

Maf nodded his tired agreement, before bidding Kunas a good night and retiring to his quarters. He was intrigued by what the future would hold but for now, he was exhausted.

# 35. Resgalar

Flin and Andira emerged from the portal in what had been the city of Resgalar. Unlike the ruins upon which Escar had been built, Resgalar had no second life. Rather, it was consigned to history and the memory of the few Ennarisi who cared to remember. Flin was one to remember. He emerged from the portal building to ruins that he had visited on very rare occasions since the rebellion's end. They always caused him to stop and remember with anguish. They did so now. The familiar sadness enveloped him, overlaying the also familiar rage at what had occurred.

Resgalar was where he had met Marjory. This was where both attended their early training for the Guides and then Mages, for Resgalar had been blessed with isolation as much as natural beauty. The Guides dedicated to Fernis and the arts of healing of body, mind and spirit, of treating the Ennarisi and their assorted trees, crops and animal life, had their school here. So, too, did the Guides following Ogun and dedicated to the arts of war. Flin had always struggled to reconcile the two, but he realised quickly that the two merely cohabited the space, without having any further links. The Guides of Fernis sought the natural beauty, while the Guides of Ogun sought the isolation to practice their war-skills.

Drewflin had been only sixteen cycles old at the time. Marjory had been but one less. Both hailed from rural villages where their gifts had manifested themselves in the usual ways. There was nothing about either of them at that time to indicate that they would play pivotal parts in the history of the Ennarisi civilisation. Indeed, both struggled to make sense of what they were expected to undertake, and it was that struggle that brought them together for the first time. Both had been assigned menial tasks for failing at relatively simple practice elements, and they found themselves paired to undertake a litter clean-up of the centre of the city. This was not a great burden, as the Ennarisi produced little waste and litter was almost unknown. The menial tasks were to ensure that they considered their futures, whether they wished to continue or not, what they were being asked to undertake.

Drewflin was tall and gangly, Marjory slightly shorter and more compact although showing clear signs of the woman she would become. Neither had finished growing into their bodies at the time they first met. Drewflin already displayed his unruly mop of sandy hair that would never be completely tamed, with a spare figure and thin, somewhat pointy nose. But his eyes were what drew Marjory in. Those intense eyes that seemed to see more than others saw, a deep green colour with flecks of amber that seemed to glow when he smiled his slow smile. Marjory already showed that she would be striking. Her dark hair already extended down her back. Her vitality shone through and was a magnet for Drewflin. The two bonded almost immediately, as though fated to be a pair. And so they were, learning much about each other for the next ten cycles of their training. The Mages, missing nothing of the intensity that existed between them, did not object, knowing that such dedication often realised greater outcomes.

They quickly outstripped their peers from their respective intakes. Drewflin's precocious gifts - for he demonstrated multiple strong gifts within a couple of cycles - resulted in the trainee Guide being in demand in the orchard regions that backed the northern steppes as well as the jungles of Ophiris around the equator, where several of the rarer raw materials were harvested from certain trees. Drewflin showed an ability to assist, support and restore any form of life, only later discovering that his healing gifts could be applied to animals and then people. He started to be discussed as one of the future powers. The depth of his gifts when, finally, he was tested as part of his path to graduating to Magehood staggered his teachers. He was unable to cause death directly without penalty, and the occasional death arising from the use of his gifts, which occurred sporadically when difficult decisions were required, caused him acute distress. This concerned some of the masters but was looked on favourably by others.

Marjory, by contrast, excelled in all the arts of warfare, both those that were physical and those that employed her gifts. It was she who studied the lore from the ancients and understood it, where for many it was arcane and confusing. It was she who demonstrated the ability to launch attacks using her gifts as weapons, and to use the exact same gifts as a shield. She could turn the beams of energy weapons aside or reshape them to pinpoint accuracy and cause them to deviate *around* objects, something no other warrior Mage had been known to do. As her training progressed, she was matched against two, then three and then four of her co-trainees in their drills and was rarely bested. Four became five and she discovered how to divide her power into multiple threads before any lessons on that matter were held. She could attack and defend at the same time in a display of prowess that astounded her instructors. Like Drewflin, she was marked for a great future. Unlike Drewflin, she could kill, and did so when required, without qualm. Marjory was the one called for when Praget, one of the stronger warrior Mages who was working to shape defensive weapons for Ennaris, suffered a tragic backlash and went rogue, killing or maiming many. Marjory confronted Praget along with Drewflin. The latter tried to break through the madness to restore the Mage, while the former was on hand to end the threat should Drewflin be unable to do so. So it had proved to be, with Marjory forced to shield Drewflin and then destroy Praget. That was the first time they had merged their gifts and their strength, for Praget had been strong and experienced.

Both had come into their full powers in this city of Resgalar. They had come into their full partnership, in spirit and body, in this same city. Both had mourned when it bore the brunt of Likud's opening attacks on the Council, specifically targeted at the schools, and especially the school for warrior Mages. Many had perished in that first use of weapons of mass destruction, a term that could in no way adequately describe the destruction and torture inflicted on the inhabitants as well as the planet itself.

In that destruction they also lost their only child, their son, a mild and even-tempered boy who followed his father's calling to nurture growth and health while, oddly, counting his mother's offensive gifts in his armoury. Marflin had been a student at the time of the attack on Resgalar, merely nineteen cycles of age. As precocious as both parents in their own youth, he had been among the most promising of the students and was nearing his own mid-graduation, the half-way mark where students were given meaningful tasks to help shape their skills. Drewflin and Marjory had searched for their son as soon as they were able, but to no avail. The student quarters were specifically targeted by Likud. The inherent viciousness of the rebel Mage was on full display, as he turned an orbital array on the building that housed many students of both of the disciplines taught in Resgalar. The building was turned to slag without warning. None of the children were seen again. Rumours surfaced periodically of young Mages or those training to be Mages, but no matter how hard they searched, the remaining Guides and Mages could find no sign of those students.

Flin now looked upon the resultant destruction once again and his spirit ... shifted. Even after thousands of cycles, there were no plants, no grasses, no weeds even. The skeletons of the towers remained. The twisted and tortured remains were like fingers pointing to the source of their own deaths as they reached for the sky, their skins burned off on that day of destruction. The radiation had been minor and was long dissipated, but no-one had sought to make use of the ruins. Popular rumours that arose as education fell away from the average Ennarisi told of unquiet spirits, strange happenings and glowing apparitions. Long ago, before the remaining Mages had withdrawn to their sporadic forays amongst the people of Ennaris, Drewflin had sought to put those rumours to rest by residing in this blasted city for four tendays, seeing nothing, hearing nothing - absolutely nothing - but his words were not heeded. No-one came near this place, even as some of the old skills started to be relearned and superstition receded.

He felt the rage building once again, the father's anguish at the loss of Marflin surfacing of a sudden. He felt himself trembling in response. The tight hold he had placed on his emotions threatened to let go. He was not sure just what would happen were that to occur.

He shook himself back to the present, taking a deep breath to centre his spirit. Andira waited, staring at the ruins around her as though seeing a dream as, Flin thought, such it would be to her. She stared at the skeletal remains and tried to imagine buildings that high and failed. She saw the ruins of the city square - for that is where the portal had been - and was unable to visualise it, despite having seen the images on the portal gate's walls. The gate was all that resisted the bombardment.

"Andira," Flin asked quietly, grimly, holding his rage tightly inside, "do you feel any tremors here, or near here?"

The woman brought her attention back to the present. This was why the Archmage had brought her along, to detect where the demon problem was.

"No, nothing," Andira replied, a little shaken at having to do this for real. "I'm sorry, Archmage."

"No problem," Flin replied. "We're still a little way from Bamjur and have a hike ahead of us. At least this will allow the first of your strength tests to occur. Let me know the moment you feel anything."

At Andira's nod Flin led the way from the portal, down the remaining steps and into the remnants of the square. The two walked through the shattered remains of Resgalar, while Flin acknowledged in his mind the ghosts of his memories, of the people he had known at the fateful time when Likud had turned a planetary-scale energy weapon on the city. Of his son. Of his life partner, also lost now.

That first part of their walk was undertaken in silence. The building rage and melancholy on Flin's part was accompanied by the anguish that was only ever just below the surface. Wonder swept over Andira. To her the city ruins seemed to extend for ever, although Flin knew that

Resgalar had been a small city by Ennarisi standards of the time. They passed from the city centre, dominated by tower ruins, into the former business sector of smaller tower ruins, following the path of the Way of the Guide, the arrow straight road that cut through the city from one side to the other. It passed through five squares as it did so, if Flin's memory was correct. And so they passed through a smaller square, the Ogunavid, the Square of Ogun, which was more open than the city's main square during the time when Resgalar was alive because its surrounding buildings had been largely residential and thus lower. On the far side of the Ogunavid Flin paused once again. He stared down a short street to where the ruins of a building blocked further progress. For a long moment Flin stared at the ruins of what had once been home for Marjory and himself.

Flin's anchor shifted. His nearly banked anger flared anew.

Flin had borne his role as the unacknowledged last Archmage of Ennaris with fortitude for thousands of cycles, sinking occasionally into despair and pulling out by his own immensely strong will and the assistance of his fellow Mages, most of whom had perished in one way or another since the rebellion's end. He had borne the loss of Ennaris as he knew it and accepted the changes wrought on the planet as the result of both misguided and unbending ambition. He had borne - still bore - the loss of Marjory with deep grief and sorrow. Long ago he had seen the last remnants of the Guides fade out and had seen the effects of Ennaris' slide into chaos and barbarity even while he was striving and failing to halt that slide. He had seen warfare return to Ennaris, conquest for the sake of conquest. There were vicious attacks on the weak as well as the deaths of many he had known over the many cycles that he trod the land, for no gain and no benefit. All of this he had borne, with snarls and curses and tears and frustration. But not with real displays of anger. His training had been too complete for that, his control too strong.

Archmage Drewflin, strongest of the Mages Ennaris had ever seen despite having no warrior gifts, fated to be the greatest of the Archmages through Ennaris' long history if he but knew it, stared at the ruins of his former home and felt that deep and harsh anger take a firm grip on his heart and grow. It took root and the tendrils followed the paths of power, spreading through the man Drewflin and into the seat of that power, in the spirit of the Guide, the strength of the Mage. Without thought the Archmage reached into his pack and grasped his staff, reduced now to little more than a gnarled stick with a greenish stone at its top. To Andira's surprise a tear ran down Drewflin's cheek but she saw that his eyes blazed, something only a few still alive had ever seen before.

The staff shimmered and grew to its full length as the Archmage stalked back to the centre of the Ogunavid, to the exact centre where once the great fountain of Ogun had bubbled up amongst a grove of andary trees, with their long and shiny green leaves and their smooth and silvery trunks reaching for the sky. And here, where Drewflin's fondest memories lay in ruins, where the knowledge of what had been lost surrounded him, the Archmage's rage spilled out. And he lost the control that he had held rigidly for all those many cycles, through all the ruin, the anguish and the pain.

Archmage Drewflin drove the blunt foot of his staff into the centre of the Ogunavid and cried aloud, an inchoate scream of fury, loss, despair and anger, raw and unbridled. The green stone clasped at the top of the staff burst into brilliant light, flooding the square, making its way through the streets of devastated Resgalar. It bathed the ruins of this once beautiful city in an emerald glow that made those ruins beautiful once again. Centred on Flin's forehead the Enchara added its own contribution. The greatest healer of Ennaris' history sent his rage, anguish, pain, fear and a challenge to his enemies - for so he now acknowledged them - through his staff and into Resgalar, and thus into Ennaris.

And far to the south, amid the southern desert where she had been delivered by Odruf, Marjory felt her life partner's cry. She felt his challenge and, to the astonishment of the desert dwellers who were watching her surreptitiously as she stood before Morrig's pavilion, she fell to her knees and responded with a cry of her own, as deep and as full of despair but with even greater depth of anger. The startled watchers saw the brilliant silver shaft spring from the brow of the kneeling woman and strike the ground, and she was surrounded with a silver nimbus that shifted and roiled. In the pack at his side, unbeknown to the Archmage, Marjory's Battle Mage's staff flared and joined forces with the Archmage's staff. The green was overlaid with silver, and the greatest Battle Mage of Ennaris' long and storied history added her very considerable weight to the power flowing into the planet. The two powers met and merged as once they had done to save Ennaris from total destruction. But on this occasion the healer took the lead and the warrior added support.

Far away, in the Citadel of the Faero, the twin Mages, builders of some of Ennaris' most beautiful towers, shocked those in the central square as they contributed their own power to the flow, tears flowing freely as they shared their Archmage's emotions, as did Trabor in the Council Chamber, he who was a master of metal and water. Varna, she who was Dharmoney-to-come, felt the remnants of her previous doubts washed away and, drawn on the currents emanating from all around her, contributed both compassion and determination, white lightning driving from her fingertips to who knew where. And across Ennaris the Guardians smiled, or uttered sighs of relief, or merely nodded sagely and added their own power to the meld.

In the hidden caverns many, old and young, were swept along and added their own share of power into what was now a planetary meld, without knowing what they were doing or why.

After a short while, the storm of his rage passed and Flin came to himself once again, kneeling in the centre of the Ogunavid with his staff grasped in his hand. The green stone was quiescent once again. He had felt some sort of reflection to his rage but was unsure what to make of it. He regretted the loss of control but accepted it, and the rage did not depart. Its fires were banked anew, and Flin knew they would remain there until the battle was done. Wearily, Flin regained his feet and turned back to where Andira awaited him. Her eyes were wide and her mouth open, having witnessed what no-one had ever seen before, and was un-likely to do again. Consciously forcing himself to straighten once again, Flin nodded to the shocked young woman and recommenced walking down the Way of the Guardians. There was some fool playing with the demon-spawn to deal with before he could take care of other far more important business.

Behind them the tendrils of power writhed and twisted, finding their way with surety. The blasted and battered stones shifted beneath the city that had been Resgalar, and the deep wells were released and purified. At first in a trickle, but then in a regular flow, the fountain that had been in the Ogunavid bubbled through the rubble and burst forth once again. It was followed by similar events at each of the other squares, at the Morrigavid, and the Anavid, then the Fernavid and finally at the great central square, which everyone called the Main Square but was in fact the Odruffavid. And in the Ogunavid the earth parted around the fountain, and first one, then two, then three and four, and finally a fifth tendril made their way above the ground, rapidly becoming silver trunks and then young trees, with shiny green leaves shot through with silver.

And Ennaris' restoration began.

A tense, eerie quiet reached across Ennaris.

Odruf found that he was nervous, which surprised him. The Guardians were meant to be objective, seeking to protect planet and people, but not individuals. However, that intent had failed when the Guardians lost three of their own.

Odruf recalled vividly when he and the others had been called by The One to undertake this responsibility. Appanu and Angor had accepted immediately, a joint decision that took no-one by surprise. They were highly popular among the Toree, the first people of this universe, and embraced the mission with gusto. Zang had been more circumspect but had joined the group after some consideration. All three had proven to be heroes of the Guardians, knowingly absorbing so much of the deadly energies released by Goroth and his rebels that they perished.

While the Guardians would honour their responsibilities there was little objectivity left. Odruf had relished his role in returning the Battle Mage to Ennaris, as Fernis had relished his role in setting her mission to the humans. She was one who the Guardians as a whole admired. Drewflin, of course, had grown into his role as Archmage, whether he had the title or not, and the Guardians' admiration for him had no bounds.

Still, Odruf was nervous. Had the Guardians been able to intervene directly in events of the past then the outcome would have been certain. They could not, however. However, though they were allowed a little more leeway now than in the past, they remained limited still and in no way were future events certain.

Goroth was at large once again and had re-united with Grensor and Likud. Goroth's act of rebellion continued to surprise Odruf when he thought of it. It had been unexpected, when the Mage's long history was considered. Even more surprising was the vicious nature of the rebellion, which saddened and enraged the Guardians in equal measure. The Prophesy, visited on Odruf in his guise as Halfgar, promised that "evil would arise anew" when Goroth renewed his campaign. This time, however, the Guardians would have a surprise or two in store for him, if all eventuated as they hoped.

The Children were to the forefront of Odruf's meandering thoughts. There had been surprise after surprise where they were concerned, with one or two more to come, he thought. Varna was a mystery whose outlines were becoming clearer, but some elements of that story remained obscured. That she was Dharmoney, that figure from deep legend, was all but certain in Odruf's eyes, but there were depths to her rapidly emerging powers that surprised the Guardians.

Blaine as the Defender was, with the benefits of hindsight, obvious. Every quality of the Defender, another legend with a long history, and more were embodied in Blaine, from extreme skills with weapons to the care shown for the people of the planet and the function he had assumed as a role model for many. That he had adopted Ennaris as his own was plain to see. How that would evolve once Goroth was defeated - an assumption that Odruf kept to even while recognising the dangers involved - would be interesting to watch.

Jalor was the puzzle. While he was the obvious leader of the Faero's forces, and a guide to Corm in many ways, he displayed no obvious qualities that conformed to the legendary roles that were ordained to take part in the battle to end Goroth's predations on Ennaris. People were drawn to him, it was true, and he inspired trust in those who encountered him. He said and did the right things instinctively. Even when injured, he had been the centre of events at the Citadel, from what Balgor had reported, with a steady stream of people visiting him and listening to his suggestions. He remained steadfast in his role for the human Union of planets, but his acceptance of a role on Ennaris had been swift and in no way begrudging. Acknowledged as a Mage by the Council Assistant based on his genetic signature, he showed no obvious signs of any gift, but Odruf had no doubt that he had a further role to play.

The Mages, those who had survived to this point, were worthy of their own consideration. This small group had stayed a long and arduous course, from the shattering rebellion of their own peers that led to a time of utter devastation and then a long period of persecution and strife. They had emerged as a tight and highly supportive unit. That the future of Ennaris and probably this galaxy would revolve around such a small group was astounding and frustrating for Odruf. He and the remaining Guardians could resolve all problems in a few hurs if they were allowed to do so, and some of his fellow Guardians were itching to do so, but that would not be allowed.

The One had made it clear that the people of Ennaris must make their own future. The One also intimated that the role of the Guardians would expand to encompass the galaxy in the near future. That would be difficult for the remaining Guardians to undertake, but there were multiple planets with emerging species that could use their help. They would need reinforcements, however. The One intimated that they would be forthcoming, but provided no further information.

Meanwhile, Ennaris was waiting. Almost all of the pieces were in place. The efforts of the Children in reaching out to key segments of Ennaris' fractured civilisation meant that all elements of Ennaris would be represented in the looming conflict. That was it should be. What was to come in the near future would shape this planet, and this galaxy, for all time.

## About The Author

James K. McVey is an author living on the New South Wales Central Coast, in Australia. The four novels that comprise *Children of Ennaris* are his first published works.

Visit www.jameskmcvey.com.au for further information and updates on these and other works.